Jumping Over Waves

Tricia Trevaskis

'Sometimes our light goes out, but it is blown again into flame by an encounter with another human being. Each of us owes the deepest thanks to those who have rekindled this inner light'
Albert Schweitzer
Nobel Peace Prize winner, 1952

CHAPTER 1

Amber stood near the adventure playground, almost hidden in the shade of the aging, peppermint tree. She had deliberately distanced herself from the other mothers. She didn't have the energy today, to even feign interest in their conversations. In the canopy above, a noisy band of hungry corellas, screeched and argued, as they tore at the foliage, sharpening their beaks, sending down showers of broken twigs and leaves. The layers of debris on the grass matching perfectly, the chaos of her own thoughts.

Snippets of their discussions, mostly about plans for Christmas and the school holidays, floated across the early childhood playground; but their talk of Christmas presents, family gatherings and camping trips were pointless to her. Amber's plan was simple: just get through the next few weeks as best she could with Marco home every day... There would be no playdates for Ruby or Arlo. That might mean she would have to reciprocate and have strangers in the house. No way! And a quiet Christmas. She didn't want to risk poking the bear.

She pretended to be on her phone when one of the women, possibly Lucy's mum, waved her over. She had a card and a pen in her hand. *Stuff it! She probably wants me to sign the stupid thank you card.* Amber pointed to her phone as if to signal she couldn't be interrupted. Two fifty-five. Surely the teacher would start sending the kids out soon? A few minutes early on the last day was hardly breaking the rules. Turning quickly to avoid the waving mother, she felt a sudden hot stab of pain across her forehead, an unwanted addition to the already throbbing ache in her cheek. Gingerly she prodded with her tongue at the inside of her mouth. Her teeth felt smooth, so hopefully they were all intact, but she still had an iron taste and acute tenderness where she'd bitten down on her cheek.

Feeling tentatively under her cap she checked her fingers, and could tell the bleeding had stopped. Bending down, she rubbed the sticky residue of blood onto the grass, but again, she had moved too fast and her head started to spin. She stood up slowly and waited for the dizziness to settle. Arlo waved at her from where he was hanging upside down on the play equipment. He was flushed from playing, happily oblivious to what had gone on before they left home. Right now, he was having fun with the other younger siblings, some he knew from kindergarten, as they waited for the pre-primary kids to be dismissed on the last school day of the year.

Amber was relieved he'd been outside playing and so didn't see Marco push her around. Not that he would be inside. When Marco was home the kids were always banished from the house. Amber pondered again the approaching dilemma of having Marco home every day from Christmas until mid-January, while he was on leave from work. It was going to challenge her on every level to keep Marco happy and the kids occupied and safe… away from him. Today, she'd been way too complacent and had paid the price. Marco didn't like mess. She should have predicted that he'd knock off work early and come home to get ready, because today was his work Christmas party. It wasn't that hard to have everything spotless, just the way he liked it, but she'd wasted time reading dinosaur books to Arlo after lunch. Marco might have ignored the dishes in the sink, and the lunch-time crumbs all over the bench, but he lost it when he tripped over the basket of washing that she was half-way through folding. That had been the trigger.

Amber was still reeling at the speed his mood changed. One second he was unzipping his work pants, giving her that lecherous smile as he walked through the door, and she was thinking, *please no, because I've got to get Ruby soon from school* and one of Marco's 'quickies' would make her late again for pickup. The next second, he tripped over the laundry basket, stubbing his toe against the bed. Before she could utter a word of apology, he'd grabbed her arm and thrown her across the room; her head smashing against the wooden doorframe as she fell. That's when she must have bitten the inside of her cheek; the pain of that secondary to the searing agony of her head-splitting contact with the unforgiving door jamb. Maybe he only meant for her to hit the wall? Maybe he didn't really know his own strength? She thought that hitting the plaster wall wouldn't have caused her so much distress.

But he wasn't satisfied with that. While she was still absorbing the pain, he grabbed her arm again, and threw her onto the bed. *Aah! That's why my arm is so sore*, she recollected, massaging her rotator cuff. The final insult came when he heaved the old wicker laundry basket at her as she cowered on the bed. She saw it coming and tried to curl her body away, but it had caught the side of her head, leaving a huge scratch across her cheek — not to mention the tender, blue-red bruise that was already developing under her skin. Stripping off his dirty clothes, he tossed them at her head, one item at a time, sneering as he disappeared into the shower: 'It serves you right, banging into the fucking basket you left lying around. You're a fucking lazy, clumsy slut!'

Amber had lain in a foetal position on the bed for a minute or two, while she mentally checked her injuries. She only had as much time to recover as it took for him to shower, so she stood up carefully and inspected the physical damage in the mirror. Blood was trickling down her forehead. She quickly mopped that up with tissues, pressing them down on the wound and putting her peaked cap over it all. The scratch where the basket had caught her cheek, looked deep, but thankfully hadn't resulted in much bleeding. She hoped it wouldn't scar. The rest of her body felt okay, but she was shaken. And terrified. Marco had pushed her around before, and been rough with her several times when she'd somehow angered him, but this was taking it to a whole new level.

By the time he came back from the shower, she knew from past experience that she should act as if nothing had happened. Sunglasses on and hat pulled down over her forehead, she said with all the sincerity she could muster,

'Marco I'm so sorry I left stuff lying around. I'll have everything tidied up when you get back from your Christmas drinks. Do you need me for anything now? Otherwise, I'd better go and fetch Ruby. It's the last day of the school year!'

Marco scowled, checking his watch as he strapped it on.

'I did have a plan for you, but Jimbo's supposed to be picking me up in a minute, so I've run out of time. Just make sure you're still awake when I get back, babe.' Grabbing his crotch, he gave her a knowing leer.

'Oh! I'll be waiting for you babe. Have fun!' Amber replied suggestively, hoping she sounded enthusiastic enough, her goodbye kiss long and lingering, as she did her best to ignore the stinging pain from the pressure of his mouth. She really was getting to be an accomplished actor... or perhaps she was simply developing a higher pain threshold.

Finally, the pre-primary classroom door opened. As the teacher spotted parents, she called out names and the kids appeared one by one, laden down with hats, drink bottles and bags stuffed with the last of their schoolwork and crafty Christmas decorations. Amber waved at Ruby and walked towards the veranda. Covering her scratched, stinging cheek with one hand, she managed a smile and thanked Ruby's teacher once again for all her help over the last few months. Keeping up the charade, she even chatted briefly with one or two parents, despite the pain that made every word a struggle to form.

There was so much noisy confusion, as everyone made their final farewells, that no-one paid much attention to Amber discreetly weaving her way through the crowds to the exit, determined to avoid scrutiny. Arlo was reluctant to leave the playground and his friends, but Ruby, after an over-the-top party day at school, was tired, and thankfully ready to leave. Coaxing Arlo with the prospect of an icy pole in the freezer, Amber was soon on her way home. Once through the school gate, she didn't mind how slowly they dawdled, relieved to be away from any further conversation or questions. She was only just holding it together as it was, her nausea and light-headedness an indication that she needed to take things slowly for a few hours.

CHAPTER 2

In a coastal town south of Perth, Lexie rolled her eyes, and smiled. *Some things never change*, she thought wryly.

'It's supposed to be *silent* ball, Blake!' she explained patiently, emphasising *silent*, and hopefully putting an end to his annoying, constant calls of 'Here! Here!'

Blake, who always pushed the boundaries, acknowledged the admonishment with a cheeky grin, before leaping up to catch a ball over his head. Just as Lexie expected, he immediately looked to throw it across the room to his mate Toby, ignoring the obvious passes right in front of him.

Mixed emotions swirled in the year six classroom at the end of the covered walkway. Excitement danced with trepidation, while anticipation played dodge with a ripple of sadness, as their final moments of primary school rolled out. Lexie, herself conflicted, felt the poignancy of these final minutes, as she always did, and indulged herself with a last quiet contemplation of the students, who had dominated her thoughts for the past year. This class, in particular, held a special place in her heart. Their twenty-seven personalities were as familiar to her as her own family. She knew their strengths and weaknesses, their foibles and endearing qualities; she would miss them all, even the challenging ones like Blake and Toby. Only Lexie appreciated how much she had needed the distraction they had brought to her life. In many ways, having to turn up each day and be accountable for them had been the only thing that kept her steady over the last six months.

Playing this final game of silent ball, their favourite end-of-day reward, was a fitting close to the year. They were in high spirits as they killed time, waiting for the siren that would sound the end of seven years of primary school, and herald the beginning of their summer holidays. Next year they would be in high school, no longer kids, but suddenly teenagers, and a new adventure would begin.

Finally, Lexie called out:

'Okay. Hold the ball, Tom. Time's up, the bell is going to go any second.'

The usual protests followed the ending of the game, but silence fell quickly. Despite the hype they were all well aware of the significance of the moment.

'Thanks everyone. Now, I know I've already said it, but I really am going to miss you all.'

Lexie smiled and paused, casting her eyes in a final sweep over her class, their faces turned expectantly towards her, as she addressed them for the last time.

'You have been such a great class to teach and every single one of you should be proud of everything you've achieved. I hope you keep it up next year in high school, at whichever school you're heading off to. Remember…if you put in the work, the rewards will come. Now, have a wonderful holiday and stay safe!' Right on cue the bell rang, and chaos resumed as the kids cheered.

Lexie called out over the noise, 'Good afternoon, everyone!'

A drawn-out chorus of 'Good afternoon, Miss Hudson,' followed, as the class broke up and began to depart. Some left with a rebellious jump, touching the green exit sign above the door in a basketball move, while others crowded around her for a goodbye hug. Several parents popped their heads in at the door for a final farewell, and Toby, with impeccable timing, dropped his still-open pencil case right in the doorway, spilling the contents and holding up everyone's exit, forcing several kids to climb over him as they left.

And then they were suddenly gone, and that unmistakable, ghostly end-of-year quiet fell, as if the room itself expelled an exhausted sigh.

Usually covered with students' work, or posters and art hanging from the display boards and rafters, the classroom was now stripped bare. Tables and chairs had been pushed against the walls, and benches cleared in anticipation of the annual holiday deep clean; thumb tacks the only evidence of what had been a lively hub of learning. Lexie knew she was being overly dramatic but she always felt that, at this moment on the last day of the year, it was as if the very soul of the room departed. She could almost envision spirits following the departing students out of the room. As the schoolyard gradually emptied and the laughter and shouts faded into the distance, Lexie remained propped against her desk, reflecting absently on her next step. For a few minutes she stayed suspended in time, even though knew she should make a move. She was well aware of what her 'to do' list entailed for the next week. Glancing at the pile of boxes behind her desk, she had just decided they could wait until tomorrow, when with perfect timing Jackie, the other year six teacher and a good friend, came to the door, bag and keys in her hand.

'Oi! Lexie! Are you coming to the pub? Brian's promised to shout us the first drink, and he certainly owes us one. It's time to toast this year farewell!'

Lexie grinned in response.

'You are dead right. The pub sounds perfect. I'll just get my bag and lock up. I'll follow in a tick,' she promised, and with a thumbs up to Jackie, she pushed herself off the desk. Shaking off her pensive mood, Lexie gathered her things and forced herself to function. She'd spent way too much time lately gazing off into the distance. Once she had packed up and left town, she hoped things would change and that she'd lose the brain fog which had plagued her for much of the year. Hefting a cardboard box full of files and resources, Lexie locked her classroom, and hurried to catch up with the year three teachers who were also on their way to their cars.

'Thank God that's the last time I have to deal with that class!' complained Pippa from class 3R. 'They definitely go down as the worst lot I've ever taught. If I had to put up with Jake Brown any longer, I'd be up on assault charges for sure! And don't get me started on his mother!'

Pippa's fellow year three teacher, Carrie, made sympathetic noises, before saying,

'I know. You did get the worst bunch. But I'd have to say my class weren't far behind. I don't know what was in the water when that cohort were born but I'm glad I'm not teaching them in year four!'

'Brian has split up a few of the more challenging ones though, hasn't he?' asked Lexie referring to the principal, Brian Weston's, attempt to balance out the classes more evenly for the following year.

'Yes, and there are a couple of tricky kids leaving which will help as well,' sighed Pippa, puffing slightly as she hauled her carry-bags into the boot of her car.

'The new teacher will probably have a much easier time, and I'll just look as if I was useless and couldn't manage!'

'I don't think anyone thinks you've had an easy year Pippa,' Lexie was quick to reassure her. 'The one bonus of leaving town is that I'll dodge that year group!' she joked, as she heaved the heavy box into her back seat. Standing up, she stretched out her back, which was complaining after the bulky load.

'See you at the pub in ten.'

Lexie waited while Pippa and Carrie pulled out, before falling in behind. The car was hot from being in the mid-December sun all day, and the air con barely had a chance to kick in before she had covered the short distance to the pub. Anzac Hotel was in the centre of the town, and parking wasn't easy to come by, but Lexie's luck was in and she quickly found a bay. Walking towards the hotel, she took a moment to admire its gracious iron railings and historic architecture. She'd had many a fun night within its red-brick walls, and the old pub was something she would miss. In fact, there was much about this town she would miss, and given a different set of circumstances she would have been happy to put down roots here.

Friday drinks at The Anzac was a bit of a school tradition, a chance for anyone who felt like it, to gather at its polished timber bar, and mark the end of the school week. However, at the end of each term, and especially at the end of the year, there was always a bigger representation. There was no pressure to stay for long, but it was always convivial, a safe space to let off steam with supportive colleagues and friends and recover from an often stressful and thankless job. Lexie knew only too well that teaching could be a solitary occupation, despite being surrounded by a class of students.

Not only was there the actual teaching, but once you added in yard duty, lesson preparation, correcting and planning, the day could go by with barely a moment to grab a coffee, or eat lunch, while simultaneously juggling emails and reading staff memos at your desk. Catching a colleague for anything but a quick query could be impossible. A chance to chat and debrief with someone who understood your issues was invaluable. *Especially*, thought Lexie, *if you live on your own*. And living on her own was something Lexie was now very familiar with.

The pub's interior seemed dim after the bright afternoon sun, but Lexie had no trouble locating her workmates. She could hear their excited chatter the moment she stepped inside the front bar. Smiling broadly, she made her way across to them, oblivious to the glances that followed her. With her long legs and thick, shoulder-length brown hair, Lexie often drew a second look, people sometimes even stopping her to ask where they had met before. Lexie thought it was her girl-next-door looks that made her seem familiar, but her soft brown eyes and habitual, open smile were more likely the reason. She was greeted with a cheer as she plonked her bag down on a chair and headed for the bar.

Assessments over. Reports sent home. Classrooms packed up. It was an infectious atmosphere of goodwill, as everyone allowed themselves a well-earned celebration after a year of hard work. Lexie felt a palpable sense of relief now the summer holidays beckoned. Even though she knew most of the holidays would be taken up with her move back to Perth, at least after tomorrow the pressure would be off for a while. Heading straight to the bar she took quick advantage of the champagne on offer from Brian. The education department didn't give too many financial rewards to their dedicated teaching staff, and principals were not paid big bucks either, so she was swift to thank Brian for his gesture.

'Thanks Brian. Cheers!' she said, clinking glasses with him. A frantic clinking of everyone's glass followed, and it was a while before the friendly disorder settled and Brian managed to reply.

'I can't talk you out of going back to Perth, can I?' he asked ruefully, taking off his glasses and rubbing the bridge of his nose, while he continued in his earnest manner.

'I don't know how we are going to replace you. You did a fantastic job with those kids. I had my doubts about some of them, but by the time they stood up for graduation, I was very proud. It was quite an emotional ceremony, knowing how far they had progressed since last year. And now you're going back to early childhood teaching. It's such a waste!' He shook his head. Noticing Lexie's quizzical raised eyebrows, he quickly added,

'I just mean, we need good senior teachers and role models as well as good early childhood teachers.'

Lexie smiled. This was a discussion she and Brian had had on many occasions. He knew her passion for early childhood teaching, but he had wanted her in the upper school, and she had to admit she had really enjoyed the challenge and the rewards. Lexie had been initially reluctant. It had been several years since she'd taught in the senior school. But Brian took a gamble on her, promising there would be plenty of support and professional development, convincing her she wouldn't regret it. And he was right. She had loved it and thrived in the pre-teen environment where hormones and angst raged a constant battle, offset, thankfully, by emerging young adults who were fun and engaging. Then, giving her a last hopeful look, he said sincerely,

'I know you need to go, but, if you ever want to come back, I'll always find a space for you. Remember that.'

Lexie nodded, briefly unable to speak. She felt a rush of emotion and knew she was on the brink of tears. In fact, she'd spent a great deal of the past few months ridiculously over-reacting like this to a few kind words. Brian had been a great support to her since she'd arrived. Always more of a friend than a boss, and he'd certainly been a sympathetic ear whenever she wanted to vent. She hadn't needed to explain to him the details, or her reasons for moving. It was enough that he respected her decision.

Realistically, she knew he must know her sorry story. School staff rooms were rich feeding grounds for gossip and intrigue. But he hadn't pried and had generously pulled a few strings with the department to get her a position back in Perth. And the unexpected bonus was, that she was going back to her old school at Thomas Street, which she was more than happy to do. It was the same school she had started at ten years earlier, and there were even some old colleagues from those days still teaching there. It would be an easy way to slip back into her old life. Not that she could credit Brian with getting her back to her old school. That was due mostly to the shortage of early childhood teachers in an urban area that was experiencing a growth in young families. Giving his hand a squeeze to show her heartfelt response to his kindness, she turned her attention towards another group of teachers who were busy debating the school's system of merit awards. Lexie listened to their chatter for few minutes, quietly regaining her composure before she interrupted.

'Stop it! Are you guys seriously discussing school? I want to hear your wild plans for the holidays. Surely you two have something exciting planned?' she gestured with her glass at the two youngest teachers.

'Please tell me you're off overseas? Somewhere exotic, to make me jealous.'

'Not quite overseas,' said Georgia, one of the year five teachers. 'I am heading to Victoria though, after Christmas, to hike the Great Ocean Road and take in a couple of music festivals.'

'And I'm going camping on the Eyre Peninsula with Jack and some of our mates. I'm going to stuff myself with oysters, and we're planning on taking our bikes and doing lots of rides. I'm even looking forward to crossing the Nullarbor, because we've never done that by road,' chipped in Jesse from year one, with a satisfied smile.

'Now I'm sorry I asked! That sounds like so much fun. I'm definitely jealous, especially since I'm going to be back living with my parents until I can find a place to move into!' Lexie made a face while the others laughed in sympathy.

Pippa complained she had her in-laws arriving in two days, so Lexie really had nothing to whinge about. Then changing the subject, she asked Lexie if she had much more to pack.

'Not too much more. It's helped that the people who bought the house were happy to keep some of the furniture, so I think some boxes will fit into Mum and Dad's garage, and I've got a storage unit for the bigger items. They don't mind they say, as long as it's not long term. Actually, they've been great at making this as smooth as possible for me'.

Taking another sip of her champagne, Lexie continued, 'Anyway. Once I pack up the last of the kitchen and my bedroom, I'll be ready for the removalist on Saturday.'

'That seems so fast, although I know you've been planning it all for ages,' remarked Pippa, impressed with her friend's ability to pull all this together, while she herself couldn't think past the in-laws arriving.

'Well, I've had plenty of time to work things out,' Lexie answered with a self-deprecating grin.

Moving a little away from the noisy chatter of the others, Pippa probed a bit deeper.

'What about Jed's stuff? Is there much left you have to deal with?'

'He cleared out quite a bit of it before we put the place on the market. The first time he came on his own, and the second time he brought Caity. I left them to it.'

Shrugging her shoulders as if she didn't care, she continued: 'Most of his stuff is sorted. There are just a couple of quilt covers I certainly don't want, and he forgot his stupid trophies, including his junior footy ones! Or maybe, she wouldn't let him take them!' Lexie laughed with a touch of bitterness, before adding,

'She's not stupid. She's probably hoping I'll throw them out so she doesn't have to deal with them. But I intend to pack them... as badly as I can!' Lexie and Pippa chuckled conspiratorially at this, and toasted each other. There was always great satisfaction in insignificant wins.

Lexie ordered another glass of champagne, but disciplined herself to sip it slowly. She had two busy days ahead of her and she needed to be on her game. The time flew by, as they shook off the mantle of work and school, reminiscing occasionally about the past year, but more importantly, talking of the holidays ahead. Lexie stayed for a couple of hours. She wasn't the last to leave, but those who were still there were also on their last drinks. After all, there was still another day of school to go. Waving a general goodbye, she felt another wave of resentment wash over her as she reflected on just how much the breakup had cost her. Never again would she trust as easily and wholeheartedly as she had trusted Jed. Having to leave these wonderful friends and colleagues, was just another item in her long list of grievances. Pulling up at home a few minutes later, she clicked the garage door remote, ruing the traffic delays that lay ahead of her next year in Perth. She doubted she would ever again find somewhere to live that was this close to her work, and to town.

The garage door went up and she drove in quickly, pressing the button to close it behind her. She was tired, and the thought of any interaction with her neighbours, no matter how nice, was just a step too far in her fragile state. Getting out of the car, she paused. *Take it easy, just breathe*, she told herself as memories once again threatened to bubble up and overwhelm her.

'*He is not, and never was, worth this self-pity*, she told herself firmly. *You are grieving for an illusion.*'

Still her anger surfaced and she allowed it to run, as she entered the house and made her way down the passage towards the kitchen, where several half-packed boxes awaited her.

When she met Jed six years ago, she thought he was 'the one'. She had dated a couple of guys seriously for a while, and both relationships were fun until they'd gradually lost steam. Each time, the parting was mutual and amicable. She had never actually moved in with either Mick or Cade, so the break-ups were relatively easy, with no messy ends to tie up. But she had thought this time, with Jed, it was different.

After she broke up with Mick, she had taken a year off teaching, and back-packed through Europe. She had turned twenty-eight and she was restless. The timing was perfect. It was a wonderful trip, and Lexie smiled involuntarily at the memories, which helped dissipate some of the anger that surfaced when she thought of Jed. Her travels opened her eyes to another world, and she came home with higher expectations, eager for new experiences. One slow weekend soon after she returned, she was aimlessly trawling a dating site, wondering if she should give dating another try, when she met Jed on-line. He was attractive rather than strictly good looking, but she liked his profile. One of the clinchers for her was that he liked to travel, to see and experience new places. He dreamed of having a holiday house in Spain. *What's not to like?* she'd thought. He seemed perfect.

From the very first date he was like an old friend. There were no awkward moments and they chatted with ease. The spark was mutual. He told her he thought she was his soulmate. Jed was thirty and said he was ready for a serious relationship. He was everything she wished for, and it wasn't long before she saw him every day, then most nights, and within six months she had moved in with him.

They were a striking couple. Jed was tall, with thick, wavy dark hair, a few streaks of premature grey balancing his boyish looks. Green-eyed and fit, he was a good match for Lexie, who was also tall and lithe.

Their dream was a house in Spain where one day, they would holiday for a couple of months a year, but in the meantime, everyday life had to be lived. Their goals were mutual, but realistic. Jed was an engineer, and for the last few years, had worked fly-in, fly-out, far up north in Port Hedland. Just before they met, he had started a new job in Perth, but was soon transferred to a mining operation past Mandurah, a couple of hours south of Perth. Their lives were closely entwined by then, so Lexie applied for a teaching position nearby.

Sick of paying rent, they decided to buy a house. Despite being late starters to the property market, they hoped their steady jobs and reasonable income would work in their favour. Fully committed, they saved every cent they could for a year, pooled their money and were approved for a loan to buy a very modest, mid-fifties house, not far from the beach. Jed enthused that they could make some money by flipping houses, until they had a luxury home at a beachside suburb in Perth, and eventually their little villa in Spain. They joked that they might be sixty by then, but it was a journey they would travel together. They had such plans. Lexie was in love and she supported all Jed's ideas. This was their future.

The renovations took a little longer than they expected, but they had fun doing them. Being an engineer, Jed was very practical and could turn his skills to many things. There wasn't much he wouldn't have a go at, and Lexie was his willing apprentice. They added on a small extension with a second bathroom and a fourth bedroom. Lexie had less time for her friends in Perth, because most weekends and school holidays were spent working on the renovation, but she hardly missed them because she was so caught up in seeing their new home emerge from the bones of the old house. Money was tight, and they gave up most of their social life, managing on a strict budget that Jed had devised. Living frugally, despite their good salaries, they renovated the kitchen, the laundry and the original bathroom, modernising and adding value to the property. For months at a time, they worked weekends, painting and tiling, even restoring floorboards and creating a new garden. They were just completing the finishing touches at the beginning of the year, and were ready to put it on the market, when Jed's boss asked him to re-locate to Melbourne for six months.

Instead of putting the house on the market, they decided that Lexie would stay living there and finish off the last few jobs, such as completing the landscaping. Once Jed was back, they'd work out where they would buy next. The short stint in Melbourne came with a bonus payment which would be handy, so Lexie had no hesitation in encouraging Jed to go. That they would miss each other dreadfully was a given, but they talked instead in practical terms, knowing this to be not only financially beneficial but also that it was a strategic move for Jed's career. An opportunity for Jed to show management just what he could do. Lexie was happy for him. The future was looking rosy. It didn't even ring a warning bell when Jed said as he kissed her goodbye,

'This will be a good thing for us. A chance to get used to being independent.'

Without thinking much of it, Lexie agreed and hugged him goodbye. Later that day, as she drove back from dropping Jed off for his flight to Melbourne, she reflected on that statement, and a small nagging thought occurred. For the first time, she wondered if she wasn't being a tad complacent, taking things for granted regarding their relationship. They did talk a lot about a future together, but Jed had never actually mentioned marriage or kids. In fact, Lexie had noticed how quickly Jed managed to change the subject when friends got engaged. She'd dismissed it, excusing him for being more focused on their long-term future. Several of her girlfriends were having babies, and Jed's response was usually to pity them, saying their life was officially over. Driving the two hours down the highway to home, Lexie began to regret the moments lost when she should have questioned him on his thoughts about having children. She knew she didn't need a wedding ring to prove that they loved each other, but all the same, she realised she did want the fairy tale of a husband and kids. He was coming back for a long weekend in a few weeks and she vowed to have that conversation with him then.

Jed had left in late January, just before school started. The early weeks of term one were always frantic with staff meetings, parent information nights and other school commitments. On top of this was her own class planning, while she got to know her students and their individual strengths and weaknesses. It seemed no time at all, before she was looking forward to Jed coming home for the March long weekend. They talked almost every day, and it seemed they were closer than ever, despite the thousands of kilometres between them. Deciding she wanted to look her best when Jed saw her, Lexie was at the hairdresser getting her hair styled when a last-minute phone call came from Jed. He should have been already in-flight. Thinking his flight must have been delayed Lexie was already preparing herself for disappointment. She was only half an hour away from setting off on the two-hour drive to the airport to collect him. She grabbed the phone to answer.

'Hi Lex. I've got some bad news.'

Lexie's heart sank.

'What's happened? How late will you be delayed?'

'Worse than that. I'm not going to be able to come back this weekend at all.'

Jed sounded disappointed. Lexie was totally devastated.

'Why? What's happened?'

'It's a long story and I'll tell you more about it if I get a chance later this weekend. But you know the gas project I've been working on? Well, they are having issues with the plant in the Hunter Valley and I've got to fly up to New South Wales and work on it. There's a team of us going from the office, and we'll be there well into next week. It might even take longer, if we can't sort it.'

Lexie could only sigh into the phone. She was completely deflated, her enthusiasm evaporating faster than her half-dry hair. Sounding pathetic even to herself, she said, 'But I was so looking forward to it! And there's so much we need to talk about! When can you come home?' then she suddenly thought. 'Or can I come over to you?'

Perhaps he was preoccupied, but Jed was quickly dismissive of this. Lexie had thought for so long about the conversations she wanted to have with Jed, face to face. Jed however, was operating on an entirely different level.

'My boss has promised me some time off and I'll be able to get back as soon as this settles down. He said he'll give me some days in lieu. Don't even think about coming over. It's way too expensive with Easter holidays coming up. And just send me a photo of what you want to talk about. Is it the side gate where it was coming off its hinge? I'll look at it, but I think it's easily fixed. I have to rush now. We can talk later. Love you!' And with that he was gone.

Lexie didn't even finish getting her hair done. She made an excuse about not feeling well and hastily paid for a wash and half a blow dry. Instead of heading up the highway flush with anticipation, she headed home, overwhelmed by the feeling that her world had just tilted, and she was scrambling for level ground.

CHAPTER 3

Ignoring the call of the half-packed boxes, Lexie sprawled on the couch in the family room, her head sinking gratefully into the head rest. Closing her eyes, she let her thoughts wander as she relived those confusing days. At the time, Lexie had been tough on herself, not allowing herself to indulge in self-pity. She had survived by simply moving forward, taking it day by day, not allowing herself to look back. It had been exhausting to maintain the pretence that she was fine. But now, deep in the final throes of packing, as she prepared to physically leave the house she had put so much of her hopes and hard work into, she gave herself permission to contemplate what she had lost.

It was three months before Jed had managed a visit back to Western Australia. The excuses piled up one after the other, as did his reasons for her not coming to visit him in Melbourne. When he stated she would be bored in Melbourne as a rationalisation for her not coming in the school holidays, Lexie knew for certain that things had changed.

She tried to tell herself this was as difficult for Jed as it was for her. She did believe he was working long hours, but she was no longer convinced that he was working these long hours for a shared future together. In fact, the time alone had allowed her to consider much about their life she had previously not questioned. Jed had always said they were a team. That everything they did would benefit them both. However, with hindsight and brutal honesty, Lexie was realising that all their supposedly shared decisions had been weighted more Jed's way than hers. Craving reassurance in his absence, she had tried to gauge what he saw their future together to be. Conditions for a meaningful conversation weren't ideal even in a FaceTime call, separated by three and a half thousand kilometres, and three hours' difference in daylight-saving time; but nevertheless, she tried. Pushing the boundaries, she broached the subject of children, and once she even recklessly mentioned that Smale's in Perth were having a sale on diamond rings. Smooth as silk, Jed had expertly evaded any commitment, even going as far as ending the conversation soon after.

By the time Jed could string four days together for a trip back, she felt as though she was greeting a stranger. Uncertain of where things stood between them, Lexie tried to act as if nothing had changed. Reassuringly, Jed had greeted her with great affection, and they had made love that first night and in the days that followed, with both passion and tenderness. Not wanting to destroy what fragile links they had in their four short days together, Lexie stupidly refrained from the one discussion she really wanted to have. Jed had bought her a beautiful gold bracelet as a surprise, his way of saying how sorry he was not to get back any sooner. There was no mention of the ring she had teased him about on the phone. Pointedly, neither was there any discussion of selling the house soon, or where they would buy next. This was a sharp contrast to the old Jed, who was constantly scanning the real estate sites for the next fixer-upper they could make a profit on. Lexie wondered about it, but thought maybe she had been over-reacting. Perhaps he wanted to wait until he came back permanently. She pushed her uncertainty aside.

Wanting to make the most of their time together, Lexie took the Monday off school to spend the last day with him. They drove down south to Margaret River and had a long lazy lunch at one of the wineries. It was a beautiful afternoon and Jed was his charming old self, making her laugh as he recounted the dorky mistakes he had made in Melbourne in his first few weeks. Lexie was beginning to relax. It felt good to just be together in their own little bubble, and despite all her previous resolutions to have the big conversation with Jed, she was still reluctant to spoil this precious time together. After all, she decided she didn't care if they were married or not. That was only just a bit of paper. They were both still young. Babies would come along soon enough. The day was perfect, and they spent a quiet evening together on the couch, watching an old movie and sipping wine.

The next morning, she left the house before Jed. He was catching a shuttle to the airport at nine-thirty and she was due at school at eight. She was upset, but stoic as ever. Jed kissed her goodbye with assurances the project was back on track, and that he would be back in WA soon, reminding her that the bonus money was just too good not to finish the contract. He held her close as he said, 'I know this is hard, but it's best if you can hold the fort here a bit longer. When I come back, we can decide what we want to do next. Soon we'll put the house on the market and celebrate all our hard work.'

Lexie smiled, 'And then we can buy something else and start it all again!'

Jed gave her a funny look, before responding with a weak laugh. When he said, 'It's been fun. I'm going to miss you Lexie,' she thought he was referring to the weekend just gone.

Lexie even shed a brief tear as she kissed him goodbye, and he gave her an extra tight hug as he said, 'Love you.'

Lexie had left him standing in the driveway when she drove off to school. She could still see him, waving her goodbye, but she also remembered that when she took a last look in the rear-view mirror before turning the corner, he had already disappeared back inside. That he could move on so quickly, rocked her slightly. Immediately she regretted her pathetic attitude of not wanting to spoil their time together with any unpleasantness. She wanted to rush back and demand some answers. But of course, she didn't. She continued to on to school, and kept making excuses for him, despite his distinctly off-hand and distracted tone, and an ever-diminishing frequency of phone calls.

It wasn't long after this that he began not answering her calls. He started to text more, apologising that he was at work and couldn't talk. Once again Lexie trawled through their conversations in her mind, trying to work out what was happening. Eventually she decided he might be unwell, and perhaps he needed her. She remembered Brad, one of the guys he had gone over to Melbourne with, whom she'd met a couple of times at Christmas work parties. She did a bit of research and sent him a private message on Facebook, leaving her phone number, asking if he could ring her because she was worried about Jed. When the phone call came through, she was out in the garden and she'd had to rip off her gardening gloves and race to the phone, so she was quite out of breath when she answered.

'Lexie speaking.'

'Hi Lexie, it's Brad here. I got your message.'

'Oh! Hi Brad. I'm sorry to bother you, but I haven't heard from Jed lately. He seems to be working really hard, as I suppose you all are,' and she laughed nervously. Suddenly this was feeling weird. She pushed on.

'I'm probably paranoid but I began to wonder if Jed wasn't well, or maybe things were getting too much for him. It's just that I haven't spoken to him properly for almost two weeks now, just texts, and he's not answering my calls.' The weird feeling was rapidly being replaced by embarrassment, as her own words echoed in her ears.

Brad gave an awkward cough.

'I saw him this morning. He's fit and well as far as I can tell. But Lexie, I don't really think this is something I should be discussing with you. It's really up to Jed. I didn't know you guys were still close. I assumed that when Jed came over to Melbourne you two had broken up.'

Lexie took a deep breath, her heart thudding as she absorbed that statement. She took a moment before answering.

'Brad, as far as I'm concerned, we are still very much together. His clothes are still in the cupboard here and I was expecting him home in a couple of weeks.'

It was Brad's turn to take a deep breath. 'You need to talk to him Lexie. My contract is up this week and I'm going back to the office in Perth, but I know Jed has decided to stay on in Melbourne. Indefinitely.' Silence followed. Lexie was reeling. She managed to stammer some thanks to Brad, and an apology for disturbing him.

'Don't apologise Lexie. I think Jed is the one who needs to apologise.' Then he added, ominously, 'You might want to ask him about Caity. You take care now Lexie.'

She hung up, her legs suddenly weak. She couldn't think straight. Why hadn't Jed told her he'd be staying longer in Melbourne? He should have discussed it with her if he was intending to stay longer. He knew she was counting down the days till he came home. And who was Caity? Furiously she grabbed her phone and rang Jed. Again, it rang out. She texted *Who is Caity?* She stared at the phone willing it to ring. A thought occurred to her, and she leapt up like someone possessed and ran to the spare room, where Jed kept his clothes. She'd always loved having the master bedroom wardrobe to herself, to spread out her own clothes. It was just one of those thoughtful things he did for her.

Throwing open the cupboard it took her only seconds to see most of his clothes were gone. She took the steps to the attic three at a time. Switching on the light, she pushed aside the cane baskets at the door. All the suitcases were also gone! Jed had packed up his life and she'd been too stupid to realise it. But when did he pack everything up? Was it on this last trip? She frantically tried to think the last time she had even opened his wardrobe. Probably not for months, possibly before he left in January.

The signs had been there but she had missed every one of them. Slowly, the jigsaw pieces clicked into place. His coolness on the phone. His reluctance for her to visit. The lack of plans for the future. Her gut instinct on the day he'd first left for Melbourne had been correct. She was right to have felt that things had been left unsaid for too long. She had been the only one who'd even contemplated that they still had a future. With heart-sinking clarity, she finally understood that his parting words, 'It's been fun,' were referring not to the weekend spent together, but to the last five years.

Her phone pinged with an email. It was from Jed.

Hi Lex,

I'm sorry I didn't get a chance to tell you myself about Caity. Brad just told me you contacted him. I'm a bit confused here. I thought you were okay with our break-up. We didn't actually talk about it but I thought we both understood that me going to Melbourne was a chance for us to re-evaluate our relationship. After all it had been a bit stale for a while before I left. It seemed to be an easy way for us both to draw a line in the sand and move on. I honestly don't think I've given you any indication that we were still a couple. And our last weekend together was such a perfect end to everything. You never said anything so I figured you were thinking the same as me; that we pretend nothing's changed, and we make it a last special time together.

The house is ready to sell and you've done a great job on the garden. No hurry to put it on the market until you decide what you want to do. I'll keep up my share of the mortgage payments until we sell. And I'm happy to keep splitting the bills. Just email me copies and I'll credit your account.

I didn't expect to meet Caity when I went to Melbourne. I swear I wasn't looking. But she's a great girl and I think you'd really like her if you ever get to meet. I really am sorry if you thought I was coming back. I can't understand how you thought this. I know we didn't actually discuss it but we always were able to understand each other so well, that I thought it was clear, and we were above all that messy angst other couples go through. We didn't ever talk much about a permanent future, just that crazy fantasy of a house in Spain. I thought you were just happy to coast along while it lasted.

My plan is to stay in Melbourne. I'm moving in with Caity, but I'll come over later in the year, and get the last of my stuff out of the house. We can decide on the furniture another time.

It's probably best if we don't talk for a while. You can always email me or text for anything urgent.

I'll always have a special place in my heart for you.

Such an arsehole! Lexie had read that email a thousand times since then. Her reactions had lurched from astonishment to anger. From grief to hatred. From confusion to embarrassment and everything in between. In fact, she'd experienced every emotion a jilted lover could. Once the hurt and pain gradually receded, she managed to coldly examine the reality of the last few years. She had loved Jed completely, and in doing so had ignored all the signs – signs that had been right under her nose the whole time. She'd made excuses that he was tired when he was cold or distant. She'd put up with vague ideas of a future together, because she didn't want to appear needy or demanding. Jed might convince himself that she knew he was leaving, but the reality was that Jed was a coward, and had taken the easy option of escape. She would never forgive him for leading her on for so long, but she also thanked the stars that she was rid of him. He would always be weak and she deserved better.

With Jed exposed for the lying minnow he was, Lexie had even felt some pity for Caity. The timeline didn't lie. He must have already been with Caity when they spent that last weekend together. Lexie was sorely tempted to warn her, but she resisted. Jed would probably lie and shmooze his way out of it anyway.

Stretching her arms over her head, Lexie forced herself to get up from the couch and move. The last of the boxes were not going to pack themselves, and she had a deadline. The new owners were due to take possession on Monday and she intended to be well gone by then. With the removalist truck booked for eight on Saturday morning, Jed was not worth any more of her time. She had already shed more tears over him than he deserved.

Heading purposely to the spare room, she made up three more boxes and set about packing the last of Jed's things still remaining in the house. She had deliberately left his stuff until the last minute, thinking that if she ran out of time they could always go in the bin. Fortunately – or unfortunately – she was well on schedule, so she decided she would pack them after all. With her care factor at zero, she took a sadistic delight in tossing the last of his possessions into the boxes as they came to hand. His cricket and football team photos went in just as they were. No protective wrapping needed. Shoes, shaving gear and even old toiletries followed, in any order. She didn't bother checking if the lids were on tightly. Old board shorts and a salty wetsuit were included, along with his pathetic collection of sporting trophies. She also managed to squash in the ugly purple vase his mother had given them one Christmas.

As she threw the last items in, she was rewarded with the tinkle of breaking glass. Not bothering to investigate, she taped up the boxes, labelling them only with JED/ STORAGE. Delivering a couple of satisfying kicks to the final box before she left the room, Lexie felt another step closer to closing the door on Jed forever.

***

The last day at school was a blur. As always, there was an obligatory professional development session, and of course, the final staff meeting with discussions on 'upcoming issues for the following year'. Lexie only half-listened, her mind on other things. Eventually, Brian released everyone back to their classrooms for some much-needed time to sort out the midden heaps of resources and files, which by the end of the year had multiplied like festering sores in their rooms. Lexie had already packed most of the stuff she wanted to take with her, but there was some filing to do, and paperwork to sort, and she was keen to leave the room in good shape for the new teacher next year. After several trips to the recycling bins, she was finally beginning to see order restored. There was the usual festive morning tea and lunch to mark the last day, and as no-one was needed for yard duty, everyone could be there. The mood was light and charged with a holiday feel. Almost six weeks of summer stretched ahead of them, and the possibilities and plans were endless.

By the time Lexie had packed the last things into her car, and made her farewells, it was well after three o'clock and time to go. There was nothing more to say. She had loved being part of this staff and school, and knew she could have stayed, but she also knew everything would always remind her of Jed, and the memories were tinged with embarrassment as well as pain. She had been a fool and couldn't yet forgive herself. It was easier just to run away. Driving out of the school car park for the last time, was a poignant moment. It had been a hard gig to keep going as though nothing had happened, when really her life had imploded. But she also felt a stirring of pride. She had kept going, done a great job, and she was stronger for the experience.

Moving back to Perth would be positive in many ways. She had good friends and family there. It would be nice to see more of her two little nieces, Hannah and Ruby. At six and four respectively, they were cute, just getting interesting. She had a job at her old school teaching pre-primary, and she was ready for the fun of early childhood again, after dealing with hormonal pre-teens. There was much to look forward to, including the sheer pleasure of continuing to suit herself.

On schedule, just after eight the next morning, the removalist truck reversed into the driveway. Lexie had been up before six, doing all those jobs that can only be done at the last minute. Once again, she cursed Jed for his absence, far away in his Melbourne love nest. Not only was she the sole person to pack up the house, but she'd also borne the burden of the constant tidying up and cleaning over the four weeks the house had been on the market. There had been two open-days and several private inspections, so she'd had to keep the house pristine. Housework was generally the least of her priorities, so having to constantly attend to it had irked her enormously. Today was another organisational nightmare for her, because the division of furniture meant that Jed's pieces had to be packed into the truck last, as they were going on to another storage facility before being sent to Melbourne.

Lexie's furniture would go into storage in Perth until she found somewhere else to live. Her boxes were carefully labelled. Those containing her clothes, personal belongings and teaching resources, were to be dropped off at her parents' place – her interim home until she either bought a new house, or found somewhere to rent. She hoped she'd be moving into her own place rather than renting. Not only did she never want to have to pack up again, but she had loved having her own place these last couple of years. The one bonus of the time with Jed was that she was way ahead financially of where she might otherwise have been.

One of Jed's least endearing qualities was that he didn't spend a cent if he could avoid it. While she credited his positive influence on her to save money, she was thankful she wouldn't be lectured about keeping within his ridiculously tight budget anymore. Until she met Jed, she hadn't considered owning her own home; rather she was thinking of setting off for Europe again. Most of her money had previously gone on travelling, and she hadn't regretted a cent of it.

***

She and Jed bought their little fixer-upper for a rock-bottom price, and soon after, housing prices had started to creep up. By the time they completed the renovations and put the place on the market, they made a nice profit – enough for Lexie to be able to buy something modest now in Perth, especially if she was open-minded as to possible areas. Lexie begrudgingly gave Jed some credit for his real estate nous, but she would never acknowledge it to him. Monday was settlement day, and once the money was paid into her account, she would never have to deal with Jed again. They had split everything fifty-fifty, as everything they had spent was equally shared. It had been yet another test of her fortitude to continue to be civil, when in reality she wanted to scream obscenities at him. However, the end was in sight.

With practiced efficiency the two removalists set to work. Lexie left them to it once they had established the order of loading, and they knew to look for the red and yellow stickers that differentiated her and Jed's boxes. Her red labelled boxes to go in first, the yellow to go in last. Symbolic colours. Strong red for her, and cowardly yellow for Jed. Of course.

The hours passed quickly as she ticked off the last-minute cleaning jobs, while the guys continued to load. Lexie was on a roll. She had been mentally preparing for this for weeks. She was vacuuming when one of the guys lifted a yellow-coded box of Jed's onto his trolley.

Catching her attention over the noise of the vacuum, he said with concern:

'I can hear something that might be broken in this box. Do you want to check before I load it?'

'No, that's fine. There's nothing important in it,' smiled Lexie, and continued with her vacuuming.

The removalists were professional and efficient. The truck was packed and on its way to Perth before noon. The last of the cleaning was finished. There was nothing more to do, other than drop off the key to the real estate agent. Lexie took time to farewell the house. She felt suddenly vulnerable, very much alone and more than a bit sorry for herself. She wandered through the garden first, appreciating her roses and succulents, most of which she'd planted as cuttings and watched them grow as if they were her own babies. She said goodbye and went inside.

Moving slowly through the house she thought back over the years, and tried to remember something that had made her happy in each room. She made herself think about the good times with Jed, before it had all turned sour. It helped. She closed the front door for the last time, and thanked the house for its memories and its refuge. And then, she got into her car and, without looking back, drove away.

CHAPTER 4

Amber stood at the living room door, a smile playing on her lips. It was a rare scene. Arlo and Ruby were sprawled on the floor in front of the TV watching ABC Kids. Arlo had one of his Christmas Lego spaceships in one hand, absently flying it through the air, while totally absorbed in *Bluey*. Ruby had her *Frozen* dolls, Anna and Elsa, arranged on the coffee table, while she clutched Olaf and zoned in on the wholesome dog-family on the screen. Amber was reluctant to disturb their peace… they'd had so little time in the holidays, to just chill and watch TV. Marco's rules that the kids had to be outside, were draining. If it was a stinking hot Perth day, and there were plenty of those in January, he'd occasionally give in and let them play in their bedroom. But there only had to be a hint of a breeze, and he'd announce the Fremantle Doctor was blowing, and order them outside.

Thankfully, all the building companies were back at work this week, and that meant Marco too. It had been such a reprieve to hear him depart at six-thirty on Monday morning. Amber was mentally and physically exhausted, trying to keep him happy and the kids invisible. Arlo and Ruby had been absolute angels. She was well aware she asked too much from them. This school holiday wasn't much fun for them, but then having fun wasn't something they expected in their lives. Since they were babies, they'd experienced so many houses, so many changes. Amber hoped much of it was only a dim memory for them.

But she remembered only too well the dilapidated housing: shared bathrooms, grimy kitchens slick with someone else's filth, and indeterminable germs. The noisy parties and unwanted interlopers. Locking herself and the kids in her room, often terrified. Woken in the middle of the night by strangers knocking at the door. Trying to protect your own food in a fridge that three other people had free access to; discovering constantly that the food you had planned to cook had disappeared! She had dreamed about having her own spotless kitchen and bathroom.

Marco had offered her that fantasy, but unfortunately the reality came with drawbacks. She worried constantly about her choice. How was living like unwanted house guests going to affect the kids long term? Not for the first time, she considered that the price of a roof above their heads might be more than it was worth.

Checking her watch, Amber knew she couldn't put the moment off any longer. It was only mid-afternoon, but she could never predict when Marco would be home.

'Sorry guys. You'll have to turn off the TV. It's after three. You can probably play in your bedroom for a while, but then you'll have to head outside.'

No complaints. No protests. A couple of sighs perhaps, as Ruby reluctantly switched the channel selection back to Nine, before turning the TV off and placing the remote carefully back on the coffee table. She was well-trained. Marco would totally lose it if he thought they'd been watching TV, and Ruby and

Arlo were terrified of Marco, even when he was in a good mood.

Amber watched them dawdle to their bedroom, her spirit sinking with every step they took. This was ridiculous! What on earth had she got them into? She'd tried so hard to make this relationship with Marco work, but as the months went on, he continued to barely tolerate the kids – her precious children – and he certainly hadn't developed any affection for them. If anything, he'd become more aggressive and bullying. Not that he'd ever hit them. Yet. Amber had vowed to herself, that would be the last straw.

Amber cast a critical eye around the lounge room – Marco's sanctuary, his pride and joy, the big TV centre-stage, the corner bar and bar fridge well-stocked – checking carefully that everything was in its place. Satisfied he'd never know the kids had been there, she returned to the kitchen. She picked a tiny piece of paper off the floor, but otherwise everything was sparkling. All this endless cleaning and tidying was draining. Resentful of the pointlessness of it all, she yearned to do something meaningful with her time.

She wished he would let her get a job. She wanted desperately to work because it was the only way she could have some independence. But Marco was adamant. He would get enraged if she brought the subject up, insisting he needed her at home. Arlo would be attending school full-time in a couple of weeks. She would have no-one at home during the day; it was her first chance since the kids were born to get a job. Marco stubbornly refused, saying he wanted to look after her, as the man of the house. Amber knew, though, the real reason was that he didn't want other blokes checking her out. His possessiveness was beyond unreasonable; it was frightening.

Apart from walking the kids to school, Marco went everywhere with her. Naively at first, she had thought him caring and keen to share the workload when he started accompanying her to the supermarket. He pushed the trolley while she collected the things on the list – the list he'd already pre-checked, the list they rarely deviated from. When they first shopped together, she put in little treats for the kids, but one look at his face as he threw the pack of Little Teddies back on the shelf, and she knew not to stray from 'the list'. And the pinch on her arm back in the car was another warning, the painful bruise a lasting reminder that there was no money to waste on the kids. Amber, however, had secretly worked out a resourceful arrangement with Erica next door. Unknown to Marco, Amber did housework for Erica, and in exchange Erica kept her supplied with little kids' treats, and importantly, some cash, which Amber kept well-hidden.

From down the street, the unmistakable throbbing of a revved-up engine announced Marco's imminent arrival home. Amber turned to warn Arlo and Ruby to get their things ready to go outside, but they were already on their way. Rushing after them Amber gave them both a big hug.

'I'll bring out some snacks for you very soon.'

'Can I have a Snake?' asked Arlo hopefully, his love of the fruity flavoured, stretchy treats making up for many an imposition.

'Sure mate. And I might have a packet of chips and a cool drink you guys can share as well. Just give me a few minutes, until Marco gets in the shower.'

As Marco's car pulled into the driveway, Amber rushed to the mirror. Giving her straight mousy-brown hair a brush, she fluffed it out, wishing she could afford to get some blonde highlights put in. She'd done that once with a girlfriend: they'd coloured each other's hair, and it had looked good for a while, until it grew out. Amber peered closer into the mirror. Was she looking tired? That was bound to piss him off. Blinking a few times, she tried to make her green eyes sparkle a bit. She'd been naturally blessed with thick black eyelashes, but some lippy and a squirt of perfume would help. Marco liked to see her making an effort. At the last second, she remembered to do up the top button of her shirt, adjusting the collar to cover the bruising around her neck. He'd only get narky if he thought she was drawing attention to what he'd said was 'an accidental squeeze.'

Checking that Arlo and Ruby had disappeared down to their makeshift cubby at the back of the garden, she made sure she had Marco's beer waiting on the kitchen benchtop. As he walked through the door, Amber was all smiles and ready to give him her full attention.

CHAPTER 5

'Look at me Auntie Lex!' called Hannah, standing in her bathers on the side of the pool. Making sure she had Lexie's full attention she executed a back-flip into the deep end, sending a shower of water over everyone including her Granny Jeanie, who had just arrived poolside with a tray of coffees.

'Fantastic!' Lexie cheered as Hannah rose blinking to the surface.

'Come on in Aunty Lex. You promised you'd swim with us!' challenged Rosie who was floating by on a pool noodle. 'And you too Dad!'

'Just give us a chance to have our coffee and we'll be in, and I'll demonstrate one of my famous safe entries for you,' Andy replied. This had both the girls squealing with anticipation. Their dad's version of a safe entry was usually a huge bomb, guaranteed to create a massive wave in Gran's pool.

'Thanks Mum, another great coffee,' sighed Lexie taking her first sip. 'If you keep this up, I may never move out you know, and you'll be stuck with me forever.'

'Oh, Dad and I don't care how long you stay! It's lovely having you back in Perth. And we get you all to ourselves.

Don't feel like you need to rush into buying your own place just yet.'

Lexie nodded and squeezed Jeanie's hand affectionately.

'I know that Mum, but I am keen to get somewhere closer to school, for a start. Andy and I have a couple of places on our viewing list for this afternoon that look really promising, but I'm not in a mad hurry to buy.'

Making a face and frowning theatrically, Amber pointed her thumb towards her brother, while whispering loudly,

'And Andy is more of a scrooge than I am, so he's not going to let me buy anything he thinks is over-priced. In fact, at this rate, I'll still be living with you when I'm forty!'

'Come on, Sis. I have a talent for these things and I know that the area along the Albany highway near St James is set to boom. It makes good financial sense to get back into the property market as soon as you can. As Dad says…' and he waited as Jeanie and Lexie took their cue and intoned together, 'The only good thing about that bloke is that he got you to save some money!'

'Otherwise,' Andy continued, 'He was an A-class dick-head!'

'Cheers to that!' said Jeanie as she clinked coffee cups with her son and daughter.

The move back to her family home, had been just the tonic Lexie needed. With the house sold and the money divided equally between her and Jed, Lexie had little to worry about. That was one tick in Jed's favour. He had been scrupulously fair. Now, with no pressing house or garden maintenance, the holidays were hers to enjoy, stretching out as an oasis of carefree time.

Best of all, the family home was a refuge, somewhere to rebuild her crushed ego and frayed spirits. She hadn't appreciated how physically tired she was after all the emotional stress of the last few months. She slept deeply every night, even surprising herself by occasionally nodding off in a chair mid-afternoon, when reading or watching television. Christmas and New Year were a blur, but now in mid-January she was feeling restored. Long daily walks and swims had had restored some of her old fitness. She hadn't dropped any weight thanks to Jeanie's excellent cooking, but she was toned and strong, and felt ready to begin the year. It wasn't until her old energy levels returned, that she understood how she'd forced herself to keep going the past twelve months. The pain from Jed's casual dismissal of their relationship continued, but the ache was receding daily. The more she thought about it, the more convinced she was that she'd dodged the proverbial bullet...

Later that afternoon, swimming duty with her nieces covered, she and Andy drove across town to check out the two houses Andy thought she might like. Grannie Jeanie was in charge of the two girls, and together they were going to cook that night's family dinner, for when their mum, Clare, returned from work at the hospital, and when Pa Ray, got home from his retirement job... golf. Quality family time with Andy, Clare and the girls was an additional bonus to living at her parents' home. Hannah and Ruby were similar in age to the pre-primary kids she would teach this year. Their obsession with *Sonic* and various Disney princesses, had already given her a much-needed update on the current interests of five-year-olds.

As Andy drove, Lexie took in the familiar sights of Perth. She had travelled to many cities, but the trip from the western suburbs past the sandstone university and along the Swan River was hard to beat. Andy spoke intermittently about the two properties they were to inspect, as random ideas occurred to him. They'd already looked at several houses together and Lexie could tell, this time, Andy was excited. Although she claimed she wasn't in a hurry to buy, Lexie was keen to have her own home again. Rental prices were through the roof and she was well past even contemplating a share-house. At thirty-three, she needed her own space, where she could hang pictures or paint walls without the worry of losing her tenancy bond. However, finding something to buy in her modest price range was another issue. Despite this, when they pulled up outside the first property Lexie's enthusiasm rose.

Her immediate impression was positive: the house was an old fifties era three-by-one, but the current owners had added another bathroom and opened up the area between the old dining room and kitchen, creating a new modern look. Lexie liked it, but after a chat to the agent, came down to earth with a thump. The owners were not prepared to negotiate, so the place would be out of her price range. Hiding her disappointment, she gave her details to the agent, who promised to contact her if anything similar came up.

Walking back to the car Andy apologised.

'Sorry Lexie. I was hoping the extra bathroom wouldn't push the price through the roof. I don't know why they don't just tell us the reserve price upfront! It's frustrating!'

Andy unlocked the car and climbed in. As Lexie slid into the passenger seat, he added optimistically,

'Anyway, I think the next one will be the best buy. I'm hoping you can get it for less than what they're asking for. It's just around the corner and still close to the highway, so you can get to school in under fifteen minutes. Depending on the traffic of course.'

Lexie shot Andy a grateful glance. She appreciated the time and effort he was putting into helping her find a house. If she'd had to do it on her own, it could have been daunting. It was so much easier to have a buddy to confer with, and since he and

Clare had recently upgraded to a new home, Andy was familiar with the current market and knew what represented good value. She was also thankful that he was realistic with what she could afford; mortgage repayments would have to be within the limits of her modest teacher's salary. There was no-one else to share the repayments this time.

They parked outside the second house. Despite telling herself to scale back her expectations, Lexie felt an instant connection. Probably built in the post-war boom, it had a double frontage, the two large windows separated by a recessed front door of opaque glass. The windows were also typical of the era with divisions on each side that could be opened to allow for air flow, while the central window gave an uninterrupted view of the front garden and street. Steps led up to a curved veranda, fronted by a wrought-iron balustrade, that was wide enough for pot plants and a couple of cane chairs. The garden consisted of a rough front lawn merging with the grass verge, as there was no fence or intersecting footpath. A few struggling plants clung to life below the veranda balustrade. The garden might need work, but Lexie was immediately in love with a grand old gumtree on the verge, casting its welcome shade across the front yard. She glanced once more at the description they had downloaded from the website, onto her phone.

Graceful older home with great potential, in need of some attention. High ceilings and carpet throughout. Three good-sized bedrooms and one bathroom. Separate kitchen and dining room, with connecting door. Kitchen suitable for renovation. Low maintenance garden at the rear. This house is sure to please a discerning buyer.

What it didn't say, and what they discovered on inspection, was that the only toilet was outdoors – a crucial point. Also, the 'low maintenance garden at the rear' featured large areas of concrete, that were cracked and overgrown with weeds. There was no garage. The carpets were dirt encrusted and the place smelled of decades of dust and use. In an ill-conceived attempt to cheer the place up, the previous owners had painted each room a different vibrant colour, the shades so deep it would need several coats to cover them. The kitchen was tiny, but the electric oven and stovetop had at least been updated in the last ten years. Lexie could see that the house had good bones. It was solid, and although the bedrooms had no built-in wardrobes, they were a good size. The house was north facing and bright, with light flooding in to show up the decorative old cornices edging the high ceilings. Lexie wandered through, only half listening to the agent. When they got to the outside loo, the agent paused, her enthusiasm tempered briefly.

'Of course, this is unusual these days, but it's a modern toilet, replaced by the owner only last year, so the plumbing is probably still under warranty,' she said in a desperate attempt to put a modern spin on a fairly primitive situation. 'And of course, if you built an extension along this back wall, the toilet would become part of the house.'

Lexie looked at the back door and the distance to the toilet. It was close. Just one step down and maybe three steps to the toilet door. But it was outside all the same. She looked at Andy who was clearly doing much the same calculation. How could they get around it? She could work with everything else in the house. It wasn't too big for her, yet big enough so she could already imagine having friends to stay, or Hannah and Ruby to sleep over.

Given the era, she was hopeful there would be decent floorboards under the foul carpet, and she was certainly not afraid to wield a paintbrush. In time, a jack-hammer would remove most of the concrete in the back yard, but in the meantime, she could live with it. The agent was right. There was plenty of room for an extension on the rear of the house, and any renovation would be easy on this relatively flat block. Lexie wanted it. Andy gave Lexie a look that only a sibling could interpret. He also thought it was worth considering. Turning to the agent, Lexie asked what the owner would accept.

The discussion was short and to the point. Clearly the agent thought the outside toilet, and the fact that hardly anything had been done to the house in fifty years (other than laying swathes of outdoor concrete and painting the rooms startling colours), was going to make this hard to sell, despite its obvious potential. Another factor in Lexie's favour was that the owners had recently inherited the house from a distant uncle, and were keen to sell quickly. Lexie didn't hesitate. She put in an offer, and within twenty-four hours it had been accepted.

Andy and Clare came over with a bottle of champagne to celebrate. Ray had heard about the outside toilet and he was less than thrilled. He also couldn't believe Lexie could cheerfully take on a substantial loan and not get a perfectly finished home for that price.

Finally, Jeanie said, 'For goodness' sake Ray! Stop going on about it. You need to stop looking up your golf handicap and check out the real estate in Perth! Prices have gone up since we bought this place, and the average loan has too.' Then she added, 'But I am worried about that outside loo, in the middle of the night. Won't you be scared, Lexie?'

Lexie nodded and laughed. 'You bet! I don't fancy going outside at night to the loo. Obviously, it's no problem during the day. But I'm hoping that between us all, we can brainstorm a temporary solution. I want to build an extension eventually, when I work out what I can afford, but in the meantime, I really don't want to hang on all night!'

'Well,' said Jeanie, 'your great Aunty Maggie always had a commode in her room. I remember going with Nanna May to empty it in the mornings.'

'That's just gross!' exclaimed Andy. 'I'm not volunteering to do that job for you Lex!'

Lexie grinned. It was such a relief to know she had her own home waiting for her, outdoor toilet or not. The settlement she offered was quick, just four weeks; another reason the sellers were keen to accept her offer. Once the bank had prepared the mortgage, handover would happen swiftly. The timing was perfect; school started in ten days' time, and the settlement was for mid February. She would have a couple of weeks to get into the swing of school and then she could move into the house. The owners had also generously agreed to allow her limited access to the house from early February, to rip up the carpets before she moved in.

With the purchase of the house finalised, Lexie made the most of the last few days of the school holidays. In between school finishing and the removalists arriving, moving back home, Christmas, and then house hunting, there had always been something to do. What a crazy four weeks, but Lexie was proud of what she'd achieved. It had also prevented her from dwelling on the past, which suited her. She told herself things happened for a purpose. *This really is a new beginning.* She was excited for the year ahead.

CHAPTER 6

Over the next few days, she indulged herself. By nature, a 'doer', Lexie's days were usually productive. Instead, she slept late, perusing the paper at her leisure over breakfast in her PJ's, so it was late morning before she even got dressed. Making the most of her self-enforced indolence, she lay on her bed reading, and if she felt inclined, watched movies in the afternoon. She jogged around her old trails and went to yoga classes. Tossing off Jed's hangover budget stipulations, she treated herself to a facial and full body massage. By end of the week, she was feeling relaxed and ready for the new school year. With the deadline of back-to-school looming, she finally contacted her old friend Kelly, who was now her new principal, and arranged to meet her at school.

Kelly was a bit of a hero to Lexie. When they first met, Kelly had been the deputy principal at Thomas Street Primary, where Lexie taught in her first year. Kelly was new to both the school and role the of deputy, and must have been quite overwhelmed as she settled into a leadership position at a new school, but had nonetheless given unselfishly of her time to Lexie, the new grad. Walking into her first class — a year six class to boot — was a challenge and Lexie well remembered the stress of those early days. She had always been given glowing, positive reports from her mentor teachers on practice rounds, so while she was nervous, she also was relatively confident of her ability to teach. She was also very naïve. Teaching an established class, already indoctrinated with routines and behavioural expectations, was one thing; starting from scratch, was another.

Lexie had arrived in her classroom, two days ahead of school commencing, thinking she was being conscientious, only to discover most teachers had already been in and out of their rooms preparing for the start of the school year for several days. Digesting this reality, she entered her own classroom to find it bare. Not only had the previous teacher taken all the classroom references and school manuals with him, but the furniture was still stacked against the walls, where the cleaners had left it. Her confidence turned to panic. She had only two days until the students arrived, and she hadn't factored in that one of those would be taken up with staff meetings and professional development! As she stood at the doorway surveying the shell of the classroom, Kelly came up behind her.

'You've got a bit to do, Lexie,' she said patting her shoulder sympathetically. 'But you've got time. You only have to be ready for the first day, not the whole year.' Then, handing over a box of files, she said, 'Here's your class list and all their files. You'll want to read through them in detail when you can, but I think for now, just look at the handover notes from their year five teachers. They are on top in the red file.'

Nodding as though all this made perfect sense, Lexie took the files wordlessly. She looked round for somewhere to put them and spotted the teacher's desk. Kelly watched as Lexie placed the files, her handbag and laptop on the desk. Admonishing herself for her stupidity Lexie's thoughts raced. *I just brought in a laptop and my handbag! What on earth was I thinking?*

She'd seen all those teachers trudging back and forth to their cars after school with boxes full of stuff! She certainly wasn't prepared, and she had no idea at this stage what 'stuff' she even needed. Feeling suddenly desperate, she took a risk. Trusting Kelly's kind eyes, and with a panicked edge to her voice, she blurted out,

'I have no idea what on earth I'm supposed to do here! I don't even know where to start! I feel so stupid that I hadn't really thought about the reality of starting off the year!' Lexie started pacing and opening drawers and cupboards randomly as she talked.

Kelly interrupted, 'Whoa! Settle down, Lexie. Take a breath!'

Smiling her reassurance, she continued: 'Don't be hard on yourself. We've all been there. If only they included a unit on starting the school year in these teaching degrees, we'd all be a lot better off. Welcome to the real world of teaching! It's hard work, but you wouldn't have slogged through the last four years of study if you didn't want to be here. Now, practical things first. Have you got a pen and paper handy?'

Lexie pulled a notepad and pen from her handbag. At least she'd thought of that! Listening intently, she scribbled dot points quickly as Kelly spoke.

'Okay. First. You need to think of how you want to set-up the classroom. Get the physical layout in order before you worry about other stuff. How do you want the kids to sit? In groups or rows? Where are you going to put your desk? Front or back of the room? Where do you want the kids' tubs to be? Together against the wall, or under the windows? Or either side of the room? Are you happy with where the computers are? You won't have much flexibility with that because of the portals, and the power-point setup, but it needs some thought.

And you'll need a space for your own textbooks and files. Also, somewhere to put artwork or PE equipment.'

Pausing for breath, Kelly added, 'You can get plenty of stuff online, but I'd also advise visiting the teacher resources in the library. They may be well picked over by now, but there are some gems there that can really help you with planning. Each room should have a copy of the school plans, curriculum and classroom behaviour documents, and I'll make sure you get a set. They use a thing called Zones of Regulation here, which I'm not up to speed on just yet, as well as a weekly Virtues Program…. but I'm sure they'll cover all that tomorrow in the staff meeting.'

Lexie wrote furiously. She knew the Virtues Program, they'd used it at her last school, and she had a fair idea about the Zones of Regulation because they had researched some of those behavioural programs at uni. Right now, she was definitely in the Red Zone! She looked up at Kelly with a wry smile, 'Thanks.'

'My next bit of advice is don't even think about planning too far ahead. You'll want to spend some time on the first day just setting classroom boundaries and expectations, and establishing a rough daily timetable. These kids have done this a few times already, so are probably better at it than you,' she said winking.

'They know the blurb, even if they don't always follow it. But you'll need to have some maths lessons prepared, and a few writing and literacy tasks. You don't want twenty-seven students sitting around with nothing to do.'

Kelly then left Lexie to work her way through the list. She'd popped in several more times that first week, giving support and a few helpful words of advice. Lexie had been eternally grateful for the quiet presence of Kelly in and out of her classroom throughout the year, and they had become close allies as the year progressed. Lexie had kept in touch with her mentor, even after she left Perth to travel, and later, to go down south with Jed. Kelly had waited loyally for several years for the former principal to retire, and in the meantime, deservedly gained the respect of the staff.

Kelly spotted Lexie through her office window as she arrived in the carpark, and went out to meet her. They embraced warmly, before Kelly stood back, her arms on Lexie's shoulders and gave Lexie one of her deep searching looks.

'It's so good to see you! But first, how are you? I don't want to hear any bullshit! I know you didn't expect to be back here.'

Lexie was touched to think Kelly knew her so well. She had thought the same thing this morning, as she'd pulled up in the staff carpark. A year ago, she would never have dreamed she'd be back at her first school. Smiling sheepishly, she said, 'You are so right! I thought my days at Thomas Street were over, but I am glad to be back here. No bullshit!' she laughed.

As they walked towards the admin entrance Kelly said, 'I'll only say this once and I won't mention him again, unless you want to. But he's clearly a dick to let you go and therefore obviously stupid, so not worthy of you.'

'Thanks, Kels. It's okay. I'm tougher than I thought, and I'm actually pretty excited to be back here. It's going to be fun working with you again, even if I'll be in pre-primary this time round. I know that's not *your* comfort zone.'

Pushing open the door as they went through, Kelly laughed.

'Shh! That's supposed to be a secret! But I'm glad you took up the offer. Importantly, you're qualified and you've taught in early childhood, so I have great faith in you. You are a fabulous teacher, and we need someone of your experience. I do love the older kids, but I'm the first to admit that we need our best teachers in the early years.'

'We're on the same page there Kel. I'm impressed you've been converted. And I'm ready for some hopefully sweet little five-year-olds,' said Lexie holding up crossed fingers.

Chatting amicably, they crossed the playground to the Early Childhood Centre. Kelly unlocked the door and handed the key to Lexie.

'It's yours now. Try not to lose it! It is such a pain if we have to get another one. The alarm was switched off this morning when the cleaners arrived, but I'll get you to re-set it before you leave. Code is,' and she referred to her phone notes, '8458. I'll text it to you.'

'No worries. The keys are safe with me,' Lexie said, crossing her fingers and giving a cheeky grin. She stepped in and surveyed her old classroom. Not much had changed since she taught here last, but there was new vinyl on the floor, and a touch screen that looked the latest in technology. It had always been a lovely light-filled space, and its dimensions were very generous. Lexie felt that familiar spark of excitement for its possibilities. Keen to start planning, she was already mentally sifting through ideas as to how she would set it up.

'This is such a great room! I'd forgotten how big it was. And I meant to ask before, the most important question. Who is my education assistant?'

'You've got Indie Greaves as your EA. She's about your age. Mid-thirties, energetic, very professional, loves kids, and the last teacher she worked with couldn't have sung her praises any more highly. I think you'll get along well; she knows this room inside-out, so she'll be able to help you set up. I had a battle to keep her here in PP. The year three teachers wanted her to work with them this year; there are a few prickly characters in that year,' Kelly grimaced as she spoke, 'but I wanted her in here with you. I think you'll make a great team. And Indie was with kindy last year, so she already has a good rapport with the class. You'll find there are a few kids who will need extra help settling into pre-primary, which is why I thought we should have our best staff on deck...you can't say I'm not looking after you.'

Lexie was touched. As educators and friends, they had always got on well. This was going to be an even smoother transition than she hoped for. Leaving the door ajar as she left, Kelly headed back to the office where more admin work awaited. Lexie watched her familiar quick-stepping gait, as she walked back across the yard to her office. In the few years since they had last worked together, Lexie saw Kelly had not lost any of her momentum. Never one to stroll anywhere, she was like a force of nature as she scurried down walkways and hurtled around corners; always busy, always rushing to her next meeting or other commitment. Turning to face the room, she sighed. She didn't need to consult Kelly's list of jobs anymore. She knew what she had to do and it was time to get to work.

An hour later she had rearranged the physical layout of the room and collected several resources. Positioning the tables in strategic groups of four and six, she was satisfied the arrangement would do for the first week or so, or until she got to know the kids a bit better. Thankfully the teacher's desk, chair and mat were exactly where she would have put them, although these days the placement of smart boards dominated the room, leaving teachers less options.

Lexie liked a portable old-fashioned whiteboard close to her chair, so she went in search of that and discovered the storeroom was bursting with fabulous play equipment and resources. Grabbing a huge container of Lego, a perennial favourite, and a couple of other boxes of construction toys, she looked around in amazement at the choices available. With no-one around to challenge her, she took whatever she wanted. By eleven o'clock, she was on a roll and making great progress. Trekking back to the car, she returned with the first box of her own resources and files.

Along the way she collected the class lists from Dana, in the office. This turned into an extended chat, as Dana was another long-term staff member whom Lexie knew from her previous time at the school. Dana was keen to find out everything Lexie had been up to over the last seven years. Luckily the phone kept ringing and Lexie managed to escape between calls, once again seeking the sanctuary of her quiet classroom. There would be plenty of opportunity for long conversations, but right now she wanted to make the most of this chance to get organised before staff meetings and professional development sessions encroached on her precious time.

Sinking into the chair at her desk, Lexie sipped her first coffee since breakfast. It had been quite a physical morning, hauling tables and chairs into place and carrying heavy boxes to her room. She ran her eye down the list of kids' names. It was unlikely the names would mean anything to her, since it was years since she had last taught at Thomas Street. There were twenty-seven students: thirteen boys and fourteen girls. It could be worse. She'd heard of some classes squeezing in up to thirty-one students, albeit with extra teaching assistants in the mix. She definitely preferred fewer students, no matter how much extra help she was given.

Lexie studied the list again, this time running an eye over the family details. It helped to know if there were other siblings, and also to check the children who had sole parents, which could be a mum or dad these days. At this point they were only names, but soon she would know their little faces and this information would become very relevant. She stopped at Arlo Evans. 'Evans', Lexie pondered. That surname was vaguely familiar.

Flicking through the accompanying family details, she searched for Evans. Mother: Amber Evans. The name jumped out at her. *Amber Evans? It couldn't be the same Amber?* Lexie dismissed it almost as soon as she thought it. She reckoned she'd taught Amber maybe ten years ago, possibly in her second year of teaching. That would make Amber about 22 or 23 now. With a five-year-old? Unlikely. She looked closer at the family information. *Ah! A sibling, Ruby. In year one. No, that made it impossible.* Amber would have been barely sixteen when she had her first baby. *Not entirely impossible though*, thought Lexie recalling the tough childhood Amber had endured when she taught her in year six.

She remembered Amber; she was hard to forget, for several reasons. Closing her eyes for a moment Lexie conjured up a memory of a thin, almost skinny girl, who was never any trouble and quite capable academically. Shy and quiet, she mostly hung around the edges of the little social cliques that existed within the class. Lexie couldn't remember any nastiness towards her from the other girls; they were a good bunch of kids that year and everyone looked out for each other. Boys and girls had synced well together, and even if there was the inevitable immaturity from the boys as they pushed every boundary, the common sense of the girls seemed to balance it out. Amber had been a lost little soul though, and she had wondered occasionally over the years what had happened to her.

Amber's mother had three children, to different fathers? Lexie couldn't quite remember, but Amber was the oldest. There were many days when Amber didn't make it to school because she was at home looking after the baby. *Two brothers! One at school and the other, only a toddler. Her mother's name was…* Lexie thought hard… *Cynthia? Sandi? … no. Cindy! Cindy Evans! Amber's dad must have been someone Evans. Or did Cindy keep her own name?* Cindy wasn't your average suburban mum. And she was more than a match for Lexie who was only in her second year of teaching at the time. Quickly, Lexie scanned the close contacts for Arlo. No sign of Cindy Evans' name as an emergency contact. The father wasn't named among the contacts either. A neighbour was listed as the emergency contact, an Erica Watson. *If this is the Amber I taught, there's a story in this, and probably not a happy one,* thought Lexie with some sadness.

Cindy had always been able to manipulate the system, but only so that it served her own purposes, never for the benefit of her children. Lexie remembered her as a selfish, almost distant mother, showing little regard for Amber, on whom she seemed to rely heavily. Amber was constantly late for school and frequently absent.

When Lexie questioned her, Amber was always loyal, saying something like, 'Mum was sick and I had to help get the baby breakfast,' or 'I slept in.' She never told the story Lexie suspected was the truth, and that was that Amber not only got the baby dressed and fed, but did the same for her little brother as well. She definitely made both their lunches before walking him to school, regardless of the weather, and dropping him off to his year one classroom on the way. Lexie always supposed Amber wrote the absence and late notes too; clever enough to disguise the writing by doing it all in capitals.

With Kelly's help, Lexie had tried to coax Cindy up to the school for an interview regarding Amber's progress, but she always had an excuse. She also knew just how far she could push the absences and late arrivals, managing to pull her head in just before they reached the reportable stage. Thin, with a mass of dyed blond hair, Cindy was really quite attractive and considerably younger than most of the year six mothers. On the rare times that Cindy did turn up, Lexie could tell that she'd made an effort with her appearance, even if her jittery manner and constant scratching gave her away. Lexie surmised there may have been money for drugs, but not for the kids.

Amber and her brother would not even have had school uniforms if it wasn't for Kelly unearthing items in the lost and found cupboard, or securing them from the uniform shop. On the days when students could wear casual clothes, Amber was always absent. Lexie surmised it may have been because her casual clothes might not measure up to those of her classmates.

Occasionally, Cindy would appear with a man. Amber didn't say much, but she mentioned to Lexie that John, who was possibly both of the boys' father, had recently moved back in with them. When Lexie asked Amber where he was from, she clammed up and dodged any further questions with vague answers, saying he was from 'over East'. Lexie finally got a good look at him when Cindy and John came to watch the sports carnival… *Robbie! Robbie was the little brother!* Lexie finally remembered his name. She also remembered sidling over to Jess, Robbie's class teacher, that day to ask what she knew about the father.

'I'm pretty sure he's just got out of jail on drug charges, maybe possession or something like that. He gives me the creeps. But I think you're right about him being the baby's dad. And he's on the enrolment form as Robbie's father as well. He's definitely been around for a while, on and off. I have to admit it scares me that Amber is in the same house as him, not to mention his dodgy mates.'

Standing together in the centre of the school oval, they'd shot discrete glances towards John, the ex-con boyfriend, each sizing him up. It was hard to see what Cindy saw in him. His scruffiness for a start was a sharp contrast to her own neat, if slightly tarty appearance. Skinny and mean-looking, with a rough grey beard and eyes which were deep set and hooded. Tattoos covered his neck, and when he grinned his teeth were yellowed and stained. He had absolutely no backside and his jeans hung low, revealing faded black jocks.

Amber didn't get to finish the year, as it turned out, which was one reason Lexie lost track of her. It was early in term four when Lexie arrived at school to see police walking into the Admin Building. Following them inside, she watched as they were ushered into the principal's office. She heard the words 'fire overnight'. Dana, who even then was working in the office, waited for the door to close before following Lexie down towards the staff room. Grabbing Lexie's arm dramatically, she whispered,

'So, there's been a fire at Cindy Evan's place overnight! Don't worry. The kids are all fine, no-one was hurt, but it turns out that her boyfriend was running a little meth lab in the garage, and it exploded and caught fire. The fire spread to the house and for once Cindy must have been on the ball and she got all the kids out. Neighbours called the fire brigade and I think the kids are staying with them. Cindy's been at the police station all night answering questions. Still there by the sound of it. I think the boyfriend got out, but apparently, he didn't stick around and the cops are looking for him!'

Dana was agog with the drama of it all, but she wasn't the only one affected. Lexie recalled just how unsettled her class was that day and in the days that followed, and she'd had to counsel the students as they processed the news of their classmate being in a house fire. When Amber returned to school later in the week everyone was genuinely concerned for her, and they all went out of their way to make her feel safe. Meanwhile, a couple of mothers from Robbie and Amber's classes set to work, fundraising for the family who had lost everything. The donations poured in. There were new clothes, books and toys, the like of which Amber and her brothers had probably never seen.

Miraculously, Cindy, being the true survivor she was, escaped any criminal charges from the police. Rumours swirled that she had been given a deal in exchange for information, but that was probably just school gossip. The family was provided with temporary accommodation, and Cindy became the model parent for a few weeks, even walking the kids to school while the initial investigations were underway. Then, towards the end of the year, Amber and Robbie were suddenly absent for three days. It was Kelly who gave Lexie the news that Robbie and Amber had been enrolled at a school in Manjimup, and wouldn't be returning. It was almost December. Within weeks, her class graduated, and Amber missed all the celebrations.

Lexie dragged herself back to the present. She was remembering many things about Amber, but she needed to concentrate on what was right here in front of her. She had twenty-seven students arriving in a couple of days, and she wanted get her head around planning, at least get something in place for the first week or two. She began reading through copies of their kindy reports, managing to concentrate for another hour, jotting notes to herself as she went, until she ran out of steam. She closed her computer and tidied the paperwork on her desk. There was no doubt that recalling Amber's tough life had rattled her. Could little Amber really have ended up pregnant at fifteen, or sixteen? Lexie had always thought it a shame she hadn't been able to finish her final year of primary school with her friends, but that would be insignificant in comparison with becoming a teenage mother. Packing some files in her backpack to look over at home, she resolved to talk to Kelly. She would know.

CHAPTER 7

It wasn't until two days later, when all the staff returned to officially start the school year, that Lexie was finally able to catch Kelly alone and ask about Amber. Kelly had been in constant meetings with new staff, or away attending briefing sessions at the regional office; her time was in high demand at the start of the school year. Finally, Lexie saw her moment as the teachers broke from a lengthy staff meeting discussing changes to the rewards system for the year. Swiftly she followed Kelly into her office and closed the door.

'What's up, Lexie?' quizzed Kelly, slightly taken aback, as Lexie rushed in behind her.

'What's up is I've got a kid in my class called Arlo Evans, and his mother is Amber Evans. Don't tell me that's my little Amber I taught here in year six?'

Instantly Kelly's face fell; she understood Lexie's concern. She nodded slowly, her face mirroring Lexie's own dismay.

'Yes. I'd completely forgotten you had taught Amber! She's had such a tough life, and I don't think it's improving the older she gets.' Sighing she went on, 'You've probably done the numbers. She must have fallen pregnant at fifteen or sixteen.

Such a hard road for her, and you can imagine the little help she would have received from her mother.'

Lexie shook her head, her fears confirmed.

'I thought it was too big a coincidence: two Amber Evans! And around the same age! But I was still hoping things had turned out better for her.'

'Well, Arlo looks like he might have some developmental issues, and we're concerned about him, and Ruby too. Both need support. Not that Amber isn't doing her best, I can't fault her on anything regarding their health and care. But they arrived half-way through last year, and Ruby had been in three schools before that!' Kelly shrugged. 'I can't believe I forgot you'd taught Amber! But it will be reassuring for her to see a familiar face. She's still as timid as she was as a twelve-year-old.'

A knock at the door signalled Kelly was being sought yet again.

'It's such a shame. But we should talk later,' said Lexie as she left.

Staff commitments over for the day, Lexie was free to get on with her planning. On her way to the Early Childhood centre she saw Indie Greaves disappear into her room, dragging a trolley of classroom supplies behind her. Even after working together for only a few hours, Lexie knew she had hit the jackpot with Indie. Lexie hoped she looked as on top of her game as Indie clearly was.

'Hooray!' exclaimed Indie, greeting her with an enthusiastic smile, as she placed the last of the jigsaw puzzles on their designated shelf. 'Freedom at last! I bet you've been busting to get back here.'

'Absolutely!' responded Lexie, rolling her eyes for effect. 'I am so over it. Everyone is. We all just want to get into our rooms and set up, and those endless discussions on Whole

School Behaviours and Reward Systems, are like sticking pins in your eyes. But look at you! I can't believe how much you've done in a couple of hours. This is amazing, thank you!'

'Well, it helped that I found out last year I was coming to this room. Knowing the set-up, I prepared a few things over the holidays and that's saved heaps of time,' said Indie, as she pointed to all the colourful, practical containers, holding a variety of pencils, crayons, scissors and glue sticks. The craft table was piled with paper and materials, and the paints were already out with a selection of thick and fine brushes, just as Lexie liked it.

Seriously, thought Lexie, *this woman is a mind reader!*

'And I've made some nametags for the first day. I haven't laminated them yet, because I thought it might be a good activity for the kids to decorate their own,' suggested Indie.

'I think it's a great idea! They can draw little pictures on them and I've got some stickers that could work well,' agreed Lexie, pleased that Indie was on the same wavelength.

The ideas began to flow between them and as they worked, Lexie pumped Indie about some of the students, and the class in general. Eventually Lexie looked up and realised the time, exclaiming,

'I'm so sorry Indie! You should have left an hour ago. I didn't mean to keep you this long. You should have said something!'

'I got a bit carried away myself,' replied Indie looking up at the clock, as she finished the last of her craft table preparations. 'And I do need to get a move on. My kids are with my mum, but she'll be well and truly exhausted by now.'

Grabbing her bag, she gave a final satisfied glance at the craft table, saying,

'I think we're almost ready anyway. Don't get too carried away yourself, either. Have a great night!' and with that she exited, walking swiftly towards the carpark.

Lexie continued to feel bad. She didn't want to wear out Indie's goodwill on the first day. She'd been teaching too long in the upper school, and she'd forgotten that education assistants finished up at three-fifteen. She made a mental note to not forget again. With most of the practical things ready for the first day, Lexie made a couple more trips to the staffroom and the office to collect the various files and forms she would need, including a hard copy of the roll for tomorrow. By five-thirty, Lexie was flagging. Whatever wasn't already done she would just have to wing.

Driving slowly through the traffic on the way home, Lexie finally had time to think through a few personal issues. She had been so focused on setting up, that she'd hardly given a thought to her private list of things to do. The removalists were booked for 26 February, and although excited, she was also a bit anxious about it all. She was hoping she would manage living there alone. It wasn't going to be as easy a move as when she and Jed had set up, both full of shared plans. This time she would have to cope with all the surprises an old house brings, on her own. Despite all his faults, Jed had actually been quite handy.

Money was also going to be tight having to pay a mortgage on one wage, let alone considering the renovations she wanted to do. And she hadn't found a solution yet for the outside loo! Weighed down by a mounting list of jobs, Lexie was quite stressed by the time she pulled into her parents' driveway, after a forty-five-minute crawl through peak-hour traffic.

Walking in through the front door, arms weighed down with files and her lap-top, she was immediately hit by the tantalising smells of Jeanie's chicken curry, an aromatic balm to her frazzled mood. A quiet domestic scene played out in the loungeroom, as Ray and Jeanie sat relaxing in front of the TV, a glass of wine in hand, watching their favourite quiz show. Lexie barely had a chance to put her bags in the study, before Ray placed a glass of cold wine in her hand, and Jeanie was asking her about her day.

All thoughts of feeling sorry for herself were quickly dismissed. She'd endured many months of solitude last year when no-one greeted her as she came home, when she'd moped around alone at night. This was such a pleasant contrast, and she didn't even have to think about preparing a meal or shopping! Her dear mum had done it all. Briefly she considered staying here and renting out the house, instead of selling. How easy would it be? But then she reminded herself that at thirty-three she was supposed to be independent – and she did know that the novelty of living at home would rub off eventually. But, for the moment she was content to enjoy the perks. As they ate dinner, Lexie told Ray and Jeanie about Amber, and her brief conversation with Kelly.

'I think I remember you talking about Amber, all those years ago. You used to worry about her. There was something about her mother? Drugs?' Jeanie asked, concerned.

'Yep. Her mother Cindy was a junkie and Amber virtually brought up her little brothers. She missed way too much school because she was probably looking after them. Then halfway through the year, this guy turned up who was actually Robbie and Sam's dad. He was the one who had a meth lab in the garage, and eventually burnt the house down.'

'That's right! And all my friends donated clothes and toys to help the family. Then they went somewhere else, didn't they?'

'Manjimup. Cindy had some connection there. And we lost track of them after that.' Lexie shrugged. 'But I'm about to find out what happened to Amber. Whatever it was, it wasn't an improvement in her life, if she ended up with two kids at barely eighteen. Such a sad story.'

'Maybe things aren't as grim as they look. She might be doing quite well,' offered Ray.

'I hope so, but I have my doubts,' responded Lexie thoughtfully. 'I always wondered if I had let Amber and her brothers down, by not pushing harder to get Child Protection involved. Amber and Robbie didn't come to school with bruises or any indication that they had been abused. But neglect? Yes, probably. It's such a fine line between potentially separating them from their mother, or hoping that eventually she would get her act together. And then they disappeared off to Manjimup and it was all out of our hands.'

'I'm sure you did what you could, Lexie. Life is not always a level playing field, and not every child has parents with the skills and resources to give them a fighting chance. And I bet there'll be more in your class to worry about, than just Amber's little fellow,' warned Jeanie realistically.

'True,' agreed Lexie, 'but I have to admit I'm more than curious about Amber. And Mum, you are so right! Life's certainly not a level playing field. Amber had so much baggage. She never stood a chance with a mother like Cindy.'

Lexie left early for school the next day, arriving before seven-thirty, and missing the worst of the traffic. Nevertheless, there were already several cars in the carpark. She wasn't the only one anxious for the first day to go well. Lexie knew she was well-prepared but she wanted to run an eye over everything and to add a few things to the home corner and dress-up box. There were plenty of construction toys in the room, which were usually pounced on by the boys and to a lesser degree by the girls, but she needed to cover all interests. She'd run out of time yesterday to create alternative areas for imaginative play. It didn't take long. Stepping back a little while later, Lexie surveyed the room just as Indie arrived.

'It looks great Lexie,' enthused Indie. 'I love that you've still got a home corner!'

'Probably a bit old-fashioned these days with such little time for play in the curriculum, but it's there if we get some free time. And,' she laughed, 'I'll make sure there is time for play.'

Nodding with satisfaction Lexie pronounced all was ready, and went to the kitchen area to put the kettle on. She hoped she would be able to at least get in a quick coffee before she had to open the door and start greeting parents. *Thank goodness for the habits started during Covid,* thought Lexie. She loved the quicker drop offs these days, parents being discouraged from lingering too long in classrooms. No more protracted goodbyes with over-anxious parents not quite willing to let go, or kids, seeing their parent hovering, getting upset and crying. Lexie was hoping for a cohort of care-givers keen to 'drop and run'.

She had only managed a couple of sips of her coffee before she heard the tell-tale sounds of people gathering at the door. She'd written a note on the white-board outside noting the door would be open at eight-thirty, but she always knew this was optimistic. Checking with Indie that she was okay to start, Lexie took a final swallow from her mug, and opened the door five minutes early. Smiling over the rowdy chaos of twenty-seven five-year-olds, their parents and siblings, she said in her strongest teacher's voice,

'Good morning, everyone and welcome! I'm Lexie Hudson, your pre-primary teacher for this year. Parents, if you haven't found it already, you'll see your child's name on a bag hook, where you can leave their bags and hats.' Pointing to a table set up inside the doorway, she continued with her instructions,

'Water bottles and fruit can be placed here on the Crunch and Sip table. There are tracing mats with the children's names on them on the tables. After that, they can read a book or do a puzzle, and once your child is settled and happy, you are free to leave. I've got some name tags here as well and I'll be busy matching each child to their nametag. I'm available if you've got any questions, or need to give me any particular information about your child, otherwise you can talk to Indie. I think most of you know Mrs Greaves from Kindy.'

With that Lexie stood aside and the excitement and chaos rolled through the doorway. Lexie quickly grabbed her container of nametags, and squatting down so she was at child height, smiled warmly at the closest child and said, 'Hi. I'm Miss Hudson. What's your name?

'I'm Ben, b–e–n,' came the very composed reply from a cute little boy, whose black curls tumbled around his face. 'And I can write my name already.'

'That's fantastic, Ben,' Lexie replied, locating his name tag and pinning it onto his school shirt with accustomed ease. 'I also love that you can sound out your name. But if you write it for me then it gives me another chance to remember you.'

Satisfied with that explanation, he took a seat at the table and began to trace his name. Lexie moved skilfully around the room, greeting parents and children, pinning on name tags and trying to make a connection with every child in some way. Most parents were content with a quick hello, knowing they would get to speak to Lexie privately at a later stage, but there were always one or two who continued to linger, wanting to corner Lexie with information, or questions. Lexie and Indie, both experienced in sifting through what was vital and what could wait for a later time, deftly managed to keep the crowd of parents flowing. Glancing up at one point, Lexie saw a very young mother enter and guide her child to the tracing mat marked 'Arlo'. Amber! This was one parent she definitely needed to speak to! She made her way over to Amber, exclaiming,

'Amber Evans! It's so lovely to see you! I saw Arlo's name on my list and thought he might be your little boy.' As she spoke Lexie examined the adult Amber closely. As a twelve-year-old she had been quite pretty, with green eyes and sun-streaked fair hair. Lexie remembered her always having a ponytail, but today her hair hung loose, a long fringe almost obscuring her eyes . The sweet face, with its tiny nose and clear complexion, was the same, Lexie wasn't sure she would have even recognised Amber, had she passed her in the street. She'd been such a skinny kid.; all arms and legs, she was one of the last girls in the class to go through puberty.

Ten years later she was still slim and petite, but even with her shoulders hunched, there was no hiding the generous curve of her breasts, and the attractive woman she'd become. Despite her fragile appearance, Lexie could imagine a wiry strength underneath that belied the dainty exterior; a theory confirmed when she felt the sinewy grip of Amber's hand when she shook it. Lexie recalled what a serious little girl she had been. Even now, there was the faint trace of a hovering frown, eyes drawn close together with concentration. However, as Lexie spoke to her, a smile of recognition burst across Amber's face, lighting up her eyes, chasing away her frown, and with it, the years.

'Hi! Miss Hudson! I'm glad to see you too! I'm really happy Arlo is in your class. He's a good boy, well, at least he is for me. And it's nice to see you back here at Thomas Street. You weren't here last year, were you? They said you've been teaching somewhere down south.'

'Yes. I was, for a few years. But it is nice to be back here and I'm really happy to see a familiar face. We'll have to get together and find out what you've been up to since you went off to Manjimup, after the fire.'

Bending down to pin on Arlo's name tag, Lexie missed the wave of agitation on Amber's face at the mention of Manjimup.

'Hello Arlo. I'm Miss Hudson. Did you know I used to teach your mum?'

Shaking his head, Arlo looked dubiously up at Amber for confirmation.

'It's true Arlo. Miss Hudson taught me when I was in year six! You're very lucky to have her as your teacher.' Bending to kiss him goodbye, she whispered, 'Now, be a good boy and I'll be back to pick you up soon.'

Cutting the conversation short, Amber stood up, abruptly apologising. 'I'm sorry, Miss Hudson, I'll have to go because I've got Ruby waiting for me outside. She's in year one; I'd better get her to her room.'

Lexie was a little surprised at Amber's sudden exit, noticing though that Amber had clammed up very quickly when asked about what she had been doing. This wasn't the time for long conversations anyway, but Lexie made a mental note to tread more carefully next time. Of course, Amber wouldn't want an ex-teacher quizzing her on her life! Watching her walk away, Lexie was struck by the unobtrusive, almost submissive way she navigated the sea of parents in the room. She certainly looked young compared to most of the other mothers, many of whom were already well into their thirties, some older still. She could easily have been mistaken for an older sister doing the school drop-off.

The day passed in a whirl, both Lexie and Indie flat out making sure the kids had as smooth a transition from kindy to pre-primary as possible. There had been the inevitable tears, when things didn't go as expected, and also a few moments when a child suddenly realised Mum had actually left and wasn't just outside the door… then, the tears could quickly escalate to hysteria, unless Lexie or Indie intervened with a clever distraction. There were also those who loved every minute, so much so, that they wanted to tear off and explore every toy in the room. Lexie had to draw on all her experience to herd twenty-seven little individuals to the mat at the same time; a process repeated several times through the day, as they moved from their tables to free activities and back to the mat.

She noted a couple of children whose behaviour concerned her, but they had already been flagged by the kindy teachers, so she could follow them up easily. All things considered; Lexie was hopeful it would be a good class. She had monitored Arlo closely, curious to gauge his strengths and weaknesses. He was unusually tall for his age, unlike Amber's tiny frame. Well-built, he seemed to have good coordination, sitting cross-legged with a strong, upright back. In all, he was a good-looking kid: blue-eyed, with thick straight fair hair. He played happily enough with the other children, although he wasn't overly friendly, seeming to prefer a bit of space. Lexie wondered at his reserve. He wasn't easy to read.

As she dismissed the class at the end of the day, Lexie managed to wave at Amber from the doorway. She called out, 'Arlo's had a good day!' which Amber acknowledged with a smile, just as a little girl, presumably Ruby, ran up to Amber, talking excitedly. Lexie was encouraged by the scene before her. Both children looked like they adored Amber, and in return Amber appeared to be very affectionate with them. Lexie watched long enough to see all three hold hands as Amber led the way to the gate, before she was pounced on by Felix's mother wondering how he'd settled in after she left that morning. Felix was one of the children who had stood out to Lexie, so she was keen to talk to his mum. This would possibly be the first of many conversations about Felix.

By the end of the week, Lexie knew the names not only of all her students, but their parents and siblings as well. Making genuine connections with the families of the children she taught, was important to Lexie. She firmly believed education was a team effort between parents or carers, and teachers. She continued to observe Arlo, and in these early days of the school year, he was one of many she was watching closely. When the bell rang on Friday afternoon of the first week, Lexie was ready for the weekend break. One by one, Lexie called the children from the mat, handing newsletters to the parents as she did so. By ten past three all the children had gone, except Arlo. This was the first time Amber had been late and Lexie stood outside the room scanning for her. Spotting Ruby waiting near the pre-primary building, Lexie called her over.

'You can come and wait inside if you like, Ruby. Arlo is just helping me finish all the jigsaw puzzles so you can help him. Mum won't be long, I'm sure.'

Ruby edged in through the doorway, almost sidling into the room, her timid movements reminiscent of her mother's. Dark-haired, Ruby had an exotic look about her. Lexie wondered who her father was, because with her dark almond shaped eyes and olive skin, she was in complete contrast to Arlo. They shared Amber's straight hair, but that was the only feature connecting both children to Amber.

While Ruby and Arlo silently tidied up the jigsaws, Lexie continued working at the computer, stealing an occasional glance at the siblings. She printed out a few things ready to be photocopied next week. Indie had brought in the last of the outdoor equipment, but volunteered to stay on for a few more minutes to keep an eye on Arlo and Ruby while Lexie raced up to the printer in the library. Lexie expected Amber to have collected the children before she returned, but she hadn't.

Remorseful that she had kept Indie late again, Lexie complained in frustration.

'I can't believe they haven't replaced the printer down here yet! Remind me to send an email and I'll follow it up next week! But thanks very much for staying.' Then in a lower voice she said, 'I thought Amber would be here by now. No phone calls, or messages from the office?'

Indie shook her head. 'Nothing. And I really don't mind staying longer when I can. I'd rather finish up before I leave anyway.'

'You're an absolute gem. I really appreciate it, Indie.'

'No worries,' Indie replied, gathering her things and taking a last look around. Gesturing with her head towards the children, she said quietly, 'It's getting on to three twenty-five. That's late for a pick-up. Do you want me to take them to the office on my way?'

'No, it's fine. I'm in no hurry this afternoon. But I agree, it is late.'

Shrugging her shoulders, she raised her eyebrows and met Indie's eyes, both acknowledging each other's concerns, before saying in a louder voice, 'Enjoy your weekend. See you Monday!'

When Indie had gone, Lexie sat on a low table nearby and watched Arlo and Ruby play. They had finished the jigsaws and now Ruby had the doll's house open, and Arlo sat beside her playing with the miniature family's car. Lexie could see they were a good team, used to playing side by side. That they were not fazed, prepared to wait patiently for Amber to arrive, also told Lexie much about them. These were resilient kids, not demanding, and used to being left alone. Hoping to find out a bit more about their lives, Lexie asked Ruby,

'How was your first week in year one, Ruby? Did you like it?

Without looking up, Ruby nodded. Lexie tried a different tack.

'You've got Mrs Pocock, haven't you? I think she likes playing her guitar. Have you been singing lots?'

Again, just a nod, but this time Ruby at least looked up.

'What's the best thing about being in year one?'

Ruby finally spoke.

'We go to the art room for art lessons. And we have enough iPads for everyone and we can use the computers. And Mr Lang took us to the science room for science. That was good.'

She speaks! 'That sounds cool, Ruby. What did you do in science?'

'We went out and collected leaves and plants and flowers. Then we had to find the stems, and the roots and the leaves, and draw them in our books. And the best part was looking at all the different roots, because that's the bit underground and we don't see it.'

Before Lexie could say anything else, Amber flew in through the door, apologising profusely for her lateness.

'I'm so sorry Miss Hudson. I got held up at home and couldn't get the car until now. Come on guys, we need to move quickly, because Marco's waiting for the car.' Amber moved like a whirlwind. What surprised Lexie even more, was the speed with which Arlo and Ruby packed away the toys, grabbed their bags and were running to the door in seconds. Lexie barely had a chance to reply.

'No worries. They are fine here with me anytime if you get stuck. Just text me next time so I know. And you can call me Lexie!' she added, as an afterthought. As they ran out across the playground to the carpark, Amber's shout of 'Thank you!' a faint cry in the distance.

Astonished at the team work she had just witnessed, Amber said aloud to no-one,

'Well, you certainly don't see that every day.'

CHAPTER 8

Amber's heart was pounding. A jack-hammer thumping in her chest.

'Great job kids. Put your seatbelts on. I'm sorry I'm so late! Marco doesn't know I took the car… so, just remember if Marco asks, say that Felix's mum picked you up. Okay?' said Amber in a rush, as she reversed quickly and skidded out of the deserted carpark.

She figured that she was safe for at least ten minutes, before Marco woke up and realised, she was gone. The school was a fifteen-minute walk away through winding side streets, even if you cut across the park. But only five, maybe less, by car. As long as she didn't stuff it up by having an accident, she thought, slowing down for the Corolla in front that was coasting along at an agonising thirty-five kilometres an hour! She prayed to the gods it would turn left at the next intersection and whooped silently when it did. She sped through the remaining streets in record time.

Braking gently a couple of houses away, Amber cut the engine and let the car cruise into the driveway. Signing to the kids to exit by her door, they unquestioningly climbed over to the front where she held the handle out, closing the car door without a sound. She would come back later on the pretext of looking for something, and close it properly. Ruby and Arlo waited. Leaning down close, Amber whispered,

'Remember. Felix's mum, and count to one hundred slowly, then you can come in.'

Not for the first time, Amber hated herself for putting this shit on her kids. They didn't ever question her though, about Marco. She knew they were both terrified of his nasty moods. Silently, Amber pushed open the back door she'd left ajar, and tip-toed inside. Marco, was just stirring in the bedroom, as she'd hoped. She expelled the breath she had been unconsciously holding. It looked like she got away with it this time, but she couldn't go on like this. Marco was getting even more demanding, more difficult. She worked so hard to please him, and she so badly wanted this to be her fairytale ending, but it definitely looked like once again, she'd stuffed up. When Marco called out from the bedroom, she froze.

'Hey babe. I thought I heard a car!'

'Yeah. I think it's Tilly, Felix's mum. She picked the kids up from school.'

'All soft cocks, the kids these days,' declared Marco as he appeared in the kitchen in his boxer shorts, scratching his balls. Walking by on his way to the loo, Marco grabbed her, roughly squeezing her right breast.

'Now if I'd let you go off and pick up the kids, you'd have missed that little tumble we had, babe. You need to listen to my good ideas a bit more often,' he crowed, just as Arlo and Ruby walked in the door.

'Here they are, the little blood suckers!'

Amber's stress levels were at breaking point. The sex and a sleep hadn't improved his bad temper, so she jerked her head towards the door, sounding harsher than she meant to.

'Go outside you two; I'll call you when it's time for dinner.'

Arlo started to protest that he was hungry now, but one look at Marco and the words dried in his mouth.

'I bet you've got both got some leftover stuff in your lunchboxes. Finish that up, and you can fill your drink bottles from the tap. Marco's been working hard all week and he needs some peace. Go on. Outside!' said Amber firmly, promising herself that she would make it up to them as soon as she could. As soon as they left, she got a cold beer out of the fridge for Marco. Trying to settle things, she gave him a hug as she handed it to him. Shrugging off the hug, he downed the beer without even a thanks, flicking absently through messages on his phone. Leaving his now empty stubby on the bench, he disappeared back to the bedroom, returning dressed in shorts and a clean shirt. With a loud, beer-smelling belch, he announced,

'I'm going to meet the boys at the pub. Keep my dinner hot, okay babe? And get those kids to bed before I get home. They're really pissing me off today.'

'Sure Marco. Have fun. I can pick you up if you want,' offered Amber with what she hoped was a supportive smile. Just then a car horn beeped.

'I'll text you. That'll be Nick. He's picking me up.'

Taking another beer from the fridge, he grabbed his crotch, smirking at Amber as he left.

'You know, I think I could be up for another workout, when I get back! Make sure you're up for it!' he threatened, slamming the front door behind him.

Amber waited anxiously. She could hear Marco call out to Nick as he got in the car, then a roar as Nick's car accelerated down the street. Finally, there was silence, the trigger for her to collapse. Amber slumped down at the kitchen table and put her head in her hands. She exhaled again, emotionally spent. That she'd got away with that, was a miracle. Marco was hell-bent on her not picking up the kids from school. No matter how often she told him it was school rules that she had to pick them up because Arlo was still in pre-primary, he didn't listen. On the days he was at work, he didn't know what she was doing but when he had a day off, it was a nightmare. Luckily, he was still driven by his dick, so the chance of an afternoon quickie and a snooze before the pub, meant he was easily distracted. Lexie was lucky this time, but she knew she needed a better backup plan.

The kids! Jumping up and feeling yet another surge of guilt, she went outside where they were listlessly kicking a soccer ball around.

'He's gone.'

That was all she needed to say. Arlo and Ruby ran up to hug her.

'Can I have special breakfast?' Arlo was straight onto the topic of food. Ruby was a little more intuitive to Amber's feelings.

'Are you okay Mumma? Is Marco coming back soon?' Amber gave them both hugs. She had so much she needed to make up to them. Would she ever sort out the mess she'd made of her life? And theirs?

'We've got the house to ourselves, probably until bedtime. And yes Arlo, you can have special breakfast.'

Special breakfast consisted of a bowl of Coco Pops, only ever given as a treat, and Amber figured being left at school for half an hour probably warranted a treat.

'What about you Rubes? Could you handle a bowl of Coco Pops?' Ruby nodded. As they walked back inside, Arlo was excited, telling her about all the things he'd done that day with

Miss Hudson. Ruby listened as he rattled on. She wished she was in pre-primary with Miss Hudson. Mrs Pocock was nice, but she wasn't young and pretty like Miss Hudson. And she loved that Miss Hudson had let them play with the toys even though they'd already been packed away. They talked about kindness all the time at school, and she could tell Miss Hudson was kind.

While the kids scoffed down their Coco Pops, Amber half-listened to their stories, her mind very much occupied on the dilemma she faced every day – living with Marco. What had seemed a good idea only six months ago, had quickly turned sour. She thought Marco would be the answer to all her problems, but he was just another mistake, in a long list of mistakes in her life.

There had been hints of what he was really like, but she'd chosen to ignore them, thinking once they were actually living together the worrying traits would magically disappear! Or at least, not be an issue. Dumb! So dumb! And once again, it was her babies who were suffering the consequences, making huge compromises and learning how to make themselves invisible. Just like she'd always had to do. History repeating.

Once they'd eaten their Coco Pops, she gave Arlo and Ruby a bowl of fruit to snack on and let them have free rein with the TV. She didn't care that they 'should' be outside playing. This afternoon they could watch whatever shows they wanted to. Leaving them to it, she cleared away all evidence of the cereal, hiding the packet among the recycled shopping bags. She was so glad she had kept secret her little arrangement with her neighbour Erica. Marco would have a fit if he thought she was wasting money on the kids. He scrutinised every docket from the supermarket and doled out every cent as if it was his last.

Foolishly, in the early days before he showed his true

colours, she agreed that most of her fortnightly Parenting Payment would go as a direct transfer from her account into Marco's account, so that she helped pay the bills. She knew he was 'careful' with money, but she was okay with that. She thought it sounded fair, because they were moving into Marco's house, and he was offering to take care of her and her two children. He kept telling her that whatever she, or the kids needed, he would provide it. He even gave her a debit card. Sweet! But it soon became apparent that this was only to be used to pay for food, and he rarely transferred any money into it anyway. Marco paid all the household bills, and had complete financial control. She was allowed to access the account only for food and Marco's beer. She learnt that very quickly after moving in, when she had tried to buy two new quilt covers, and pillows for the kids' beds. She'd come in laden with the packages, when he said in a cold voice,

'What the hell do you think you're doing?'

At first, she failed to understand the nuance in his tone and showed off her purchases, proudly telling him she'd bought them on sale. His only response had been to ask for the docket. Amber produced the docket from the bags, stammering that it would brighten up the kids' room and make them feel more at home. She would never forget the look of total distain he had cast over her as he said, '*K-Mart*. Good. Take it all back and get the refund. Now!'

It cut right through any illusion that he actually cared about her or the kids, and it shocked her. She understood now that this was a relationship that centred solely on Marco. At first optimistic, like the fool she'd always been, she thought she could change that. Of course, she couldn't, and both her and the children's lives, became dependent on his meagre goodwill. She had been so unhappy living in the chaotic shared house, that when she met Marco, a single guy with his own home, she desperately wanted him to be her Prince Charming. He didn't have kids of his own. No extra baggage! She'd met him at the pub on a rare night when Krystal, one of the other mums she lived with had offered to babysit Ruby and Arlo. He bought her a couple of drinks. He made her laugh. He was a bit older, but she liked that. They danced. She took him home for the night. Within weeks he was a permanent fixture, turning up at all hours, usually when the kids were in bed. Was she so starved of any excitement in her life that she'd thought he was interesting?

Once or twice, when she could get a housemate to mind the kids for the night, she stayed over at his place. Every cell in her body coveted what he offered. A house of her own! A kitchen and bathroom she didn't have to share with numerous other people. It was a dream come true when Marco suggested she move in. Money was always so scarce. Every cent she had was set aside for her share of the rent and bills; gone before it even arrived in her account. With Marco, she would have a roof over her head, and the kids would have a home. No more rent to find! And finally, she would have someone on her side, they could work together as a team. The father-figure the kids needed! However, in all her daydreaming about a better life, she'd not stopped to consider that Marco hadn't spent any time with the kids to get to know them, or even with her, as it turned out.

Most of their time together had been late at night when the kids were in bed, and hence, out of the way. She knew what he liked to drink and what kind of sex he preferred, but she didn't really know what made him tick. Right from the start though, she realised he liked to be the one to take control. What did it matter? Lots of blokes thought they were the only ones with a brain. So keen was she to escape the seediness of shared housing, she figured she could put up with anything. Which she did.

Hiding her true feelings, she gave in to all his demands. She wore the clothes he liked her to wear. She stopped seeing her girlfriends because he didn't like them. She even pretended to take on board his theories on child-rearing. Arlo and Ruby were like ghosts, hardly visible when he was home. He showed no interest in them other than wanting to know when they'd be in bed. Marco was a brickie. He worked long hours, often gone by seven in the morning and not back till after five, maybe later if he stopped in at the pub after work. Fortunately, he also took on a few extra 'cashie' jobs on the weekend, so she and the kids occasionally had the house to themselves. His work ethic was their salvation; without his intimidating presence at home, they could relax and be themselves.

Christmas had been tough though; as had the first couple of weeks of January, when all tradies had a break. Things really soured then, with the kids on school holidays and around all day. Amber had finally come to terms with the fact that Marco wasn't in love with her, and she wondered if he'd ever had any genuine affection for her. He had probably only suggested she move in because he was sick of having to spend nights at her place when he wanted sex. He could have all the sex he wanted, on tap, if she moved into his place. Despite all his theories about rearing kids, he was really just a big mummy's boy himself. He wanted a cook and a cleaner, with fringe benefits. He had never intended this to be anything more than a convenient arrangement.

Trying to justify this to herself, Amber knew that her part of the bargain was not having to pay a bill or worry about rent. The kids had shelter and food. But she still had barely a cent to her name and struggled to buy them basic clothes and shoes out of what Marco doled out of her government parenting allowance. There was never a trip to the movies, or the beach, and she and Marco hadn't been out together since she moved in.

Added to this was his obsession about not spoiling the kids. He boasted he'd always walked home from school on his own, and picking them up was just making them weak. He was scornful when she argued it was school rules that kids be collected. He countered that the school rules were 'bullshit.' She worried constantly that the day would come when she couldn't get to school, and her children would be stranded; afraid the school would report her to Child Protection, if she was too late. Marco also liked to check her movements on his phone app. Not that that concerned her. There was nowhere to go, other than the supermarket, and he usually drove her there himself. She had no car, no money. Her only outing was taking the kids to school or a playground.

But above all, she was terrified of him. He was a heavy-set man, tanned from working outside all day, and muscled up from years of laying bricks. He liked to show he was in charge by hurting her in little ways. Minor things like grabbing her arm and leaving a bruise, or pinning her against the wall to make a point. The occasional slap across her face. Just little things, but they hurt, even though he would laugh them off and call her a sook if she complained. She knew very well how quickly this could escalate and she worked hard to not provoke him. The pretence was exhausting and she longed to get out. But there was the eternal problem. No money and no support. She didn't have an option. She was trapped.

CHAPTER 9

Lexie's unease over Amber and the kids' frantic departure stayed with her through the weekend, so on Monday morning she was watching out for Amber to arrive. When she spotted her saying goodbye to Arlo at the door, she waved her over. Amber hesitated, but she knew she needed to explain. Kissing Ruby goodbye, she told her to go up to her own classroom, so she could talk to Miss Hudson. Ruby ran off and Amber followed Lexie to her desk, giving them a little privacy. She came straight to the point,

'Okay, Amber. What was that all about on Friday?'

Amber blushed, she was embarrassed, but looked Lexie straight in the eye.

'I can't always get to school to pick the kids up, especially if Marco's home. He thinks they should walk home by themselves.'

'Doesn't he know we are not allowed to let kids in pre-primary leave the school unless it's with a designated care-giver?' asked Lexie.

'I've tried to tell him but he thinks that's a lot of crap,' said Amber quietly, adding, 'He thinks that I baby Arlo and Ruby.'

Coming to the conclusion that this was an issue that needed at least a temporary solution, Lexie acted swiftly. 'Okay. I'll send you my number. If you can't pick the kids up for whatever reason, text me and I'll look after them. Just remember not to panic. The kids will be safe with me and I'll get them home to you. Okay?'.

Amber's relief was immediate and visible.

'Oh, thanks Miss Hudson. I can't tell you how much that means to me,' tears appearing in her eyes at this unexpected gift of help.

'Call me Lexie. But we need to talk. Can you come in on Friday when I have my planning day? Anytime that day is fine. We'll see if we can talk through all this, and hopefully work something out.'

Amber nodded. She was trying to brush her tears away without making it too obvious to anyone watching. Lexie added reassuringly,

'Sit here, take a minute…as long as you need. And we'll talk about it on Friday.'

Amber sat down at Lexie's desk, her head in her hands, ignoring the curious stares of the children in the room. Arlo came over and put his head against her arm. Eventually, his concern and the touch of his little hand on her shoulder gave her the impetus she needed to get up and quietly leave the classroom, just as the children were being called to the mat to start the day. Luckily, for once, the usual groups of parents loitering outside had already dispersed. Relieved, Amber made her way across the school grounds and began the walk home, deep in thought.

Lexie. It would feel a bit weird to call her that. She'd only ever thought of her as Miss Hudson. Lexie had at least given her some peace of mind over the immediate problem of getting the kids home from school. Most of the time it would be okay, because Marco was currently working on a build in one of the outer suburbs, and it took him until around five to get home. But that could change at any time. Sometimes they moved from job to job. Also, if it was too wet, he'd be home early. Or, a job could finish before schedule, and he could get the afternoon off, like he had last week. It was such a relief to know the kids would be safe if she couldn't get to them, that she almost gave a skip. But her insurmountable problems remained.

It had taken Amber until Arlo was six months old to build up the courage to leave home, and start out on her own. She had never looked back, cutting Cindy from her life completely. In true form though, Cindy hadn't tried to stop her. Cindy. She refused to ever call her Mum; she'd never been a mother to her. By the time she walked away from Cindy, there was little left between them. And, no matter what she tried, things just kept getting further and further out of her reach. It had taken her four years to salvage the scraps, and to build herself back up to this point.

Amber liked to think she was strong, but this crazy situation she was in with Marco was becoming dangerous, and she berated herself for thinking there would ever be an easy way out for her. She had first put her name down on a Public Housing list when she was eighteen. Four years later, there was still nothing, and finding somewhere to live had been a constant roller coaster. Some of that had been her own fault. She'd done things over the years that she regretted. Just additions to the ever-growing list of bad decisions she was constantly accruing.

When she finally left the house in Manjimup, she left with nothing. Her parenting allowance was always spent on food and necessities, and usually, it had to cover whatever her brothers Robbie and Sam needed as well. Cindy had stepped up for a while in those early days, when John was back inside, but it was short-lived, and once John was out, they were both using again in no time. Amber was still the only one caring for her younger brothers, so she just kept doing what she'd always done, which was being a mother to the boys, and in time, to her own babies. She had no close friends. Pregnant at sixteen, she'd left school before it was obvious. Whatever friends she had, quickly lost contact with her. She got a part-time job at a news agency, but once her pregnancy became obvious, she didn't get as many shifts, and Cindy ridiculed her for trying.

When Ruby was born, there were follow-up visits from the hospital and a social worker was assigned to her. This was when Cindy suddenly became mother of the year, putting on a brilliant show of caring, assuring everyone she would look after her 'precious little mother'. The act lasted only for as long as Cindy knew the social worker had 'stopped nosing around', and the Single Parent Allowance kicked in. Amber was a good mother to Ruby and later to Arlo, when they were babies, breast feeding each for as long as possible, because she wanted to give them the best start. Realistically, she probably couldn't have afforded the baby formula anyway. And they hadn't lain crying in wet or dirty nappies. They were always clean, dry, and well fed. She'd protected them like a lioness, from the craziness of the drug saturated, violent household she lived in.

However, when the police started paying more attention to Cindy and John's activities, and her brothers were beginning to attract attention from Child Protection, Amber knew she had to get out, or her own kids might get caught up in the crossfire. She had to save them. She found a woman's refuge in the city, and she was accepted there. While she didn't quite fit the conventional picture of an abused woman, no-one doubted that she was fleeing an unsafe home environment. It wasn't the first time they had taken in someone who was at risk from an abusive parent.

Amber knew too well the loneliness that resulted from absence of a mother's love, and she vowed her children would not know that void. Sadly, she had discovered the hard way; love alone was not enough to guarantee your kids a safe and happy life.

She'd stayed at the refuge for several weeks, resting and getting some much-needed practical help. For the first time in years, she could loosen the knot of tension that was always in her stomach. Living with Cindy and John meant living in a constant state of anxiety. She'd not slept one night without fear. Even in the daytime, she worried about her babies' safety in a house where so many people came and went without question. It hadn't occurred to her either, until new clothes were given to her, Ruby and Arlo, just how destitute they must have looked. With fresh clothes, a safe bed to sleep in and meals provided, Amber thought this must be what a holiday was like. There were women of all ages there, some with kids and some without. It didn't matter. Many shared a similar dull weariness about the eyes. Studying herself in the mirror, Amber wondered if she looked the same.

There were helpful sessions on basic childcare, cleaning and first aid. A nutritionist talked to them about good food choices on a budget. Amber had been caring for her little brothers all her life. She didn't need tuition in these areas, but she did find the talk on budgeting useful. She longed to be able to live independently and make some decisions with her own money. Looking back, that had been a happy time in her life, despite the dire circumstances. It was a time when she had dared hope for better things ahead. After her time at the refuge, she was given accommodation in a more permanent hostel arrangement. The refuge was just to get you to a safe place. The hostel aimed at giving you the skills to stand on your own.

She made some good friends at the hostel, allies in each other's shared secrets. It was then she had first applied for public housing which was known to be scarce, but at least she was on the list. A token amount of her allowance went towards her food and board at the hostel, and without having to support an entire household, Amber's money slowly began to mount up. She stayed in the hostel for several months. Relieved of all responsibility for her brothers, she could at last just be a mother to her own children. Eventually, it was time to move on. There was no way she could afford to rent a house on her own, but when the chance came up to share a house with two other women and their kids, Amber took it.

Katy was twenty-five, her little girl Sasha, five. Amber liked Katy, although she was painfully quiet. Sasha said even less. They were hiding from Katy's ex-partner who was also Sasha's father. As far as Katy knew he was still living in Melbourne. She had escaped one night, after a particularly violent beating, taking Sasha with her. Despite a broken wrist and other injuries, and with the help of family, she had made her way to Perth, which was as far away from her partner as she could get. Katy knew no-one in Perth outside of the refuge. Mel was older. She was twenty-eight with two boys, Rex who was eight and Nate, six. Three mums, five kids…but together, with their combined incomes they could afford a house. Family services found the house, and more importantly, a landlord who would take three fractured families. After that they were pretty much on their own.

The arrangement worked well, for a while. The three older children were enrolled in a school nearby, and Mel even managed to get herself a job stacking shelves at the supermarket at night, while Katy and Amber minded her boys. Financially, it was great. Amber could pay her share of the rent, buy clothes and shoes for herself, Ruby and Arlo, and occasionally, even have some money for treats. Then Mel met up with a friend from the old days and she started drinking. Amber didn't know much about her previous life. Mel had been pretty tight-lipped, but Mel's slide back into drinking, and then using, was swift and destructive. Within weeks she had stopped her job, and stopped coming home, leaving the boys alone for days at a time. When she did show up, she was often bruised and bloodied. No-one knew where she slept at night. Katy and Amber covered for a while, but eventually, she was picked up by the police, then Child Protection became involved, and the boys were taken into foster care. Even that didn't stop Mel. One day, a social worker arrived and packed up her belongings. Mel was in rehab and wasn't coming back. Katy and Amber cleaned out her room. They never found out what happened to her. They didn't ask. They weren't sure they even wanted to know.

Finances were tight without Mel sharing the rent and the bills. They tried to get someone in, and there was a revolving door of women and their kids from the hostel, but none stayed more than a couple of months. Katy and Amber stuck close throughout, supporting each other when things got tough. Then, about twelve months after they had moved in together, Katy had an unexpected phone-call from her mother. Her ex-partner, Sasha's dad, had been charged with manslaughter, after a one-punch hit. The guy he killed was a much-loved, young doctor and there had been a great deal of anger about it in the community. He was expected to spend several years in prison.

Katy's mother wasn't well-off, but she did have a spare room, and with the threat of Katy's violent partner removed, she begged Katy to come home. Amber was happy for Katy, but she knew there was no fairy godmother coming to rescue her. Katy and Sasha went back to Victoria to live with her mother, and Amber looked for somewhere else to live.

When the child protection unit had acted so swiftly to take Mel's boys into foster care, Amber's fears increased. She knew she was always at risk of close scrutiny because of her age. She'd had two children before she was eighteen and that alone was cause for alarm bells. Any chance of public housing still looked like being years away.

Desperate for accommodation, Amber took a monthly lease on a caravan in a caravan park out towards the airport. It meant she would be isolated, because she didn't have a car, but it was cheap. She didn't have a driver's licence either, although she did know how to drive. John had taught her, so she could run jobs for him. She had a fake licence, but she knew it wouldn't pass a police inspection. Whatever. Owning a car was way out of her league.

The caravan park had mostly long-term residents, and nearly all were hard luck stories. Poverty and desperation dripped off the spindly tea-trees that marked each site. Amber was lonely, but she avoided the other residents, keeping to herself. During the day she walked to the shops and playground, with Ruby and Arlo in the second-hand pram she been given at the refuge, staying away from the caravan park for as long as she could.

Her little caravan had a toilet and shower, in an attached lean-to shack on the side of the van. She had to use the communal laundry facilities, but otherwise she was self-contained. At night she locked the lean-to door and barricaded it with a heavy lounge chair that she zealously hauled into place each night. Then she locked herself, Arlo and Ruby in. On several occasions, when she was woken by loud noises, or people screaming obscenities across the camp sites she was glad to be anonymous. Occasionally, when the sirens and flashing blue lights heralded the arrival of police, she worried in case Ruby or Arlo woke up. But the place was cheap, and despite its shortcomings, she lasted there for six months.

Amber had maintained contact with friends from the refuge, so when one of them let her know a room was available in a share house, she jumped at it. She gave notice at the caravan park, packed up her little family's meagre possessions, hired an Uber driver with a van, and moved in. This time there were four tenants, and not all single mums. There was Daniel, a Chinese student who chose the rental to be close to his part-time job. He was only there to sleep because he was either working or at uni. Sue, who was in her sixties, kept to herself, and had her first wine with a late breakfast at around eleven. Ellie was also a young single mum, with a four-year-old. Amber met Ellie through a friend of a friend, which was how she found this particular share house. Given the circumstances, she and Ellie bonded quickly.

Just as Amber was beginning to feel hopeful that this arrangement would work, Sue went to the pub one afternoon and brought back half the pub to party at midnight. The party got out of control and the police were called. Things got messy and the landlord came the next day, asking questions. It was the start of several more moves; constantly in and out of share houses, some better than others, but most cockroach infested, or in danger of being condemned. A series of unsuitable housemates followed; some left with rent unpaid, others just left the kitchen a mess or the bathroom filthy. One held parties that often got of control. Some parties Amber joined in, but there were others when she bolted herself and the kids in her room, until the party goers left or crashed.

There were times she regretted, when just by being there, she had put her children at risk. There were a couple of messy relationships and several one-night stands, usually leaving her feeling used and discarded once again. By the time she met Marco, Amber was ready to do anything to escape the merry-go-round of temporary housing and the resulting complications. However, desperate as she had been, she'd at least had her freedom, and the kids were happy. Under Marco's control, she could see Ruby and Arlo changing, becoming faded versions of themselves. She hated to see their frightened looks when Marco, beer in hand, started on one of his rants.

Walking up the driveway to the empty house she had once dared to think might be a home for her family, all Amber could think was, how could she escape?

CHAPTER 10

Lexie arrived at school on the day she was to take possession of her new home, with a skip in her step. She had only seen the house once since her initial inspection, and that was when the carpets had been ripped up. She was naturally impatient to get another good look at the house, especially with the floorboards exposed and polished. The real estate agent had suggested four o'clock for the hand-over, and the plan was for Andy to meet her there, along with Jeanie and Ray, who would be seeing the house for the first time.

Before all that could happen, she had things to do. Friday was her planning day. Lexie loved Fridays. This was when she had a whole day free from teaching so she could review her program, and plan her next steps. She was itching to get stuck into a more targeted literacy program, now she knew the kids better. As usual, there was a huge range of abilities in the group, but the kindy teacher had covered the basics thoroughly, so the bulk of the class was well on the way.

Arlo was one of those who would need more help, but considering he had frequently changed schools and missed most of his kindy year, he was probably progressing as well as could be expected. Lexie had met with Amber for her interview the previous week and it had proved an eye-opener. Life had certainly not been easy for Amber and it seemed her current situation was no better.

The interview had been scheduled for eleven. Fetching two coffees from the staff room, Lexie had taken Amber into a quiet room, where they could chat undisturbed. Lexie was struck by how little emotion Amber showed, as she talked about some of what had happened over the past four years. She was quite matter of fact, explaining that Cindy was probably still in prison, that her brothers had been placed in foster care soon after their mother was arrested, and that she herself had left the family home just before it all occurred.

She made no mention of her own children's fathers, and Lexie decided this was not the time to ask. Listening to Amber's sorry tale of constant moving and relocating, Lexie had wanted to reach out and hug her. Despite her setbacks, Amber had tried her best to be a good mother; Ruby and Arlo were always her number one priority. However, when they came to the subject of her current living arrangements with Marco, Lexie could tell things were not going well.

'Tell me about Marco. What's this about the kids walking home on their own? I can get Kelly, Mrs Brunn the principal, to speak to him about our school policy if you like?'

Amber shook her head saying emphatically, 'No! Please don't. He'll know that I've been talking to you about him, and that will make him really mad. It's been working so far, thanks to you Lexie. Most of the time he has no idea I pick the kids up. It's only if he's home that he even cares. He just thinks I baby them too much.'

Alarm bells were ringing furiously in Lexie's ears as she listened to this. She decided to push a bit further.

'Are you afraid of him, Amber? Does he hurt you?'

Amber gave a shrill, nervous laugh. She denied that he hurt her, protesting that she was sure he'd never hit her or the kids. Although Lexie was dubious about this, she could see Amber was getting flustered, and she gave her the benefit of the doubt. However, Amber's next words again gave her reason for concern, when she said, 'You're not going to report me to Child Protection, are you? You can't do that! I'm a good mum. I look after Ruby and Arlo! You can see that! They're happy kids!'

'No! No! Of course not!' Lexie was hasty to reassure her. 'Don't worry, Amber! I know you're a good mum and I can see Arlo and Ruby are really well cared for!'

This time she did reach over to give Amber a firm hug, patting her on the back.

'I can't lose my kids, Miss Hudson, I mean Lexie. They're all I've got.'

'Don't worry. That's not what I meant. I'm just checking if you need any help. Is Marco a good man?'

Sniffing, Amber took a tissue from her pocket and blew her nose before answering,

'He's a good man,' she responded softly. 'He's got a steady job. He works hard. He's given us a home and he pays the bills. What more does he have to do?'

'That's a good start,' Lexie smiled, and changed the subject. She'd almost pushed Amber too far then, and she didn't want to lose her trust. Every instinct Lexie had, told her that Amber was unhappy and frightened, but her hands were tied.

Long after Amber left, Lexie continued to mull over their conversation. Amber had said nothing to raise any alarms, but taking into account all she had told her about her constant battle over the last few years to find some permanent housing, Lexie believed Amber was prepared to go to any length to make this Marco situation work.

Above all, Lexie was blown away by Amber's resilience and strength. She couldn't imagine how hard it must have been for a teenager with two babies to make her way in the world. While the details of their conversation were still fresh, she typed up some notes, mostly in relation to the children's history of temporary housing. The constant upheavals in Arlo's early years may very well have an impact on his later learning. Her fears about Marco, she kept to herself.

She'd only needed to help Amber out on a couple of times since that first week of school, both times it was just to keep Arlo and Ruby in the classroom with her after school until Amber could get there to collect them. And both times it was because Marco had come home unexpectedly in the afternoon, before heading out again. Lexie wondered if it was a form of control, a need to check up on Amber – but she said nothing. She hoped she would have no issues this afternoon. With no parent interviews scheduled, and it being her planning day, she was looking forward to making a quick getaway.

The day went like clockwork and Lexie powered through the tasks she'd set herself, including the never-ending paperwork demanded by admin. She, and every other teacher, constantly complained of this to Kelly, who simply smiled and passed it on saying, 'I totally agree, but it's not me doing the asking. Take it up with the Education Department'.

By three o'clock, Lexie was ready to exit soon after the students, when she received a text from Amber. *Marco came home early. We are out. Can you keep the kids for a while? Maybe till four?* Lexie sighed. Four!! That was complicating things. She really didn't want to be late for the handover of her house keys. Reckless with frustration, she texted back: *Give me permission to take the kids in my car, and I'll drop them back to your house when you get home.* Lexie's heart was in her mouth. This was a whole new level and she knew Kelly would not approve, but she was torn between wanting to help Amber and her own plans. She justified it to herself saying, that if Amber was a friend there would be no problem in driving the kids home. It was just a bit tricky to explain …

Amber's reply was swift.

I, Amber Evans, give permission for Lexie Hudson to drive with my children, Ruby and Arlo in her car, at all times.

Lexie was impressed. Amber was certainly no fool. She would have realised that Lexie needed this to look as official as it could without the usual paper copy and signature. Lexie vowed that if they got away with this, she would make sure she was legally covered with the correct paperwork, just in case there was a next time.

While Arlo packed his school bag, she collected Ruby from her classroom, then quickly walked them over to her car. By lucky chance, she had a booster seat in the boot, which she kept in case she was driving either Hannah or Rosie somewhere. Arlo and Ruby were both tall for their age; Ruby was old enough not to need the booster and Lexie was confident that Arlo's tall frame, plus the booster seat, would be enough to cover the seatbelt rules. Once again, she was amazed at Arlo and Ruby's flexibility in accepting this change of plans. She was also slightly flattered that they were prepared to trust her to look after them. Fastening their seatbelts securely, she stowed their bags. Fortunately, there were no other teachers in the carpark to observe things and ask difficult questions. Before she started the car, she turned to Arlo and Ruby.

'Your Mum wants me to look after you until she gets home. But I have to go somewhere first, so we can't just stay at school. I have a new house, and I'm getting the key to it this afternoon, so we are going there before we go back to your mum. I can get you something to eat when we get there, but if you want, you can eat any leftover stuff from your lunchboxes in the car. Is that okay?'

Ruby, quiet as ever nodded, but Arlo was more upfront.

'I don't have any lunch left. Can we get something from the shop?' he asked hopefully.

'Of course, Arlo! We can definitely get something from the shop, but you might have to wait a bit, because I don't want to be late for my appointment.' Arlo seemed satisfied with that and Lexie started the engine.

Reversing out of her car bay, she glanced at her watch. Three-ten. She was well on time. This would be a good test of just how long it would take her to get to her new home from school. Arlo kept up a constant chatter, asking questions and telling long stories. Lexie listened with some amusement. She'd had Arlo in her classroom for three weeks and he'd hardly said a word. Now he was chattering away so much, he'd barely drawn breath.

With a sudden flash of insight, Lexie realised he was excited. Amber didn't own a car, and by the sound of it they went nowhere with Marco. He'd probably rarely been in a car. From his booster seat he had a view of everything, and she watched him in the rearview mirror, looking eagerly out the window, taking it all in. How many experiences in life that most kids took for granted had these two kids missed? Ruby also had her head turned, straining to look out the window. Lexie wondered at the places they'd never seen.

Within twenty minutes she pulled up at the house. This was going to be wonderful! Such a relatively short commute to and from school, compared to the almost hour-long trek each way that she'd been making while staying with her parents. Definitely nothing compared to the five-minute drive she'd had when she lived down south, but for Perth's commuters, this was a rare convenience. The first to arrive, she parked with a sense of ownership in the driveway just as Mary, the real estate agent pulled up across the street. Lexie helped Arlo and Ruby out of their seatbelts, saying, 'Come on. You can be the first people to see Miss Hudson's new house!'

As the kids got out of the car, Mary strode over to greet her.

'Hi Lexie! Congratulations! I hope this is an exciting day for you!'

Seeing Arlo and Ruby, she did a bit of a double-take before asking,

'Who are these gorgeous little ones? Are they your brother's?'

Lexie shook her head, and figured Mary didn't need the whole story.

'No. This is Arlo and Ruby. They are a friend's children. She couldn't pick them up at the last minute, so I offered to help. Say hello to Mrs Piper.'

When both children looked the estate agent in the eye and said clearly, 'Hello Mrs Piper,' Amber's parenting stocks rose even more in Lexie's eyes. Despite everything she'd had to juggle, Amber had still managed to impart the basics of good manners to her children.

Shifting a couple of heavy bags from one hand to the other, Mary said, 'I meant to get here before you and have everything tickety-boo, but you've beaten me to it. If you give me a tick, I'll get myself organised and we can do a proper handover.'

Lexie wasn't fazed. 'Take your time, Mary. I'm waiting for Mum and Dad anyway. They shouldn't be long. Anthony's coming as well. He's keen to look at the house again.'

'Lovely!' said Mary walking purposely towards the front door. Lexie took Arlo and Ruby's hands, steering them towards the side entrance. A bit over a metre high, the strong wire gate hung the width of the driveway. There was a carport on the other side of gate. Lexie pondered briefly if she could be bothered with the rigmarole of unlocking this gate, driving her car in and locking it again behind her, every time she used the car. Maybe the gate could stay open.

'Come on kids! Let's check out the back yard. I think there's an old swing there…'

Spying it immediately as they rounded the side of the house, Arlo and Ruby took off, fighting to have first go. With a well-timed shove, Ruby pushed Arlo off course, just long enough to get her legs over the seat of the swing first. Fearing an injury, Lexie had already taken off towards Arlo's sprawled figure, when she saw him jump up laughing, and run behind the swing, to give Ruby a helpful push. Just then, a dog barked and raced into the backyard. Making a beeline for Arlo, it jumped up and licked him, before taking off to mark its territory, peeing on the agave plants along the fence line. Belatedly, Anthony appeared sprinting after the dog, calling to him.

'Radar! Radar! Come here!'

The dog responded in an instant, obediently charging back to Anthony, who rewarded him with a pat.

'Good boy! Good boy, Radar!' he praised, continuing to pat the dog. Then grabbing him by the collar, he walked him the few steps over to Lexie.

'When did you get him Anthony? I didn't know you were getting a dog! He's beautiful! A German shepherd?'

Unable to resist the soft eyes looking up at her, Lexie stroked his head and was rewarded with a lick, and a gentle bump as he rubbed his snout against her hand. Abandoning the swing, the kids ran over to meet the dog. This time it was

Anthony's turn to look surprised, as if to say, 'Where did you guys come from?'

'Anthony. This is Arlo and Ruby. Arlo is in my class and Ruby is his big sister,' Lexie said before getting on tip-toes and whispering in his ear, 'I'll explain later.'

Arlo and Ruby gave Radar a couple of tentative pats, and the dog took off happily, racing up and down the back yard. They immediately chased after him, laughing and calling out his name. To complete the chaos, Ray and Jeanie walked in through the back gate, Mary following them and looking slightly dismayed at the growing cast of characters.

Jeanie watched Arlo and Ruby chasing Radar around the yard, and turned to Lexie, eyebrows raised in question. She had recognised the school uniforms as being from Lexie's school, and knew straight away something was up. As Lexie introduced everyone again, she added, to Jeanie, 'These are Amber's kids.' Jeanie nodded in understanding, recalling the chat she and Lexie had about Amber.

Radar continued to do circuits of the backyard, before stopping to take a big drink of water from a container near the garden tap.

'He looks like he's been here before!' said Lexie laughing at her brother. 'Tell me. Where did you get him from? He's just gorgeous!'

'Well,' started Anthony, pausing to put his hands on his hips, 'I'm glad you like him.'

'So am I!' interjected Ray, before getting shushed by Jeanie.

'I'm glad you like him because... he's yours. Radar is my solution to the outdoor toilet problem. He's still only a pup — well, two years old — but he comes highly recommended as a guard dog by the staff at the rescue centre. With him in your back yard, I promise no-one is going to climb over the gate and be waiting outside the toilet for you.'

'What! Mine?' Lexie's voice went up a level. She wasn't sure if she was happy or not. She hadn't figured on having a dog in her life! She didn't really want that responsibility. Shaking her head, she said firmly,

'I don't know Anthony. I'm not so sure I want a dog.'

At this point Mary chose to chip in.

'Welcome everyone! Maybe we can discuss this later. Right now, we have keys to hand over. Let's go inside and have a look at your new home Lexie.'

With practiced expertise, she managed to steer everyone back to the front of the house, while Anthony shut the gate, the gate suddenly very handy with Radar in the backyard. Then she arranged everyone including Arlo and Ruby, for a photo on the front steps of the house, before videoing Lexie ceremoniously unlocking her front door for the first time. With great pomp, Lexie swung open the door and with a grand sweep of her arm, welcomed everyone into her new home.

Mary had already been inside working her magic. On the kitchen bench was a bottle of champagne cooling in an ice-bucket, along with six matching champagne flutes and a platter of cheese and biscuits. While the adults opened the champagne, Mary magically produced a can of coke each for Arlo and Ruby and a packet of chips to share. They were more than happy with the deal, and soon disappeared into the back yard to play with Radar, while the adults admired the house, including the lovely old floorboards that had been exposed when the carpet was ripped up.

Mary didn't stay long. She left the glasses and platter as a housewarming gift, along with a beautiful pot plant and made an exit, citing Friday afternoon traffic as her excuse. As Lexie walked her out, Mary took the opportunity to say,

'I know it's not my business, but I think the dog is not a bad idea. This is a good area and we tell all our clients it's generally very safe, but personally, I think a dog provides extra security. Definitely a deterrent to intruders, and this outside toilet is not ideal when you live on your own.'

Touching Lexie's shoulder in a show of support, Mary continued,

'Think about it. In any case, this house has great bones. I'm looking forward to seeing what you do with it. I wish you all the best and I hope you'll be very happy here.' Then she hurried down the steps to her car, giving a cheery wave goodbye.

Walking back to the kitchen where the family had gathered to finish off the champagne, Lexie took a quick look at her phone. Two messages. One from Amber. Great. *I'm home in ten minutes. Marco still at the pub. Thanks Amber.* The message had only come in a few minutes ago. She texted her back. *The kids are fine. We'll be at yours in about half an hour. Okay?* The reply was a thumbs up emoji.

Anthony gave her a hug as she stood next to him. 'Are you mad at me? What do you want me to do with Radar?'

'No. I'm not mad. He is beautiful, and he's obviously good with kids! Are you sure he'll even bark at a stranger?'

'I promise you. He's been well trained. The family who had him before said no-one came near the house without them knowing. They had to find another home for him because they were returning to England and they couldn't take him with them. But if you don't want him, there are at least two families in our street who will take him. He's been staying with us for the past few days and people have been eyeing him off.... a bit warily at first, I have to admit,' he joked.

Lexie looked through the back door at Radar, ears cocked and alert as the kids ran around him. She sighed deeply, pondering the pros and cons. In a possibly rash decision-making process, she made up her mind. It was a time for new beginnings after all, and then she remembered; Jed had always been very negative about getting a dog…

'Okay. I'll keep him!' she said impulsively, turning to hug Anthony. 'Thanks bro. It's a great idea!'

'Phew!' said Ray, who had followed them out of the kitchen. 'I wasn't sure if you'd agree and I'm not so sure I would have gone ahead like Anthony did, without checking. I do think it's a good idea though. Even without the outside loo, I certainly feel happier that you've got Radar here for some added protection and company.'

'I'm glad too,' chipped in Jeanie coming over to join in the conversation. 'But what is going on with you having Amber's kids?'

'Oh! I've got to drop them back to her! Come with me in the car Mum, and we can talk about it. It won't take long. She lives near the school.'

Jeanie looked at Ray to see if he wanted to come as well.

'No Love. You guys go. Anthony and I will set up Radar's kennel and his bed. We came prepared, Lexie, so it's lucky you said yes. You won't believe the gear this dog has! We'll probably still be here when you get back.'

Lexie called Arlo and Ruby: 'Time to go, kids.' Reluctantly they gave Radar final pats, before following Lexie and Jeanie to the car. Lexie didn't say much, but Jeanie kept up the conversation asking the kids questions. Most were fairly routine, such as their ages and birthdays. She also told them some stories about Lexie as a little girl, which made them laugh;

like how she couldn't ever say the word 'hospital' and said 'hobsticle' instead. Then she asked,

'Does Mummy have a job? Does she go to work?'

'No!' answered Ruby. 'Marco doesn't want her to work!'

'What does Marco do?'

'He's a brickie,' said Arlo. 'He builds houses and stuff.'

'That sounds like a great job,' said Jeanie, turning to smile at Arlo. 'Have you ever been to work with him? Has he shown you what he does?' Jeanie watched the children's faces shut down. The response was silence and a double shake of the head from Arlo.

Eventually, turning her face to the window, Ruby replied, 'We don't do anything with Marco.'

Fearing that she had crossed a boundary, Jeannie changed the subject, asking Lexie instead about her plans for moving into the new house on the weekend. By the time they arrived at Marco's house, the kids appeared to have recovered their usual happy natures. Amber must have been watching for them because she came out as they pulled into the drive, hugging Arlo and Ruby tightly as they got out of the car, with their school bags. Amber looked upset, strung out.

'Thank you, so much Lexie. I was so worried about them. This is so kind of you to help me out. You are amazing.'

'Don't be silly. I'm sorry I couldn't bring them straight home but I think they've had fun anyway, haven't you?' she smiled at the kids.

'We met Miss Hudson's new dog! And we saw her house!' said Ruby triumphantly.

'And she doesn't have any beds or chairs or tables in her house!' announced Arlo in amazement.

'Well not yet,' laughed Lexie. 'But I promise next time you come I will have lots of furniture, even a TV!'

'Okay. I can't imagine a house without any beds or tables, mate,' said Amber smiling. 'Now you guys go inside while I have a quick chat to Miss Hudson.'

'Is Marco home?' asked Ruby, in a way Lexie could only describe as fearful.

'No Rubes. You can watch some television, and there's a snack on the kitchen bench for you both. Now don't forget to say thank you to Miss Hudson for looking after you after school.'

Calling out their thanks, Arlo and Ruby raced each other into the house. Jeanie had remained in the car. Catching Amber's eye, she wound down the car window and said hello. Lexie belatedly made the introductions.

'This is my mum, Jeanie. And this is Amber, Mum. Arlo and Ruby's mother.'

Looking nervous, Amber plucked at her sleeves, pushing them up, as if she was suddenly hot, and immediately pulling them down again.

'Hello Amber. It's lovely to meet you. You have two beautiful children there; you must be very proud of them.'

'Oh! Thanks, Mrs Hudson. They're pretty good kids most of the time. It's really nice to meet you as well. But I better get inside and see what they're up to.'

Despite her smiles, Amber was agitated, glancing up and down the street several times, clearly watching for someone. Picking up on the cues, Lexie got back into the car.

'Well, we probably need to get back to dad. We've left him holding the fort with my new dog. The kids will tell you all about Radar, I'm sure. We can talk more about this later. But I'm glad you thought to ask me. I'm more than happy to help, where I can.'

Giving Amber a quick wave, Lexie backed her car out the driveway. Amber stood there until they had turned at the end of the street. Lexie watched her also, in the rear-view mirror. She could almost sense Amber's sigh of relief that Marco wasn't home to see the kids being dropped off. It didn't take a genius to see Amber's fear.

'Whoa!' said Jeanie. 'That is one frightened girl. What is going on there? Did you see her arms?'

'Her arms?' questioned Lexie a bit confused.

'Yes, her arms,' repeated Jeanie for emphasis. 'She pulled up her sleeves for just a few seconds, without thinking. I think she was distracted by meeting me, and then she pulled them straight down again, when she probably realised what she'd done. They were covered in bruises. Great black and blue marks all up her forearms, as if she's been grabbed roughly, manhandled. What's going on? And is it safe for you to be involved in all of this, Lexie?'

'Well, I didn't notice her arms, but come to think of it, she's almost always wearing long sleeves whenever I see her. She is clearly afraid of this Marco, and it seems she's literally got no-one to help her out. It's the least I can do, to keep an eye on the kids after school.'

Lexie had already told Jeanie about Marco's odd stipulation that Amber not walk the kids home from school. They'd discussed it at length, especially the instances of Marco's controlling behaviour, but this was the first time Lexie had evidence that he was possibly violent towards her.

'And I didn't like the scared look in Ruby's eyes when we asked about Marco. That girl is in way over her head, Lexie. Mark my words. I think she needs help.'

'Which is exactly why I had them with me today.'

Lexie drove, barely registering the Friday afternoon hectic traffic, as she and Jeanie talked through possible scenarios of what Amber's life might be. None of them were positive. Both women shared a growing fear, that Amber was very much afraid of Marco, and probably for a good reason.

CHAPTER 11

Lexie continued to worry about Amber, Ruby and Arlo, her disquiet simmering away like a slow-cooker in the background. For the next few days, however, her priority was moving into her new home in St James. She'd had several weeks to plan for this day, and had booked the following Friday off school for the move. Lexie efficiently directed the removalists as to where the big articles of furniture and boxes were to go. Beds, tables and chairs were easy. The hard part came later, when she started unpacking and discovered annoying details, such as the house's lack of conveniently placed power-points.

Ray and Jeanie were on hand, as always, making sure most things were put somewhere near their final resting places. Clare and Andy turned up mid-afternoon, both their girls at play dates, so they were free to help as well. At five o'clock, after a huge day that had started, for Lexie, well before the removalist van arrived at eight, they ordered an early dinner of Chinese take-away. While Jeanie collected the girls, Clare and Andy set up Lexie's new smart TV, adding her to their family streaming services.

Everyone was physically exhausted, but as they shared dinner, there was a great sense of family, and pride in a job well done. Lexie felt very fortunate as she hugged them, thanking each of them for their support. Despite this, she was more than happy to wave everyone goodbye when the gang left. She was ready to crash on the couch and do nothing.

She was just about to close the back door, when she caught Radar looking hopefully at her through the fly screen. Guilt took over.

'Okay big guy. I guess you have been very patient all day. Let's go for a quick walk to the park and I'll toss you some balls.' Radar pricked up his ears as if he had understood every word, and began circling excitedly while Lexie collected the ball and the dog collar. Locking the back door as she left, she pocketed the keys and set off towards the park. By the time they had walked there and back and Radar had fetched a dozen or so balls, it was getting dark, and Lexie regretted not bringing her phone with her.

She also made a mental note to buy one of those nifty ball throwers the other dog owners had at the park. *Way more efficient and definitely easier on the arm*, she thought, as several rarely used muscles began complaining. As Radar settled down contentedly on his day bed at the back door, she retrieved a wineglass from the cupboard and poured herself a glass of wine. She raised a solo glass to Clare, for her thoughtfulness. Clare had brought along a box of food essentials for the first day or so, and had thought to include a bottle of wine. What a great sister-in-law! Sitting on the couch, Lexie stretched out her legs, plonked her feet on the coffee table, took her first sip, and surveyed the lounge room with some satisfaction.

The two tan leather couches looked good, one in front of the TV and the other adjacent to it. A couple of sixties-styled low armchairs set against the spare wall, completed the three-way seating arrangement. It would work well when she was here alone, but she could also imagine herself entertaining, or sitting around chatting with friends. The cream cushions would do for the moment; in time, she might find something more stylish. An old pine table from Ray's garage, which she had cleaned up and stained, stood under the big window at the front. The table and its odd assortment of chairs would suffice as a dining table until she could afford something better. In the meantime, she decided it actually suited the room, with its high ceiling, quite well.

Over the next few days, she would hang some prints and a lovely old mirror she had picked up at a second-hand shop some years ago. Jed hadn't liked it, so it never made it on to the wall of their house. It was definitely going to make the cut this time! She grinned happily at the thought that she could do whatever she wanted. A ping on her phone reminded her that she hadn't glanced at it for hours. Now she saw there were several messages from friends, wishing her luck. And, as if he was clairvoyant, one from Jed!

Good luck on the move into your new home. Maybe we can have coffee soon.? Would love to see you. xxx JED

Lexie read it twice before it sank in properly. *What the hell? Wanting coffee? Would love to see you?* She checked the sender again. She was intermittently, stunned, confused and annoyed. She had heard through mutual friends that Jed had returned to Western Australia recently. She also knew that he and Caity were still very much together. There was no way that she was going to engage in any sort of liaison, platonic or not, with Jed. If they accidently meet one day, she hoped it would be civil, but there was no need to be friends. He had destroyed their relationship, and she had no desire to go down that road again. She shook her head that he could treat her so heartlessly, then imagine that he could send a text and she would be so grateful that she would be ready to forgive and forget it all!

Dismissively she deleted the text, resisting the urge to text back a scornful reply. She considered briefly, that maybe it was time she moved on, and started trawling dating sites, as her friends were constantly suggesting. Instead, she spent what energy she had left, catching up on her emails and other messages.

By eight o'clock she was ready to crawl into bed. A thousand things on her to do list, sifted on rotation through her brain. Tuning out the mindless random thoughts, Lexie soon succumbed to the warm familiarity of her own bed and the special joy of clean sheets, eventually managing to fall into a deep, dreamless sleep.

The sun was well and truly up when she woke, desperately needing to relieve her bladder. Slightly disoriented by the new room, and still half asleep, she stumbled to the back door, unlocking it, before bumping into Radar, who was right there, on alert, waiting. Lexie smiled. Going outside to the loo in the daylight wasn't a problem, but she could see Andy's guard dog solution working well for her at night, if she ever needed it.

CHAPTER 12

Amber had been up since daylight. She'd crept out of bed without Marco even stirring, grateful once again for the small bonus of him being such a deep sleeper. *Mind you*, she thought cynically, *who doesn't sleep well with a gutful of booze, and a night of rough sex; especially when you're the one delivering it...*

The first thing she did was to check on the kids. Careful not to make a sound, she opened their bedroom door and peered in. Relief! They were still asleep, snuggled close to each other in Ruby's bed, Arlo's pyjamas a tell-tale pile on the floor. She realised guiltily that must have been why Arlo had called out to her in the night, and she made a mental note to change the sheets as soon as they were awake. Marco was inclined to ridicule Arlo if he wet the bed, and he would continue to make Arlo the butt of his jokes all day. It was his way of imposing his ignorant child-rearing theories on Arlo and Ruby. She wondered again what Marco's childhood was like, because he certainly had some archaic ideas on raising kids. It probably also had a fair bit to do with why he had absolutely no contact with his own family.

Marco hadn't let her go to Arlo. He was too intent on his own needs. She'd had to listen helplessly to Arlo's faint calls, while Marco had thrust deeply and aggressively inside her, finally collapsing with one leg and arm on top of her; effectively pinning her beneath him so she could hardly breathe, let alone move. Trapped, she picked up an occasional quiet murmur coming from Arlo and Ruby's room, until the house grew quiet, and the only sound was Marco's satiated snores. Eventually, she'd managed to wriggle away from underneath his crushing weight, able to breathe easier at last, before she fell into an exhausted sleep.

Closing the door, she went to the bathroom to examine her latest bruises. A purple mark was forming near her eye where he'd backhanded her. He was getting careless and didn't seem concerned if the bruises were visible anymore. In the beginning, they had just been on her torso, where no-one could see. Now, she had to wear long sleeves and jeans, even on warm days, to cover the evidence of his temper. She knew Lexie's mum had spotted her arms when she absently pulled up her sleeves the other day. That was stupid, but then she had always been stupid, hadn't she? It was her one crowning achievement in life to be constantly stupid. Marco being her dumbest mistake so far.

If she could trust that he would confine his violence to her, maybe she could bear it. She had a high pain threshold and the bruises healed eventually. To give her kids a stable life and a house that was safe was all she'd wanted. But Marco's drinking bouts were increasing, and she wondered when he would turn his temper on Ruby and Arlo. After all, he didn't have much patience for them, even when he was sober. How long could she protect them from his weekend drinking benders?

She stared at herself in the mirror. Was she really only twenty-two? She felt so much older. It seemed she was forever doomed to be in fight mode, just to stay upright in the world.

Not that she cared any more about herself. She had long ago stopped comparing herself to other girls her age. How she envied those carefree lives she followed on Insta and Tik Tok, the glamorous photos of nights out, with exotic drinks and gourmet dinners in stylish clubs and restaurants. There was a whole other world out there, that had passed her by.

As much as they depressed her, she had a weird obsession with following perfect families. Families, where the kids were dressed in cute, trendy clothes, and had parties with impossibly decorated cupcakes; or *Spiderman* and *Frozen* themed birthdays. Where the mums sported trim bodies in black gym gear and dads smiled broadly, besotted by their kids…and their wives. She regretted so much that her babies never experienced that. And they were certainly never going to get that from Marco. He could barely stand the sight of them.

Back in the kitchen, Amber stood at the sink and rubbed gingerly at her arms. Her upper arms were seriously every shade of purple, and so sore! What was his current obsession with squeezing her arms until she bruised? She almost wished he would go back to punching her in the back and ribs, just so her arms had a chance to heal. Why did she not see this side of him until it was too late? Should she have spotted this? Could she have?

When they'd met, he seemed quiet and she judged him a bit of a loner. She actually felt sorry for him and thought she and the kids could bring a bit of happiness to his life. He didn't want to talk about his family. In fact, he was emphatic that he never saw them, hadn't seen them in ten years, did not want to answer questions about them. Well, Amber could understand that. Apart from her brothers, whom she still worried about, Amber didn't care if she never saw her mother again. She'd accepted that Marco was a bit socially awkward, but she had long since given up hope of meeting Prince Charming. Marco had a house and a job. She would make herself fall in love with him, if he was prepared to take her and her children on.

To give him credit, he hadn't looked excited about the fact that she had kids, his disappointment that she was the sole parent, so there would never be any kid-free weekends, was obvious. But in her optimistic state, Amber chose to ignore that fact, blissfully thinking that once he got to know Arlo and Ruby, he'd see what great kids they were, and love them. Or at least like them. But he definitely had baggage she had no comprehension of, and the longer she spent with him the more afraid she became.

She understood now, that the reason he hadn't had a relationship, or even a girlfriend, before, was because he was emotionally destitute. He was incapable of love, or empathy, or kindness towards anyone female. He had mates he would do anything for, but he was a misogynist, harbouring a deep-seated hatred for women, treating them with undisguised scorn. She'd been so desperate to get out of the share-house craziness, that she was willing to take on anyone, given half a chance. And he had seemed okay initially; so much so that she had taken him home that very first night.

She was attracted to him at first, with his olive skin and dark hair, wide soft mouth below a straight nose. His deep-seated brown eyes were his only flaw. Even in her most optimistic mood, she could only describe them as beady. His forehead, framed by dark curls, was creased by frown lines… lines she'd assumed were due to working in the sun, but later decided were probably caused by his permanent scowl of disapproval with the world. He was physically fit and toned from long days laying bricks, but she'd grown to fear the strength in his body.

Amber still wasn't sure what he'd seen in her. Undoubtedly, he'd been looking for a girlfriend without success for a while. She suspected that her compliant, naturally quiet nature, and her obvious willingness to place few demands on him, sealed her fate. It helped that she had no family or friends that she could turn to. Once she'd crossed that threshold into his house, she was trapped. Wryly she thought of the line in a film she'd once seen, where the wise friend warned his buddy, 'Careful what you wish for.' Well, that had been her undoing. She'd wanted a home so desperately, she'd ignored all the danger signs until it was too late.

In giving Marco access to her bank account, and her Parent Payment details, she'd given up her independence entirely. Marco now controlled every aspect of her life, physically, emotionally and financially. She was nothing more than a possession to him; she existed only for his pleasure. She knew he wouldn't let her leave without a fight, and the thought of his simmering anger made her blood run cold. She was a prisoner in this relationship, and powerless. No money, no car, not even a driver's licence. The useless waste of space that Cindy had always told her she was.

She, Arlo and Ruby tiptoed carefully through their days trying not to earn his displeasure, but it was draining. Her luck couldn't go on forever. Her guilt at creating this life for her kids, forcing them to live in the shadows, ate at her constantly. Marco's complaints about them were escalating, and it was surely only a matter of time before he carried out his threats and gave them the good old-fashioned belting, he said they needed for their own good. Aware that she was going to have to act soon, a ragged sigh escaped her. Did life always have to be hard? How was she going to be able to escape this mess?

Ruby threaded her arms around Amber, squeezing her and bringing her back to the moment.

'Good morning bubba,' said Amber softly, bending down to cuddle Ruby and cover her with kisses.

'Arlo wet the bed,' whispered Ruby. 'It's okay though, I found him some new pyjamas. We called out, but you didn't come!' There was a hint of disappointment, even accusation in her voice. Despite this, Ruby continued hugging her, patting Amber's back reassuringly. At the end of the cuddle, Ruby drew back slightly to look at Amber, and in that moment, Amber saw Ruby's eyes widen in shock. It was Amber's turn to hug Ruby tightly and say,

'It's okay, baby. It doesn't hurt. I just bumped into the door last night on my way to bed. I'm fine really.' She smiled conspiratorially. 'Come on, let's get breakfast and maybe we can watch some TV before Marco gets up. Go and see if Arlo is awake yet.'

Ruby nodded, before laying her head on Amber's shoulder just for a moment. Amber knew in that instant she hadn't fooled her, instead she had added yet another burden to Ruby's backpack of worries. In a sickening flash of recognition, Amber realised that Ruby was re-living a version of her own childhood. Despite her best efforts, Amber had to acknowledge the truth: she was no better a mother than Cindy, except that she actually loved her kids and cared about them. Amber slumped. Even her heart felt limp. Over-wrought and emotionally depleted, she could almost taste defeat. What good were the best of intentions if the result was always the same?

It was Saturday and Marco liked to sleep late on weekends. She could usually count on a couple of hours' peace, when the kids could laze around before he got up, and they were yet again banned from the house. Once awake, Marco usually propped himself in front of the TV for the day, placing bets on the races and watching non-stop sport. It was Amber's job to bring him snacks and keep Arlo and Ruby out of his way. He'd start drinking early, but not till after lunch…he had his standards. Once he was ensconced on the couch, he wasn't to be disturbed. As the day progressed, and depending on his betting success, he would become more and more belligerent, until inevitably a text from mates sent him scurrying off to meet them at the pub. Once he was gone, and only then, could she and the kids dare to occupy the lounge, and touch the remote. It was the moment they waited for all day; when he disappeared down the driveway and they had the house to themselves.

Amber watched as Ruby moved soundlessly across the kitchen towards her bedroom. As she did, the door opened and Arlo took a tentative look down the passage, checking to see if Marco's bedroom door was still shut, before also quietly stepping out. Ruby jerked her head towards the kitchen, Amber felt her heart breaking as she saw them both creep silently towards her, afraid to make a sound in their own home. This was no way to live.

Putting on a bright fake smile, Amber scooped Arlo up in a bear hug, her bruised back complaining at his weight. He was getting to be a big boy.

'How did you sleep, mate? Ruby told me you had an accident. I'm sorry I couldn't come. Did Rubes help you?'

Drawing back from her tight embrace, Arlo looked at her solemnly. He nodded.

'Yep. Ruby helped me. It's okay.'

Then he put his hand very gently on her bruised cheek,

'Does it hurt, Mumma?'

Shaking her head, Amber said in a cheery voice, 'I'm fine. Now, what do you say to pancakes for breakfast?'

Amber was rewarded with big smiles, so she shooed them to the lounge and the TV while she set about mixing up the batter. When she returned a little while later with the pancakes, she let them eat in front of the TV, a rare treat, and sat with them while they watched episodes of *Bluey*, enjoying the antics of this happy dog family… whose carefree life was totally foreign to theirs.

Eventually the tell-tale sound of the blinds being raised alerted them: Marco was awake and moving around. In a well-rehearsed scenario and without the need for a prompt, the kids scooted off to the bedroom to get dressed, while she cleared all evidence of their breakfast from the lounge, careful to exit *ABC Kids* before switching off the TV. By the time Marco emerged, Arlo and Ruby were already on their way outside, hats on and water bottles in hand. They were almost at the back door when Marco called out,

'Hey! Arlo! Come here!'

Arlo stopped, reluctantly turning to face Marco, standing outside Arlo and Ruby's bedroom. Amber felt physically sick. In trying to spend some happy time with the kids, she'd forgotten to get rid of the evidence of Arlo's wet bed. Every step Arlo took towards Marco was torture. As he neared him, Marco suddenly shot out his hand, grabbing Arlo roughly by his arm and dragging him in the room, towards his wet bed. Amber held her breath.

'What a baby you are,' Marco sneered. 'What are you? Five? Almost six? At school, and still wetting the bed?'

Then putting his face right up into Arlo's, he taunted him, 'I think I'll take you to school on Monday. Yeah! I'll take you. And then I'll tell all your little mates what a baby you are, wetting the bed. And, I'll tell that stupid teacher of yours as well, Miss fucking Hudson, what a little loser you really are!'

By now Amber had finally found the wits to move, but even though she flew at him, Marco had already dragged Arlo to the bed, roughly thrusting his little face into the wet sheets. Holding him firmly he pinned him, face down in his own cold urine, while he laughed. As Amber reached Marco, she grabbed at his arm pleading with him to stop. His response was brutal and swift. Releasing Arlo for a moment he gave her a backhand across her already bruised face, before pushing her viciously across the room, where she hit her head on the edge of the windowsill.

'Stay out of this, you slut!' he growled.

'If you weren't such a pathetic excuse for a mother with all your babying ways, this kid might stand half a fuckin' chance. You're the one whose made him such a pathetic sook. Wetting the bed every night! He needs a nappy! Maybe I'll take him to school with a pack of nappies,' he sneered cruelly.

'Yeah! Let's do that! I'm happy to buy him some fuckin' nappies. It' d be cheaper than all this wear and tear on my washing machine,' he continued, once again thrusting Arlo's face into the wet sheets.

Amber's head was stinging with pain. Although dazed from the contact with the windowsill, she turned swiftly back to Marco, ignoring the bile rising in her throat; the sight of Ruby trying to pull Marco away from Arlo, was the adrenaline rush she needed. Within an instant, she was up on her feet, tearing wildly at Marco's arms. Frantic, she hit at him with her fists, trying desperately to shield Ruby. As ineffective as her punches were, she at least managed to distract him so that when he threw Ruby off, she miraculously landed on the bed, and not hard against the chest of drawers.

Focusing his anger back on Amber, he pushed her roughly against the bedroom wall, holding her there by the neck, and trapping her with his forearm, so she could hardly move. As she struggled to breathe, she was conscious of Arlo coughing, gasping in air, before crawling over to cling to Ruby on the bed. Writhing, and desperate to escape from the strangle hold Marco had on her, Amber managed to get her hands free, beating wildly at Marco's chest. Then, just like a light being switched off, he suddenly released her, and stepped back. Amber fell to the floor. Marco stood over her, his lips curled in derision.

'Fuck, you are pathetic. Here I am, just trying to help you out with these kids and you go all fucking psycho on me,' he sniggered malevolently.

'Don't come crying to me when the kid has no friends because he's a loser, a mummy's boy. Fucking baby he is.'

Then, kicking her in the ribs as she lay cowering on the floor, he said in a ruthless voice,

'Now get my fucking breakfast. And get those bloody whingeing kids out of my sight, before I give the three of you a taste of what you really deserve.'

With a final snarl, he swaggered off to the bathroom. As soon as the door closed, and the noise of the shower could be heard, Amber put out her arms. Arlo and Ruby rushed to her.

'Are you okay?' whispered Amber checking each child desperately. The kids nodded back, clearly in shock as tears rolled down their faces.

'I hate him, Mumma,' breathed Ruby into her ear. Putting her finger to her lips, Amber nodded and mouthed at them, 'I know. I hate him too. We'll talk later.'

Ignoring the shock of pain in her ribs, she gingerly got up from the floor. No time to feel sorry for herself. Time to act. Her mind was made up in an instant. Thinking fast, she grabbed the kids' backpacks, frantically stuffing them with spare undies, track pants, T-shirts and windcheaters. Pushing through the pain of her injuries she moved quickly to the pantry. Indiscriminately, she snatched up packets of biscuits, some bananas and several apples, cramming them into whatever space was left, before pointing to outside. Once Arlo and Ruby had followed her out of the house, she handed them their drink bottles. In a low but firm voice, she gave them serious and concise instructions.

'I want you to go to the park and stay there, until I come for you. Don't talk to anyone, and don't go anywhere with anyone. You know all about stranger-danger, Ruby. You have to watch Arlo and stick together. If you are too scared then you can run back here, but try to be brave. I'll come and get you as soon as Marco goes to the pub. Can you do this for me?'

Terrified into complete submission, Arlo and Ruby nodded, the fear evident in their eyes. Kissing them both, she told them she loved them and gently pushed them to go, her heart in her mouth at leaving them on their own, but her fear of keeping them anywhere near Marco greater. She watched them walk away, but only long enough to see them turn right towards the playground. Then she hurried back inside to start Marco's weekend breakfast of bacon and eggs, with all the trimmings.

She had just enough time to get the hashbrowns in the air-fryer, when Marco sauntered out naked. Flicking his penis towards her, he smirked,

'If you play your cards right, I might just give you a taste of this after breakfast. You are one *lucky* woman!' he laughed as he strolled back to the bedroom to get dressed and lay his first bet of the day.

Amber expelled the breath she'd been holding. She had to keep moving. First priority was to get a perfect breakfast served up, so he wouldn't have any reason to turn on her again. She knew she had overstepped boundaries big time by rushing in to defend Arlo, and she was terrified how this would all play out. If she could get through the next few hours, she was determined to leave this nightmare. By the time Marco returned to the kitchen, the bacon was sizzling gently, the coffee machine was primed, the eggs ready to go, and the hash browns were starting to crisp. A miniscule amount of the tension building up inside her diminished. Faking a smile and acting as if nothing had happened, she said cheerily,

'Perfect timing. Breakfast is almost ready. Do you want orange juice or just coffee?'

'Don't give me perfect timing, bitch!' he said and roughly pushed past her. Caught off-balance she fell against the kitchen bench, resulting in another sudden stabbing pain from her ribs. As she grabbed instinctively at her side, Marco pulled her hair, dragging her face towards his.

'Don't try that sooky stuff with me, or I'll give you something to really complain about. You're as big a baby as that fucking bed-wetting kid of yours.' Then shoving her aside, he snarled,

'Now do yourself a favour and clean yourself up. Have a shower, you look and smell like shit. I bet that pee- soaked kid's been all over you. Piss off!'

Stopping only to serve up his breakfast, and needing no further encouragement to escape the kitchen, Amber found some clothes and retreated to the bathroom, leaving Marco to eat and scroll through his phone. As quietly as she could, she slid the bolt across the bathroom door, thankful for a few minutes' respite. Sinking to the edge of the bath, she allowed her tears to fall. The back of her head throbbed where it had hit the windowsill, and her body ached with new bruises. Reaching up carefully so as not to hurt her ribs, she felt the sticky patch of blood at the back of her head. She hoped it didn't need stitches. There would be no time for that today.

Forcing herself to move, she turned on the shower. Teeth gritted against the pain, she examined her body in the mirror, while she waited for the hot water to come through. She didn't think anything was broken, but every breath hurt where Marco's foot had connected with her ribs. There were several new marks on her legs and torso, added to the purple bruises already there. However, she could still move, still function. And she needed to be able to function.

Her brain was on steroids, racing through her options, thinking up one desperate plan after the other. All the while, she was conscious not to linger too long in the shower. She didn't want to anger Marco again. Today he'd reached new level of violence. He'd never had such an aggressive outburst towards the kids before. His contempt and bullying had been constant, but he'd never actually laid a hand on them, and the thought of what he might be capable of, shocked her. Whatever happened, she couldn't risk another beating to herself in the next few hours. She needed to be fit and ready to move when the opportunity came. And she knew she must give him no reason to suspect that she wanted out.

Moving with care, she patted her aching body dry, then dressed as quickly as her pain would allow. Examining her face closely in the mirror, she opted for no moisturiser. That would be too painful, but she did put on mascara and perfume, so Marco would think she was making an effort. Then, very carefully she applied some lip-stick. It would have to do. Although every instinct screamed at her not to open the bathroom door, she knew she had to face him again. He was absolutely capable of breaking the lock and she figured that scenario would be worse for her. Taking several deep breaths, before she exited the sanctuary of the bathroom, Amber tried to act as if nothing had happened. Marco looked up as she walked by.

'That's an improvement at least,' he grunted, searching her face for any hint of dissent. Amber nodded and smiled, hopefully placating him.

'Yes, you were right. I was a mess! I feel so much better after a shower. How was brekky? Can I get you another coffee?' she asked, as she walked through to the laundry, where she dropped her bloodstained nightie in the dirty washing basket.

'Yeah! Another coffee would be good,' he replied sounding somewhat mollified by her evident change of heart. 'Where are the fuckin' kids by the way? It's pretty quiet out there, even for those two losers.'

'I finally took your advice babe. I've sent them off to the park, or wherever, and told them they are on their own today. You are so right. I've been babying them for too long.'

As Amber said this, she gave Marco a hug.

'So, we have the house to ourselves,' she smiled suggestively. 'Or, we could even go out somewhere, if you want to.'

Marco nodded; his lips pursed together in a self-satisfied smirk.

'I'm glad you are finally listening to me. My mum never cared what I was up to, and I was lucky if my shitty dad even remembered my name. Didn't do me any harm. You're just overthinking it.'

Just then his phone buzzed with a message and Marco once again began scrolling through to check it. Amber placed a fresh coffee in front of him, then busied herself cleaning up while he went back to his all-important Saturday morning job of working out his bets. Suddenly, he exploded, with a loud, 'Fuck!'

Amber froze: her hands still in the sink. What had she done? She didn't dare look at him.

'You and your little shitheads made me fucking forget! I was supposed go round to Jimbo's to help him with his side fence today. He expected me an hour ago! Fuck! Now it'll probably take most of the day.'

'That's a bummer! I'm so sorry we stuffed up your morning,' sympathised Amber, trying to look every bit as devasted as Marco was by this news. 'It would have been nice to do something just the two of us. But then, he helped you with that bit of plumbing a couple of weeks ago, didn't he?'

'Yeah. I do owe him,' admitted Marco begrudgingly. 'Also, I think he said we could bring the kids over for a barbeque later today.'

Amber felt her heart lurch in her chest in panic. She was speechless until Marco began laughing.

'Don't look so terrified Amber. You don't think I'm going to let you go out in public and let everyone see what a klutz you are, always bumping into doors and giving yourself bruises.'

Amber managed a short, almost hysterical laugh. In her twisted reality, she was actually thankful for the bashing that had left her with visible bruises. They certainly would take some explaining in front of his mates. Her laugh was short-lived though. Instead, she flinched in pain, as Marco, on his way to get changed into his work gear, flicked her cheek with his thumb and fingers…one last insult to remind her who was the boss.

In the meantime, Amber tried to make it seem as if she was going about a normal Saturday, putting on a load of washing, and taking meat out of the freezer for dinner. As Marco picked up his keys, she asked,

'What about spag bol for dinner? That way if you get home late it doesn't matter?'

'Yeah sure. We'll have a few beers probably. I'll see you when I see you.'

Before leaving he gave her a long kiss, stamping his claim on her. Despite a serious urge to bite down hard on his tongue, Amber returned the kiss, trying to appear submissive, and making sure she reinforced his illusion that she had learned her lesson.

'And do yourself a favour. Chill out while those kids are gone. It'll do you good,' he announced magnanimously, slamming the door as he left. Amber could scarcely contain her relief at this reprieve. It was such an unexpected miracle that he would be gone this early on a Saturday! At best, she'd hoped that he might meet his mates at the pub perhaps late afternoon, but this was a bonus. She watched from the kitchen window as he strolled to the car, giving his balls one final scratch and adjustment, before getting in and starting the engine.

If she could have, she would have punched the air in celebration, or cartwheeled, like Sam Kerr after a goal. This surely equalled an Olympic winning moment, but her body pulsed with pain at the mere thought of any unnecessary movements. Standing back from the window, out of his sight, she watched as he reversed down the driveway, still holding her breath. But once she heard the car accelerate down the street, she sank her head down on the kitchen bench, and allowed herself a few seconds to breathe and to calm her racing heart. Old mate Jimbo's fence job had probably given her at least five hours' start, more if that lot got stuck into the beers after the job. She wouldn't need all of that, she would be long gone.

However, right now, she did need to think things through, to plan their escape.

First priority was money. She had a hidden savings account with about a hundred and thirty dollars in it. When Marco insisted early on that she hand her debit card over to him so he could 'manage her money for her,' she'd dutifully handed over one card, but some sense of preservation had kicked in. Despite her bubble of optimism, she'd kept the existence of her other account a secret. She collected the card now from under the potato bin in the pantry, where it was safely tucked away in a plastic zip bag.

Next, she hit the bedroom, going through Marco's drawers and the pockets of his clothes. No-one used cash much these days, but Marco and his mates always had a few 'cash jobs' on the go. He would never have shown her where his stash was, but she had already worked it out. She needed a step ladder, but the climb was worth it, as she found three hundred and seventy dollars in the old biscuit tin at the back of the wardrobe shelf. There was another fifteen dollars from his pockets and bedside drawer. He had a glass jar of coins he used for spare change. She emptied it all into an old purse. It would be heavy, but she would make sure she used the coins before the notes.

She calculated she had a bit over four hundred in cash, plus the money in her own account. The final stash was in her own sock drawer, which she had accumulated from her cleaning job at Erica's, next door. This money usually went to pay for extras the kids needed at school, like the Mother's Day stall, or an excursion. Another forty-odd dollars. She didn't have time to count it but she reckoned on roughly four hundred and sixty dollars. She would need every cent.

She put the notes into her wallet and split the coins into two purses. Her next priority was food. Using up all the bread, she made cheese, Vegemite and peanut butter sandwiches, wrapping them in clingwrap. She grabbed packets of plain biscuits, a knife and the remaining cheese, and, as an afterthought, the peanut butter and Vegemite too. They went into the bag with all the apples, bananas and mandarins in the house, and a container of sweet biscuits. Then she added some black garbage bags, a plastic tablecloth, and a roll of paper towel. Stopping, she forced herself to think logically; all possible scenarios running through her head.

The kids had a backpack each, so she could put more spare clothes into a carry bag, and eventually they could pack them into their own bags. She grabbed toothbrushes, undies, spare track pants, tee- shirts and jumpers; it was probably better to have warm clothes as a priority. She included their school uniforms at the last minute, even though she figured the likelihood of getting emergency housing in this area was remote. They would probably have to go to another school. She hated having to put them through all this again, but she knew there was no alternative if she was going to keep them safe.

Packing her own clothes with ruthless efficiency, she filled up her own backpack and another soft carry bag. She had nothing of value, other than a small photo-book that held some baby photos of her and her brothers. She checked her wallet. No Medicare card! When did she last use that? She was going to need documentation! What had she done with all that stuff? Not her! What had Marco done with her important documents? Amber knew every inch of this house, and apart from the money stash tin, she couldn't think of where else he would keep things. She looked carefully through the pile of household bills and his files. There was nothing there. Why hadn't all this control over every aspect of her life not rung serious alarm bells earlier? *Think girl! Think!*

Climbing up the step ladder once more she searched the high wardrobe shelf, hoping for inspiration. Then she saw it. A key! Blu-tacked against the wall at the back of the shelf. It was still a stretch for her, but she got finger-tips to it, and flicked it closer. It was old and looked like it would fit an old wardrobe…and she knew just where to look. Panicking – time was moving on and she was terrified Marco would return unexpectedly – she half-ran, half-limped outside to the old shed. She rarely had a reason to go in there because the garden was Marco's domain, but she did remember it was dominated by a shabby old wardrobe. The bolt on the shed door was ancient and stiff with rust, but at least it wasn't locked. It took what seemed an endless amount of tugging and twisting, all the while conscious of time ticking by, to get it to finally slide across – and at last she was inside.

Thankfully, the old key was easier. With just a few jiggles, Amber had the wardrobe open. Several files were stacked neatly in a plastic container. Ripping the lid off, she scanned the notations on the old A4 binders. One simply had a capital A on the spine. One quick look at the contents and Amber found, not only her Medicare card with Arlo and Ruby's names on it, but also their birth certificates. There were official letters from Centrelink, as well as her MyGov details and passwords. She didn't even remember handing all this over! Why had he hidden this information from her? Once again, it confirmed her stupidity. What a fool she'd been!

Cursing herself for being so gullible, she pulled the plastic sleeves from the file, before replacing it in the box. Hopefully, if she left everything as it was, and put the key back in the bedroom wardrobe, Marco wouldn't discover for a while that she was really gone. She might gain some time. Fighting all her instincts just to leave everything and go, Amber again wrestled to close the garage door bolt, wasting precious minutes. Methodically she worked backwards, covering up all signs that she had found Marco's money stash and the key to the wardrobe. Putting the step ladder back in the laundry, and breathing heavily from her efforts, she mentally took stock of what she had.

Money. Food. Documents. A few clothes. At the last minute, she pulled a blanket from Ruby's bed, folded it and pushed it over the top of her carry bag. Looking round one last time, she grinned at the half-done dishes and the unmade beds, including the still gloriously wet sheets on Arlo's bed. With a flash of insight, she remembered the tracking app Marco had installed on her phone so he could follow her movements. She switched it off and deleted the app, turning off her phone for extra protection. Then, wearing her coat despite the warmth of the day, her backpack on, a carry-bag in each hand and a soft overnight bag slung over her right shoulder, she left the door to the house wide open, and walked away, ignoring her aching body's objections.

CHAPTER 13

Lexie indulged herself with a second cup of tea and basked in the sheer joy of having the house to herself. She'd become used to her own company last year, to doing her own thing at her own pace. She wondered briefly if she was getting a bit set in her ways. Then just as quickly, decided she didn't actually care. And it was so pleasurable to simply sit and enjoy this lovely old house with its high, decorative ceilings, and mellow timber floors. A part of her itched to begin renovating, and her head buzzed with possibilities, especially painting those garish walls! All ideas were quickly squashed, when she considered the limitations of her current budget.

Sitting back and stretching her neck, she thought of the positives. For a start, the plumbing was definitely up to scratch. The water was hot and the pressure great. No need for major renovations in the bathroom, other than new tiles and a bit of paint. Baby steps, she reminded herself as she gulped down the last of her tea. Dishes first, then she would attack the last of the kitchen boxes. By the time she was midway through the second box and delighting in finding her favourite heavy frypan, she heard the familiar toot of Ray's car as he and Jeanie turned up to help. Within minutes, Jeanie was knee-deep in the contents of the linen press, arranging it into some sort of order, and Ray had started on re-assembling the spare beds. The three of them worked harmoniously, and it wasn't long before all the boxes, including the assortment of tools and gardening utensils destined for the outdoor shed, had been unpacked.

At two o'clock they stopped for a late lunch, congratulating themselves on an excellent morning's work. While Jeanie and Ray had a well-deserved rest, Lexie dug out the sandwich maker and produced cheese toasties all round.

'I need a trip to the supermarket, before I do anything else tomorrow,' said Lexie sitting down to join her mum and dad, surveying the growing pile of flattened boxes with great satisfaction. Just then a loud bark came from outside the back door.

'I think you're forgetting someone,' laughed Ray. 'I'd say Radar's telling you he wants a walk. And he'll need walking too, otherwise he'll dig up the back yard for sure. German shepherds need exercise.'

'I will walk him today, but at some point I want to go to the pet shop and buy one of those ball-tossers. Then we only need to walk as far as the oval. It's just a couple of streets away, and I can toss the ball to him there. Mind you, walking will be good exercise for me as well … not that I need any more exercise today. I'm stuffed,' laughed Lexie. 'But thanks so much Mum and Dad. You've been such a great help.' And reaching across the table she gave them both a hug.

'I'm going home to watch the cricket for the rest of the afternoon,' announced Ray..

'And I might just join you,' threatened Jeanie, standing up and stretching. 'At least we've broken the back of it for you, Lex. You can take your own time to sort out the bedroom and the bathroom. You know where you want everything. We'll leave you in peace now. We'll probably catch you later in the week.'

'Save some jobs for us,' Ray added. 'We can come around one day next week and give you a hand. Maybe even get stuck into the garden and clear some of those weeds. You might want to think about what you could do with the garden. I don't think it's had much attention and some new plants won't cost much.'

'Yep. I'll need to go to Bunnings for some storage containers as well. I can give it some thought, and maybe look at their plant section too. I'd better get moving, and take Radar for a walk, or the neighbours will be complaining about his barking,' replied Lexie, frowning as Rader barked again loudly. Another reminder that he wanted attention.

'I'll get him on the lead for you, while you get ready,' offered Ray. 'And then we'll leave you to it.'

Ray headed outside and Jeanie shooed Lexie away from the dishes, saying she would clean up. Figuring it was easier to do as she was told, Lexie found her joggers and applied sunscreen. By the time she walked around to the front, Ray was deep in conversation with one of the tradies Lexie had noticed the day before, working on the house across the road. With Ray gesturing to her to come and say hello, Lexie had no choice other than to put on a forced smile and meet the poor fellow Ray had bailed up at the front of the house. He had his back to Lexie as she walked over, laughing at something Ray said, but as Lexie approached, he turned round to face her, smiling politely.

Hmm! Nice eyes… thought Lexie involuntarily, as she briefly contemplated two striking hazel eyes, while also taking in an attractive face and collar-length curly red hair. Shaking his hand, Lexie noticed a confident strength in his grip. Ray introduced his new friend Josh, and began to describe the renovations Josh was busy with on the house over the road. Although he responded politely enough, Josh was clearly distracted, appearing completely charmed by Radar, who he patted and talked to like a besotted dog lover.

Lexie couldn't help but be slightly miffed that Radar rated more highly than she did, but to be fair, she had to acknowledge she was possibly looking a bit jaded after the last few days' labour. And she was in some very un-flattering working gear.

'Welcome to the neighbourhood,' said Josh, eventually turning his attention back to Lexie. 'You must be happy to be settled into the house. It's one of the nicest around here, and it's got a great backyard for young Radar. He's a beautiful dog.'

Lexie was not too sure what to make of this guy. He was certainly a bit over the top about Radar. She took the dog lead from Ray, and gave Radar a proprietorial tug, keen to establish ownership. Patting Radar one last time, then running his fingers through his own thick, red curls, Josh said ruefully,

'He's just like my old dog Bruce, so forgive me if I'm a bit besotted. Bruce died two weeks ago and I'm still missing him.'

Then he directed a deadly smile at Lexie, who was afraid her mouth had dropped open in response. In the face of such a charm offensive, she was prepared to forgive him for anything. She managed to mumble her condolences, before hearing herself say,

'Oh! Please feel free to visit any time… um, Radar loves attention, and I'll be out all day, during the week.'

Then, stating the obvious she said brightly, 'I'm just taking him for a walk now. Bye Josh. Nice to meet you. See you later Dad.'

Simultaneously blushing and cringing at her own awkwardness, Lexie made a hasty exit with the dog. When she looked back some minutes later, Jeanie had joined Ray, and they were both comfortably chatting like old friends with the neighbour's handy man, or whoever he was. Lexie rolled her eyes at herself and blushed again, her cheeks flushing hot with embarrassment. *Are you thirty-three, or thirteen? Who gets lost for words because of a pair of hazel eyes? 'Please feel free to visit anytime!' He must think I am an absolute nutcase!* Then Lexie laughed out loud at herself, causing Radar to look up from his sniffing, his ears on alert.

'Okay Radar, I'll admit it. Not just nice eyes but a seriously handsome man! Maybe I am finally getting over Jed!' she chuckled, as Radar dragged her all the way to the park.

When she returned an hour later, Jeanie and Ray were well gone and there was no sign of the handsome Josh. Lexie didn't doubt there was an adoring 'partner' waiting somewhere at home for him to return. After making herself a cup of tea, Lexie sat down and wrote out her shopping list. She really couldn't be bothered going to the supermarket, but she forced herself. It was only ten-minutes by car, and if she had the time, she could even walk there occasionally, especially if she didn't need a big shop.

Today, however, a big shop was definitely required. By the time she had the basics to set up the pantry, and thought about a couple of meals for the week ahead, Lexie had spent a small fortune. She was also ready to put her feet up and do nothing for the rest of the day. Nevertheless, she unpacked the bags of groceries slowly, enjoying the initial chance to arrange everything in the pantry. Hands on hips, she surveyed the neat rows of cans, packets, condiments, spices and assorted containers and announced to the empty room,

'I really should take a photo because it will never look this neat again. Good job, Lexie!' She gave herself a thumbs up.

Glancing at the clock which was edging towards six, she declared, 'Wine o'clock.'

There was still yesterday's open bottle in the fridge, and soon Lexie was relaxing on the couch, wine glass in hand, flicking channels to find the news, when Ray rang.

'Dad? What's up?'

'Oh! Hello love. I just wanted to tell you before I forgot, that Josh... you know the guy who was working on the renovations on the house across the road?'

'Yeah?'

'Turns out he's an architect, and he can draw up plans for you if you decide to renovate. He said he's more than happy to have a look at the house and give you a few suggestions.'

'An architect? What's he doing on the tools then?'

'Very interesting chap. He likes to see a project through, apparently, so he contracts the work out and supervises the job. Sometimes, like today, he'll go in and finish off a minor job, so the sparky or plumber can make a start on Monday. It's a huge reno. He said you're welcome to have a look at it anytime.'

'Okay Dad. Sounds good. Maybe I will. But I'm not too sure if I can afford much at the moment. I may have to be patient.'

'All the same. It might be worth your while having a chat with this bloke. He's a very nice fellow.' Lexie could hear her mother saying something in the background, to which Ray replied with a 'Hmph.'

'What did Mum say?' asked Lexie.

'Just stupid stuff about him being easy on the eye. Ignore her. We'll talk later. Goodnight, love.'

'Good night, Dad,' chuckled Lexie, ending the call with a grin. So, the old girl wasn't immune to a pair of good-looking eyes either. *Good taste must run in the family* she thought. Still smiling, she filed Ray's information away for another day.

Maybe it would be good to get a bit of an idea of what she was up for financially, if she did renovate.

***

By the time Amber arrived at the park her arms were screaming with the effort, and every muscle in her sore body was now aching with a vengeance. The ten-minute walk had felt more like thirty, her injuries protesting at every step. Why did he have to kick her in the ribs? Just breathing was an exercise in pain-management, especially when she forgot and took a deeper breath. It didn't help that she was stressed out that the kids would even still be there! Dozens of scenarios played out in her mind, most involving them being snatched by a paedophile, while she doggedly made her way to the park. She had never left them on their own like this. Her only excuse, she told herself, was that she'd had no choice. Despite the risk, they were definitely safer away from Marco and his volatile temper. When she neared the park and saw two little figures sitting on the swings, scuffing their shoes in the gravel as they swung gently back and forth, her relief was almost euphoric.

Spotting Amber, they both came running. Arms outstretched, she managed to hold them at bay so their hugs didn't overwhelm her, and bring on another burst of pain from her ribs. Kneeling, she held them close, while she praised them for being so brave without her.

'I'm hungry,' whimpered Arlo on the verge of tears. 'You took so long, Mumma!'

'I'm hungry too,' complained Ruby. 'We finished all the food ages ago. We were scared you wouldn't come.'

'I know. I'm so sorry, but I've got sandwiches and some fruit. I had to make sure we didn't have to go back to Marco's, so it took me a while to pack stuff. Help me carry this and we can sit down and have some lunch.'

Reassured, now Amber had arrived, and cheering up visibly, Ruby and Arlo took one of the carry bags from her, sharing the load between them. Amber led them through the park, and down an incline to where the park converged with the edge of the public golf course. She was keen to get out of sight of the road, just in case Marco drove home this way, although it was highly unlikely he would. The most probable outcome was that he wouldn't get home until around eight o'clock, half-pissed, after lots of drinks with Jimbo. However, after this morning's events she wasn't going to take anything for granted. All her senses were on red alert, and right now she needed to rest and regroup.

Choosing a grassy spot in the shade, Amber spread the blanket, and sitting cross-legged, opened the backpack containing the sandwiches. For a few minutes all three were silent as they munched on the food she had prepared. When they'd eaten their fill, Amber loaded up on Panadol, and they all lay down on the rug, their heads resting on the backpacks and bags of clothes. It was only about four in the afternoon, and although both had long since stopped needing afternoon naps, Arlo and Ruby were quickly asleep. Amber felt their bodies grow heavy beside her, as the drama of the day caught up with them. Amber managed to doze off a couple of times herself, waking each time feeling stronger and more refreshed.

Despite their dire situation, Amber felt ridiculously happy and optimistic. She was never going back to Marco. She had hit rock bottom and things could only improve. She hadn't fully realised just how deeply unhappy and stressed she was with Marco, until she escaped his sphere. Somehow, she would make a better life for Ruby and Arlo. But they couldn't stay here. She had to find somewhere safe for the night. Past experience had taught her she would be unlikely to get any emergency accommodation for the three of them at such short notice, especially on a Saturday. Her best chance would probably be on Monday. Once the kids were at school, she could start doing the rounds of the shelters, or even try contacting old mates from her refuge days. Someone might be able to offer them a couch for a few nights.

Amber was reluctant to risk going to a government agency straight away. She feared someone might assume she was a bad mother and take her kids from her. She'd read the look in people's eyes when they saw she had two kids. As a young single mum, they expected her to fail. She wasn't going to give those 'do-gooders' any reason to take her kids away. Going back to her old share house would be too risky, because that might be the first place Marco would look. She just needed time to work things out. And, she did have a plan. At least for tonight.

The knowledge that this day was coming had never been far from Amber's mind. She was prepared. They just needed to wait another hour or so until it got dark. Refreshed by the rest, and with the Panadol finally taking some of the edge off her aches, Amber began to sort their worldly possessions. She repacked the kids' backpacks and her own, so she only had one carry-bag, calculating bleakly that, as their food supply diminished, the bags would get lighter. It was getting on to dusk when she woke Arlo and Ruby, telling them it was time to go.

Loaded up once more with backpacks and bags, Amber led the children along the sheltered path next to the golf course boundary. It offered some tree cover, even though it was a longer route, but it would be worth the effort to be less visible from the road. Eventually she left the track, and as darkness fell, cut across a couple of side roads, taking the kids back through familiar streets that ran towards the school. Eventually Ruby complained, stopping in her tracks.

'Are we going to school, Mum? It's not a school day. And it's all dark!'

'Come on keep moving, Rubes. We're not going to school, just close by. Now we need to be quiet for a bit,' replied Amber putting a finger to her lips. Gesturing to Arlo and Ruby to stay close, Amber hugged the fence line, on the watch for cars and passersby. Then, stopping outside a dimly lit house, she checked in all directions. Not a soul around. Holding on to each of the children's hands, she walked brazenly down the side of the house, praying that there was no hidden security light to announce their arrival. Ruby's eyes were like saucers as they crept around the back of a stranger's home. Arlo stumbled and his backpack hit the side fence with a clang. They all froze, listening for sounds nearby. Nothing happened. Not even a dog barked. After a minute or two, they continued down the side path, and around to the back veranda. Inside the house, a light was on, throwing a weak beam outside, but it was clear that no-one was home. Amber gathered Ruby and Arlo close to her and whispered:

'When I was walking home the other day, I noticed the people who live here packing their caravan. The lady was on her phone out the front and she was telling someone they would be away for six weeks. We should be safe here. And if we just stay on the back veranda, we're not doing anyone any harm. We've got a table and chairs… and look at the cushions! We can sleep here for a couple of nights until I work out what to do. We just have to be as quiet as mice, and make sure no-one sees us here in the daytime. Okay?'

Arlo and Ruby nodded. They were good kids, and after such a crazy day, they were ready to agree to anything. Amber added another shovel-full of regret to her ever-increasing pile. Yet again, she had failed them, but she was also incredibly proud of how they were coping with everything she threw at them.

'It'll be like camping. It will be fun!' Amber smiled confidently. None of them had ever been camping.

'And I promise we'll get MacDonalds for breakfast tomorrow. And ice-creams! You guys deserve some treats, because you have been so brave for Mummy. But we just have to make do with the food we've got left tonight. We can make a better plan in the morning. Marco will never find us here, so we are all safe. I promise.'

Then hugging them both again as tightly as her bruises would allow, she set about making their improvised shelter as comfortable as she could. The covered veranda at the back of this house was an absolute windfall. With so little money, a motel was out of the question. Marco could check any motels within walking distance anyway. What he would never expect, was that she would be so close to home, at the back of a random house; the owners of which were complete strangers to her. The veranda was open to the back lawn, but each side was closed in. One end appeared to contain a small greenhouse, filled with plants. The opposite end was like a storage area, with shelves for shoes, and mats on the floor. There was an outdoor table setting. If she spread the chair cushions on the mats, and tucked everything in close to the wall, Amber thought, it would be comfortable enough to sleep there. Night had fallen, wrapping them safely in its darkness, but they had the advantage of the security lights from inside, so she could still see enough for them to move around.

Rummaging in her backpack, Amber produced a note pad, a Barbie colouring-in book, a zip bag of felt pens, three Matchbox cars and a couple of Pokemon characters. The extra weight had been well worth it as Ruby's eyes lit up and Arlo showed the first signs of animation in hours. Placing them near the glass back door where the light was best, they both sat down; while Ruby drew, Arlo ran his cars along the back step, quickly involved in his own imaginative play. Amber got out the last of the food.

There were two rounds of sandwiches left, and she put those out on the plastic tablecloth, and spread some of the plain biscuits with peanut butter and some with cheese slices. She chopped up two apples and broke up the mandarins into pieces. The bananas she kept for the morning. At the end of the veranda near the plants, was a tap, and she filled their water bottles from that. The kids had eaten most of the packet of sweet biscuits she'd left them, but she rescued what was left, and placed an unopened packet on the table if needed.

She switched on her phone and immediately it pinged with several messages.

Where the fuck are you? Marco was obviously home. She switched it to silent so the kids wouldn't hear the pings. She'd thought about blocking Marco's number, but felt it might be better to know what he was thinking. Her phone would run out of charge eventually. She looked along the back wall of the house. Did houses have outside power points??? Marco's did for when he used the blower... bingo!!! There were two! She only needed one. She was beginning to think this crazy spot might actually work. She could feel her phone vibrate in quick succession.

You better get home soon you slut. The house looks shit.
Did those loser kids get lost on the way home?
Then a change of tack.
Okay. I'll come and pick you up. Where are you?
Come on babe! You need to come home. I know things got a bit rough,

but it was your fault. You just pushed my buttons.

Fuck babe. It's getting late. I'm over this.

I'll fucking really give you something to cry about if you don't get here soon.

Amber read the texts and felt sick. There was no going back, but the possibility he might find them terrified her. She turned her phone onto flight mode, blocking any messages. That way she could still use the torch function. She watched Arlo and Ruby play for a few more minutes, then catching their eyes, she gestured to them to come and eat. Clearly hungry, they ate everything in sight without a complaint. They were such good kids. No way did they deserve the crazy life she'd inflicted on them.

Once they'd eaten, she let them play for a bit longer while she made up their bed for the night. The plastic tablecloth became the ground cover for the big flat square cushions, handily shaped to fit the backs and seats of the outdoor chairs. Placed together on the ground they were perfect, easily long enough for the three of them to stretch out on, and their backpacks would do for pillows. It was going on seven o'clock when she brought out their toothbrushes, trying to bring some normality into this insane day. They put on extra jumpers and trackpants, and huddled together under the blanket for the night.

Arlo and Ruby were a bit wound up about sleeping outside, nervous and excited at the same time, and Amber doubted they would sleep anytime soon. In a whispering voice, she told them a story, making it up as she went along, about two brave dinosaurs called Ruby and Arlo, who had amazing adventures when they went to the park alone. It took several tales of these adventures before they finally fell asleep.

Amber needed to satisfy herself with a last look around the

back yard. Creeping out of the makeshift bed, she explored the boundaries of the yard. From somewhere close, the unmistakable smell of meat grilling on a barbecue, wafted by, carried enticingly over the cool night air. The neighbour's house to the right was in complete darkness, so Amber wondered if anyone was home there either. Peeking over the opposite fence she could see lights and the blue flash of a TV screen. They clearly had no idea who was next door. No dogs barked, alerting them that something was amiss, which Amber put down to good karma, or sheer luck.

Occasionally things had to go her way. It was certainly good luck that she happened to walk by as the caravan was being packed two days ago, and there was a reason she had committed it to memory. She had been mentally preparing for this possibility for weeks now.

She gave her aching body a tentative stretch. She couldn't imagine that she would get much sleep tonight. It had been four hours since her last dose of painkillers, so she took two more Panadol to help relieve some of the pain. Then she eased herself back into her spot between Arlo and Ruby, careful not to disturb them. Settling back on her make-shift pillows, tiredness hit her like a train. Closing her eyes, she shifted cautiously trying to find a comfortable position, and, despite her sore body, her anxiety about the future, and her self-recriminations, fell into a deep sleep.

CHAPTER 14

The sun was just visible over the trees, when she was woken by Arlo and Ruby tugging at her to get up. Six-twenty. They had all slept unexpectedly well, but it was time to start moving. Fighting off her drowsiness, Amber dragged herself groggily into the new day and into action.

First, clothes. She took a critical look at Arlo and Ruby still dressed in yesterday's gear. Ruby had managed to stay stain-free. Arlo's T-shirt needed changing, but Ruby was good to go. Amber decided her clothes would also last another day, and they all changed into clean undies. Amber packed up the bedding and carefully returned the cushions to their chairs. Packing what they would need for the day into one backpack, she folded everything into the other bags, and hid them behind some boxes on the veranda. If a casual observer walked through the backyard, they wouldn't notice anything amiss.

There were only bananas left of the food rations, and they ate them quickly, but Amber planned to get well away before they needed more food. Quietly they tip-toed around to the front garden. Checking carefully to make sure there were no other people in sight, she led them down the street, past the school, and towards the main road to a bus stop. After a short wait, they caught a bus to the Westfield Shopping Centre on Albany Highway. It was too early for anything other than Macca's to be open, but that was perfect anyway. The kids were in seventh heaven; they hadn't had takeaway for a long time. After choosing whatever they wanted, and scoffing it down ridiculously fast, they had free range of the in-store kids' playground, which was deserted at this early hour. As long as they were happy, Amber was happy to chill out and drink her coffee, quietly contemplating her next move.

This was such familiar territory for her. When she was still in primary school, all those years ago, before the fire and before they moved to Manjimup, the family had lived within walking distance of Westfield. She had spent many a day here looking after her brothers, while Cindy and John were partying, or sleeping off the effects of the night before, and she would take Robbie and Sam away from the house to keep them safe.

The shopping centre had expanded and changed since those days, and she was confident she would easily be able to fill in several hours there. For a start, once the shops opened, there were the toy aisles in both the major department stores for the kids to explore. Robbie and Sam used to love spending hours there, examining the toys in detail, even though examining the packaging was as about as close as they ever got to playing with them.

Later, when the midday movie sessions started, she would sneak Robbie and Sam into the cinema for free. Careful observations over many weekend visits had made Amber an expert on dodging security and cinema ushers. They might miss the first few minutes, but once the film was running, the young usher checking the tickets was usually called away to the start of the session at the next cinema … Hopefully, she hadn't lost her touch, and they could do the same today. Money was tight.

While Ruby and Arlo chased each other through the brightly coloured plastic tunnels in the playground, she began contacting the emergency housing numbers she had. At eight o'clock it was too early to contact friends, but she hoped the emergency contact staff at the Women's Refuges would be answering phones. Several calls later, the fight was starting go out of her. The adrenaline that had sustained her in flight yesterday was ebbing like a tide, draining slowly away. There was nothing available in the short-term, even for a few nights.

She begged the last lady, who sounded as worn out and exhausted as Amber herself was, to find her something. Relenting eventually to Amber's pleas that she didn't even have a car to sleep in, she suggested Amber try a crisis centre in Joondalup. There was a chance a room might be available later today. However, she made no promises.

Amber bought the kids more pancakes and herself another coffee. Carefully composing each text, she went through all her old share-house and refuge buddies to see if anyone could help her out for a couple of nights. Sipping her coffee, she stared at her phone willing a solution to appear. Gradually the replies came in.

From Sasha; *Sorry Ambs. Having a few problems with my new boyfriend. Not a good time but let's catch up soon. Love ya!! Xxx*

Lisa wasn't any better; *What a shit Marco turned out to be! Who would have thought? Sorry I can't help I'm broke right now. Back with Mum at the moment. Things not really working out. Maybe we can get together again… Keep in touch girl. xxxx*

Eventually Melissa answered. She'd counted on Mel, they'd been through so much together; *Sorry to hear things are bad. I'd love to help, but I've moved down south. Remember Toby, from Albany? We've been together for a few months. It's going well. If you can get down*

With each text Amber grew more depressed, and her anxiety rose. The kids came running back because someone had pushed Arlo and he was crying. It was time to go. The shops were open now. Amber really wanted to stay where she was, but she dried Arlo's tears and forced herself to move. Holding Arlo and Ruby's hands, her backpack slung over her shoulder, she guided them through the shopping centre, to the department stores where they spent almost two hours looking through the toy sections. By the time the kids declared themselves hungry again, and began bickering over nothing, Amber was numb with fatigue, and her aching ribs were becoming seriously painful.

Claustrophobic after so long in the shopping mall, and overloaded with half-baked plans, and vague random ideas, her brain had given up. Amber headed to the southern exit at the end of the building, dragging the kids outside and into the fresh air. From across the road came the pungent smell of a sausage sizzle, where a charity group were turning sausages on a barbecue in the car park of Bunnings Warehouse, bringing back more memories for Amber, and momentarily, a renewed sense of purpose.

Skilfully dodging traffic, and with Arlo and Ruby's hands firmly grasped, Amber made a beeline for the barbeque. The aroma of onions, sausages and hamburgers cooking was the oxygen she needed to continue functioning for a little bit longer. A can of Coke each (she didn't have the energy to care), and a sausage in bread topped with tomato sauce, and all three of them were restored. Bunnings didn't exactly have a toy department, but it did have variety, and with nothing better on offer, it would have to do for a bit of a wander around.

Amazingly, Arlo and Ruby seemed happy enough, perhaps entertained by the sheer novelty of it all.

In the last aisle next to the gardening section, a godsend! Arlo spotted a kids' playground area, mercifully located next to a coffee shop. As Arlo and Ruby ran off to play, Amber ordered a coffee and sat down at a table where she could keep an eye on them. Not even a double shot of coffee this time could quell the feeling of utter defeat Amber experienced as she sat there, wondering if they could safely spend another night in the same backyard.

It was still too early to ring the women's refuge office in Joondalup, and she didn't want to risk going all that way if she wasn't going to be guaranteed a spot. This would mean a new school for the kids…maybe a couple of new schools before they got settled again. More change and uncertainty in their lives, the remorse and anxiety pressing down even harder, physically deflating her, so that even taking a breath was a struggle. Placing her head in her hands she closed her eyes, immobile, conscious of just breathing in and out, her mind a blank. On a distant level she was in tune with Arlo and Ruby's chatter, but otherwise for a few minutes, she gave in to utter exhaustion.

Lexie had driven to Bunnings that afternoon with the sole purpose of buying storage containers, and was now distracted by the gardening possibilities on offer. Walking down the aisle towards the plant section, she saw two kids who looked familiar, tearing around the playground next to the café. Looking more closely, she spotted a young woman at a café table, head slumped on folded arms, fair hair covering her face like a shroud. She didn't need to see the face to realise immediately it was Amber. Her gut told her something was very wrong. Not wanting to startle her, Lexie approached slowly.

When Amber felt a hand on her shoulder, she jerked upright and looked round frantically. Had Marco found them? It took her a few seconds to realise it was Lexie, concern written all over her face. As recognition dawned on her, Amber's relief translated into tears that streamed uncontrollably down her cheeks.

'Oh Amber! What's the matter? It's okay,' soothed Lexie, grabbing a chair, and sitting down next to her and wrapping a comforting arm around her shoulder. Amber's defences fell away. She had nothing left. Deep wracking sobs overtook her and she gave in, the dam finally breaking on the river of tears she had stored up inside. Spotting Lexie with Amber, Ruby and Arlo left the play equipment and ran over to them. Lexie was surprised when they both threw themselves at her, little arms squeezing around her neck and clinging onto her free arm.

'Hello Arlo! Hello Ruby! What's happening? Is everything alright?' Lexi was alarmed. Amber continued to sob, and Lexie feared she wasn't going to stop any time soon. Looking at Ruby, Lexie asked again:

'What happened? Why is mummy so upset?'

Ruby suddenly burst into tears herself. 'Marco hurt Mummy. He hurt her lots and then he pushed her so she hit the wall. Really hard. He tried to hurt Arlo as well but Mummy wouldn't let him hurt Arlo, and that's when he got really cross and we had to hide. And we slept at the back of someone's house last night! And Mummy's tummy and her sides are sore as well.'

Arlo added in a loud whisper, 'So we're hiding from Marco. And Mummy says we don't ever have to go back, but I had to leave my toys there. But I don't care. I hate Marco.'

Amber's tears continued unabated but she did put her hand up to stop Arlo and Ruby saying any more. Eventually finding her voice, she tried to explain,

'I'm fine. Just a bit tired that's all.' Straightening up, she attempted to make light of it, brushing away tears as they fell. Nothing however, could cover the defeat that was in her eyes, or the tell-tale bruises on her face.

Lexie had heard and seen enough. Gently she pushed back Amber's hair, revealing more cuts and bruises, and a very swollen eye. As Amber turned away from Lexie's scrutiny, her shirt collar moved exposing angry red marks on her neck, marks that stood out against her otherwise pale skin. Lexie didn't think twice about it. Picking up Amber's backpack from the back of the chair, she helped her to her feet. Ignoring Amber's protests, she took hold of Amber by her shoulders and steered her towards the exit.

'Come on, guys. Can you help me with Mum? My car is out this way. Stick close, and follow me.'

Arlo and Ruby didn't need any further encouragement. They had never seen their mother like this. She was all floppy and crying, and that frightened them. They trusted Miss Hudson, and they were used to doing what she asked. What anyone asked, really. Amber's tears continued, but her protests quickly dried up. It was all she could do to stay upright, the fight in her swiftly evaporating. She submitted to Lexie. She had nothing left.

At the car, Lexie settled Amber in the front seat, before she put the children in the back. With no spare booster this time, she weighed up briefly the legality of it all, but at least she made sure the seatbelts fitted across their bodies, before clipping them in. The need to get them somewhere safe, far outweighed any other risk. Placing the backpack at Amber's feet she asked, 'Is this all your stuff? It doesn't seem much…'

Amber shook her head, and murmured the address of the house where they had stayed the night.

'You mean Wallis Street, near school?'

With Amber in an almost catatonic state, Lexie decided just to go with it. She could see Amber was crashing fast, and she wanted to get her home where she could rest. All thoughts of the kitchen storage containers and rubbish bin she had gone into Bunnings for, were consigned to the non-urgent category. She could get that sorted another day. The traffic was reasonably light for a Sunday afternoon, and she made good time to Wallis Street. Amber had closed her eyes, and hadn't moved. Turning into the street, Lexie asked Ruby which house it was they stayed at, and what the people's names were.

'Oh! We don't know the people. We slept outside. Just like camping! It's that one there with the big tree,' said Ruby helpfully, pointing to the correct house.

'We sneaked in!' added Arlo. 'We slept in the backyard! Mummy said the people were on holidays and it was okay.'

Amber tried to rouse herself enough to speak, but couldn't. She had simply, suddenly, lost all strength. But Ruby was on to it.

'So, first, you have to make sure no-one's looking, and then we can go down the path. Mummy stashed our bags behind some boxes. Then we can sneak back to the car. The people are on a caravan holiday, so it's okay. No-one's there.'

'*Whoa!*' thought Lexie. '*This is definitely living on the wild side.*'

She considered leaving the bags there and driving away, but one look at the state Amber was in and she decided not to stress her any further.

'You wait here with Mummy, Arlo. Ruby can help me get the bags, then we'll go to my place and you can have a play with Radar. Okay?'

Arlo nodded and gave a thumbs up. Lexie got out of the car with a confidence she didn't feel, attempting to appear as though she had every right to be there. While Ruby hopped out, she looked nonchalantly up and down the street. She didn't spot a soul. Taking Ruby by the hand, she walked purposely down the side of the house to the backyard. As they came to the veranda, Ruby put her fingers to her lips and pointed out the place where Amber had hidden their bags.

'Where did you sleep?' whispered Lexie. Ruby showed Lexie the little nook they had slept in before running over to the cushions that Amber had carefully replaced on the chairs, and mimicked sleeping on them. Lexie nodded. Resourceful Amber! This was a story she was looking forward to hearing in detail. Making sure she had all the bags, she followed Ruby down the path, pausing briefly at the front of the house to check again there was no-one watching, before walking quickly to the car.

Lexie crossed her fingers no-one was behind any of the windows in the street, writing down her licence number, ready to report her to the police for trespass. Belatedly she thought of security cameras on houses. If anything was reported she had an explanation, and decided she'd deal with it then. She dropped the bags in the boot, while Ruby got in the car. Wasting no time, Lexie started the car and accelerated quietly. It was only at the end of the street that she turned around to Arlo and Ruby, giving them a big grin and a thumbs up. Arlo clapped. Even at five years old, he knew they didn't want to be seen walking in and out of a stranger's backyard.

As she drove, Lexie rang Jeanie on the hands-free, relieved when she answered after a couple of rings.

'Hi Lex. How is it going? Did you get the stuff you needed at Bunnings?'

'No. I can get all that later,' she paused and continued in what she hoped was a serious tone, emphasising her words so Jeanie would catch-on that this was no ordinary conversation. 'Actually, I ran into Amber and the kids at Bunnings. I've got them in the car with me now.'

'Right,' said Jeanie cautiously, picking up on the change in Lexie's voice. 'Is there anything you want me to do?'

'Could you and Dad come over? I know it's supposed to be a rest day from my place for you guys, but I think we need you. Also, can you bring your first aid kit Mum? Amber might even need to go to a doctor.'

'Yes! Absolutely. Dad and I will head off in a few minutes. We'll meet you at the house. Are the kids, okay?'

Mentally, Lexie thanked her mother's nursing background and her practical nature. She didn't waste time with pointless questions, she was ready to move, and Lexie totally trusted her medical judgement. She would know what to do.

'Yep. The kids are fine, aren't you? Say hello to Jeanie. 'Hello Jeanie!' came the chorus from the back seat.

'Okay. See you soon Mum.'

Lexie hit the hang up switch on the car phone, and took a quick look at Amber who had stopped crying but was still very subdued. Sensing Lexie looking at her, she turned and mouthed 'Thank you.'

Amber felt removed from reality, out of the frame, looking down at herself, sitting shrivelled and hunched in the front seat of Lexie's car. The moment Lexie had touched her; any last vestiges of resolve had collapsed. Surrendering completely, she'd given up, placing herself in Lexie's hands. It was such a relief. For the moment she felt safe. Cocooned. And when she turned to look at Ruby and Arlo, she knew she could relax because they were also safe. This warm feeling of trust was an unfamiliar one. There had been so few times in her life when someone wanted to look after her. Despite all this, Amber's hands remained tightly clasped together on her lap, her body taut, tight, a shell threatening to fracture into a thousand pieces at any second. Occasionally, she felt Lexie reach over and give her hand a gentle squeeze. It helped.

The trip home was quick, and the Sunday afternoon traffic kind to them. Lexie drove carefully, conscious of the fragile cargo she had on board. She didn't want to alarm them with any sudden moves. Even when she parked in the driveway and got out of the car, Amber stayed motionless in her seat. Lexie had to open the car door and take her arm as if she was an invalid, physically helping her from the car, guiding her up the steps of the house to the front door. Arlo and Ruby walked behind, also subdued, as Amber's zombie-like behaviour continued. While Lexie settled Amber at the kitchen table, she suggested to Arlo and Ruby that they could watch TV.

'Ray sorted out Netflix for me yesterday. I'll show you how to get it on in a minute. Just let me put the kettle on for Mum. Okay?'

The prospect of TV was a welcome distraction and undoubtedly the perfect suggestion for two over-wrought kids. Before Lexie could make it back to the loungeroom with two glasses of water, tech-savvy Ruby had already switched on the TV and was flicking through the Netflix options, settling for *Sonic*. Deciding that was suitable, Lexie hurried back to Amber, and the boiling kettle.

While Amber stared listlessly out the kitchen window at the neighbour's roofline, Lexie made the cups of tea, in between stealing glances at Amber. With the light falling on her face, Lexie could clearly see her cut and swollen lip, the bruises and swelling around her eye, and a nasty graze on her chin.

Bastard! Lexie fumed inwardly, noticing Amber wince in pain as she shifted in her chair. Hearing a car door slam, she blew out a discreet sigh. *Back-up!* She hadn't even realised she'd been holding her breath while she worried about Amber. *Mum will know what to do!*

She was just placing a cup of tea and a sweet biscuit in front of Amber, when Jeanie bowled into the kitchen with her first aid kit of medical supplies, Ray heading towards the lounge room with a couple of Paddle Pops in hand. *So much for the apple option,* thought Lexie.

Taking one look at Amber, Jeanie began talking in a soothing voice, her movements slowed to a beautiful dance of gentle probing and careful examination. Delicately, she smoothed back Amber's hair from her face for a better look.

'Oh! I bet this all hurts quite a bit, doesn't it honey?' she murmured. 'I've got some dressings that will help. Lexie! Can you run a nice warm bath for Amber?' she suggested.

'A bit of a soak in the bath first and then we'll get you patched up and into bed. I can have a look at your back and ribs if you like, to see if we need to get you to a doctor. Is that okay with you?' she asked again, brushing Amber's hair back gently with her fingers, looking concerned, but in control.

Amber managed an imperceptible nod as unchecked tears started coursing down her cheeks once more.

'You're safe now, my girl. We'll look after you. Just drink up that tea, and here's a couple of tablets that will help with the pain.'

Lexie left Amber in Jeanie's capable hands and went to run the bath. Only yesterday she'd unpacked some fragrant fresh bath salts, a forgotten Christmas gift from a past student, which she quickly located. As she ran the warm water and sprinkled in the bath salts, she gave the bath a critical look. It was old and an unfashionable pink, but it was a good-sized bath and very clean. Leaving the tap still running she ducked down the passage to check on Arlo and Ruby.

The kids were in zombie mode themselves, oblivious to the world, utterly absorbed in Sonic's exploits while licking the remains of their ice-creams. Ray was ensconced on the couch between them, and noticing her concerned look, gave Lexie a discreet nod to let her know he had things under control. He was in grand-dad mode, and there was no-one more competent in the role. Lexie smiled, mouthing, 'Thanks Dad.' By the time she got back to the kitchen Jeanie had her arm around Amber's shoulders and they were disappearing down the passage towards the bathroom.

Hands on her hips, she stood at the kitchen bench. There was a lot going on. She could hear Jeanie talking to Amber through the now-closed door of the bathroom, but it was just an indecipherable murmur. With everything in hand for the moment, she sipped at her own cooling tea, relishing a few seconds' peace, and running through a vague plan of action in her mind.

First thing was to get beds made up for Amber and the kids. It was unlikely that Amber had any plans if she had spent last night sleeping rough, so at the very least she needed somewhere to stay... maybe even for a few days. And if she did have to go to hospital, someone would need to look after the kids. She could do that. Should they go to the police as well? She certainly would if *she* had been assaulted, but what did Amber want to do?

Putting all that on the back-burner, she opened the fridge door tallying the contents. She had planned to make a vegetable lasagne, and freeze some portions for later, but she figured it would do as a meal for all of them, including Jeanie and Ray if needed. Then she spotted the mince steak! Yes! She'd intended making some tacos later in the week; she could whip up a meaty lasagne for tonight.

The bed in the second bedroom was already made up with fresh sheets, thanks to Jeanie's work yesterday. There was a pull-out couch in the study, and Lexie thought the two kids could sleep on that together.

Swallowing the last of her tea, Lexie was juggling whether she'd start cooking dinner or making beds, when Jeanie came back into the kitchen. Widening her eyes expressively, Jeanie shook her head, saying quietly,

'Oh my God! That poor little thing!'

Ray had also heard Jeanie return to the kitchen, and he came out to hear what she had to say.

'She has bruises all over her! It's shocking to even think of what she's gone through. The brute has stopped short of breaking anything, though. He's a moron no doubt, but he knows enough about how to inflict a beating without breaking a bone. I wish she would go to a doctor, or the police, but she says she doesn't want to report it. She's very upset, but she is firm on that. No police.'

'But should we take her to a doctor, love? She looks bad,' Ray stated with concern, still processing that anyone would do this to a defenceless young woman.

'I'd like to, but I am reasonably confident that a doctor wouldn't be able to do much more for her at the moment than

I can. As I said, nothing seems broken. I'm sure her ribs are bruised, but they'll heal on their own eventually. The best I can do is patch her up. She has a gash on her hairline but not deep, and it's probably best fixed with a butter-fly bandage anyway, rather than stitches.'

Jeanie continued ruefully, 'I think the thought of going to a doctor, or reporting Marco to the police terrifies her more… and I haven't got the heart to force her into anything right now. The best thing for her is rest. We can always see a doctor in a couple of days, just to make sure everything is okay.' Jeanie sighed, 'I can't even imagine what it must be to endure a beating like that.'

Lexie put her arms around her mother, and they stood holding each other for a few moments, gaining strength from each other. Ray joined in the group hug, saying,

'I'll let the kids watch TV for now, then they can come with me to take Radar for a walk. That will get them out for a bit while you two look after Amber.'

'Thanks Dad. That will be great. Mum and I can get some dinner organised and see what Amber needs. I think it's the kids she's most worried about. She's terrified of going to the police in case they call in Child Protection and they take the kids away, which I can understand.'

'They can't do that, can they?' asked Jeanie, concern bringing quick tears to her eyes. 'She's a good mother. Surely that's what counts?'

'We know that Mum, but she's feeling very vulnerable and completely traumatised, I'm sure. At least she's safe here, out of that awful situation. We can work out what she wants to do about it all later, when she's recovered a bit. In the meantime,' Lexie repeated firmly, 'they're all safe for now.'

CHAPTER 15

Ray returned to the adventures of Sonic, while Lexie started on dinner. Jeanie waited a few more minutes, then knocked on the bathroom door with a clean pair of Lexie's pyjamas in hand. Amber was like a rag doll, as Jeanie washed and rinsed her hair. Helping her out of the bath, she sat her on the edge, carefully drying her, trying not to aggravate any of the bruises scattered on her body like batting marks on a cricket bat. With her extensive first aid kit in hand, and her nurse's training to the fore, she attended to Amber's cuts and bruises, applying antiseptic creams and bandages wherever needed.

Amber was clearly grateful for Jeanie's care, but she was incapable of doing much more than murmuring her thanks, and answering with a nod or shake of her head. Deciding that her unresponsiveness was no more than a case of shock and complete exhaustion, Jeanie was keen to get Amber into bed, knowing that a good sleep would help restore her strength.

Jeanie was just smoothing back the blankets for Amber in the spare bedroom, when Ray turned off the TV and said it was time to take Radar for a walk. As they were about to race each other down the passage to the back door, Ruby and Arlo spotted Amber in the bedroom. Their exuberance stilled; they weren't used to this frail version of their mother.

Slowing to a walk, they crept silently into the bedroom where Amber was sitting on the bed. Amber held out her arms and they snuggled carefully into her, the three of them speaking a language that required no words, but conveyed everything. After a moment, Amber released them and without a fuss they kissed her and left the room, immediately resuming their race out to where Radar was pacing at the back door.

Ray followed at a slower pace, restoring order as the dog jumped excitedly at the sight of the leash. The pandemonium continued for several more minutes, finally fading into the distance as the three of them, plus an over-active Radar, finally got going. Peace reigned for another hour. By the time Lexie heard the kids' and Ray's voices heralding their return, dinner was well on the way and Amber was sleeping deeply.

Ray and Jeanie stayed for an early dinner, helping Lexie get the kids bathed and into bed. Arlo and Ruby were crashing fast. It had been an eventful couple of days for them as well, and they were more than ready for sleep. They wanted to look in on Amber first, and even though Lexie was loath to agree in case they woke her, she understood their need for reassurance that their mother was safe. After this, they gave in and went willingly to bed. In fact, Lexie thought they may even have been asleep before she turned off the light and partially closed the door. It was only six forty-five.

Ray and Jeanie began collecting their things to leave. As Lexie walked them to the door, she remarked,

'Amber's packed both kid's uniforms in their bags, and their lunchboxes and drink bottles are there too, so they have everything they need for school tomorrow. I think it's best if the kids go to school as normal, and that way Amber can have the day to herself. She can sleep all day if she wants to, but it would be good if you could check in on her, Mum. Just to make sure she's okay?'

'Of course I will. I'm going to worry about her all night anyway, so I'll certainly be here straight after my morning Pilates class. I want to make sure there's no infection in that gash in her head, as well.'

'Thanks guys,' said Lexie hugging them both again. 'I couldn't have done this without you. And you've already helped me so much lately, with the move and everything.'

'Rubbish!' said Ray, 'That's what we're here for.'

Then dropping his voice to a whisper, he added, 'It's such a shame Amber doesn't seem to have anyone to call on. It just doesn't seem fair.'

Jeanie put her hand on Ray's shoulder to steady herself as she went down the steps in the fading evening light. Lexie watched them walk to the car. They were only in their sixties, still very fit and strong, but Lexie could see what a toll the last couple of days had taken on them. They looked tired. She felt a pang of guilt for all the hours they'd spent helping her move into the house, but she knew she couldn't have managed without them today.

Having Jeanie and Ray as backup support made all the difference. Vowing to herself to make it up to them soon, Lexie waved goodbye and locked the front door for the night. For once, she had managed to get Jeanie out before she could start washing up, so despite the wave of tiredness that rolled over her, she forced herself to clean up the kitchen and stack the dishwasher, putting it on for its first cycle. Mary, her trusty estate agent, had assured her it was quite new and a reliable brand. As it hummed into its eco-cycle, it seemed Mary had been telling the truth.

Lexie carefully laid out the kid's school clothes ready for the morning, using her hands to smooth out any creases that remained from being squashed in their bags. Washing their lunch boxes, she sourced some savoury biscuits and two muesli bars from her tidy pantry, that would do for snacks, deciding to make the sandwiches fresh in the morning. She already knew that Arlo had a chopped apple every morning for recess, packed in his lunch-box. Suspecting that Arlo and Ruby were rarely given much choice in what they ate, Lexie nevertheless thought she would check their preferences in the morning.

Even though it was still early evening, Lexie was also craving her bed, but she forced herself to have a cup of tea and watch some news, before she gave in. As she stepped outside to the toilet, she couldn't help but brace herself, staring intently into the darkness beyond the light. She was sure Marco would never find Amber here; in fact, she wasn't even sure he would bother looking for her, but after checking that Radar had water, and the gate was shut, she locked the back door. Then she did another inspection of the whole house, making sure that everything was locked and the curtains drawn.

She left a passage light on and their doors ajar in case Amber, Arlo and Ruby needed to get up in the night, and the faint glow lit up her bedroom with unfamiliar shapes. This bedroom was still a stranger to her. It would take a few more nights before it would feel like home. The knowledge that there were others in the house was also a new sensation, making her more alert than usual. Despite her tiredness, Lexie thought she may have trouble sleeping. She was wrong. She slept like a log.

***

Amber was the first to stir, at around six. Her first instinct was to snuggle deeper into the bed, but then the events of the last couple of days surged like floodwaters into her swampy mind, dissolving the last remnants of lethargy, so that she was instantly awake and alert, her heart suddenly racing. Amber figured she'd been asleep for something like fifteen hours straight. The house was silent. Gradually she took stock of where she was and her heart steadied. She moved gingerly onto her back, her ribs instantly protesting, repaying her with excruciating, sharp stabs of pain. She was still sore in so many places, but Jeanie had worked wonders with her bandages, and her wounds felt better. Reaching up, she touched her head where Jeanie had thought she might need stitches, and was reassured. The butterfly bandage felt dry the wound no longer weeping.

Creeping out of bed, she tiptoed down the passage to check on Arlo and Ruby. They were nestled together still asleep. Some of the tension went out of her. They were safe. Still moving quietly, she noiselessly opened the outside door, patting Radar on her way to the loo. Back in bed, another wave of drowsiness crept over her. Despite her long sleep, she knew she could easily fall back into a doze. Silently, she thanked whatever cosmic powers had sent Lexie to Bunnings at that precise moment; even though she was quite embarrassed that Lexie had caught her at her most vulnerable. In a little while, she was sure she would have rallied enough to creep back to the house in Wallis Street for the night. Maybe she could have stayed there a few more nights, and the kids could have gone to school from there? It would have been tough, but not impossible.

Even now, she had no idea of her options for the future. Hopefully, she could contact the refuge in Joondalup today, she thought. Perhaps, Lexie would be okay with them staying for a couple of days until she could get herself sorted. She promised herself that one day she would repay her for this kindness. Hearing a squeak of the floorboards she opened her eyes to see Arlo's face only inches from her own, peering anxiously at her.

'Hi Bubba,' she said affectionately, pulling back the blankets. 'It's okay. Mum's good. Come on, hop in.'

Just as Arlo climbed up into the bed beside her, Ruby appeared at the door. Smiling, Amber motioned to her to hop in the other side; Ruby almost flew across the room and jumped up onto the bed. As they cuddled in close to her body, Amber felt a little hand plant itself on her cheek, softly curling around her face like a silky leaf. Two brown almond eyes stared at her, taking an inventory of her bruises and cuts; Ruby's eyes filled with tears, as she gently stroked her mother's swollen lips with her finger.

'Don't worry darling. I'm feeling much better. Jeanie has fixed me up and I'll be fine soon,' whispered Amber reassuringly, before stifling an urge to cry out as Arlo accidently nudged her bruised rib with his knee.

'We're safe here. Marco won't find us, and I promise we don't have to live with Marco ever again. I mean it! Never again!'

As Ruby lay back on the pillow, Amber continued, 'We're okay here for now. I don't know yet where we will live, but you guys don't have to worry. Mummy will work something out, as soon as I can,' she said, kissing them both.

Just then, Lexie popped her head into the room, and caught the end of Amber's promise.

'Hi guys. Did you all sleep well?' All three nodded in unison, as Lexie went on. 'Well, it's a school day today, and I need to leave at seven-forty-five, so it's probably time to get moving. And,' raising her finger in the air for emphasis, 'as your mum just said, you don't need to worry. You can all stay here until she decides what to do next. That is, if that's okay?' finished Lexie, looking quizzically at Amber for an answer, and getting a very grateful and decisive nod in return.

'Now, let's get dressed for school!'

'Yes Miss Hudson,' they chorused, as they exited the warm bed, and tore through the door to get dressed. Making way for them, Lexie pressed herself against the wall and laughed. Amber started to get up as well, but Lexie was quick to urge her to stay in bed.

'Now, you don't have to get up. Stay there. You've got the whole day to get dressed, or not. Just relax and rest up. No-one knows you are here, and we can talk about what you want to do next, when I get home. Jeanie said she'll come over to see if you're okay, but I'm sure she'll text beforehand, so you'll know when to expect her.'

Overcome with Lexie's continuing kindness, Amber started to tear-up again. She tried to say, 'I can't thank you enough Lexie. This is so kind of you,' but after the first few words, the rest was just a blubbering mess. 'Sorry. I can't stop crying,' Amber sobbed, trying without success to take control of her emotions.

'Hey!' shushed Lexie, sitting next to her on the bed and hugging her reassuringly. 'You are physically and emotionally spent. Just go with it. Cry as much as you need. I'm here for you and the kids. You know I'll take good care of them and I can keep an eye out for them all day at school. All you have to do is rest and get back to your old self.'

Closing her eyes, Amber was about to take Lexie's advice to rest, when a thought suddenly occurred to her, and she grabbed Lexie's arm in fright. 'What if Marco turns up at school!'

'He can't do anything. He's not on the list as a contact, and I will make sure the office gives him no information.'

'But what if he sees them? He might try something! He's very angry with me! I don't know what he might do. He doesn't care about the kids, but he might use them to try to find me!' Amber was becoming more agitated by the minute. Kicking off the blankets and despite the shooting pain, she stood up quickly, ready for action.

'Okay. Listen. Calm down. You know the school has a fence around it. He can't just walk in without anyone seeing him. I'll make sure Arlo only plays inside today, and Ruby can spend recess and lunch in the library. That's the best I can do. And it's Monday. Won't he be at work anyway?'

'Yes. But he scares me… And I know he will be furious!'

'I'll alert all the staff on duty to look out for anyone lurking. He's tall, right?'

'Yes. He's like, six foot two, and not fat, but heavy-set. Brown hair, curly, and he's got a beard, so he looks hairy. Brown eyes too…' then breaking off she added, 'I wouldn't call him handsome but I used to think he was nice enough, so he's sort of attractive in a rough way.' After a pause, Amber added, 'Now I hate him.'

Lexie put her arms around Amber.

'Hopefully you will never have to see him again. I do think it will be good for the kids to go to school, and have some normality. You stay here and rest and I'll ring you to let you know what's happening during the day. Agreed?'

It took a few more reassurances to convince her, but when Amber saw how excited the kids were to be going to school, she knew Lexie was making sense. She did get up though, and made the kids' breakfast, which also brought a sense of routine to their day. She even waved them off with a smile that belied her worries, while inside every cell was screaming, 'Don't go!'

Despite everyone's fears, the day went smoothly, and there was no sign of Marco. Lexie even did a reconnaissance swing-by of the school first, with Arlo and Ruby on the floor of the car hidden from view, while she checked for Marco's blue ute. The discussion with Kelly was much more difficult. Lexie knew that Kelly, as the Principal, needed to know what was happening to students in her school, especially when it involved domestic violence and possible danger to the children. She was torn because she also felt loyalty to Amber, and she had to respect her wish not to press charges, or report this in any way.

'Come on, Kelly,' pleaded Lexie as Kelly started talking about involving the police, and reporting the situation to Child Protection. 'I know we have mandatory reporting, but… if the kids seem fit and well to you, and they are no longer in a dangerous situation at home… then surely, we don't need to report anything.'

'I will have to report it, Lexie,' said Kelly sternly, looking down her long nose, and simultaneously pursing her lips, in a well-practiced move, guaranteed to send fear into the hearts of recalcitrant students, but one that had minimal effect on Lexie.

'However, I think we can monitor it. I will let them know the children are in a safe environment, and perhaps Community Services can assess the family instead. We should get a psychologist to see both of them though. Max Green would be good. I'll certainly be documenting this, but it will help to be guided by Max, to see if we need to get them any further help.' Kelly finished with a warning,

'I know you want to consider Amber's wishes, but if I think those kids are in danger, or they have any on-going emotional issues that impact their well-being, I'll have no alternative other than to call in Child Protection immediately.'

'Fingers crossed it doesn't get to that, Kel. But I agree a chat with the school psych might be good for them. I'll get Amber to sign her permission tonight. And thanks. I know you have to report it, I understand completely. But at the moment Arlo and Ruby are in a safe situation, and you know how much pressure Child Protection are under. Besides, I've got Jeanie on the case and she's busting to help Amber.'

Kelly laughed at this, despite her misgivings about the situation. She knew Lexi's mum from years ago, and could well imagine Jeanie's zeal with a project like Amber's little family to rescue. Nevertheless, Kelly followed through with the departmental guidelines and reported it, but she did make a couple of discreet phone calls to confer with Child Protection, and assure them that currently the children were safe. Whether Amber approved or not, rules were rules.

As an added precaution, she alerted the staff to watch out for a man of Marco's description lurking near the school grounds. However, no-one reported seeing anybody suspicious. Fortunately, it turned out an uneventful day all round. Neither Arlo or Ruby minded that they didn't get to play outside, because it was a rare treat to have indoor time and total run of the construction toys and iPads. Also, before she left school for home that afternoon, Lexie was again careful, walking through the car park, checking for any sign of Marco, before beckoning the kids to the car. By the time she got home she was satisfied, convinced that for at least today, Marco had been nowhere near the school.

Amber was watching for them when they pulled into the drive. She couldn't wait to hear how their day had gone, and see that her precious little ones were okay. She'd even managed an afternoon sleep, and was feeling more like herself, albeit still sore and bruised. Jeanie had popped over and changed her dressings and praised Amber for healing so well.

She had also come bearing gifts: a nourishing chicken soup, along with crumbed chicken pieces, a potato bake, and a salad for dinner; all ready to heat and eat, with only the chicken pieces to cook. Not only that, but she had contacted her Nanna network and had some second-hand clothes in Ruby and Arlo's sizes, complete with some new undies and singlets she'd picked up at Target. She'd bought Amber a couple of T-shirts, some jeans and underwear, even down to guessing the correct bra size. Lexie was amazed at her mother's ability to be a step ahead, anticipating what everyone needed.

Once home, Arlo and Ruby took off outside to play with Radar, and in the meantime, Lexie filled Amber in on the day's non-events. No-one mentioned Marco. Amber cooked the chicken pieces while Lexie and the kids took Radar for a walk. By the time they had eaten Jeanie's delicious dinner, Amber could see that Ruby and Arlo were again ready for bed. It had been an emotional weekend for them, and no doubt they were still feeling the effects.

Amber, after a quiet day, was keen to be involved in the children's bath, story, and whole bedtime routine, while Lexie busied herself with the dishes. It was going on seven when Amber kissed them goodnight, and Lexie, flattered at being included, was summoned for a goodnight kiss. She was discovering though, that even when kids looked dead on their feet, they could hype themselves up with a late surge of energy. The moment the light went out, giggles turned to complaints, and arguments back to giggles. For a while Lexie thought they would never sleep, but after a few stern words from Amber, the chat turned to whispers and eventually all was quiet.

While Lexie made tea, Amber readied the school bags for the next day. Once the tea was poured, they settled down in the lounge room together, sipping at their tea in companionable silence, the television on low. Looking across the couch at Amber, Lexie was comforted to see how much better she looked already. Several bruises were darkening to shades of purple, but her swollen lips were healing and almost down to their normal size. Amber's hair was washed and brushed, glossy in the lamp-light, and her eyes alert and alive once more. Lexie thought she looked strong and ready for a chat. Sensing Lexie's thoughts, Amber met her gaze confidently. She was ready, and she wanted to talk. She switched off the TV.

'What do you want to know?' asked Amber bluntly.

'Amber, you don't have to tell me anything you don't want to,' Lexie protested sincerely. 'I'm just happy you are here.'

'I want you to know, though. You've been so kind, and you knew me before…and everything.' Amber broke off shrugging.

'Okay, why don't you start with when you left Perth after the fire? I heard you went to Manjimup, but what happened after that?' Lexie prompted gently.

Amber took another sip of her tea and began.

CHAPTER 16

'Yep. We went to Manjimup. You remember it was late in term four when we left? After the fire we stayed in a motel for a few nights… and then we got all those beautiful new clothes and toys from the school. People gave us such nice stuff,' said Amber remembering a rare time in her life, when she'd had something new. She looked at Lexie.

'I remember you gave me the *Matilda* book and two *Harry Potter* books…I loved those. I read them over and over again.' Smiling, she added, 'And you gave Robbie and Sam books too, and some jigsaws as well.'

'I'd forgotten that,' laughed Lexie. 'That's such a teacher thing to do. I probably should have given you all vouchers to Target so you could buy whatever you wanted. Toys for the boys, or whatever you were into at the time.'

'Oh no! Definitely not! Cindy would have grabbed those vouchers and spent them on herself! The books and puzzles meant we at least had something of our own,' said Amber emphatically.

'Anyway, we ended up in Manjimup where John had family and contacts. The police were asking lots of questions about the fire, and of course they eventually pinned John for cooking up stuff. I'm sure that's why we moved to Manjimup. He decided if he had to do time it would be better if Cindy was in Manjimup where his family could keep an eye on her, especially if she got any ideas about going to the police. With his two older brothers close by, he knew Cindy wouldn't be game to step out of line… not that he had to worry about that. She thought the sun shone out of skinny old John, and she always put him first…certainly above us kids. He was Sam and Robbie's dad, and she hung on to that like a crab clinging to a rock. He gave her a house to live in and paid for everything… not that they lived a high life, far from it, but she wasn't out on the street.'

Curious, Lexie asked, 'What about Cindy's parents? Your grandparents? Why didn't she go to them? Did you ever see them?'

'She grew up in Geraldton, and she was an only child. From what Cindy used to say, and she never spoke much about them…I think she was a very spoilt child. They gave her everything, but they also hovered over her constantly, and their expectations for her were probably too high. When she came home pregnant at seventeen, they were bitterly disappointed. She wanted to run off with her boyfriend, my father, who was some German backpacker she'd met working at MacDonalds.' At this point Amber took a couple of sips of tea and a deep breath. 'She couldn't have known him long because she barely knew anything about him, or even what town he was from. All she told me was that his name was Hans Schuster… but who even knows if that really was his name?'

Lexie had to strain to hear, as Amber's voice fell to a whisper. Placing her cup carefully on the coffee table, Amber leaned forward, resting her head in her hands. Clearing her throat, she took a few seconds before going on in a stronger voice.

'When Cindy confronted young Hans with the news that she was pregnant, he took off and vanished. Poof! Just like that, never to be seen or heard of again. Apparently, my grandparents were good Christians, and a pregnant daughter with no husband was too much for them. They bought her a one-way bus ticket to Perth, gave her some money, and told her never to return to Geraldton again. So, even if they were still alive and I could find them, I can't imagine them welcoming me with open arms. Me! An unmarried mother with two kids! So, no point looking for help in that department,' Amber scoffed.

'In fact, my birth certificate has *Father Unknown* on it.'

Looking up and stretching her neck, Amber said flatly,

'According to Cindy, she sent photos of me to her parents every Christmas for three years, always with a return address, but she never heard a word back, and by then she'd decided they could just get stuffed. As far as I know she never contacted them again.'

Lexie nodded in sympathy. In unison, as if they wanted to get a bad taste out of their mouths, they took a swallow of their rapidly cooling tea. Amber continued:

'I know Cindy didn't have many choices after that. There were probably a few blokes, but the only one I remember was Jimmy. I was only little, but I know he used to bash her up…one thing John never did, which is probably why she stuck with him… Anyway, we lived with Jimmy for a year or so, until he got caught for armed robbery at a service station and ended up in jail. It wasn't long after that Cindy met John and got pregnant with Robbie, and then Sam, and the rest is history, as they say. She did do it tough, but all the same, I'll never forgive her for everything she did, or I should say, didn't do. She was, is, a crap mother.'

Amber sank back, resting her head against the back of the couch, and closed her eyes. Lexie worried that Amber was too emotionally vulnerable for this conversation.

'We don't have to do this Amber. You don't have to go through all this now. You're tired and we can do it another time if you want. Just have a rest and I'll get you some Panadol. Or another cup of tea? This one is cold,' said Lexie taking the half-drunk cup of tea away to the kitchen.

Returning a few minutes later with a fresh cup of tea each and a block of chocolate, Lexie was surprised to see Amber sitting up straight, and even more surprised when she declared she wanted Lexie to know her story. Taking the two Panadol and the chocolate Lexie offered, Amber swallowed the tablets, washing them down with water, before popping a piece of chocolate in her mouth. As she sipped her hot tea, the melting chocolate flooding her taste buds with sweetness, she continued her story.

'So, we leave Perth and we get to Manjimup. The cops catch up with John and arrest him. He's convicted but he only goes to prison for a while, in the end. First conviction.

'Child Protection and Community Services were called in, and they visited regular, like, for a few months, even though Cindy swore she was innocent and didn't know what John was doing. Cindy was as useless as ever in between the case-worker visits, but when she thought a visit was due, she cleaned up the house, and the fridge actually had food it, instead of wine. I can't remember exactly, but it was less than a year before John was back home in Manjimup, because I was still in first year at high school.

'The first year or two weren't too bad. John and Cindy weren't on the gear as much. Cindy even got a job at the local supermarket for a bit. And John used to drive trucks for his brother. We had a house just on the edge of town, and I could walk Robbie to school, and also Sam, when he started. The high school was only a block away from the primary school. I made a few friends, the girls were mostly nice, and sometimes I was invited to parties at their houses. Not that they ever came back to my place. John wouldn't let us bring anyone home. He didn't want anyone snooping around, he would say.'

Lexie broke off some more chocolate, handing it to Amber, who dunked it into her tea, before sucking on it. Lexie watched as Amber's eyes narrowed and her expression hardened.

'So, life went on, and we started getting regular visitors to the house. When they came, Cindy would give me a look, which I knew meant I had to get the boys outside and take them off somewhere for a walk.'

Suddenly, Amber put her cup down and stood up. As Lexie leaned forward to see if she was okay, Amber put her hand out to stop her.

'I'm fine. I just need to move a bit.' Bending forward, she put her hands on her knees, taking a deep breath. She was clearly agitated.

'Okay. This is the short version. So, by now John was back dealing but this time he had some new mates in on it with him. He was actually way out of his league. Apparently, John had always been delivering drugs, along with his truck freights, around the south-west and out towards the wheat towns in the state's mid-west. But that had only been small-time. Now, when he got back from picking up a delivery, there would be a bloke waiting for him. John would park the truck up against the shed. We were on a couple of acres. Cindy and John and whoever the visitor was, would disappear into the shed for hours. Under the new arrangements, I had to keep the kids away from the house until it was almost dark, and only then could I bring them home, feed them and get them into bed. The special visitor usually stayed a night or two, and a few more regular people would arrive, usually during the day when we were at school. And then the visitor would go, and John and Cindy would take off in the truck for a couple of days, and that would be it. Until the next time.'

At this point Amber was almost hyperventilating, forgetting to breathe as she relived the memories. Lexie wasn't sure she wanted to hear all this, but she also felt that Amber needed to tell her story, so she sat quietly and listened.

'I was only just fifteen when Snowy turned up. Snowy was a bit older than John. Probably around forty, and he was a Kiwi. He was tall and skinny, not much hair, but he had long white goatee, hence the name. He chain-smoked. Finish one and light another. I could always smell the nicotine on him. I knew John was scared of him right from the start. And Cindy simpered at him, laughing at all his jokes. Making him coffee or getting him beers…whatever he wanted. I told you how these guys used to stay the night. The first time I met him, he looked at me in such a creepy way. He stared at my boobs before he looked at my face, and he even said, 'Nice tits.' And then he grabbed his crutch.' Amber's face puckered in disgust.

'He made me feel really uncomfortable. Usually, I got the boys to sleep in my room the nights he stayed over, but one night I forgot, and I was fair game.'

Having been pacing for several minutes, short steps across the room and back, Amber now stopped. She squared her shoulders and continued in a deadpan voice.

'That night, while they were all partying, he sneaked into my room. I heard him come in and I pretended to be asleep. That was dumb. I should have run instead. He tried to kiss me, and I said no, stupidly thinking that would do, but he's on me straight away; his dirty old jeans down, and he's pulled off my pyjama pants before I get the message that he doesn't care that I'm saying no. I never stood a chance. Maybe I should have run but I was naive. I thought he would stop.'

The pacing resumed briefly, before another abrupt halt. Lexie strained to hear the tortured whisper that followed.

'When he raped me, I tried to call out! I thought Cindy or John would help, but even if they'd heard, they were too scared of Snowy and his bikie mates to do a thing! Anyway, Snowy just laughed at me and covered my screams with his huge hand. He had ugly big hands. I couldn't breathe. I can still almost taste his palm, pushed against my teeth. I thought I was going to die. He kept pushing down hard on my face. I don't think he would have cared if I suffocated. It was easier for me to shut up and take it. Besides, there was never going to be any help on the way.'

Amber had remained standing, hunched over, arms wrapped around her sore ribs, as she told her story. At this point, she fell silent, taking a moment to sink carefully into the armchair opposite Lexie. Exhaling deeply, but deliberately making eye contact with Lexie, she continued,

'He was like a heavy bag on top of me. I think he fell asleep. I remember feeling squashed but too scared to move. When he woke up, I was terrified he'd do it again. My heart was seriously pounding in my chest, so loud I thought he would hear it. But he just rolled off the bed. He didn't say a word. I could see him putting his pants on again in the dark, and then he left and went back to the party.'

By the time Amber finished, Lexie was lost for words. She had listened in horror, Amber's awful ordeal conjuring up disturbing images that wouldn't fade; the very air in the room was thick with the terror and brutality of her experience. She managed to say, 'Oh Amber!' her throat tight, choking on the current of evil that Amber's story unleased. Shocked and heartbroken for Amber, Lexie fought back tears she felt she didn't have the right to shed. This was Amber's pain and she didn't want to diminish it with self-indulgent weeping. Amber sat for a while with her eyes closed, the only hint of her pain in the set of her mouth and the slight, rocking of her body, forward and back. Eventually, Lexie broke the silence.

'That is dreadful! Did Cindy know?'

Amber grimaced. 'Oh yeah! I'm sure she knew. She was cagey the next day. She even asked me if anything had happened, but I didn't tell her… I was so angry with her… and I blamed her for everything, anyway. I think she was relieved when I said nothing had happened. She and John were terrified of Snowy. They were just glad that while I was distracting Snowy, he wasn't causing them any trouble. He was a very dangerous man, and the last thing they were going to do was worry about my fifteen-year-old feelings.' Then with a shoulder shrug and a sigh, she added, 'He terrified me as well.'

'You didn't tell anyone at school? Or try to go to the police?'

'I didn't tell a soul. For a start, I knew telling the police would mean Cindy and John's little business would be exposed and it would not end well for any of us. If Snowy's mates found out I'd been to the police, I knew we would all be in danger, including Robbie and Sam… and I wouldn't be able to protect them. I certainly would never have told anyone at school for the same reason. And my life was so far removed from what my friends knew as normal, that I couldn't even imagine telling them I'd been raped by a bikie.'

Lexie moved over to Amber, and sitting on the arm of the chair, circled her with her arms. 'I can't imagine how you survived all this! It's all so wrong!'

Holding Amber in her arms, Lexie patted her back as you would a child, tears streaming unbidden, despite her best intentions. After a few moments, she felt Amber shudder, and she realised Amber was quietly sobbing. Lexie murmured words of comfort, and support, while in her heart she grieved for her, deeply shaken by the trauma Amber had experienced. As Amber's sobs gradually lessened, Lexie gently extracted herself and fetched tissues and a glass of water. Nodding her thanks, Amber sipped the water, blew her nose, and bravely told the rest of her story, her tears spilling down her cheeks.

'Sorry. I'm okay. It's in the past. I'm just a bit emotional after Marco and everything.'

Sniffing and wiping her eyes, she continued. This time there was bitterness in her voice.

'I went to school just the same the next day. I got the boys up as usual, made their lunches and left. Everyone was still asleep after the big party the night before. By the time we got home from school, Snowy was gone. Cindy hung around me a bit. I could feel her watching me. That's when she asked me if anything had happened, but I didn't give her any satisfaction. I knew she knew. But what was the point in talking about it? She wasn't going to suddenly produce any motherly concern for me. So, I just let it go. Then of course, after a few weeks, Snowy came back.'

Amber shook her head and bit her lip before going on. 'I went into Sam and Robbie's room thinking I'd be okay there. But that didn't stop him! In fact, it was worse because I was scared the boys would wake up, and he'd hurt them too, so I couldn't make a fuss. By this time, Snowy expects I'm just available for him. I don't even know if rape was in his vocabulary... I tried staying away at friend's places, but that's not always easy midweek when it's a school day. And anyway, if he spotted me around home, he'd make me go with him. He'd just have to look at Robbie and Sam, and back at me and I knew if I wanted them to be safe, I'd have to do whatever he said...he didn't care where we did it... usually in my room, though.'

Lexie couldn't help herself. This was all so disturbing. She blurted out, 'How long did this go on for? Is this when you got pregnant?'

'Yes, but he never knew a thing about it. It went on for a few months. I was pretty dumb. I wasn't thinking I'd get pregnant! I was more concerned with working out ways to dodge him. Then, suddenly the deliveries stopped. Cindy and John would go away for days at a time, but there were no more visitors for a while. No more Snowy! But I was always scared he would be back. One day I dared to ask Cindy what was happening. First, she got all angry and said it was none of my business. Then she goes,

'I can tell you one thing though. Snowy won't be back. Some bastard knocked him off his bike, then went back and ran him over. He's dead. Business has been a bit quiet since. There's stuff going on though. Nothing to do with us. Looks like Snowy had a side hustle that hasn't gone down well with the boss... and we're just making sure the boss knows we're loyal.'

And that was that. I was so happy to hear he was dead. It felt like I'd been given such a big present. I was free! He was out of my life! I know that I'm probably a bad person to be happy he was dead, but I can't help it. I still can't feel sorry for him.'

'No-one could think you're a bad person Amber, for feeling like that.'

'Maybe…I don't care. Anyway, he never knew about Ruby. I didn't even know myself for ages. As I said, I'm pretty dumb,' Amber gave a self-deprecating laugh, and waved away Lexi's protestations.

'You ever see that TV show called *Bump*? It's where the girl only finds out she's pregnant when she's actually having the baby. And she's at school when she goes into labour, in the toilets, and they have to get her mum, who of course is a teacher at the school, and then they call an ambulance, and it's the ambulance guy who tells her she's having a baby.'

Lexie smiled. 'Yep. I saw it. It's a bit far-fetched.'

'Well, I wasn't quite as dumb as that, but not too far-off,' Amber rolled her eyes. 'I'd missed a couple of periods, but then I was always irregular, so no biggie. And I knew I was getting fatter because I couldn't do up my jeans anymore. So, I tried to not eat snacks and stuff, but it didn't make much difference, except…' and she paused for effect, 'I did feel my stomach rumbling a fair bit. Duh! I was lying in bed one night when I got this big rumble and all of a sudden it occurred to me that it wasn't a rumble, it was a baby! I was six months pregnant by then.'

Shaking her head, she continued, 'By the time I got myself to a doctor, I was way past being eligible for an abortion. I was sixteen by then. Sixteen and a half. I didn't tell anyone who the father was. I just made out I'd slept around and didn't know. Cindy knew of course. And John. But they weren't letting on to anyone either. None of us, least of all me, wanted to go down that track. So Ruby was born without a dad. And I know only too well how that feels.'

'Did you ever think about giving her up for adoption? You were so young!'

'I thought about it lots. But by the time she was born, I wanted her. I just couldn't let her think she didn't even have a mum who cared about her. And I wanted to prove I could be a good mum. I wanted to be the best mum in the world, and I really thought that if I loved her, and cared for her, she'd have a better life with me.'

Amber's eyes lit up briefly when she spoke about loving Ruby. Lexie glimpsed the young Amber, determined to be the kind of mother she never had. Then in a flat, matter-of-fact tone, she continued,

'But after a while, babies need more than just love, and even with Parenting Payments, I couldn't afford much. I didn't mind giving up school. I loved her so much, that I wanted to be with her all the time. And Sam and Robbie helped me when they got home from school. I would have loved to get out into a place of my own, but I didn't have enough money…and I knew that Robbie and Sam needed me. I couldn't leave them. I was the closest thing to a mother they would ever get. I couldn't just go.

So, I stayed in my old room with the baby, and it was mostly fine. Only…' she paused, throwing her hands out in frustration.

'Now I was home all day, Cindy had an excuse to get shit-faced all the time, and left all the work to me. The best times were when she and John would go off making their deliveries, and the boys, Ruby and I had the place to ourselves. It was like a holiday when they were gone and there was far less mess to clean up.' She finished angrily, adding,

'So that's Ruby's story. I'll tell you about Arlo, but first I need a trip to the loo, and I'd love another cup of tea, please.'

'Amber. You don't have to tell me all this. And you look tired. Let's leave it for another day, and only if you want to.' Lexie suggested, concerned.

'Nah!' said Amber almost recklessly. 'I want you to know. I want you to understand my story and Ruby and Arlo's stories. I don't think I can sleep anyway, until you know.'

Amber was fired up, and Lexie understood from her own experience, that sometimes you need to share. She was only too happy to be the supportive listener if it helped Amber deal with some demons.

'I'll make us another cup of tea, while you take a few minutes to yourself. We could even drink it outside if you like. It's a beautiful night, one of Perth's best.'

Ten minutes later Amber and Lexie had exchanged the couch for two comfy cane chairs on the veranda out front, yet another cup of tea in hand. Lexie was thinking wine, or even a stiff whisky would be more appropriate, but even though she was discovering intimate details about Amber's life, she didn't even know if Amber drank alcohol. They relaxed into the cushions, caressed by the warm evening breeze. A myriad of stars lit up the western sky; in the distance, traffic hummed, while closer, somewhere in the damp soil, crickets chirped. With the sounds of the night as background, Amber resumed her story.

'Well, you may think very differently about me after you hear this, but you need to know, because what happened next really had nothing to do with Cindy. And you have to believe that I really tried to be a good mum to Ruby. Like… she always had a clean nappy, and she wasn't ever hungry. I fed her myself, so it was all good breastmilk, like they tell you the baby needs. I stayed home and did everything right, so she was safe and healthy. And I talked to her and read her books. I looked after

Sam and Robbie, as well. I made sure they got to school every day, and had lunch and clean clothes. But, when Ruby was about ten months old, I definitely had a bit of a meltdown.

I used to see on social media how my old school friends were out partying and having fun, and going on dates, and hooking up with guys… and I was jealous. I still loved being Ruby's mum. You know, I loved her so much, that sometimes I could have burst with happiness just looking at her. But then these cranky moods would sneak in and I'd get FOMO so bad, it would just unsettle me for days.'

Amber grimaced and shrugged. She appeared uncomfortable, but continued to tell her story, as honestly as she could.

'So, Cindy and John were still doing their special deliveries. The business had really cooled off for quite a few months after Snowy died, but when nothing bad happened, and the boss seemed happy with the deliveries, things started to ramp up again. It was around this time that Cindy and John got a bit more *entrepreneurial* as John would say, and they began supplying to a few locals again. Obviously, once the word spread, we began getting visitors again at all odd hours. Sometimes a few regulars would turn up with grog, and after they'd got their gear from John, they'd stay on and soon enough it would be party time, and Cindy and John were always up for a party; especially when they were making a profit and having a good excuse to get on the gear at the same time.' Amber gave a wry grin.

'Usually, I'd get the boys to bed and make sure Ruby was asleep in her little cot in my room, and just close the door on all the noise. But then one night, all these kids I'd seen around town arrived, and I just couldn't resist. It had been so long since I'd even talked to someone my age!'

Amber's voice rose defensively at the memory. She took a sip of her tea.

'I put Ruby in with the boys. I could trust Robbie to put her dummy in if she woke up, and he knew to come and get me if she cried. And I put on a summery dress like the girls were wearing and headed out like I was part of the party. Most of the kids were high already, but they were happy to talk crap to a stranger. None of them knew each other that well anyway because they were from all over the place. They had holiday jobs on the wheat bins around the district and they'd come in to Manjimup to party. Cindy and John's place being just out of town, and away from the coppers, looked safe enough I suppose. They didn't even ask where I was from, but they would have guessed I was local.

'I had so much fun that night, I went again the next night. Eventually, I used to hang out for those party nights, when the crew from the wheat bins were in town. It wasn't always the same gang because the work came and went as the crops came in, and it depended which town's wheat bins were loading or unloading. I never did any drugs. I didn't even smoke a spliff, or drink more than a beer or two. I was always perfectly in control of myself, except for one thing… if a guy noticed me.'

Amber paused. This was painful to say but she'd long since admitted it to herself, and she'd learnt the hard way, just how pathetic she was. Every time she admitted it to herself, it still churned up all sorts of bad feelings inside her, the self-disgust bubbling up and spilling over.

'I was such a sad case. I just glowed under the attention I was getting. No-one had ever told me I was pretty, or attractive, so when I discovered these guys were interested, and thought I was cute, I was as addicted to that as any of the drugs Cindy and John were dealing. I thought I was so careful because I did make sure the guy had a condom, but it seriously only took a bit of flirting and a couple of kind words and I was off behind the shed, into the bush, or the back of a car in no time. I don't even think I really enjoyed the sex so much as the seductive feeling of power I had over them. I remember being with maybe six different guys over the few weeks they were around.

'Then suddenly, the crops were all in and the bins filled, and the gang disappeared back to Perth, or wherever they came from. I didn't even know their family names. They were all nicknames like Thomo, or Slatsy. Once again, by the time I had worked out how pathetic I was, sleeping with every bloke who smiled at me, and before I'd even considered condoms might not be the safest form of contraception, I was pregnant again. The fantasy that I could be like other girls my age, was over. I wasn't even eighteen and having my second baby. How dumb is that?'

Amber fell silent, wrung dry by her outpouring. This was a conversation she had had with herself many a time, and she still felt the same surge of anger at her naivety. Lexie began to say something in support, but Amber, holding up her hand, silenced her. Shaking her head, she indicated she wasn't yet finished. In a flat, expressionless voice, she told the last part of the story.

'Once again, Cindy was useless, other than to say that if I had the baby, I would get extra in child support payments. I didn't really expect any help from her. This was always going to be my decision. I'm not religious or anything, obviously, but I just couldn't bring myself to end the pregnancy. I loved Ruby and I knew I could love another baby just the same. And of course, now, I can't imagine not having Arlo…I'd do it all again, exactly the same because I can't imagine life without him. But I constantly feel bad that I can't ever tell Arlo who his father is. That's something I can't forgive myself for, and I have to live with it every day. But I'm hoping that if I love him as much as I can, that will be enough.'

Somewhere close by, a kookaburra spat out its harsh cackle into the night. The sound echoed and faded. The two women sat there in silence, together in time, but a world apart in what they'd experienced in their lives. Amber slumped back, totally drained. Her eyes now dry, she gazed out defiantly at the night sky. She had confessed it all. Lexie studied Amber carefully, her own heart wrenching at the young woman's anguish, although well aware her distress was merely a fraction of Amber's torment.

Reaching over, she took Amber's hand in hers, giving it what she hoped was a reassuring squeeze. Lexie knew she had probably made up her mind when she'd first noticed her in Bunnings; the moment she had seen the emptiness and defeat in her eyes. This was a big step for her, but it was something she genuinely wanted to do. If anyone deserved a helping hand it was Amber; maybe it would give her a chance regain some control over her life. She waited until she thought Amber was calmer, choosing her words with care.

'Amber, none of this story changes anything about how I feel about you, Arlo and Ruby. I want to help you – let me. I have plenty of room in this house, enough space for all of us together. I want you to feel safe, and for Arlo and Ruby to feel safe. And I know I have the back-up of Jeanie and Ray. They both really like you, and Ray is definitely in full granddad mode where Arlo and Ruby are concerned. And,' attempting a joke, she said, 'I think if you go, Radar will be very confused. He likes all the extra attention he's been getting from everyone.'

Right on cue, and with uncanny perception, Radar chose this moment to wander over from where he'd been sniffing.

Putting his head on Amber's knee and nudging her hand for a pat, he broke the solemnity of the moment and made them both smile.

'And I mean it. Stay as long as you like, not just for a few weeks until you get sorted, but think of it as your home… a chance to start a new life. You've never had anyone look after you, let me and my family step up. We won't be perfect, but I think we can bump along alright. It's entirely up to you how long you want to stay, but up-front, I want you to know there is no time limit or expectations.'

Amber was stunned. This was an unbelievably generous offer, and she really had nothing to offer in return. She thought once Lexie knew how silly and reckless she'd been, that she wouldn't want anything more to do with her. And it wasn't just her! She was a package with two kids!

'Are you sure Lexie? Two kids can be annoying at times. They do have their quirks and they don't always do what they're told.'

'I pride myself on having extreme tolerance where kids are concerned,' laughed Lexie. 'But you're right. I haven't ever had to live with children. But I want to give it a try, and maybe we can work it out as we go.'

Standing up Lexie reached out a hand to Amber, pulling her to her feet.

'You look absolutely exhausted. Go to bed and think on it. I don't need an answer straight away. But remember, I mean it when I say that I would love you to stay, to think of this house as your home.'

Amber was very emotional and teary as she gave Lexie a hug. 'Thank you. Thank you. I just can't believe how lucky I am. I do want to stay here! You can't even begin to understand how much this means to me!'

As Amber broke away, she moved to grab their now empty mugs, thinking she would wash them, but Lexie took them from her. Giving her a gentle push, she said, 'Just get to bed Amber, before you fall in a heap. I'll see you in the morning.'

Walking back inside, Lexie watched Amber check on the kids before making her way to bed. It was nice to have someone else to think about for a change, instead of dwelling on her own dramas. And it did feel good to know she could make such a difference to someone's life. She had wasted a year being self-indulgent and feeling sorry for herself, but she could change that now.

CHAPTER 17

Following her cathartic, tell-all conversation with Lexie, Amber slept deeply. She was so exhausted that she barely stirred the next morning when Ruby and Arlo tiptoed in to kiss her goodbye. Even then, she had to fight her way up through layers of unconsciousness to sleepily acknowledge them before once more falling back to sleep. When she finally woke at almost nine o'clock, the house was silent. She lay there for a few minutes, her thoughts scrambled, until she remembered exactly where she was, and recalled the events of the night before. There was an immediate surge of guilt that Lexie had got the kids up, dressed, and off to school, all while she had slept like a zombie. Despite that she realised she felt content, even happy…and this was a rare emotion for Amber.

Stretching her arms and legs, she made the most of the queen-sized bed, luxuriating in the unfamiliar treat of having slept-in, and still incredulous that despite having told Lexie everything, every relevant sordid detail, Lexie had asked her to stay! She'd had no idea Lexie was even contemplating they should stay longer with her, let alone ask her to think of it as their home! Amber had just wanted Lexie to know her story, the bare facts without any Hollywood drama or gloss. It was important to her that there be no secrets between them because Amber could tell that Lexie's concern was genuine. She knew Lexie felt sorry for her, but she had to know that Amber wasn't the victim in her own life. She had made some bad choices, and lots of mistakes, and she'd paid dearly for them. But she did have two beautiful children, and she would do it all again just to have them in her life. It was as simple as that.

Amber was aware she had taken a massive risk, confessing everything, but she wanted Lexie to know the kind of person she was. If Lexie couldn't handle it, then, no worries. Amber would survive. She was already enormously grateful to Lexie for what she had done. When she tapped her on the shoulder in Bunnings, she was at her lowest, frightened and desperate. For the first time in her life, she was truly homeless, and she had dragged Arlo and Ruby into a dire and dangerous situation. They deserved so much better than her for a mother. She'd even fleetingly considered, sitting there in Bunnings, as every plan crashed around her, simply getting up and walking away. A brief fantasy which she knew she would never carry out, but the temptation was there. In that moment of weakness, she was ready to give up.

Now here she was, after a couple of good sleeps in a safe space, refreshed and ready to fight once more. The conversation last night had depleted her, eating up the last of her reserves. She'd bared her soul. Much had been said and there were more things to tell; or not. Going over all that old stuff, things she'd rather forget was very disturbing. It was like a wrecking ball smashing through her already fragile self-respect, which was a delicate construction at the best of times. But at least now Lexie knew. She knew and she said it didn't matter! Amber was still a bit stunned, taken aback by Lexie's generosity; at the same time, she was terrified that Lexie would change her mind.

Agitated by such negative thoughts, Amber kicked away the blankets. Lexie had offered her a home here! Could she really be this lucky? A flood of panic coursed through Amber's veins. *Did she mean it? Maybe when she thinks about it properly, she'll reconsider.* Pessimistic scenarios from Lexie kicking them out, to being back homeless in Bunnings, flashed through her imagination. Amber paced around the empty house; wild possibilities playing out in her mind.

With her thoughts scattering out of control, she finally stopped still, forcing herself to take several deep breaths, concentrating on the belly breathing she'd learned in a group session at the Women's Refuge. It was a technique she'd used many times since. *Get a grip.* Breathe. *Be positive.* Breathe. *Trust Lexie.* Breathe. *Whatever happens, you'll manage.* Breathe. *You always manage.* Breathe. Soon enough her breathing returned to normal, her heart slowly resuming its normal beat. *For the moment we are safe* she reasoned to herself. *Even if it's only for a while, the kids have a home. Marco is out of our lives. We've got somewhere to live while I make a plan. Just don't blow it by doing something stupid. You've got a lifeline here girl! This is a chance to get on your feet. No more constantly scrambling from one crazy day to the next.*

This was a conversation Amber would have with herself many times in those early weeks, as she learned to trust Lexie. She had eventually pulled herself together that morning, and by the time Lexie and the kids arrived home from school, she was back in control. Even weeks later when she thought about it, she still could not believe the lucky coincidence that led Lexie past her table at the café in Bunnings that day. Despite her fears, Lexie was true to her word. She really did mean what she said when she opened her home to them. Gradually, like shedding layers of heavy winter clothes, the promise of the first kiss of warm summer air on her skin, so Amber slowly grew used to feeling safe and welcome. And, as if in a choreographed dance, she and Lexie found their way, gradually getting used to living together.

Amber's role as Arlo and Ruby's mum, was never in doubt, but Lexie stepped up to help out when she could. They ate earlier than Lexie usually preferred, but as long as Amber was happy to cook, Lexie was flexible, happy to fit in with child-friendly meal-times, which were also much more entertaining than the solitary dinners she endured last year. Amber was proving to be quite a talent in the kitchen, and Lexie, by nature a reluctant chef, saw this as a decided bonus. Although she did take her turn at cooking, mindful not to take advantage of Amber's good nature. Meanwhile, Amber slipped efficiently into the role of house-keeper. Being home all day, she had done most jobs before Lexie and the kids arrived home from school, and besides, she reasoned to Lexie, it filled the day for her.

Not that her days exactly needed filling. Life was a breeze without trying to live up to Marco's exacting housekeeping standards. Amber gave an involuntary shiver, recalling how he would punish her if things weren't just so. He could get angry if he saw as much as a teaspoon out of place in the drawer. He was obsessively tidy, with a place for everything. She'd learned very early in their relationship about his fussy little routines. In the honeymoon stage, she had thought it would be nice to be with someone who was so particular. She was keen to please him, and went to great lengths to keep the house perfect, and of course that meant the kids couldn't make a mess, or leave toys around. Even though she used to clean constantly, he always found something wrong. Looking back, she couldn't believe she took so long to realise he would never be satisfied.

Instead of worrying about Marco, and trying to second-guess his moods, she enjoyed her quiet days at home, slowly recovering from her injuries. She looked forward to Ray and Jeanie popping over occasionally. Sometimes they took her shopping, and often, she and Jeanie would cook together while Ray pottered in the garden. Occasionally, all three of them would take Radar for a walk, or she would help Ray in the garden while Jeanie kept them company, giving instructions from the shade of the porch.

It was Ray's suggestion that she get her driver's licence, a suggestion Amber jumped at. Having been driving unlawfully for the last five years, Amber was very keen to be legal. She was already a competent driver; or at least good enough to avoid ever being pulled over for a driving infringement, and lucky enough to have never had an accident. Ray, who had taught both Andy and Lexie to drive as teenagers, couldn't believe what a star pupil he had this time, and Amber felt herself glowing under his constant praise. Praise was something she was unused to and initially she was embarrassed by the attention. Still, she was proud of herself when he booked her in for her official driving test after only a few lessons.

Amber felt like she was living in a dream. Life was good and she dared to hope that even better days were on the horizon. She was even beginning to believe that she was wrong about Marco not stopping until he found her, thinking that possibly she had over-estimated his need for control. Perhaps he really would leave them alone after all. By infinitesimal amounts, she began to unravel the knots of tension she had lived with for so long. Even so, when she was alone in the house, she could not resist the urge to periodically go to the front room, tweak aside the curtains and surreptitiously check the street for Marco's car.

Lexie also watched out for Marco when she arrived at school, scanning the carpark before she allowed the kids to get out of the car. At the end of the day, she repeated her cautious routine. She would go to the car first, survey the surroundings, then signal to Ruby and Arlo, waiting in the shadow of the school walkway, to follow. So far, there had been no sign of him.

Amber was also proud of the way Ruby and Arlo had adapted to the new living arrangements. *They certainly have survival skills* she thought with justified pride. They'd settled into Lexie's home like the true chameleons they'd been forced to be all their lives. Amber was confident that this time, their new experiences were happier, in line with the freedom and joy every child had a right to expect.

Lexie had also maintained her vigilance over Arlo and Ruby at school, seeking Ruby out at recess and lunch. She reassured Amber that her daughter was always busy, having fun and interacting with friends. Ruby's teacher, Jane Pocock, was also in the loop and reported that Ruby was switched on, progressing well academically, and appeared happy and engaged in class. As Arlo's teacher, Lexie was delighted with how quickly he was developing his reading and writing skills. He was certainly trying hard, but he also laughed lots and smiled often. Amber knew that Arlo adored Lexie and probably wanted to please her, but she also suspected his and Ruby's happiness, and academic progress, had a great deal to do with no longer being constantly afraid. Their fears about what mood Marco might be in when he got home were now a fading memory.

CHAPTER 18

Lexie was dozing in bed, enjoying a lazy start to the day, when squeals of delight disturbed the morning's calm. Soon Radar joined in the action with some crazy barking. Lexie could hear Arlo shouting, 'Go! Go!'

Ruby's squeals turned to shrieks.

Amber's voice rose above the bedlam outside the back door, admonishing the kids to be quiet, so as not to wake Lexie. It was too late for that. Glancing at her phone charging on the bedside table, Lexie thought she had done pretty well for a Sunday morning. Seven fifty-three. Not a bad sleep-in with two kids in the house.

The mayhem continued for a bit, until Lexie heard the back door slam, then the clink of the back gate, then silence. *They've taken Radar for a walk*, Lexie surmised. *Good idea.* It was going to be a scorcher, so the earlier the better.

Closing her eyes, Lexie wriggled further down under the blankets. There was nothing urgent to get up for, although she was hoping to fit in a morning bike ride or a run, and maybe a swim at the beach before the sea breeze came in. She had no set plan. Life was definitely easier now that she had Amber to share the housework, although, to be totally honest, she was first to admit that Amber was doing the bulk of the jobs around the house. Last year, she'd had to juggle everything, keeping up with the housework and maintaining the garden and yard, so this was a bit of a reprieve. She didn't want to take advantage of Amber's good nature, but Amber was so dammed efficient, she rarely left anything for Lexie to do!

She was hoping though, that soon Amber would think about her future. Lexie had higher ambitions for her than cooking and cleaning. Amber had wanted to get a regular job for a long time. They'd discussed it on many occasions, and this was probably the first time that it was a real possibility for her. Her ribs and bruises had healed well. Amber was looking forward to getting her driver's license, so she could start to look properly for work.

Lexie could appreciate how important it was for Amber to get paid employment, and to actually have some positive choices in her life. She was also quietly hopeful that in time Amber would think about doing some bridging courses for further study. As her teacher, she had known that Amber was capable of so much more academically, but the odds had always been stacked against her. Wishing she could wave a magic wand and change it all in an instant, Lexie reluctantly acknowledged that Amber first needed time and space. Jeanie had reminded her several times, that Amber's first priority should be to recover from her injuries – physical and emotional – and feel safe, so she had purposely refrained from any overly 'helpful' suggestions, or heavy discussions about the future. Amber's dreams would take shape in good time.

Lexie surveyed her bedroom contentedly, enjoying the ambience of the dappled sunlight, as it crept through the blinds, casting a rosy morning glow over everything. She was more than happy with the room's dimensions. The high ceiling with its decorative pressed metal cornices, created an airy feeling of space, while the solid, dark floorboards lent a sense of substance. A generous double window, large for the era of the house, faced east, perfect for catching the morning sun and the afternoon breeze. Her thoughts began to wander over the improvements she wanted to make to the house; the lack of an inside loo, being the one she most pondered on these days. With four people in the house, the need for a second toilet was becoming a pressing issue. Lexie swung her legs over the side of the bed, stood up, and completed several good stretches, while she tossed up whether to have a shower or get dressed.

Standing close to the window, she could feel the radiant heat of the sun through the bedroom's blinds, and decided against pulling them all the way up. It was already hot and there wasn't a cloud in the blue sky. If they were going to the beach, they probably should get there early, and then maybe drop by Ray and Jeanie's on the way home, for another swim in the pool. Her bike ride could wait until late afternoon. It would be more pleasant anyway, at that time of day. A beach lover herself, she was keen to get Arlo and Ruby to the beach, because she wanted them to learn to love it too.

Amber had already mentioned that the kids had never seen a beach, except in the movies. Lexie couldn't believe her at first. Who lives in Perth and had never been to the beach? But when you don't have a car, and you live in an inland suburb, and buses and trains cost money you don't have, it's not a priority. And there was no way Marco would have taken them to the beach. He hated the beach. Amber had asked him once and he complained so much about the prospect of getting sand in his car, and then got angry that she had even suggested it, that she'd spent the rest of the day placating him. That meant keeping the kids out of his way, and being on her best behaviour. She never mentioned the beach again.

Lexie was also discovering other experiences Amber and the kids had missed out on. Last weekend, Lexie thought it would be a good idea to spend Saturday afternoon at Ray and Jeanie's making the most of their pool, while the warm weather lasted. However, with their exposure to swimming pools, limited to Ruby's brief in-school swimming lessons last year, Arlo and Ruby were way out of their comfort zones. They had barely seen a pool, let alone swum in one, and certainly not one where the water went over their heads. It took a fair amount of coaxing before either child even got wet.

Andy was there with Hannah and Rosie, who were constantly jumping in and out, diving under and splashing everyone with their antics, while Arlo and Ruby stood frozen stiff in their new bathers, looking terrified. Very much surprised at their timidity around water, Lexie berated herself for not fully grasping just how restricted Amber and the kids' lives had been. There was so much she had taken for granted in her life, trusting that others had similar opportunities. She'd always known that in every class she'd taught, there were a few kids for whom life was not so easy; not everyone had access to the same chances. Nevertheless, she was still confronted that Amber, Ruby and Arlo's experience of life had been so narrow.

Lexie didn't give up easily, and with Amber's support, they eventually managed to get both kids into the pool, even though it meant Ruby clinging to Ray and Arlo hanging on just as tightly to Andy. Determined to fix this fear of water, but mindful not to push too hard, Lexie suggested that Arlo and Ruby could do beginner swimming classes after school.

'You know, in fourth term the whole school does a two-week intensive swimming program. It might not be so scary if they can get used to a big pool before then.'

She needn't have worried. Amber was also clearly well aware that Ruby and Arlo needed to be able to handle themselves around water. She wanted her own kids to have the life she'd never had, and swimming was something other people did. Her kids were not going to miss out.

'I think that's a great idea! Ruby was terrified when she did swimming lessons in pre-primary. I went along one day to look and she just stood in the baby pool, holding on to the edge. The swimming teacher couldn't get her to do anything more. But, how much does it cost? Will I be able to cover it with my parenting payments?' asked Amber, concerned.

One of the first jobs Jeanie had undertaken with Amber, was to open a new bank account for her and sort out new passwords to her MyGov and Centrelink accounts. Of course, with the benefit of hindsight, Amber understood what a red flag Marco's offer to manage her money had been… the start of complete control over her life, and the emotional and physical abuse that was to follow. With Jeanie's help, she had quickly cancelled her old bank account and established a new account, grateful she was finally in control of her own finances again.

'Don't worry about that,' reassured Lexie. 'If you can sort the lessons out, I'll pay and you can pay me back. The kids need to learn to swim, and I think they'll love it.'

It took her a few phone calls to find a swimming lesson with two vacant spots, but Amber persevered. On Wednesday, Lexie left school earlier than usual to pick up Amber and go to the pool together for beginner swimming lessons. As they approached the entrance, the kids were unusually subdued.

Lexie led the way through the turnstiles, her mind on other things. However, when Amber stopped at the office to sign in and pay, Lexie turned to check if Ruby and Arlo were following, she almost knocked them over, they were so close behind her. Two sets of arms grabbed hold of her legs, and suddenly she was rooted to the spot, unable to move. Looking down, she saw pure terror in their eyes. Belatedly she realised that she should have prepared them for this.

For a start, Arlo had never been in an indoor pool setting, and the clamour and chaos of the crowd of parents and kids, punctuated by the piecing sound of several swimming teachers' whistles blown at once, was almost overwhelming. Added to that was the cavernous setting, that housed not one, but three pools – a fifty-metre competition pool, a twenty-metre learners' pool and the smaller baby pool.

Tiered seating ran along both sides of the building, where families sat watching on. Dotted at intervals around the two main pools, were swim teachers with their groups of students kicking and splashing. It was organised pandemonium. Arlo had put his towel over his nose; the humidity and strong, chemical smell of a heated, indoor chlorine pool, a foreign element in his sensory knowledge. And, although Ruby had been to the pool before, her experience had not been positive, and she wasn't reacting well to the idea of going back into it. Berating herself for not being sensitive to this, Lexie knelt down to their level, and spoke calmly.

'It's okay, guys. It's okay. We're just going to have a try at this, and your Mum and I will be really close by. You don't have to do anything. You don't even have to get in the water. Maybe we'll just watch first and see what you think.'

Just then there was a cacophony as twenty whistles were blown simultaneously and each teacher called their group to the pool's edge, signalling the end of lessons. Arlo almost leapt into Lexie's arms at the ear-piercing sound, and she had to steady herself not to topple over. Adding to the tumult, several groups of soggy kids surged past them in wet streams, as they made their way up into the stands where parents waited with towels and dry clothes.

'Whoa!' said Lexie laughing as the last swimmer rushed past. 'I didn't realise we were blocking the track! Come on! That was a bit funny, wasn't it guys?'

'What was funny?' asked Amber, coming up with their paperwork in her hands.

'We nearly got runned over by all the kids!' said Arlo, his happy nature slightly restored.

'Well, let's get out of the way and set ourselves up over on these chairs,' suggested Amber, pointing to some seating alongside the smaller learner pool. 'The lady said this is where we should wait for your teacher, Elle. She's going to have a number four on her vest.'

Right on cue, Elle arrived with a clipboard and a box, and a welcoming smile for the five little swimsuit clad pupils waiting warily, goggles strapped tightly onto their heads, their small bodies tense and slightly hunched. Despite her apparent youth, Elle was a seasoned swim teacher. Dropping the clipboard at the side of the learners' pool and slipping off her Crocs, she counted out five different-coloured rubber sharks from a plastic box, motioning to the children to follow her to the baby pool. By the time she had demonstrated how the toys filled up when she squeezed them underwater, she had every child captivated.

With great fanfare she proceeded to squirt them in turn across the water until the kids were all jumping up wanting to have a turn. Holding the sharks above her head, she threw them into the middle of the baby pool, where the water level was about knee high for an adult. Not one child hesitated. They all ran as fast as they could into the water, falling over and getting up, until they could pounce on their own shark. Calling them back, she repeated the exercise several times encouraging the kids to go as fast as they could.

After a few turns of this and some squirting competitions, every child was wet from head to toe. Then, holding their sharks underwater, she got them to crawl through the water, with just their heads out, in a game of 'shark follow the leader'. When they assembled back at the pool edge, there were only a few minutes left in the lesson, but Elle had them hanging off every word. When she asked them to get into the deeper water, up to their armpits, and hold onto the side of the pool, again not one child hesitated. Elle soon had the group holding onto the pool edge and kicking, even putting their faces into the water. But the final challenge was getting them to open their eyes underwater which she accomplished by asking them individually to open their eyes underwater and tell her how many sharks she was holding. Lexie and Amber sat totally entranced, nudging each other occasionally in amazement, at Elle's skills, and the small miracle she had just achieved.

'Thank the Lord for Elle,' laughed Lexie as Arlo and Ruby finished the lesson, dripping wet, big smiles plastered on their faces.

'Was that fun? You guys did so well!' enthused Amber, after Elle had dismissed them and they ran over to her and Lexie.

'Can we have another swim? Pleeease?' asked Ruby.

'Yeah! Another swim!' shouted Arlo, dropping his towel and heading back to the baby pool. Ruby didn't wait to hear Amber's answer either, following Arlo into the pool, discarding her towel at the edge. Amber jumped up to save the towel, calling out,

'You've got fifteen minutes!' but they were already out of earshot and playing with a couple of other kids from their lesson who had also run straight back into the water.

'So much for the *they'll never learn to swim drama*,' laughed Amber as she settled down again next to Lexie. For a while they watched the kids splash and clown around, not quite going under the water but showing much more confidence. It was a sight that had them both smiling.

'You know, I've been thinking maybe I could get into the pool and swim some laps, even though I'm a really crap swimmer. Actually, I can barely swim, because I missed most of the school swimming lessons myself,' said Amber thoughtfully, studying the lap swimmers in the main pool.

'I can probably only do about ten metres, but I could improve,' mused Amber buoyed at the sight of a very ungainly swimmer, an older man who was rolling his way down the slow lane, while several faster swimmers passed him.

'What? Didn't you do swimming lessons when you were in my year six class?' questioned Lexie, wracking her brain for specific memories of that year and the intensive swimming program.

'I didn't have any bathers that fitted, for a start. And it cost money, so Cindy wasn't interested. By the end of that year, I was a bit of an expert at avoiding school on swim days.'

'But the lessons went for two weeks! Surely, I would have noticed you were absent for two weeks!'

'It was certainly much easier in year six, because by then I could pull the old I've-got-my-period excuse. No-one ever queried that.'

Lexie was stricken with remorse. 'I'm so sorry Amber! I can't believe I was so stupid. I really let you down.'

'Nah!' Amber shook her head. 'Don't be so hard on yourself. Cindy wouldn't have signed the permission form anyway. I used to go to the year one room and help out. I probably had more fun doing that.'

'Oh Amber! Too many people have let you down over the years. I should have followed up on this!'

'Lexie. Seriously. It's okay. But… you know, I think I might get wet next week and see if I can remember anything.'

CHAPTER 19

Lexie thought remorsefully of that conversation now, as she opted for bathers, shorts and a long-sleeved loose shirt to wear over the top. Just listening to Amber casually refer to the harsh realities of her childhood, and the tough years after she'd left school, made Lexie mourn for what Amber had missed. While Lexie hadn't always appreciated it, she had to acknowledge just how privileged her own upbringing had been. Amber's aim had been to simply survive each day. Going to the pool, or the beach, were things other people did. Lexie again wished she could wave a magic wand and rectify everything at once. It saddened her to think how little joy Amber had experienced in her life.

Lexie made up her mind. A trip to the beach was definitely the priority for the day, and it would give Amber a chance to swim, or at least paddle. If they got their act together and arrived early enough, the conditions would be perfect. Living in Perth, summer was synonymous with hot sunny days and trips to the beach; hours spent chasing waves or splashing in and out of the shallows. And because Lexie had always been a water-baby at heart, the excitement of running across the burning sand and plunging into the blue Indian ocean, were some of her favourite childhood memories.

Lexie was just finishing breakfast, when she heard Arlo talking non-stop, from down the street. Perfect timing. Swinging into action, Lexie downed the last of her cup of tea and within minutes, had the cooler bag out, ice bricks in, and cool drinks and water sorted. She was starting on some sandwiches when Amber and the kids bowled in through the back door, Ruby shoving Arlo away so she could get to the fridge first.

'Mum said I could have first pick!' complained Arlo, pulling Ruby back from the fridge door.

'I know where they are, so I'm just getting them for you,' responded Ruby bossily, pushing his hand away. Before Arlo could make his next move, Amber had skilfully wedged herself between them and had taken control of the fridge door handle.

'Both of you can wait, or I'll change my mind about having an icy pole before ten o'clock in the morning.'

Scowls replaced any potential disagreements. Amber's threats were not idle, and neither child was prepared to risk missing out on an icy pole. Swiftly locating the frozen treats, she handed them each the same orange fruit flavour simultaneously, so there would be no further disagreement. Placated, they went outside to Radar, to enjoy them.

'Sorry about that,' apologised Amber, shaking her head. 'I still can't believe how much fuss they can make over who gets to the icy poles first. I mean, what difference does a few seconds make?'

'It's obviously a big deal to them,' laughed Lexie, waving her hands at the slices of bread she had just spread out. 'I thought it would be fun to go to the beach today. We probably should take some lunch if we want to stay for a while. What should I put on the sandwiches? We've got ham, cheese and salad stuff. Or do the kids just want Vegemite or peanut butter?'

'The beach! That will be fantastic! Honestly, they won't care what they eat. Just peanut butter for them both, and I'd be happy with ham and tomato. Can I help though? I'm happy to.'

'No, I can sort this. If you get the kids and yourself ready with bathers, towels and hats, we can go soon. I've already got my bathers on, so it won't take me long. We can do sunscreen when we get there.'

Twenty minutes later, Lexie had loaded the sandwiches into the cooler bag, along with some fruit and snacks. She found two low beach chairs for herself and Amber, and put everything into the boot. Once Ruby and Arlo found out they were headed to the beach, they slurped up the last of their icy poles, and raced inside to don their gear, while Amber packed a beach bag. They were so excited, they were in the car, seatbelts on, a full ten minutes before she and Amber were ready to leave. Backing out the drive Lexie caught sight of Arlo's face. He was agog, his blue eyes open so wide, they were almost out on sticks. She put out a hand to pat his knee.

'This will be fun, won't it mate?' All he could do was nod, jiggling animatedly in his seat.

Lexie and Amber chatted on the way to the beach, with Arlo and Ruby uncharacteristically quiet. This was not the reaction Lexie was expecting, thinking they'd be full of questions, but when she swung onto Ocean Drive, and they got their first good look at the rolling waves of Scarborough Beach, their cheers more than made up for it. A flood of exclamations followed:

'I can see sand!'

'It's so blue. Look Mummy! Its blue!'

'I can see waves! Can we stand in the waves? '

'Can we go in? Is it cold? Where do we go?'

'Mum! Look! There's a boat! And flags! And people on surf boards! Can we watch them?'

By the time Lexie pulled into the carpark, the kids were straining at the leash, frantic with impatience, while Amber put on their sunscreen, and made them wear hats and thongs.

'I won't need shoes,' said Arlo throwing his back into the car.

'Oh, I think you will,' said Amber patiently retrieving them. 'I can see glass and stones here in the carpark, so you're definitely wearing thongs.

'And be careful! The sand will be hot,' warned Lexie as she locked the car, hoisting the chairs on one arm and the cooler bag over her shoulder.

'Hot sand!' laughed Arlo, thinking Lexie had made a joke, but nevertheless he put on his thongs and skipped happily beside the adults as they wove through the parked cars and along the sandy track that led to the beach. Once on the sand, he ditched his thongs, and holding them in his hands, took off running barefoot towards the water which was glinting enticingly. It took only a few steps before he stopped dead with a 'Yeouch!!!' Jumping from one foot to the other, he threw his thongs down and jumped back into them.

'I did warn you,' laughed Lexie. 'Once you get down onto the hard sand, it won't be as hot.'

But her last words were pointless. Arlo was already off again, with Ruby close behind. They didn't pause at the top of the path, as Lexie and Amber did, to take in the perfect blue sky, rolling waves and golden sand. Instead, they headed straight down to where the water foamed and swirled, as waves rolled in and sucked back at the water's edge. Barely breaking stride Arlo had his shorts off, dropping his towel and kicking off his thongs, leaving them scattered just above the tide line. Ruby was a fraction slower and a tad neater, managing to drop her gear at least in the one spot.

Watching them run helter-skelter, towards the sea, Amber tried to call out to them to stop, fearful that they were both about to rush headlong out into the deep water. Her voice was lost above the squawk of seagulls, the crashing waves and the happy shrieks of bathers, but she needn't have worried. Arlo and Ruby halted at the shallows, content to let the water roll over their feet, splashing them safely up to their knees.

Lexie and Amber collected the strewn clothes and towels, and found a clear spot on the sand to bunker down. Arlo and Ruby were already running in and out of the water, jumping over the waves, before racing them back to shore. Perhaps it was instinct, or perhaps just sheer luck, but they managed to escape the occasional bigger swell that threatened to swamp them. Amber stood close by in the shallows, laughing with them, soaking up their pure delight, as they experienced the beach for the first time in their lives on such a glorious hot day.

Lexie joined Amber to watch Arlo and Ruby's antics from the shoreline. Arlo was a whirlwind, leaping over waves, kicking swathes of water at Ruby, or squatting as the ocean swirled around him, before finally lying down with Ruby on the wet sand to let the water ebb and flow underneath them. Lexie was keen for a swim herself, but she also couldn't resist observing both children, and enjoying vicariously their joy, as they discovered for the first time, the fun of being at the beach.

Wading through the shallows, Amber watched every splash with an intensity worthy of an Olympic event; she was glued to the scene, torn between jubilation and self-recrimination. How many times in their lives had they been this happy? Possibly never. Tears threatened, but she held them back. She would not allow any sentimental blubber of her own to spoil this precious moment. Frustrated yet again with herself for making so many bad choices, she added another regret to her list. She had been such a shit mother! Why had she been so pathetic that she had never taken her kids to the beach? It didn't matter that Cindy had also never taken her, Robbie or Sam to the beach. She had vowed to be better, and she had failed them. Lexie stood beside her, and as if reading her thoughts placed a hand on her shoulder, drawing her close.

'Come on,' she whispered. 'Let's lift them up over the waves.' Taking Amber's hand, she led her over to the kids.

'Hang on to us,' Lexie called to them. 'We'll take you out deeper.' Motioning to Amber to take Arlo, Lexie held Ruby under the arms and lifted her over the breaking waves to stand in deeper water. Ruby loved it! In between waves, she clung on to Lexie's hand, jumping up and down. Lexie looked over to where Amber was doing the same with Arlo, who was squealing with delight, for once not talking because he was laughing so much. Lexie had no idea how long they playing in the waves, but eventually she'd had enough.

'Okay. I'm exhausted and I need a swim. Back you go Ruby, unless your mother has enough energy to lift you both.'

'No. I'm pooped too. Go for a swim Lex, I'll take them back and watch them. Or do you guys want something to eat?' asked Amber, before suddenly calling, 'Watch out!' and belatedly attempting to lift them both, as the next wave, much higher than the last, rushed over their heads, drenching them. They had to struggle to get their footing, before stumbling, laughing and squealing back up to the shore.

It had only been the slightest change in the breeze, but the waves were starting to come in with more force. Lexie took her chance to escape, diving under the next couple of waves until she was out where the water was calmer. Allowing herself to float gently with the swell, she relaxed into the glorious sensation of the cool clean, silky water running over her, massaging her body. There was pure magic in the refreshing power of the ocean, and it never failed to invigorate her.

What was the line Jed used to say? 'You never regret a swim.' So true. But idle thoughts of Jed were not to be encouraged, and Lexie struck out into the waves, swimming until she ran short of breath. Content, she stayed in the water for a while, plunging occasionally beneath the surface, using the time to clear her head.

She had guessed when Amber was standing stiffly in the shallows earlier, that she was ruminating over something. She was pleased to have interrupted whatever dark mood Amber had been swept up in. Lexie could tell by her stance that something was wrong, and when Amber rewarded her with a grateful smile, she was glad to have broken the spell. *The poor kid certainly has some baggage*, thought Lexie despairingly. Jeanie is so right when she tells me not to rush things. I can't just click my fingers and all will be well. Body surfing in, she made a vow to herself to be patient and let time heal. Amber was a survivor. Lexi had to give her that. Lexie doubted she, herself, would have done as well, alone, broke, with two children and no-one at her back.

By the time Lexie emerged dripping from the surf, Amber and the kids were eating lunch. A strong breeze rolled across the sand, and by the time Lexie had wrapped a towel around herself, the waves had turned choppy, with whitecaps visible every few metres. The Fremantle Doctor was in; its fresh breeze sweeping through the western suburbs, cooling down the streets. They stayed a while longer, Arlo and Ruby happy to build sandcastles and run intermittently in and out of the shallows, while Amber went in up to her waist, tentatively at first, diving under the choppy waves, but building her confidence with each attempt.

Finally, Lexie and Amber decided everyone had had enough sun, and they packed up, the trek back to the car taking longer than their initial run down to the beach, a much wiser Arlo happy to wear his thongs.

On the way home they stopped at Jeanie and Ray's for a quick dip in the pool, to cool down again and wash some of the salt off. This time it was a different story. While Arlo and Ruby weren't quite ready to take a flying leap into the pool, they were far more confident. Ruby ventured down the steps into the pool as far as she could before it got too deep, and then she had a go at holding onto the pool noodle. At first, she needed Amber in the water to hold her, but eventually she kicked off on her own, content to float for a bit, but still with a close eye on Amber.

Arlo sat on the steps, watching Ruby before he had a go with the noodle himself. He took a little longer to find his confidence, but eventually he also kicked away on his own. They both got braver by degrees, even staying in the water when Amber got out to sit with the other adults.

'Well. That's a sight I didn't expect to see after last week's performance. I didn't think we'd ever get them into the water on their own,' remarked Ray, cracking open a can of beer, and relaxing back in his pool-side chair.

'You can say that again,' chuckled Lexie. 'But their swim teacher, Elle, who looked about twelve years old, was just amazing, wasn't she Amber?'

'Yep. She was great. I'm so proud of them,' smiled Amber, clapping Arlo who had worked out how to twist his body so he swirled around in the water. Ruby copied him immediately.

They were quickly discovering that they were perfectly safe as long as they hung onto the noodles.

'Now Amber,' said Ray, taking a swig before he went on. 'I've worked out a little program for us for the next few days. You're still quite a long way short of completing your logbook for the driving test. When Lexie and Andy did it, it used to be only about twenty hours, but these days, you need one hundred hours of supervised driving signed off. I figure we are up to about eighty, give or take a few, so we need to plan a few long drives this week, if you're up for it.'

'I'm up for it. I can fit in with whatever you have in mind,' Amber replied eagerly.

'Well, I'm thinking we may as well make the most of the last of this great summer weather, so I thought we could do a few drives up and down the coast. If Jeanie can bear to miss golf, then she can come too, and we can make a day's outing of it. We could drive as far north as Lancelin, possibly. That will give you some country driving as well. And maybe we could go down to Mandurah one day to get you used to the highway. We could do a fair bit of exploring down that way.'

'That sound great! All of it!' agreed Amber enthusiastically, her eyes still on Arlo and Ruby floating in the pool. Then turning to Ray, and looking slightly self-conscious, she asked, 'Do you think we could stop and visit someone in Mandurah?'

'Of course, we can. No worries,' reassured Ray.

'Who do you want to visit Amber?' asked Jeanie curious.

'My brothers, Robbie and Sam. They live there, or that's where they were living the last time I heard.'

'Do you know where they live? Are they with your mum?' asked Jeanie slightly puzzled because this was the first time Amber had mentioned them. Lexie was curious herself; she hadn't thought to ask about Robbie and Sam either. She had just assumed Amber didn't know where they were.

'They're with their foster parents in Mandurah. Sally and Neil. They looked after them when Child Protection services finally caught up with Cindy.'

No-one else said anything as they digested this information. Amber seemed to be weighing up her options before she continued, lowering her voice so Ruby and Arlo couldn't hear.

'After I left, things went downhill fast. I was lucky to be gone…First, the police came for John. He was caught with enough shit, sorry, drugs and stuff, to send him away for a long time. Cindy protested she knew nothing, but the cops weren't having any of that and she was locked up as well, pending bail. Community services were called in of course, and then Child Protection. The house must have been in a pretty bad state. Once I was gone, and with Cindy on the gear and John useless, it was always going to be a disaster. Robbie probably tried his best but he was only twelve, barely old enough to look after himself, let alone Sam. I think he was relieved when someone finally came for them. And they got lucky. They got Sally and her husband Neil. Good people. I've met them two or three times.'

'How did you meet them?' asked Lexie fascinated by yet another crazy chapter in Amber's short life.

'Well, it was soon after the boys first went to Sally's. They had only been living with her and Néil for a few weeks, because I was still in the women's refuge place. They came to visit us. I'd heard about the bust, and I'd been asking around if anyone could find out for me where the boys were. The social worker at the refuge was great, and when she tracked the boys down, she gave Sally all my details so we could meet.' Amber smiled at the memory.

'We met in a park, not far from the refuge, so it was easier for me. The best thing was, I could tell straight away that Sally and Neil were good people. I didn't even have to ask Robbie and Sam. You see, I got there early and I was waiting with Ruby and Arlo. I was pushing Rubes on the swing and I saw them get out of the car… and I could see Robbie laughing at something. And then they saw me and started running over, and Sally called out to Sam that he forgot his hat. And he just skipped back and grabbed it, no fuss, and took off again. They looked like a family…even if they weren't. But when they got to me, and I looked at their eyes, I could see they were happy.' Amber shrugged. 'You know. They just had happy eyes.'

'Happy eyes,' repeated Jeanie, emotion in her voice. She walked over to Amber who was sitting on the pool lounge. Without a word she sat next to her and put her arms around her. Amber leaned in, resting her head on Jeanie's shoulder, and closed her eyes. As Jeanie made comforting noises, Ray noticed that Arlo and Ruby had stopped playing in the pool, and were looking with concern at Amber.

'Well! What have we here?' he boomed. 'Two fat fish floating in my pool! I think I'll catch them!' and he made a big show of standing up, taking off his T-shirt and stretching, before stomping towards the pool steps.

Arlo and Ruby shrieked and started kicking wildly to escape. Pandemonium reigned courtesy of Ray, allowing Jeanie to take Amber into the house while the kids were distracted. Lexie stayed outside, laughing at Ray's exaggerated fishing efforts, and encouraging the kids to escape. Inside, Jeanie sat Amber at the table. Dropping her head into her hands, Amber had a little cry, while Jeanie patted her back. Then Amber brushed her tears away, and shook her head in apology.

'I'm sorry Jeanie. I thought I was getting over all these sooky tears. I just can't hold it together lately. I'm so pathetic.'

'Don't be silly. A bit of a cry every now and then does you good. I'll make us a cup of tea. You don't have to talk. Just lie down on the couch. Close your eyes and have a rest.'

Amber took Jeanie's advice and, for a few minutes, stretched out on the couch with her eyes closed, until the cup of tea arrived. Outside, the kids were still playing in the pool, and she marvelled at Ray's energy and patience. She could also hear Lexie give a five-minute warning to the three of them, (Ray having ended up in the pool), that it was time to get out, but they appeared to be taking little notice. Jeanie placed the cup of tea in front of her, and Amber sat up, ready to talk about why she had essentially abandoned her brothers. She'd never admitted to anyone how much it had cost her to leave the boys, and she'd never forgiven herself for leaving them.

She hesitated, searching for the right words.

'I hated leaving the boys behind with Cindy. I didn't want to do it. But I knew things were turning bad and if I got caught up in all the police stuff, I'd risk losing Arlo and Ruby to foster care.' Amber had both hands wrapped around her mug of tea, and she leaned in closer to Jeanie to make her point.

'You see, I was terrified they'd be taken away and I'd never get them back. But I felt so guilty about deserting Robbie and Sam. They needed me too, I was all they had, and I loved them so much. I hated myself and I'll never forgive myself…even though I know it's worked out okay.'

'Amber. Listen now,' said Jeanie sternly, taking Amber's hands in her own and holding them tightly. 'You can't keep blaming yourself for all this stuff. You were… What? All of eighteen years old? You had done your best, and besides, it did work out in the end. No more of this going over the past. You need to forgive yourself and move on.' Then in a softer tone she asked,

'Now tell me about the boys. How often have you seen them over the last few years?'

Amber sighed. 'I saw them two more times after that. Once, Sally came and picked the kids and me up and we had a Christmas Day all together. That was our best Christmas ever.' Amber smiled at the memory.

'And we met in a park another time. But because I have no car, and Sally and Neil live in Mandurah, and they're busy people, I didn't like to bother them. Every now and then, Sally would send me a text about how they were going, and sometimes photos, so I know they've grown heaps.'

Amber smiled broadly at Jeanie. 'You know, I think they'll both be taller than me now.'

Then her smile turned into a grimace. 'When I moved in with Marco, he wouldn't let me see the boys. Said he didn't want me taking on any more losers. And he even used to check my phone to see if I'd messaged Sally. So, I actually haven't heard how things are, for ages.'

'Well, that's going to change this week!' said Jeanie emphatically 'You message right now and find out when you can visit Sally and Neil, and the boys. Tell her anytime this week. Next week. On the weekend. We are at your disposal. Go on.'

'Go on what?' asked Lexie opening the door and catching the last of the discussion. Quickly analysing the situation, she could tell Jeanie had everything under control and that Amber was looking more like her normal self, so she continued. 'I have two drowned rats here who need drying out, and then we need to make tracks because I've got some jobs I need to get done before tomorrow.'

'Maybe they can just go straight in the shower now, and get dressed here. Save a bit of time when you get home,' suggested Jeanie.

'Great idea, if you don't mind them wrecking your clean bathroom,' said Amber, looking up, as she typed a message to Sally on her phone.

'Yep! Great idea, Mum,' agreed Lexie, shepherding the kids toward the downstairs bathroom. 'I don't suppose you've got any leftovers for us to take home for dinner, have you?' she asked hopefully.

'No. I haven't got leftovers, but I did make you guys a quiche this morning. I figured you'd be too tired after a beach day to be bothered cooking.'

Lexie walked back down the passage and gave Jeanie a big hug, whispering in her ear, 'You can fill me in later, but you know you really are the best mother in the world.'

As Lexie headed towards the bathroom where Arlo and Ruby were waiting, Amber's phone pinged with a reply.

'She's texted straight back! She says, *Anytime! I can make sure the boys are home even if I have to pick them up early from school, or it can be a weekend. Robbie and Sam will be so excited to see you, and they've got lots of news for you as well. Sally xxx*

'Well. We can certainly make that work. That's great, Amber,' said Jeanie high-fiving her.

***

Amber drove home from Jeannie and Ray's with the L-plates on. Every thirty minutes of driving counted towards her logbook. Underneath her outwardly calm exterior, she was deliriously happy. Thanks to Jeanie's candid and unreserved support, and even if she still couldn't completely forgive herself, it felt better knowing someone else understood why she'd done it. She didn't quite dare put it into words yet, but she was beginning to believe that she could actually move on from her old life.

Glancing in the rear vision mirror, she could see Arlo and Ruby were close to nodding off. Don't you dare fall asleep two minutes from home, she thought. I'm planning on getting you guys into bed early, because you've both had a huge day, and it's a school day tomorrow.

'Who had fun today? Didn't you just love the beach?' she asked them brightly.

Ruby managed to spark up a little. 'Yeah! It was cool mum. I loved it. I loved the waves. Next time I'm going to go out deeper!'

'You won't! I bet! You're just a scaredy cat! I'm better at going under the waves than you anyway!' retorted Arlo, making sure Ruby didn't get too big a head for herself.

'Okay settle down guys,' warned Lexie, as Ruby kicked out at Arlo from across the seat, missing him completely and getting the back of Lexie's seat instead.

Mission accomplished. Both kids were now wide awake. The timing was perfect. Seconds later, Amber turned the corner into their street. Swinging into the driveway, she braked abruptly, shocked at the scene confronting them. Simultaneously Lexie cried out,

'What the hell!'

Josh, the nice builder-slash-architect from next door, was on her lawn, picking up garbage and the contents of the recycling bin that were strewn across the driveway and front yard.

'Why are the bins pushed over?' Ruby asked tearily, over-wrought from her big day and upset at the rubbish everywhere.

'We'll find out, Ruby. Maybe it was just the wind. Remember how windy it got at the beach today?' said Lexie, trying to make light of it all.

All three bins were on their sides though, as if deliberately tossed, their contents spread across the lawn and the driveway. As they got out of the car, Radar, already barking furiously, elevated his complaints to a new level.

'Quiet! Radar! Stop it boy!' Lexie called out, surveying the dismal scene.

'What's happened Josh? Who did this?' asked Amber, unable to believe her eyes.

'I'm assuming it's kids. It's probably partly my fault. I heard Radar barking, but I ignored him. I thought he was just bored, and that you'd be home soon. By the time I came out to the street, this mess was here, and no-one in sight. Seriously, it must have only happened in the last half-hour.'

'Thanks so much for helping, Josh,' said Lexie. 'I'll just get some gloves and I'll pick up the rest.'

With a meaningful glance at Amber, and knowing how tired Arlo and Ruby were, she said 'Why don't you take the kids inside? They're dead on their feet. I can deal with this. It won't take long.'

'Okay,' said Amber torn between wanting to help, and getting the kids inside. Gathering the beach gear from the car, she checked, 'Are you sure?'

'Oh yeah!' laughed Lexie. 'I'm sure. Put Mum's quiche in the oven, and let's get them fed before they totally crash. And maybe they can distract Radar before the whole neighbourhood comes out to see what he's been barking about.'

By the time Lexie had pulled on her gloves, Josh had collected most of the rubbish. Lexie tried to tell him she was okay to finish up, but he wasn't listening. Shrugging her shoulders, Lexie concentrated on picking up the recycling stuff, before they both started on the green waste. This muck was by far the most unpleasant, because vegetable scraps and food, were mixed with bones and tea-bags, and it seemed deliberately scattered everywhere. It looked like the perpetrators had tried to create the worst possible result. When at last the job was done, they stood together, hands on hips surveying the now mostly clean lawn. The remaining bits of trash would be mashed up by the mower the next time the lawn was cut.

'I can't thank you enough Josh. I owe you one.'

'Don't mention it. Your dad, Ray, has made me quite a few coffees since you moved in, for which I'm very grateful. So, this is no big deal.'

'That sounds like Dad. He loves a chat, but you probably already know that,' laughed Lexie. Walking to the kerb, Lexie gestured up and down the street. 'But what's your take on this? Why do you think they targeted us? Especially with Radar going off his head? It doesn't look like anyone else's yard was hit…'

'Yeah! It's a bit strange. But it looks like something stupid kids would do. Maybe for a dare?' Josh shrugged, 'It probably pays to be a bit more vigilant, though. Maybe keep the bins inside the gate, rather than out here where they are more exposed… Anyway, it's getting late, so I should go.'

He paused before saying, 'By the way, your dad has asked me to take a few measurements and give you an idea of what you might be able to do with the house. I understand you still have an outside loo? Are you happy for me to do that any time soon?'

'Yes. Yes, absolutely. Especially now I seem to have a full house. Ideally, I'd also like an extra toilet and bathroom as well. If you could give me some suggestions, I'd be very interested. Although I have to say upfront, I'm not sure I can afford to do much just yet. But, maybe one night this week? After I get home from school. I can get home earlier if need be. The kids have swimming on a Tuesday at four, but otherwise I'm usually home by about four-thirty.'

'Okay. I'll keep a look out for you. I should be here a couple of days this week. Even if I'm in the office, I can probably pop around anyway.' Opening the door of his ute, Josh collected a card from the dash.

'Here. Take one of my cards; you can ring me when you've got time.'

Lexie took the card thanking him, and started towards the house. Once in the car, Josh wound down the window, and joked,

'Good luck getting those kids into bed, after all this excitement.'

Lexie was still smiling as she walked into the kitchen, where the kids were sitting at the table eating dinner.

'Thank goodness the two of you had your showers at Jeanie's, because I am definitely bagging the bathroom, so I can shower off this disgusting smell after picking up all that rubbish,' said Lexie making a funny face at the kids.

'It was yukky, Lexie,' said Arlo seriously. 'I think you do need a shower, and you better use lots of soap like Mummy always says.'

'I will Arlo. Good advice,' nodded Lexie. She collected some clean clothes from her bedroom and trekked back through the kitchen to the bathroom.

'Did you have a nice chat with Josh?' asked Amber, a knowing smile on her face. 'Nothing like a good pile of rubbish to inspire romance, I always say.'

Making sure the kids weren't looking, Lexie gave Amber the finger before she disappeared into the bathroom. She could still hear Amber laughing, even when she turned the shower on.

CHAPTER 20

Amber was apprehensive as she drove down the highway, a few days later, towards Mandurah, but it had nothing to do with her Learner driver status. Even with Ray supervising from the passenger seat, and Jeanie chatting away in the back, it felt like her stomach was digesting cardboard, and the feeling hadn't eased in the long drive from the city. Jeanie had given up her usual golf day, for which Amber was extremely grateful. Knowing she had Jeanie there, helped. The irony in all of this wasn't lost on Amber. She had always prided herself on being strong and independent when things went wrong… and plenty had gone wrong over the years. Yet, here she was, within a few weeks of meeting Jeanie, ready to trust her with all her secrets and fears. On cue, as she slowed the car and pulled up beside a mid-nineties suburban home, there was, a reassuring squeeze of her shoulder from the back seat.

Ray was praising her on her excellent driving, when the front door of the house flew open, and two gangly teenagers leapt off the front porch. Within a couple of steps, they were at the car door. Amber's heart cartwheeled with joy at the sight of her brothers. Tearing open the driver's door she fell into both sets of arms at once. Tears and laughter flowed equally, as they stepped back to look at each other before all three embraced again, standing close together, lost in the moment. It had been too long since they had seen each other.

Amber pulled back to take a good long look at Robbie and Sam. Oh! They had changed so much! At seventeen, Robbie was a head taller than her, and Sam, thirteen, was already looking her in the eye. Sam was around the same age Robbie had been, when she left them. He looked so young! Remorse engulfed her like a dust storm.

Stop it! Enjoy this moment! There's time for all that later, she admonished herself. Both boys were talking at once. Amber shook her head. She was struggling to take it all in. Reaching out, she took Robbie by the shoulders first.

'Robbie. You have grown so handsome! I love your hair a bit long. You always had such gorgeous curls! Come here and give me another hug.' She squeezed Robbie, her hands only reaching around waist-height these days. Then she turned to Sam.

'Sam. When did you get so grown up? Oh! I've missed those beautiful green eyes! Come on. Another hug from you too.' Another group hug followed. Breaking apart Amber spotted Sally who had followed the boys out at a slower pace, watching from the veranda and smiling. Ray and Jeannie were also out of the car, looking on at the siblings reunited after so long. While Amber made the introductions, she could barely contain her excitement. She had no patience at the moment for formalities. She was itching to get the boys on their own and talk. But she needn't have worried. After Sally had ushered them all inside, she took Ray and Jeanie to the kitchen to meet Neil, and sent Amber and the boys to the back patio, to 'spend some quality time together,' as she put it.

There were snacks and cool drinks, already laid out, and apart from Sally bringing Amber a cup of tea, the three of them were left alone. The knots in her stomach eased as she soaked up the sight of her brothers, to whom she had been more mother than big sister. Their voices were deeper and their cheek bones more chiselled, but occasionally they would say something, or laugh, or there would be a facial expression, reminiscent of a younger Robbie or Sam, and the years would fall away.

Robbie was in year twelve. He wasn't sure what he wanted to do, but he was getting good marks, and Neil was helping him look at some courses at uni. He was playing hockey and loved it, and he was pretty good at it, he revealed almost shyly. Sam interrupted, debunking Robbie's modesty by saying Robbie was in the State Under 18 squad, making sure Amber knew that was a big deal.

'Neil was a hockey player, so he's given me lots of tips along the way which help. I'm not sure if I'll keep my spot in the squad but I love all the training. And Sam's pretty handy with a hockey stick too,' Robbie said proudly. Then he paused before saying earnestly,

'Hockey was the thing that really helped us when we first came here. Neil gave us a hockey stick each and he used to take us down to the hockey pitch whenever he thought we needed to get our mind off stuff. We'd spend hours down there just dribbling and hitting shots. Playing little competitions. It sort of settled us. You know.'

'Oh. I can imagine,' said Amber, impetuously kissing each of them on their foreheads.

Not only was Robbie doing well at school, but he was a Faction Sports Captain, a fair runner, and had several good mates to hang out with. Sam's news was just as positive. He declared he loved school. He was in year eight at the same high school as Robbie and he also had good mates. He liked hockey as well, but he was also keen on cricket and played both. Sam had no idea yet what he wanted to do after school, but he finished by saying whatever it was, he wasn't going to be a loser like his dad, John.

'You're nothing like John, Sam. Don't even think that. You will never do the bad stuff he did.' Then changing the subject, she asked, searching both their faces for clues.

'But tell me about Sally and Neil. Are you still happy here?'

Robbie nodded emphatically. 'We don't even have to think about being happy, do we Sam? It feels just like we're a family. Sally and Neil are fantastic!'

Robbie's face was serious as he recounted what had happened on that final day at their parents'.

'We were so scared that day before they picked us up. Cindy was screaming, "Don't take my kids!" while the cops were taking her away, like she even cared about us! And there were sniffer dogs, and so many cops! This lady from the government, just walked in and helped us pack our clothes. And we waited in an office in town for ages. Then in come Sally and Neil, all smiles, and they tell us everything will be okay and that they'll look after us. And they're still looking after us. They haven't let us down, ever.'

'They do get cross sometimes if we mess up. And there are "Sally's rules" we have to mind,' said Sam, making quotation marks with his fingers.

'But they really care about us, and it feels good when someone cares, even if they get cross…you know it's 'cause they actually want the best for you,' said Sam, with a wisdom beyond his years.

Despite reliving those last days with Cindy and John, there was not one word of recrimination about Amber leaving them. She finally accepted that neither of her brothers blamed her for going when she did. It was time to forgive herself.

Eventually, Sally popped her head in and said that some lemon slice, coffee and chocolate milkshakes were ready in the kitchen if they were up for it. Robbie and Sam bolted at the mention of milkshakes. Sally walked slowly back to the kitchen with Amber, wanting to check if everything had gone well.

'All good, love?' she queried.

'Oh! Thank you so much Sally! They are marvellous! And they're so happy! I really can't thank you enough. It's just wonderful to see them again. I didn't forget them, I wanted to come… it's just that things have been…difficult for me,' Amber confessed.

'I know. Jeanie told me,' said Sally, sympathetically putting an arm around Amber.

Stepping into the kitchen, Amber could see everyone was getting on well. Ray, Neil, Robbie and Sam were talking hockey, and Ray, ever hopeful of a new convert, was trying to convince them that if they were good at hockey, they would probably be good at golf, and was busy offering Robbie his old clubs. Jeanie was looking at photo books Sally had made for the boys. Sally's affection for Robbie and Sam was obvious.

It was a lovely finish to what had been a momentous Saturday afternoon. During their protracted goodbyes, Robbie asked Amber to bring Ruby and Arlo next time.

'I definitely will. They would love to see their two favourite uncles! We might even come and watch a hockey match. I'm sorry I didn't bring them, but just this once I wanted to get you boys all to myself,' said Amber giving them both a kiss and hug in turn, before taking the driver's seat once more for the return journey.

'Another three hours on the logbook today. She's going for her test next Thursday, so keep your fingers crossed,' Ray informed them proudly through the passenger window as they were leaving. 'Hopefully next visit they'll be P plates, not L plates. Cheers!' he called, as Amber, rolling off smoothly, gave a toot and final wave before accelerating down the street.

***

Amber's mood only got better listening to Jeanie talk about Sally and Neil. As only Jeanie could, she had managed to hear their whole life story within the first hour of meeting them. In a nutshell, they couldn't have children, and so in their forties, they decided to take in foster children. They'd cared for all ages, from tiny babies to teenagers. Most children stayed a few months, some only a few weeks. Very rarely they'd had children for over a year, but they both knew that the longer they cared for the children, the harder it was to say goodbye. It was especially hard, when they weren't convinced that the parents were going to be any better at it a second time. At one time they had up to six kids in the house, and no siblings in that mix. It had been a chaotic ride, but they were glad they'd been able to help. Jeanie continued, relating Sally's story.

'Sally said they almost said no, when they were asked to take on Robbie and Sam, because they were emotionally scarred after a particularly difficult foster placement. But when they met Robbie and Sam, they were so glad they said yes. For a start, the boys had beautiful manners, which is apparently unusual in these kids, and they thanked them for everything they did. She said they'd had kids who were so traumatised by their experiences, that they didn't speak for weeks. But they could see that even though the boys were dreadfully neglected by their mother…' Amber scowled involuntarily at this…

'Sally and Neil could tell that at some stage; someone had really looked after them well. Of course, they found out later that they had a big sister, Amber, who had been like a mother to them.'

Amber blushed profusely at this praise from Sally. Jeanie continued,

'You should be proud of yourself, keeping those boys safe, as well as Ruby and Arlo. Sally certainly thinks you're wonderful, and we do too, don't we Ray?'

'Yes. You are amazing Amber. Especially as you can concentrate on the road with Jeanie yabbering away. Now, Jeanie let the girl just focus on driving. She's going for her licence next week, and she needs to practice.'

A long, exaggerated sigh could be heard from the back seat, but silence prevailed. Amber stole a look in the rear vision mirror at Jeanie, who eye-rolled at her. Amber chuckled to herself, but she did appreciate the peace and the chance to focus on her driving, and quietly savour the events of the day.

CHAPTER 21

Lexie had tried to leave school earlier than usual but it was still almost four-thirty when she, Ruby and Arlo arrived home. She had arranged for Josh to come and take a few measurements, and hopefully give her a few ideas about the much-discussed renovation. She was optimistic it would include a solution to the outside toilet, and perhaps, the addition of another bathroom and toilet.

Josh was already there, having a coffee in the kitchen with Amber. Lexie made one for herself, then she and Josh went outside to look at the rear of the house. Amber was making Ruby and Arlo their after-school snack, when Ruby announced she had found a party invitation in her bag, but she wasn't sure who had given it to her yet. She was very animated as she unzipped the backpack and pulled it out.

'I found it in my bag! Whose party, is it? Can I go? I couldn't open it. It had too much sticky tape everywhere,' she jabbered excitedly, handing the envelope to Amber and jumping up and down to take a better look.

'Hang on,' said Amber, laughing and trying to slice through the envelope with a knife. The invite was pink and covered in balloons. Opening it, Amber read the first line when the smile froze on her face.

Dear Ruby,

You are invited to a special birthday party. Please bring your mother, the slut, and her whore girlfriend. I promise there will be lots of fun games….at least lots of fun for the birthday boy!

You and Arlo can play anywhere you want for the day. Maybe ride your bikes on the freeway, That sounds like fun.

RSVP Don't worry. I'll be in touch.

'Tell me Mummy! What does it say? Can I go? Whose party is it?' nagged Ruby, repeating it louder each time because Amber wouldn't answer her.

Amber looked at Ruby's eager face, unable to think straight; the alarm bells going off and feeling of dread, almost paralysing her. Finally, she smiled brightly at Ruby.

'Oh! I'm sorry Rubes, it's actually not for you. It's for someone called Judy. Almost your name, but I think they got the wrong bag. And it doesn't even say who it's from!! That's pretty silly isn't it? Did anyone see who gave it to you?'

Ruby looked disappointed. 'Are you sure it's not for me? There's no Judy at school!' she protested.

'I'm sure. Look. It's a fancy 'J'. It must be another class!'

Amber waved the invite quickly at Ruby, hoping she wouldn't insist on a closer look.

'We can have a party this week ourselves. Hey! If I pass my driving test, let's have a celebration night. That'll be good fun. We can have party pies, a cake and fairy bread, and even play some games with Lexie! Maybe Ray and Jeanie will come over?'

Ruby didn't quite react with the enthusiasm Amber was aiming for, but she did eventually drop the subject. Throwing all the usual rules out the window about no television after school, Amber shooed her and Arlo into the lounge to watch TV. She needed space to think, and she needed them where she could see them. Her heart was in over-drive, and she kept looking out the front window, in case Marco suddenly appeared. How did he manage to get that invitation into Ruby's bag? Did he know where they lived? Maybe he did. He certainly knew about Lexie. She was dying to show her the invite, but she'd have to wait until Josh was gone. In the meantime, she paced from the front window to the kitchen, re-reading Marco's words, and liking them less each time.

Lexie, oblivious to Amber's angst, was thoroughly enjoying herself. Josh had some great ideas, which he sketched out for her, simple sketches but clear, so she could readily imagine them. He was proposing an L-shaped addition across the back of the house and along the left side fence. The outside loo would remain where it was, but instead could be accessed through the existing laundry. The addition to the rear of the house could be used as a study or games room, and a master bedroom and ensuite could be built along the side fence, with windows facing a landscaped courtyard…a courtyard that wasn't there yet, but could be in time.

Radar would still have plenty of room to roam, as it wouldn't take up more than about a third of what was quite a generous back yard. Best of all, Josh was assuring her it was a relatively easy build. Though she tried to remain detached, Lexie was excited by Josh's ideas. She could visualise them, and they made good sense.

Josh was very professional, encouraging her to get some other proposals; however, he was absolutely on her wavelength and Lexie had to control herself not to agree too enthusiastically to all his suggestions. *He really is a most attractive man*, she thought, surreptitiously checking out his strong physique. After a while, he began talking about some of the costs involved.

Josh was suddenly all business, as he moved on to more practical matters, bringing Lexie back to earth with a bang. Putting on what she hoped was an astute face, Lexie pushed aside all distracting thoughts.

'Anyway. Let me give you ballpark figure before we go too far down the track of what you can do. I'll take some measurements now, and I'll work out two quotes. One for the whole L-shaped construction, which includes the extra bedroom and ensuite, and another for an addition along the back that will enclose the outside toilet, and give you – initially at least – another living space here at the rear of the house. You can always add on the extra bedroom and ensuite at a later stage if you choose to. What do you think?' he queried, with a deadly smile that had Lexie ready to agree to anything.

'Yep. That sounds good, Josh. I need to have a think about it all, and a ball- park figure of what it might cost would be great.'

As Josh moved off with his measuring tape in hand, Lexie asked if he needed any help.

'No, thanks. I'll give you a yell if I need anything. I shouldn't take too long.'

Lexie wandered back inside, excited by Josh's ideas, despite her attempt to maintain an objective mindset. She also resolved to be more pro-active. Just because Ray thought Josh was a genius, she didn't have to get him to do the job. After all, she had been the project manager and had dealt successfully with all the tradies when she and Jed had renovated. She made a mental note to check out some of Josh's other construction and design work, although from what she had seen of the work going on across the road, it looked like he did an excellent job.

Lexie was putting the coffee cups in the dishwasher when Amber handed her Ruby's invite. Lexie read the text, the shocking words jarring with the innocent images of pastel-coloured balloons.

'Holy shit!' she swore, looking at Amber, whose stricken face said it all.

'Do you think he knows where we live?' Amber whispered.

'I think he might. How did Ruby get this?' Lexie was even more worried after Amber filled Lexie in on Ruby's story about finding it in her bag.

'How did he manage that? Was he in the school? Maybe he got a parent, or another student to do it? You know I'm going to have to tell Kelly this. And, I think we should go to the police ourselves.'

Amber nodded. 'I know. I understand. Do what you have to, but I'm not ready to take it further.' Amber held up her hands as Lexie protested angrily.

'I know the school has to know. I get it that they have to follow it up. I think it's best if the school reports it. I can't face going to the police myself, because I'm scared about what he might do to the kids. I'm terrified that he can get this close to Ruby.'

Lexie didn't quite understand the logic behind Amber's thinking, but she let it go, for the moment, giving her a quick hug instead. 'Okay Amber. But he crossed a line when he did this. It's an outright threat.'

Lexie stewed over the invitation all night. The next morning, at her first opportunity, she knocked on Kelly's office door, with the invitation in hand. Kelly took a cursory look, before frowning and re-reading it.

'How did he get it into Ruby's bag? Are you sure it happened at school? I can't believe no-one saw him at school. With all our safety protocols, I hate to think that a random man could just walk through the school. How can you be sure it is even from Marco?'

'It has to be. Who else would want to be that threatening to Amber? I've been thinking about it all night. It has to be him, and Amber didn't even consider for a moment it wasn't him. But how did he do it? There is no way he could have wandered into school unnoticed. He must have got someone else to put it into her bag. I mean, a pink envelope looks innocent enough, doesn't it?'

Kelly sighed. 'I'll follow it up. Leave it with me.' Then she looked at Lexie. 'Are you okay? I mean he's referring to you in this. Don't you feel a bit concerned for yourself?'

'Yeah! I'm not thrilled about it. He is a bully and he's threatened me. I have to admit that I do feel anxious about what he might do. But I think he's made a mistake with this. I mean he hasn't put his name to it, but it's in writing. If I can get Amber to go to the police, and report his abusive behaviour, then this should be more evidence.'

'It is a police matter. I have to report it. Why is she avoiding this?'

'She's scared of him. And she's scared she might lose her kids.' Lexie put up her hands in defence. 'I know. It is crazy, but I'm still trying to make her understand that the best option is for her to report him herself.' Lexie shrugged. 'She's terrified of him.'

'Be careful, Lexie. I just hope you haven't taken on more than you can handle. Keep me in the loop,' said Kelly very seriously. 'This is all very stressful for you, so if you need some relief time today, let me know. I can swing some your way.'

Ideally, Lexie wanted nothing more than to leave school and go home to Amber, but her conscience overruled. There were so many things she had planned to get through today. Tuesdays were the only day she had the class without interruption, and she had a few things she wanted to finish. Besides, Ray and Jeanie were coming over to take Amber driving, because she still had several hours in order to complete her logbook; and Ray was a stickler for the rules. She knew Amber would be safe. Ruby and Arlo had swimming after school, and after seeing the invitation, they had already planned to all sleep at Ray and Jeanie's. They didn't know if Marco knew where they lived, and it was possibly a bit over the top, but Amber looked relieved when it was suggested, and Lexie had to admit she was happier being cautious.

The day went well. Lexie managed to keep the class on track and when she looked over some of the tasks the children had completed successfully, she could see her lesson had gone well. Lexie gave herself a tick of self-congratulation. She looked over Arlo's work carefully. He had managed the maths concepts easily, and she was really pleased with the revision of sounds she had given him. She made a mental note to tell Amber how much he had progressed in just a few short weeks.

In no time at all it was three o'clock, and Lexie flew around the room, tidying up and preparing a few things for the next day. Indie, was as always, a step ahead of Lexie. She knew most of what was going on, not all of course, but enough to know Lexie was anxious to be off.

'Go! Go!' encouraged Indie, shooing the kids and Lexie out the door. 'You've done most of the packing away. I'll finish the rest.'

'Goodbye, Mrs Greaves,' Arlo and Ruby chorused in sing-song voices as they took off after Lexie, who was already halfway across the playground.

While the kids put on their seatbelts, Lexie quickly checked her phone. There was a message from Amber. *Don't forget we've got swimming. I'll have the kid's bather's and stuff ready. Jeanie and Ray are here. I've made snacks so we can go straight there. xx*

Perfect, thought Lexie. *I'm glad everyone is on the same page.* Glancing at her watch, she began to relax. They had plenty of time to make it to the pool, especially as it was just going to be a quick stop to pick up Amber. She took a deep breath and made herself slow down. Surely all this drama was not good for one's health she reasoned, as she tried to get her blood pressure back to normal with a few slow breaths.

The traffic was kind. Amber was waiting with all the swimming gear and the snacks, and they made it to the pool with twenty minutes to spare. Plenty of time for the kids to get changed and even have a quick play in the pool before Elle started the lesson. And time for Lexie to leisurely get herself and Amber a coffee from the kiosk. Not for the first time, Lexie reflected on just how busy life with two kids was, even though Amber was the one doing most of the caregiving work; she was just an extra pair of hands, occasionally useful. While Amber headed to the changerooms with Arlo and Ruby, she could sit back and sip her coffee. By the time Amber returned with the school clothes stuffed into their back-packs, her coffee was only lukewarm. Amber had also changed into bathers, and stood, sipping her coffee with just a towel wrapped around her waist.

'I thought I might have a swim after their lesson, if you can keep an eye on them. Is that okay?'

'Yes! Knock yourself out! You should make the most of being here. I'm happy to watch them.' smiled Lexie.

'Well, I'll probably be hopeless, but I'll give it a go and it will be good to get a bit fitter.'

'You have to start somewhere. I'm not a brilliant swimmer myself,' confessed Lexie, 'but I've had to teach it at times, and maybe I can give you some pointers.'

'That sounds good. I figure if Arlo and Ruby are learning to swim, I have to at least keep up with them,' Amber laughed.

Elle worked her usual magic, and was full of praise for how far her little group had progressed in the last week. Only a quick dip was required in the baby pool this time, with most of the lesson being spent in the waist-deep water of the learners' pool. At one point, she introduced kick-boards and within minutes every student was happily holding on to a colourful foam board, kicking out towards the middle of the pool.

The final challenge was to wrap their arms around the boards, lie back and float. There were a few failed attempts, but eventually they all trusted in the buoyancy of their kickboards and managed to float on their own for a short period. Amber and Lexie weren't the only adults clapping and high-fiving their children, as they emerged dripping and excited from the pool. Floating was a major step. A quick drink and a snack, and Arlo and Ruby were back in the water.

Amber took this opportunity to slip quietly into the slow lane of the fifty-metre pool. The water was warm and inviting. She adjusted her goggles, and pushed off from the edge of the pool. Stifling a smile, she wanted to laugh out loud, as she slid through the water. What a great feeling! She felt so light, so buoyant, the water rolling smoothly over her body as she came back to the surface. Kicking energetically, she started to swim, her head at first above the water. She knew she wasn't quite ready to put her head into the water yet.

After about thirty metres she grabbed hold of the side of the pool, already puffed, and needing to guzzle in air. Regaining control, she pushed off again, determined to make it the next twenty metres to the end of the pool. Once more, she clung onto the side, her lungs bursting with the effort. Proud of herself for getting through fifty metres, she prepared to go again, back down the pool. Her breath semi-restored, this time she managed to swim three or four stokes with her head in the water, before raising her head, taking a breath and continuing.

She made it through another fifty, with a midway stop again. This was way beyond her expectations! As she rested at the end of the pool, Lexie came over and made a couple of suggestions, before returning to her lifeguard duties with Arlo and Ruby. Lexie's advice was helpful, and Amber tried turning her head to the side every two strokes, to take a breath. Amber was surprised how much easier this was, although she could feel herself tiring. She had to stop twice on the third fifty. By the time she pushed off for her final lap, Amber was really proud of herself. She hadn't imagined she would last this long.

Stopping for the last time down the final fifty, Amber had just pushed off, determined to make it to the end of the pool, when she saw him. Marco! Just standing there! On the far side of the pool! Watching her!

Her goggles were a bit fogged, and she had water running down her face, but she was sure it was him. Floundering to a stop in the deep water, and panicking, she inhaled too quickly, choking immediately on a mouthful of water. Kicking hard, and coughing uncontrollably, she tried to stay afloat, while she looked again for him. But he was already moving away. By the time she reached the safety of the edge, tearing off her goggles to see better, he was gone.

Still coughing, Amber searched desperately for sight of him. Knowing Arlo and Ruby were somewhere in the pool, and in possible danger, she thrust herself up and out of the water in one swift movement. Running towards the learners' pool, her heart beating wildly in her chest, she searched frantically for Arlo and Ruby. A young pool attendant tried to caution her for running, but she shrugged off the teenage part-timer, as she continued to pace up and down.

Spotting Amber looking like a crazy woman, Lexie went quickly over to her.

'Where are they? Where are my babies?' she begged Lexie, out of her mind with fear.

'Look! They're over there, near the waterslide. They're fine. Everything's okay. What's the matter Amber? What's happened?' Amber was attracting attention and several curious looks. Lexie tried to calm her down, as she pointed over to where Arlo and Ruby were happily chasing some other kids around the pool. Spotting them herself, Amber slumped forward with relief, hands on her knees for support, suddenly weak, as the adrenaline that had been pumping drained away.

'He's here! Marco! He was here! I saw him, just then!' she stammered, looking around wild-eyed, desperately scanning the cavernous recesses of the pool complex. 'We should get them out! We should get home! He saw me! He was watching me swim!'

'Fuck!' swore Lexie quietly. 'Are you sure? I mean there are so many people here,' raising her hands in query as she looked around.

'I'm sure. I spotted his silhouette. Just a flash, but I'd know that body anywhere! That made me look closer, and when I stopped, he looked right at me. He knew I'd seen him, but then I started panicking and choking, and by the time I looked over again, he was gone.'

'Okay,' said Lexie decisively. 'I'll get the kids out, and you get yourself sorted. We'll pack up and then... I don't know!

Maybe we can walk out with a couple of families to the car? We'll wait till it looks safe.'

Amber took less than a minute to put her clothes on over her soggy bathers, plus shoes. *In case I have to run*, she thought. She made Arlo and Ruby put on their school shoes as well. Arlo complained of course, because he couldn't see why they were getting dressed over wet bathers, when the last time they just walked out wearing their towels and thongs. Ruby didn't fuss. She could see both Amber and Lexie were edgy and she had learned long ago that sometimes she needed just to do what Amber wanted.

Trusting Amber and wanting to please her mum, she gave Arlo a push and told him to shut up. Amber hushed them both, and it was a very subdued group that departed the pool area. Once in the foyer, Amber scooted ahead to see if there was any sign of Marco. There wasn't. She gave Lexie a thumbs up. Just then, a dozen or so gym-clad participants fresh from a Pilates class, emerged from a side room, chatting as they walked towards the exit. This was their chance. Mingling smoothly with the group, they left. Relying on the safety of numbers, Lexie held Ruby's hand, while Amber had a vice-like grip on Arlo's.

Once in the car, Lexie didn't hesitate. She locked the doors and was reversing before the kids even had their seatbelts fastened. The return journey was silent. By now, Arlo was no longer complaining. He knew something was wrong, and from his booster seat in the rear, he stared anxiously at the back of Amber and Lexie's heads for clues. The plan was for Ray to meet them at Lexie's house so he could take Radar in his car. Amber rang ahead while Lexie was driving, to make sure he was there. Ray greeted them with a worried look, and a question ready on his lips, but he was quickly shut down by Amber. With a cheeriness she didn't feel, and a warning glance towards Arlo and Ruby, who were all ears, she over-rode his question.

'Hi Ray! We've had such a great swim. But we need to move quickly if we're going to pack up our stuff. So! Come on guys! Shake a leg. I'll get your school clothes ready, but you need to get your PJs and whatever toys you want to take. We don't want to keep Ray waiting.'

It took less than ten minutes to gather changes of clothes, toothbrushes, and some things from the fridge. Lexie was careful locking up. She didn't want to make it easy for any unwelcome visitors, especially since they had decided not to leave Radar at home. The house would be more vulnerable, but they also were reluctant to put Radar in danger. Lexie drove ahead, Ray following behind with the dog.

It wasn't until later that night, when the kids were in bed, that Amber gave Jeanie and Ray a full debrief on what had happened at the pool. Ray suggested she might have made a mistake, because it happened so quickly, but Amber would have none of it. She was adamant she had seen Marco, even though neither Arlo nor Ruby had seen him. Despite a long discussion, during which they rehashed the situation over and over again, no-one came to any satisfactory conclusion. Was Marco serious with his threats? Or was he just wanting to frighten them? Eventually the adults went to bed, hoping that Radar, on guard in the back yard, would alert them if Marco came creeping around.

Next morning, in the light of day, their fears were allayed for the time being and everyone appeared more at ease. Lexie had to leave earlier than usual, so as to get herself, Ruby and Arlo to school on time. Jeanie was also up early for her Wednesday ladies' golf game. With no-one else there, Ray took Amber for a long drive around the streets near where she was due to take her licence test in a couple of days. Amber executed hill starts and parallel parks with aplomb. She spotted pedestrian crossings, slowed down in fifty-kilometre zones, and indicated perfectly as she entered and exited roundabouts. Ray was as confident as he could be that she was ready. Amber tried not to get her hopes up, but she did appreciate the distraction preparing for the test gave her. Far better that, than the sight of Marco watching her from across the pool, playing on an endless reel inside her head.

CHAPTER 22

'Good luck, Mum,' called Arlo for the tenth time, before he ran out to the car. Lexie lifted her bag containing files and her laptop, into the front seat. They were already late leaving for school, and she was worried the traffic would be heavy. It was a longer drive to school from her parents' house, but worth it because everyone had felt much safer.

There had been no further sign of Marco. Kelly had reported the party invitation to the police, and her fears that it was related to domestic violence. They were going to investigate it further. Also, after talking about it to Jeanie and Ray, Amber had decided to go to the police herself. Understandably, she wanted to get her driving test out of the way, but after that, she vowed to go to the police with Ray, 'First thing tomorrow morning.'

Everyone was relieved she had finally made the decision to report Marco. With fingers crossed that she would pass the driving test, they planned to have the party she had promised Ruby. A celebration would do them all good, and they certainly could do with the distraction after the last few days. Ray had engaged a security firm to put in an alarm at Lexie's house, which they would activate at night, and cameras were to be installed front and back next week. That, plus Radar, would give them a greater sense of safety. With all that in place, the plan was for Lexie and Amber, and the children to return home that evening.

Amber was going to apply for a restraining order on Marco, to keep him away from her, Arlo, or Ruby. This was a huge step forward for Amber, and while Lexie hadn't wanted to push Amber into going to the police, she knew this would be the only way that their dysfunctional lives would return to some semblance of normality. She was already looking forward to getting back to her own bed, and her home. The long commute to school from her parents' place was an added stress she didn't need.

Amber waved them off, and as was her new habit, looked carefully up and down the street. Seeing Marco at the pool had really unnerved her. He clearly hadn't given up. Amber wasn't exactly sure what it was he wanted, but she had every reason to suspect that, at the very least, he wanted to hurt her somehow. Hiding her head in the sand about his controlling behaviour was a dangerous thing. Amber knew, when she finally left, thwarting his power and daring to stand up to him, that he wouldn't let her go without a fight. When she didn't hear from him for a while, she hoped he had given up; but that was just foolishness.

It frightened her now, even more, that he had taken his time, before allowing himself to be seen. How long had he been plotting this? When she'd blocked him on her phone, she had no idea what he was thinking, but she'd assumed correctly that a leopard doesn't change his spots, as the old saying goes. Even through the fog of her goggles, and the distance of eight swimming lanes, she couldn't mistake his sneer, nor the aggressive set of his shoulders as he stared at her, his face black with fury. She shivered at the memory, terrified to think what evil he might be capable of.

Having already had so much help from Lexie and her family, Amber didn't want to expose them to any danger; the possibility that Marco could harm them, was a big influence on her decision to finally take action. Reluctant as she was to subject herself to scrutiny, she had to trust that they were right, when they assured her going to the police and asking for a VRO, wouldn't put her at risk of losing her children. She couldn't bear that, after fighting so hard to keep them all these years.

One last glance up the street before she shut the front door. All clear. It was time to get ready for this driving test. The closest Department of Transport office wasn't far, but Ray wanted to arrive early, so she didn't feel rushed, and could prepare mentally. Amber dressed demurely, in a knee length denim skirt and white shirt. She wore the flat slip-on shoes she was used to driving in. Not only did she want to avoid any unexpected wardrobe malfunctions, but she wanted to look as mature as she could.

Ray had washed the car and vacuumed the inside, and it shone in the sun, as good as a showroom vehicle. If there were credit points for the cleanliness of the car, Ray would have scooped them all. At the Department of Transport, they sat in the waiting area with several other prospective candidates, all wearing anxious expressions, like guilty students outside the principal's office. At ten forty-five, and right on time, a formidable looking, tall, moustachioed man appeared, wearing the traffic authority uniform and bearing a clipboard. Amber said a silent prayer that he wouldn't be her assessor.

'Amber Evans!' he called imperiously, in a thick, heavy accent. Amber's heart sank. This guy was definitely ready to fail her at the slightest mistake. Sitting close beside her, Ray noticed the slight drop of her shoulders, as she stood up.

'That's me,' she said timidly, raising her arm.

The assessor jerked his head towards the exit, indicating that Amber should follow. Ray moved quickly to reassure her. Putting an arm around her, he gave her an encouraging squeeze, saying,

'He might look tough, but he can't fail everyone, or he wouldn't have a job. You'll be fine. You've got this!'

Amber nodded. She still felt nervous, but this driving test was happening right now, and she needed to give it her best shot. Straightening her shoulders, she followed him outside where they stopped on the footpath. After brief introductions and a quick perusal of Amber's paperwork, her assessor, who had introduced himself as Herman, pronounced they were ready to begin. Amber unlocked the passenger door of Ray's car, allowing Herman to get in first. Ray gave her a thumbs-up and a big smile as she walked around to the driver's side. Sending a last look of terror towards Ray, she composed her face, then slipped behind the wheel. Ray said a few rusty prayers, watching intently as Amber started the engine, put on the blinker, looking expertly in the rear-view mirror before she accelerated slowly off.

Noting the time on his watch, Ray walked to a nearby café and ordered a takeaway coffee. After ten minutes he was back outside the Transport Office, sipping his long black, and checking the time. From harsh experience he knew the longer she lasted, the better her chances were of passing. He remembered only too well that Lexie had failed her first test, within two blocks of the Transport Office, when she hadn't come to a complete stop at a stop sign. Immediate fail! Lexi hadn't been a bad driver, but she was too nervous. There had been no time to get a coffee that day because she was back in less than five minutes.

Amber was a very competent driver though, and she deserved her licence. Today he was more confident, but you never knew what could go wrong. Time ticked by. Ray's coffee was long finished, and Amber had been gone for thirty minutes before Ray spotted his car turning left into the street where he waiting, drive slowly towards him, and come to a stop. He could see Herman talking to Amber and pointing out some things on his paperwork, while Amber nodded. They were both smiling as they got out of the car, and Herman waited for Amber to walk around before shaking her hand.

Catching sight of Ray and assuming he was Amber's grandfather, he said, 'Your granddaughter did very well. I was most impressed.'

Ray was happy to go along with the charade, thanking Herman, before he disappeared inside to collect his next victim.

'Thanks Grandad,' said Amber with a big grin. Then in answer to Ray's hands open in query, she high fived him saying, 'Yes! I passed!'

Over the moon with jubilation, and still laughing at the grandad joke, Amber and Ray went back into the building. This time they went over to the counter labelled, New Licences, completed the required forms and collected the two red probationary P Plates Amber would need to display for the first twelve months of driving. Ray expected Amber would want to drive home, but even though she could now drive officially, she was so mentally drained by the driving test, that she was happy to be a passenger and let the world slide by. Holding her brand-new driver's licence in her hands, she looked at it several times, basking in her own success, while Ray drove home. She was proud of herself. Achieving anything in her life was rare and she knew she owed it all to Ray.

'I don't know how I can ever repay you for helping me get my licence, Ray. Even though I knew I could drive. I didn't think I'd get ever the chance.'

'Listen, girlie. Don't worry about thanking me. I've thoroughly enjoyed the lessons, and even if Lexie and Andy don't want to hear it, you've been by far my easiest pupil.' Looking at Amber, he said meaningfully, 'The next thing is, to get you a car.'

Amber nodded, but didn't reply. Getting a car was a dream, but realistically, a long way down her list of priorities. First, she needed a job. She had recovered well from her injuries and was keen to be independent, not having to rely on government assistance. At almost twenty-three, she'd never had a proper job! Amber yearned to go off to work every day, like other people her age. She wanted to feel this good all the time.

She was still young enough to make something of herself, be someone Ruby and Arlo could be proud of. Maybe this was the start of a new chapter in her life. She felt a flutter of excitement. She vowed that if she got a job, whoever employed her would never regret it. She would prove she could work hard, save some money, and give Arlo and Ruby all the things she never had.

For the hundredth time, Amber thanked her lucky stars that Lexie had walked past her at Bunnings all those weeks ago. Through everything, Lexie hadn't wavered, and Ray and Jeanie had been incredible too. Even so, Amber's past experiences nagged at her. She still half expected it all to come crashing down one day, and she wanted to be prepared, in case she had to cope on her own again. Glancing once more at the paper in her hands, Amber put aside her plans for the future. Right now, she was going enjoy the moment and celebrate a red-letter day with these wonderful people.

Jeanie came rushing out of the house when they pulled up, full of questions and congratulations. Ray told her the story of Herman, who had terrified them both with his stiff manner, and also being called Amber's grandad! Jeanie loved that, chortling with laughter.

'I wouldn't be too concerned, Ray. It's probably not a reflection on you looking old. It's more to do with Amber looking barely seventeen!' she said, which went some way towards mollifying Ray's vanity.

After a late lunch, Amber packed their bags and helped Jeanie stack the party supplies, in Ray's car. Ruby was going to get the party she had been promised. The plan was for Ray and Amber to go ahead, and Jeanie would finish icing the chocolate cake that was still cooling, and come over a bit later with Radar. Amber was keen to get there, so she could share the good news with everyone when they arrived home from school. This time she did feel like driving, and the traffic was kind so they were back at Lexie's with time to spare. Amber parked carefully in the driveway, inching forward so the other cars could fit behind when they arrived. She was about to get the bags, when she noticed Ray stop, one leg out of the car, his face stricken. Her eyes followed his gaze, seeing clearly what had stopped him in his tracks. Spray painted, in large red letters, over the front of the house was, *Leso Sluts*.

Amber dropped the bags and ran, scaling the front steps three at a time to get to the writing, where she rubbed futilely at the red letters, giving up when she realised the paint was already dry.

'Has to be Marco!' said Ray angrily as he walked closer to the house. 'He's not exactly a wordsmith, is he?'

Amber remained speechless, tears of frustration and anger

threatening. Ray was matter-of-fact. There was no time to waste.

'Okay. Let's get this stuff inside first, and we'll work out how to deal with this,' he pronounced with authority, conscious of the need to clean it up before Lexie got home with Ruby and Arlo.

They moved swiftly, stashing groceries on the kitchen bench and bags indiscriminately into the bedrooms. A search of the laundry cupboards revealed Gumption cleaner, sugar soap, and an opened bottle of graffiti cleaner that Lexie might have needed sometime at school. Armed with these, plus buckets of soapy water, brushes and cleaning rags, they rushed back outside. Before they started to clean, Amber took a few photos, from several angles. This would be more evidence for the police tomorrow.

Amber had immediate success with the parts of letters that had been painted over the front windows. They came off easily with the sugar soap and a bit of scraping with the hard plastic handle of the scrubbing brush. The graffiti cleaner was also fairly successful. It certainly took out the red colour, smudging it enough so the words were difficult to read, but nevertheless leaving a visible residue on the grey walls of the house.

'We're going to need more of this graffiti stuff. It's working pretty well, and if we hurry the kids straight around the back, they probably won't even notice. We can give it a quick lick of paint tomorrow,' Ray said, taking a brief rest from scrubbing.

'And if I put up a couple of balloons, that will help as well,' Amber said, standing back to survey their efforts. The word *slut* was still visible on the wall near the front door. Amber was tempted. She wanted it all gone. Bunnings was so close.

'They won't be home for another forty minutes at the earliest. Do you think you could do a quick run to Bunnings for paint? Or I could go? What do you think?'

'Yeah. We've got time,' said Ray decisively. 'I'll go. I could be back in twenty minutes and we'll have this finished. They won't know this was ever here. You keep working on the window, and do what you can with what's left of the sugar soap. I'll be back as soon as I can.'

Checking quickly in his jeans for his wallet, Ray jumped in the car and took off. Amber continued scrubbing, concentrating intently on removing the paint with sugar soap and scraping away what she could with the plastic brush. She barely looked up.

There was no way the kids were going to come home to this confronting sight if she could help it. Totally engrossed in her task, she didn't even consider the fact that she was alone. Nor did she turn her head, when she heard the familiar sound of a ute pulling up, assuming it was Josh, from next door. Suddenly it occurred to her that the familiar car sound didn't belong to Josh. It was Marco's ute she'd heard! Amber froze in terror. All too late, she sensed Marco standing behind her. She turned around slowly, fear streaming through her veins.

'Hi babe. I've missed you,' Marco taunted, leering as he stepped forward.

Amber tried to run, but she was nowhere quick enough. In seconds he had her trapped in a tight bear hug, his grip like steel, his breath warm on her skin, as he snarled softly into her ear.

'Now, just relax babe. This doesn't have to get ugly. You're going to come home with me where you belong. You know this has just been a little… holiday… but now it's time to come home. You know you want to.'

'Marco! Please!'

Gripping her shoulders, his fingers digging painfully into

her back, Marco held her at arm's length. If anyone was casually watching from the street, they would not have guessed this was anything more than a couple having a conversation, or perhaps a serious chat.

'Marco please!' he mimicked in a whining voice. 'See! You're already begging me to get you out of here.' Amber opened her mouth to scream, but the sound was cut off when he clamped a heavy, meaty hand over her mouth and nose. His voice became menacing, warning her not to speak or react.

'This is what's going to happen. First, give me your phone.'

Amber glanced down to where it was on the windowsill. Grabbing it, Marco tossed it into the garden.

'Now, you and I are going to get in my car. You don't want to make a fuss because I've been watching you for a long time. I know every move you make and I swear I will get to those kids, as easy as buttering toast. They can stay here with your girlfriend. She can look after them for you for a bit, and then we'll see if you deserve to see them. It depends entirely on your attitude now, babe.'

Gripping her left arm, his other hand squeezing the back of her neck and forcing her forward, he propelled her down the front steps of the porch, towards his ute. Amber stumbled as she tried to resist, but the resolve had gone out of her. Even though the rational part of her brain told her he couldn't get away with this, she was still processing his threat to come after Ruby and Arlo. As he pushed her into the car, she begged him to forgive her.

'I'm so sorry Marco! Please. Can't we work something out?'

Marco's reaction to this plea was to slap the side of her head, a sharp practised move she was only too familiar with. Her panic escalated. Sobbing and shaking, she looked desperately for someone who could help. Josh was often around at this time of day; but he was nowhere in sight. The street was empty. Her thoughts racing, Amber went quickly through the possibilities. Ray was probably only a few minutes away. Jeanie would be there soon. She could try to delay Marco. But Lexie could also arrive home any minute with Arlo and Ruby. She didn't want to risk Marco being anywhere near her babies.

'Don't even think about fucking moving!' Marco threatened, locking the car for the few seconds it took him to walk around to the driver's side. Unlocking it again, he got in swiftly, immediately thrusting his arm against her neck, suffocating her and pinning her to her seat. His eyes held hers, a gleam of madness in them. Then he relocked the car, before starting it. Amber felt physically sick. She knew that look. She would pay a heavy price for leaving him.

'Seatbelt, Amber!' he said sneered, 'We don't want the cops to pull us over, do we?'

With shaking hands, Amber reached for the seatbelt, the sound of it clicking into place, an ominous full stop to the past few minutes. His face was set in a scowl. She sensed the waves of hatred pouring from him, fuelling her rising fear. She had been terrified of him for good reason. He'd never loved her, but he would also never forgive her for rejecting him. This was all about him, his ego. With a jerk, he released the handbrake, and throwing the car into reverse, swung out of the driveway before skidding off down the street. Amber thought she saw a glimpse of Josh's work ute turn into the street behind them. Too late.

Marco drove recklessly. Fearlessly. He knew his way, taking corners sharply and not slowing at intersections, avoiding the tricky no-through roads in the area. Amber could tell this was not the first time he'd driven these streets. He'd obviously stalked her many times before he made his move. Reaching

Albany Highway, he swerved into the right-hand lane, flicking on his blinker at the last moment. The lights had only just changed to red. They waited in silence, the rhythmic tick of the blinker the only sound, apart from Amber's stifled whimpers. She looked straight ahead, hardly daring to breathe. She wanted desperately to check behind, but she was too afraid. Perhaps Josh had seen Marco speed off and had followed? That was the best she could hope for. At one point, Marco grabbed her hand and thrust it between his legs. He was hard. Repulsed Amber quickly drew her hand away.

'See what effect you have on me babe?' he chuckled mirthlessly. 'We're going to have to do something about that very soon.'

Amber shrunk further back into her seat, as far away as she could from him, twisting her head away. When the light turned green, Marco veered out of his lane, the car rocking slightly as he pulled overly fast onto Albany Highway. She expected him to turn off at the next exit, which led towards his house and the school, but he continued down the highway heading south, driving at the edge of the speed limit, and passing other cars at every opportunity.

'Where are we going?' she finally dared to ask.

Marco smiled a self-satisfied smirk, taking his time to reply.

'You'll see. I thought it might be best if you had a bit of peace and quiet for a while. A place where we can have some *quality time* without anyone interfering. I think you'll appreciate it.'

Amber's terror increased and a feeling of dread came over her. If he took her to some remote spot, no-one would ever find her. She suddenly realised Marco was not just being vindictive. He wanted more than payback for a lover scorned. He was acting crazily. Perhaps he was mad! Frightened into action, she tried another move. Pushing away her revulsion, she turned to him, suggestively placing her hand on his leg, caressing him. In a honey-sweet voice she pleaded,

'No Marco! Take me back to your place. I can look after you again there. I can make you happy there; we were happy. Remember? I was stupid to leave. I know that. Let's just go home together.'

Amber tried to be convincing. She continued in a baby voice, making wild promises, trying to flatter him into changing his mind. Marco placed his hand briefly over hers, giving it a squeeze. She felt a flicker of hope, until he increased the pressure, crushing her hand painfully before returning both hands to the steering wheel. Twenty minutes later he slowed marginally, indicated left, and turned onto an outer suburban road.

Once off the highway, Marco sped up again, racing along empty streets, and housing that grew increasingly sparse. Eventually his wild dash through the outskirts of Perth came to a grudging halt, as he came up behind a truck, heavily laden with a container, forcing him to slow down to fifty kilometres an hour. Impatient, he kept sliding out right, checking for a clear run, his foot constantly on and off the accelerator and the brake; each time he was thwarted by traffic coming in the opposite direction. Amber held her breath. Surely, he wasn't going to try and pass here?

Just then he saw his chance, a clear path straight ahead. Swerving out abruptly he accelerated into the right-hand lane. He was halfway along past the truck, when a four-wheel drive suddenly appeared out of a side street ahead, making a left hand turn straight into their path. There was no time to think. Marco could brake and hope he didn't hit the car head-on, or he could accelerate and trust he'd make it past the truck without hitting the car. He chose to accelerate.

Time stood still.

Everything happened in slow-motion.

Marco's ute surged forward as he accelerated.

Reduced to a blur, the gap between the approaching car and the front of the truck diminished rapidly. Amber was close enough to see the startled look on the driver's face in front as he presumably, hit the brakes. Almost on one wheel, Marco's car flew past the truck's front right fender. Miraculously, he swerved back to the left-hand side of the road, missing the other car, by a fraction. The truckdriver must have also hit the brakes, giving Marco precious space.

Amber could see a clear road ahead. They were almost past the truck and safe, when Amber felt the ute hit something, and shudder. At the very last second, the ute's tail bar had caught the edge of the truck's massive front bull bar. Designed to be rigid, the bull bar didn't give an inch. Marco's luck ran out. The ute absorbed all the force of the heavily loaded truck. Spiralling instantly out of control, in seconds they were airborne, rolling several times. Sparks flew! The noise as the ute's cab struck the bitumen road again and again, was like a bomb exploding. The truck driver struggled to stop, his load jack-knifing across the road. Marco's ute finished on its roof, skidding across the road, before finally coming to rest; the driver's side crushed against an unforgiving brick wall.

Amber blacked out when the car went into its second roll. She lay unconscious, trapped in her seatbelt, the engine still turning. Marco lay beside her, his arm pressed against her throat, his head twisted at an unnatural angle. His open eyes stared lifelessly at Amber. Marco was dead.

CHAPTER 23

Ray arrived back at Lexie's exactly twenty-five minutes after he had left. Calling out to Amber that he was back, he went straight to the shed to collect some newspaper and paint gear, so he could make a quick start. He wasn't concerned that Amber wasn't out the front. He assumed she was doing something inside the house. Ray's mind was firmly on the job at hand, removing all evidence of Marco's unsavoury message. He was keen that none of the family should see it; he wanted them to have a happy evening, celebrating Amber's success. Ruby, Arlo and Amber had had few chances to celebrate over the years, and Ray was determined that nothing would spoil it. He would explain the sudden paint job to Lexie later.

Working quickly, he had managed to cover the remains of the message, just as Lexie's car appeared in the driveway, Jeanie following closely behind. Chaos ensued as Radar, freshly escaped from the confines of Jeanie's car, took off across the lawn to Arlo and Ruby and began barking excitedly, turning circles and jumping about in front of them. Lexie unloaded school bags, simultaneously calling out to Radar to 'SIT!' and asking Ray what he was doing painting the house. Over all this, Jeanie called out for help with all the shopping bags. No-one missed Amber for several minutes, until Lexie, giving up on getting anyone's attention, left them all to it and went inside to find her.

Lexie sensed it immediately. Something was off. For a start, Amber always met the kids at the front door, keen to find out about their day. Besides that, the house was eerily quiet, an emptiness in the air. Dumping all the bags in the kitchen, she hurriedly searched every room. There was no sign of Amber. She stepped outside. The toilet door was ajar and she wasn't there. The backyard was deserted, until Ruby chased Radar around the side of the house and began throwing his ball for him. Lexie's fear was escalating. Where the hell was Amber? Arlo had joined Ruby with Radar, and while they were playing, she raced back through the house to Ray who was coming in through the front door, dutifully laden with even more supermarket bags.

'Dad! Where's Amber?' Lexie hissed at him, so the kids didn't hear.

Ray froze. His face turned white. 'She's here, isn't she? I didn't check when I got back. I thought she was here.' Frantically, he also started checking rooms.

'What do you mean, when you got back? Where did you go?' demanded Lexie confused and agitated.

'Oh love! I just did a quick trip to Bunnings for paint. I was gone barely twenty minutes. I didn't check when I got back. I just thought she was busy inside. You know how she's always doing little chores,' Ray remonstrated, looking absolutely devastated.

'But why did you go to Bunnings? What was so important that you left her here on her own?' quizzed Lexie.

'Left her on her own? Where is Amber?' demanded Jeanie, carefully carrying the celebration cake she'd been working on all afternoon, into the kitchen, and catching the end of the conversation.

Ray quickly filled them both in on the graffiti across the front of the house, and how they didn't want the kids to see it. Lexie was shocked at this new development. Things really were getting out of hand. She could understand why Ray had tried to paint over it. Ruby would definitely have been able to read it. However, they still had no idea where Amber had gone.

'Do we assume the worst?' asked Jeanie fearfully. 'Has she just gone for a walk, which would be totally out of character, or has that brute got her?'

Lexie rang Amber's phone, while Jeanie began searching the kitchen benches, lifting up anything placed there in case there was a note underneath. Ray followed the ringing sound outside, discovering it at last in a garden bed. Suddenly, his legs gave way and he had to sit down on the front steps, feeling every bit his sixty-eight years. This, on top of Marco's painted message, had really shaken him.

'Do you want me to ask the neighbours if they saw anything? Do you think we should ring the police?' he asked, his voice breaking.

Lexie took one look at his hangdog expression, and quickly decided she would ask the neighbours herself. Ruby and Arlo would need to be distracted, but Jeanie was already a step ahead of her with after-school snacks in hand. Spotting Josh walking towards his ute, Lexie waved and called out to him. Hopefully he knew something.

He smiled and waved back, waiting as Lexie jogged across to where he was standing. 'Josh!' she started breathlessly, 'have you seen Amber? She's disappeared!'

'No, I haven't seen her,' he replied slowly, 'but when I got here, can't have been more than twenty minutes ago, I did see a dark blue Hilux ute leaving your place. It took off like a cracker, swerving all over the road. Why?'

'Did you see anything else?' she asked anxiously.

'No, nothing. I really only noticed it because it was going so fast, way too fast for around here. And also, because it didn't look like any of the cars I'd ever seen at your place before.'

'Thanks Josh. I need to contact the police. I think Amber's ex has got her, and he's a scary guy.'

Lexie yelled the last bit over her shoulder as she raced back to the house, calling out to Ray and Jeanie.

'Mum! Dad! We have to call the police! Josh saw Marco's blue ute here! Maybe twenty minutes ago. He sped off down the street! I bet he's got her! She'd never go anywhere with him willingly, I'm sure. We have to report it.'

Lexie went into action. Dialling triple zero, she paced distractedly from the kitchen to the loungeroom, as she went through the system until she got through. Speaking as calmly and clearly as she could, she reported Amber was missing. Then she gave Marco's name and the make, model and colour of the car. They promised to send someone around as soon as possible. However, Lexie's hopes for a fast resolution were quickly dashed, when the policewoman, a Constable Todd, began asking several key questions that soon established this was not regarded as an emergency.

'I'm sure we can look into this but I need some further information first if that's okay.'

'Yes. Yes,' replied Lexie earnestly.

'Right. How long has your friend Amber been estranged from her partner?'

'About five weeks.'

'Has there been any contact from him before this?' the policewoman quizzed.

'No. I don't think so other than messages when she first left. She had to block him. He was being abusive.' Lexie explained.

'Would there be a possibility that he could have contacted her to discuss their relationship?' The police woman's question was reasonable but Lexie rolled her eyes in frustration. She replied angrily,

'No! She hated him! She was afraid of him. He bashed her up! She would never have gone with him willingly!'

'Just so I understand this. He used to physically assault her?'

'Yes. She was terrified of him,' Lexie replied earnestly, wondering why Constable Todd wasn't already raising the alarm.

'And did she ever report this to the police? Are there any hospital or medical records we can access?'

Lexie sighed as realisation dawned on her. 'No probably not. She was too scared of him and she worried he would hurt her children.'

'Are the children safe? Did she leave them alone?'

'No! Yes!' Lexie said quickly, hasty to reassure the Constable. 'The children are safe with me. They live here with me. She's a good mother. She would never just leave them without letting me know. And we've found her phone here! Who does that?'

'Okay, Lexie. We can send someone round, but it might be quicker if you go to your nearest police station, and make a statement. I have the details regarding the blue Hilux. It would be helpful if you could get a registration number as well for us. Also, maybe you could establish for certain that she hasn't reconciled with him. Perhaps check to see if she is at his house and if she is actually safe?'

Feeling stupid, but raging internally that the situation was being so lightly dismissed, Lexie could only agree and thank

Constable Todd for her help. Clicking off, she swore under her breath. Ray had followed her into the loungeroom, overhearing the last of the conversation. It was clear from Lexie's reaction that things hadn't gone well.

'They don't believe me, Dad! They want me to check if she is with Marco and that she actually might have reconciled with that creep! I just want to scream!'

'Okay settle down. Let's go for a drive. You and me. The kids are fine here with Jeanie and that way if Amber does turn up, there will be someone here. Let's establish if she's there or not, and then we can go to the police station and make a statement. You can't blame them not wanting to rush off and arrest him on your hearsay over the phone. Let's go through the process,' said Ray trying to calm Lexie down.

Lexie nodded. 'You're right, Dad.' Giving him a big hug, she said, 'Good common sense as always.'

Just then there was knock on the front door, and a discreet cough. While Ray went to tell Jeanie what was happening Lexi answered the door. Josh stood on the porch.

'Oh Josh! I'm sorry I was acting a bit crazy back there,' she said apologetically, as she pushed open the flywire door.

'No worries. You're upset, obviously. I was just wondering if there's anything I can do.'

'Thanks Josh. I'll let you know. Dad and I are going to drive over to Marco's house, Amber's ex-partner, and see if Amber is there. And then we'll go and make a statement if we still need to. The police want a bit more evidence before they get involved. I just got a bit carried away.'

'Maybe not. He took off driving like a madman, so I think you're right to be concerned for her. And she's such a sweet kid, and pretty vulnerable I imagine.' Josh paused, 'I'm happy to come with you and Ray. Just in case you need backup?'

Lexie started to say thanks, but no thanks, when Ray spoke over the top of her,

'I think that's a great idea, if you don't mind. I'm not sure what we're getting into. Hopefully, just a case of knocking on the door and asking for Amber, but you never know. Are you sure you've got the time to do this?'

'Yeah. No worries. I was just heading home, and I've got no plans. I'm happy to help,' said Josh, nodding at Ray.

Lexie quickly saw the commonsense in this. She was also relieved to have Josh as back-up, in case things went sour. Lexie got in the back of Ray's car while Josh, with his long legs, and at her insistence, took the front seat. On the way they filled Josh in on some of the events that had led to Amber and the kids living with Lexie. They also told him about Marco painting the house, and that Amber had actually intended to file a complaint against Marco to the police the next day.

'Maybe, if we pick her up now, she can make a statement tonight. Kill two birds with one stone,' observed Ray.

Lexie fell silent in the back, desperately concerned for Amber, and terrified about what Marco could be doing to her while they were on their way. A lot could happen in an hour. She worried if they just turn up knocking on the door, asking for Amber, things could get ugly. She doubted he would just let her go of her own free will, even with Josh there. As they got closer to where Marco lived, Ray slowed down while Lexie pointed out the house.

The driveway was clear. There was no sign of anyone at home.

Nevertheless, they all got out of the car. Ray knocked on the door, Josh beside him, and Lexie just behind Ray. They waited, knocking several times and calling out, but there wasn't a sound. Just to make sure, they went around the outside, peering in windows and checking doors, where they could. From what Lexie could see, everything was neat and tidy. There was no sign that Amber, or anyone else, was there.

'Oh well. We can rule out that she is here,' said Ray ruefully. 'This makes it even more of a mystery. Where on earth would he take her if he was trying to convince her to come back with him?'

Josh looked concerned. 'I know it's not my business, but I think you should get to the police station and make that statement. I saw the way he drove off. That was an angry driver at the wheel. He could be taking her anywhere. Do you know if you can get the car rego?'

'Yep. Let's do this,' said Lexie decisively. 'Do you mind coming with us as well, Josh? You can describe the Hilux. And hopefully, they can look it up on a data base. I mean, how many dark blue Hilux utes can there be?

Ray drove as fast as he dared, straight to the nearest police station, located conveniently about halfway between Lexie's and Marco's houses. Giving the statement didn't take as long as they thought, and this time Lexie felt that her concerns were being taken seriously. The two officers were very interested in the graffiti incident and the party invitation Lexie described. Unfortunately, there was no evidence linking Marco with the rubbish bin fiasco, other than a strong motive, and everyone's now well-grounded suspicions.

By the time they got home it was almost seven-thirty. Arlo and Ruby had eaten, showered and were in their pyjamas when they heard the car. Before Jeanie could stop them, they had run outside, fully expecting Amber. Their disappointment was obvious. Ruby ran back inside, curled herself into a ball beside the couch and sobbed. Arlo kept asking, 'Where's Mum?' over and over again, getting more and more agitated.

'Keep me updated if you can,' said Josh as he took his leave. 'And let me know if there's anything at all I can do. I'm a handy babysitter as well, if you need someone. I've had practice. Lots of nieces and nephews,' he offered as an explanation.

'Thanks Josh. You've already been a great help,' said Lexie, impulsively hugging him, giving him a squeeze of gratitude. 'I'll let you know if anything happens.'

Then, anxious to console Arlo, she raced up the steps, gathering Amber's precious little boy into her arms, cuddling him tightly, all the while making soothing noises to pacify him. This was going to be a long night if they didn't hear from Amber soon.

***

It was way past the children's normal bedtime, before they finally fell asleep. They were both distraught by Amber's disappearance, and took a long time to settle. Lexie gave up her bed to Jeanie and Ray, while she slept in Amber's bed. Or rather while she lay there all night, checking her phone and going through possible scenarios. Sometime in the early hours of the morning, she remembered to text the school, to say they would need to get a relief teacher for her class. There was no way she would make it to school today. As faint light began to creep around the edges of the blinds, she got up, dressed, and tip-toed to the kitchen to make a cup of tea. It was just before five.

The kettle had not long boiled, and Lexie was taking her first sips when she heard a knock on the door. Checking through the lounge window, she saw a police car parked out the front. Heart thudding in her chest, Lexie tentatively opened the door. She was realistic. Police arriving on your doorstep at this hour would rarely be bringing good news. Two young female police officers stood solemnly in front of her.

'Good morning,' said the taller one in a pleasant voice, a look of compassion in her eyes. 'First, I apologise about the early hour. I'm Constable Woods. This is Constable Wilson. We wish to speak to Lexie Hudson regarding her friend Amber Evans.'

'I'm Lexie Hudson.'

All niceties forgotten she blurted out, 'Has anything happened? Have you found her?'

'We have a person fitting her description, who was a passenger in a blue Hilux, similar to the one you mentioned in your statement,' Constable Woods said reassuringly. Then her demeanour changed as she continued, 'However, she has been in a serious car accident, and is currently in Fiona Stanley Hospital.'

Lexie gasped. Jeanie had also heard the discreet knock on the door, and coming up quietly behind Lexie, overheard everything. Shaken, she grabbed Lexie's arm for support.

'Oh my God! Is she alright?' Jeanie blurted out.

'Yes. She has some serious injuries, but she is in a stable condition. We need you to come to the hospital to confirm it is Amber,' explained the other policewoman. Pulling out her phone she referred to some notes.

'We have your statement and your description of Amber. Your statement also indicated that Amber probably had no identification on her, and was seen leaving this house in a blue Hilux. Based on this, we believe the patient from the accident is Amber, and we are anxious to confirm this.'

'Of course. I'll just get my jacket,' replied Lexie rushing back into the house.

Quickly Lexie checked with Jeanie. No words were needed. One look and a returning nod from her mother, and Lexie knew the kids would be fine while she was gone.

'And don't even think about taking them to school,' said Lexie, needlessly. 'They need to rest, and hopefully, if this is Amber, we can bring them in to see her.'

Lexi went with the two policewomen, making a crossed fingers sign to Jeanie as she left. The traffic flowed smoothly and it took very little time to get to the hospital. Lexie asked if the driver of the car was in the same hospital. Constable Woods expressed her commiserations that the driver hadn't survived; Lexie felt nothing. They parked close to the emergency entrance. Constable Woods got out first, and opened the door for Lexie. Lexie followed the policewomen, through the hospital lobby to the trauma area where Amber was being cared for. There was no need for them to ask if it was Amber. Lexie's reaction said it all.

Pushing past the two officers, she gasped as she saw Amber lying unconscious. It was almost too much for Lexie to take in. Amber had multiple cuts on her face and traces of blood streaked across her skin. Her neck and throat were splotched with deep red and purple bruises. A cannula was in her right arm, with an IV drip attached; her left arm was cradled in a support cast and lay limply across her chest, at an odd angle. Lexie called her name, but Amber's eyes remained closed. Taking Amber's right hand gently, she repeated her name, saying,

'It's Lexie, Amber. I'm here.' Tears welled in her eyes. Amber looked so vulnerable, so young. Carefully, she smoothed out her hair, which tumbled messily across the pillow.

A nurse came over to check the IV. Looking up at Lexie, she gave an encouraging nod.

'She's doing okay,' she reassured Lexie. 'I'm glad the police were able to locate the family.' She glanced at the two officers, who quietly excused themselves, having got what they came for.

Lexie ignored the reference to family. She was anxious to find out more. Understanding Lexie's angst, the nurse waved over a registrar, who was nearby doing her rounds. The young doctor came over quickly. She had been on-duty when Amber was brought in. She smiled, sympathetically, and introduced herself.

'I'm Doctor Edwards. As you probably know… Amber?' she paused to confirm the name. Lexie nodded. 'Amber's been in a high-impact car accident. She was unconscious when she was brought in, but did gain consciousness briefly. We were initially concerned she had significant blunt laryngeal trauma, as she presented with dyspnea, or rather, shortness of breath. She had obvious difficulty breathing, but that seems to have settled. Dr Neville, our trauma specialist, performed a flexible fibreoptic laryngoscopy, to evaluate her airway. He seems satisfied that the severe impact of the accident, while causing the bruising you can see starting to appear, hasn't seriously damaged her larynx, which is good news.'

Lexie nodded although she was having difficulty keeping up with the lingo. She could tell by the doctor's body language that everything was positive and that was all the information she needed.

'Dr Neville also ordered chest, and cervical spinal X Rays, as well as a CT scan. Amber had those done a couple of hours ago and the indication at the moment, is that the results are clear as far as any spinal injury is concerned. We're still waiting on the full report from the radiologist because it looks like she has a fracture on her upper arm. And definitely a dislocated shoulder, with possible ligament damage. We should know more when the report comes back.'

Lexie knew she had a stunned expression on her face. This was just so much to take in.

'Will she be alright?' she asked, anxiety evident in her voice.

'Dr Neville, will be able to tell you more when you see him, but its looking promising. She should make a good recovery. She's a lucky girl, though. We've given her something to keep her sedated for now, and to make sure she isn't in any pain. You know the driver didn't make it?' she commented quietly, moving away out of Amber's possible hearing. Lexi nodded. *The least of my concerns at the moment*, she thought. It took her a few seconds before she realised the doctor thought that Marco was either a good friend, or Amber's partner, and that the news of his death would be upsetting. This wasn't the time or place to go into it all, so Lexie simply said, 'Might be best if we don't even mention anything to her. I'm not sure how she will be affected.'

'Okay. I'll make a note of it. There are several forms to fill out, now we know who Amber is. I'm hoping you can help, unless there is someone else who is next of kin?'

'I'm probably the closest person at the moment. Amber lives with me. We house-share,' Lexie added hastily, as the nurse who appeared with the forms, hovered her pen over the 'partner' column.

'And she's estranged from her family,' Lexie added quietly.

Dr. Edwards left Lexie to complete the forms and continued on her rounds.

The paperwork took a while. Evie, the nurse who was caring for Amber, took Lexie through every aspect of Amber's general health, challenging her knowledge at times. They sat a distance away from where Amber lay, so Lexie quietly told some of Amber's story. She wanted this nurse to understand that Amber wasn't just another young woman who had been in a car accident with an ex-boyfriend. They were just finishing up when Dr Neville arrived with an orthopaedic surgeon at his side, who he introduced as 'the brilliant Professor Jim'. They had just reviewed the results of the Xray's and CT scans. Dr Neville repeated much of what Dr Edwards had told her, but the second time it made more sense to Lexie. Professor Jim took over to deliver the bad news.

The fracture to the proximal humerus, which was close to Amber's shoulder, was a displaced fracture and would need surgery to repair it. He wouldn't know the full extent of the damage until he operated, but it would require a plate and screws, at the very least. The shoulder was also dislocated as a result of the impact, and that would be carefully manipulated back into place under anaesthetic at the same time. It could be a long operation, he warned, but with appropriate care and physio, Amber should get full use of her arm back. His explanation was short and to the point. Within minutes Lexie was signing more medical permission forms, and Professor Jim was off to theatre to prepare for Amber.

Dr Neville continued examining Amber, gently prodding her larynx area, as orderlies arrived to take her to theatre. Lexie had just enough time to go over and give her a kiss and squeeze her hand, before she was wheeled away. She could already see the bruises deepening on Amber's throat. Dr Neville's concern showed on his face and he walked over to the computer nearby, and began tapping more information into it.

'Is everything alright?' Lexie asked nervously. She was feeling queasy, and longed to get out of the overheated emergency department, but she needed to know the whole prognosis. She sensed Dr Neville was holding something back. In the close atmosphere of the hospital environment, and after a sleepless night and no breakfast, she was desperate for fresh air, but she was dogged. Ignoring her nausea and light-headedness, she stood her ground, waiting for him to reply. He finished typing and turned to her almost apologetically,

'I am a bit concerned about the trauma to her larynx. It looks like a blunt force, as if the seatbelt caused it, or possibly even the arm of the driver may have contacted her throat during the impact. The laryngoscopy was clear, but these injuries can be complex and she may have voice damage as a result.'

Raising his eyebrows in a non-committal gesture, he finished with an unsatisfying, 'We'll have to wait and see.'

One thing at a time, thought Lexie, grabbing her bag and following him out of the room. While he turned right into the labyrinth of the hospital Lexie headed to the public bathroom, where, her stomach churning, she retched into the toilet bowl.

CHAPTER 24

Voices. Mostly unknown. Occasionally, Amber recognised one. Caring, kind voices. Speaking to her. Telling her things Then, a familiar voice. One she knew and trusted.

'Amber. Amber. It's me, Lexie. You can wake up now. You're safe. You're in hospital. I'm here. Amber. I'm here.'

Amber tried. Her eyelids felt heavy. It was so hard to open them. She was aware of a hand holding hers, gently squeezing and rubbing it. She thought she squeezed back, but she wasn't sure. Finally, her she managed to flicker her eyes. Just for a second, but long enough to see Lexie's face smiling at her. She tried again, several times, before they opened. By now, the nurse had nudged Lexie to the side and was speaking words of encouragement to Amber as she peered at her and fiddled with a screen above the bed. Amber opened her mouth to speak, but the effort brought instant pain to her throat. Oh! Her throat was so sore! She tried to swallow and that added to the pain.

'Hush! Don't try to speak, Amber,' instructed the nurse. 'Your larynx has been quite badly bruised and you need to rest it. Do you understand? Just for a little while.' Amber nodded. Groggy and confused, she searched for Lexie. What was happening?

'It's okay, Amber,' soothed Lexie, quickly moving to her side, as the nurse completed her observations and returned to monitor the equipment. 'You've been in a car accident. Do you remember that?'

Amber frowned. A car accident? She tried to concentrate. Then from the edges of her mind came a flash-back of a car becoming airborne, rolling and skidding. A car? Whose car? Then suddenly the memory hit her and her eyes opened wide in terror. There was no mistaking the moment she recalled the accident. Lexie was quick to continue.

'Yes. Do you remember being in Marco's car? It was a very serious crash. You've got a few injuries, but you're going to get better. You're going to be okay.'

Amber could only blink and nod, as Lexie briefly explained the events of the last two days. It was a lot to take in. She discovered she had a dislocated shoulder, and a broken arm. Glancing down, she noted the plaster and the sling. Lexie talked about tests and an operation she'd had. She couldn't believe all this had gone on, while she'd been asleep. No. Not asleep. Lexie was saying she'd had concussion and had lost consciousness. The doctors had put her into an induced coma while they examined the extent of her injuries. They had been very concerned about her larynx, but the prognosis was looking good, with fairly minor damage. *It doesn't feel minor*, thought Amber, as she became gradually more lucid. Her throat certainly felt bruised and it hurt, even to breathe.

Suddenly it dawned on her. Where were the kids? Where were Ruby and Arlo? She tried to look around but the quick movement of her head made the room spin, and nausea rise. Lexie could read the panic in Amber's eyes and rushed to reassure her.

'Don't worry about Ruby and Arlo. They're with Jeanie and

Ray, and they're happy and safe. They know you've been in a car accident. And they know you're going to be okay. Jeanie will bring them up for a visit as soon as you feel up to it. You just need to rest up and get your strength back. Everyone is very relieved to know you are safe.'

Amber was relieved. She knew the kids adored Jeanie and Ray and that they would be safe with them. That's all that mattered. She had never felt this level of complete and utter tiredness before in her life. At the moment she couldn't imagine being able to sit up, let alone look after the kids.

'You even made the papers! No-one knew who the mystery woman was in the car accident.'

Lexie gave an apologetic laugh. 'Also, I know it's the last thing that you would want, but somehow, they got hold of your name and published it in the follow-up story today. It's only a small paragraph in the West, on page five, so with a bit of luck, no-one will notice anyway.'

Amber nodded, accidentally moving her shoulder in the process, then grimacing, as she felt a sharp, hot thrust of pain. She could feel herself getting drowsy. She wanted to go back to sleep. But she had to know the answer. Making eye contact with Lexie, she mouthed one word. 'Marco?'

Lexie held her hand and softly replied, 'He didn't make it Amber. He's dead.'

Closing her eyes, Amber began to drift off. She hadn't imagined it; she just needed it to be confirmed. Deep down she already knew. She remembered floating in and out of consciousness while she was trapped in the car. Flashes of sirens and urgent voices. Feeling Marco's arm against her neck, pinning her down. His head rolled to one side. Seeing his eyes. Knowing they were lifeless. She wanted to forget that moment.

Pushing the memory down, she willed it away, as her body gave in and she sank into her first natural sleep in days.

284

CHAPTER 25

Amber was ecstatic as she left hospital a couple of weeks later. She couldn't wait to get back to Lexie's which, she realised with some trepidation, she had begun to think of as home. Her shoulder still ached, especially if she moved it too quickly, but she was on a much lighter dose of medication, and the occasional stab of pain was a small price to pay for being able to think clearly. The headaches from her concussion had also eased, and it was great to feel more alert and mentally switched on again. Since the accident she'd felt like a sticky goo had invaded her brain, and it was only now starting to dissolve.

The final concern was her larynx. Her doctor's advice was to continue to rest her voice, along with regular sessions with the humidifier, and another round of antibiotics and steroids. Her specialist, Dr Grey, had cautioned her not to push trying to talk. She assured her that there was no lasting damage, but that she should listen to her body. Amber herself would know when it no longer felt constricted and tight; like a rusty hinge that needed oiling, it would relax and soften and being able to speak would feel natural.

Jeanie and Ray picked her up from the hospital, and drove her carefully to Lexie's, before going home themselves for a well-deserved rest. It was Easter school holidays, so Lexie, Arlo and Ruby were all waiting at home for her to arrive. Lexie had outdone herself with her thoughtfulness. Amber's bedroom was inviting, the bed newly made-up with lots of pillows, so she could prop her broken arm up comfortably. Fragrant fresh flowers sat cheerily on the chest of drawers, and there was a jug of iced water at her bedside, along with soothing barley sugar lozenges. Amber didn't mind being silent. There really were no words for Lexie's many acts of kindness, and it was easier to just smile and hug her friend. She wouldn't have been able to speak without weeping, anyway.

For the first hour Ruby and Arlo were constant visitors in and out of the room, chatting away and proudly displaying the Welcome Home signs and pictures they had made for their mother's return. At first, Amber relished every moment with the kids. She had missed them so much in hospital, but despite her best intentions, she could feel herself tiring rapidly. It had been a big day already, just being discharged and making the journey home had been exhausting. Even getting in and out of the car had been an effort. Thankfully, Lexie soon decreed that she, Ruby and Arlo were taking Radar for a walk to the park, and that Amber was to rest.

A flurry ensued to find shoes and hats, and then all was silent. *Pure bliss*, thought Amber adjusting the pillows, sinking back into them and closing her eyes. It was the first time she had been alone for a while. In a busy hospital, there was always someone in and out of your room. For a brief time, she luxuriated in the silence and the peace. In fact, she was probably truly alone for the first time since the day Ray had left her at the house, while he went to Bunnings. Unbidden, her thoughts circled, as always, back to that day. Once again, she replayed that fateful afternoon in her mind.

Marco. She shivered involuntarily. He had terrified her. His behaviour had been out of control, and he'd acted like a crazy man. But still, she hadn't expected the tragedy that followed.

She remembered the fear, that numbing dread that had overtaken her, her breath held in fright, as he'd continued along the highway, instead of turning towards his home. She still didn't know where he had planned to take her, but her gut feeling remained that it wouldn't have ended well for her, had they reached Marco's intended destination.

She tried to feel some sympathy and grief for Marco, but her heart was cold. She'd never wished him dead, but she was undeniably relieved that he was out of her life. In the few months she was with him, she had lived with constant and escalating anxiety. Her fear was ingrained, a habit, hard to shake. She told herself repeatedly, he couldn't hurt her or the kids ever again. The psychologist who had visited her in the hospital told her she needed to manage these thoughts. She had to think of a happy place and imagine herself there. *Breathe in slowly, count to five and breathe out slowly. Breathe in, hold, breathe out, hold. Repeat.* Eventually thoughts of Marco faded.

Marie, the hospital psychologist, was a kind, confident woman in her mid-forties, with an air of quiet competence. Amber fell quickly under her spell. Marie obviously had done the talking, and Amber managed to communicate with her through notes and nonverbal exchanges. In the last session they'd had, she asked Amber to think about the sort of future she would wish for herself. Amber had modest dreams. She wanted a simple, but safe life. A future where she was the person in control of her own well-being and happiness, employed, managing her own finances, making good decisions in her life, and providing Arlo and Ruby with a secure home.

Marie suggested when she began to spiral with negative thoughts, that it might be helpful to think about this future.

Breathing slowly in and out, Amber tried to think of this utopia. It was a routine she would need to follow for many months. The accident, and Marco's death, would probably haunt her for the rest of her life, but she would deal with the memories and trauma, until they faded with time.

Slowly her heart rate settled and she began to breathe normally once more. Still restless, she logged on to her phone and started optimistically looking at job vacancies; until she remembered she had a broken arm and couldn't speak. A one-armed mute! Fairly useless once again, but she wasn't going to leave it any longer. If anything, this setback was making her more determined. Her arm would heal, and even if her voice didn't, there must be something she could do. She wanted a job. She wanted to recapture the optimistic feelings she had after she got her licence. She wanted to prove she could do more; she wanted to be independent and strong. She was going to change.

CHAPTER 26

Over the next few days, Lexie treated Amber like a princess, making sure she had every chance to rest and recover. Once term two started, they slipped back easily into their routine, with a few minor adjustments. Lexie had taken over all the meal preparation, ably assisted by Jeanie who had, so far, dropped off a lasagne and her legendary quiche, cookies and chocolate cake, with the promise of more meals to come.

With everyone gone for most of the day, Amber could rest and concentrate on getting better. Ruby and Arlo were happy to have Amber home with them again, and once they were back at school, they were soon back to their normal selves, as if nothing had happened.

Amber's injuries were healing well. She continued her daily regime of exercises, and the pain gradually lessened in her shoulder and arm. However, her voice was another issue. While the prognosis was that she should have been able to use her voice by now, Amber was still mute. The children had developed a sign language to use with her, and the three of them communicated freely, but every time Lexie asked her how her throat was feeling, Amber just shook her head and gave a thumbs down sign, indicating there was still pain there.

It was late one Saturday morning, when Lexie heard a knock at the door. A quick glance through the front bedroom curtains revealed an unfamiliar car parked on the verge. Arlo and Ruby were in the backyard taking turns to throw the ball for Radar, and Amber was just emerging from the bathroom, dressed for the day, after her morning shower. Lexie had no idea who would be randomly knocking on her door, especially since they were driving an expensive luxury car.

Opening the door, she faced two complete strangers, a man and a woman, both smiling nervously at her. They were neatly dressed, in fact very well dressed, and looked to be in their seventies, but obviously fit and healthy. He was a distinguished old guy, with a grandfatherly, almost farmer-like look about him, in his chinos, pale blue shirt and tailored jacket. The woman was also stylish, in navy linen pants and a white linen shirt, set off by a colourful silk scarf. There was something familiar about the woman, that Lexie couldn't quite put her finger on. Her fair hair was straight, and well-cut, finishing just below her jawline, with only a touch of grey around her face. She had interesting green eyes, and Lexie thought she must have been quite a looker in her day. Her first thought that they might be Jehovah's Witnesses, was quickly dismissed. They looked uncomfortable and edgy, and they didn't have any pamphlets.

'You must be Lexie Hudson,' the man said. 'I'm Kevin Evans, and this is my wife, Joan.'

Lexie looked blankly at him, trying to place him, not really taking in the names. Should she know these people? And how did they know her name?

'We believe our granddaughter Amber is living here. Is that correct?' said the woman, a slightly shrill touch of urgency in her voice.

Lexie stared at them, confused. Grandparents? Amber's grandparents? None of this made sense. She stared back at them like a stunned mullet, her mystified look clearly giving the message that Lexie knew nothing about them. The visitors rushed into an explanation.

'You see, we read about the accident in the paper,' Joan began, before Kevin interrupted her.

'We saw the name! Amber Evans! We weren't sure if it was our Amber, but we had to come and find out. The hospital wouldn't give us any information, so we've been door knocking in the area, all over St James, until we could track her down. Someone told us they thought the girl from the accident lived here,' Kevin finished hopefully.

Lexie's brain was working overtime. Amber had barely mentioned grandparents, other than saying how Cindy had left Geraldton all those years ago because her parents had kicked her out. Surely these weren't the grandparents from Geraldton?

'Are you sure you have the right Amber Evans? I have to ask where you are from, because I'm not sure if you have the right Amber, either.'

Curious at hearing her name mentioned, Amber appeared behind Lexie at the door, just as Arlo and Ruby let an over-excited Radar into the house, promising him a walk. Radar charged through the house to the front door, creating total confusion for several minutes, while he sniffed out the two strangers, jumping about in front of them for attention. Lexie apologised profusely and tried to settle Radar, ordering him to sit. Amber was the only one to hear Joan answer,

'We're from Geraldton. Cindy is our daughter.'

It was Amber's turn to freeze, her eyes darting wildly from one supposed grandparent to the other. Grabbing Lexie's arm to get her attention, she pointed agitatedly at the couple, at the same time nodding emphatically, her eyes wide with shock. Joan repeated her words. 'We're from Geraldton. Cindy is our daughter.'

This time Lexie heard. Her brain finally switching into gear, Lexie said simply,

'You'd better come in.'

***

Joan and Kevin sat close together on the couch. Lexie placed a tray with a jug of iced water, several glasses and a plate of Jeanie's cookies, on the coffee table in front of them. She proceeded to pour water for everyone, while Amber sat stiffly in an armchair examining Joan and Kevin as though they were a foreign species, looking for clues to explain their existence. Ruby and Arlo had squeezed themselves next to Amber, each silently checking out these new people who had suddenly come to visit. Absently, Amber nodded when Arlo and Ruby reached out to take a biscuit each. She placed a protective arm around her children when she noticed how Joan couldn't take her eyes off them.

Joan saw this and apologised. 'I'm sorry Amber. I just didn't realise you had children. You see, we had no idea what happened to Cindy and the baby…you.' Joan broke down at these words and Kevin patted her hand in comfort. Lexie took control, and tried to speak with authority.

'Why don't you tell us what you're doing here? Amber is still unable to speak as a result of the accident, so I'll try to answer anything you want to know. But you need to know right away that, if you're looking for Cindy, we can't help you.'

She had no idea who these people really were and what their agenda was. If they were really Cindy's parents, why had it taken

292

them this long to find her? This was all a bit too much to believe and she was wary of a scam.

Nodding, Joan dabbed constantly at her eyes, while Kevin cleared his throat. She wasn't sure what Kevin would say, but her gut-feeling was that the kids didn't need to hear it. Barely taking her eyes off him, Amber shooed Arlo and Ruby out of the room, miming that they could watch the television in her room. This was a no-brainer for them. The new visitors kept looking at them funny, and seemed pretty boring, so they were more than happy to escape, each clutching another biscuit.

Kevin started slowly, his voice a bit croaky, the raw pain of his emotion as clear to read as the pages in a picture book.

'I have to go back more than twenty-three years, just before you were born, Amber. There have been so many times when we would give the world to go back to that time, and do it all differently, but life rarely gives you that chance. Sometimes you just make terrible decisions, and we have paid for that terrible decision. Every day of our lives since.'

This elicited another sob from Joan. Lexie reached across to the box of tissues on a side table and discreetly put them on the coffee table. Kevin patted Joan's hand reassuringly. He coughed quietly, clearing his throat.

'But the story started even earlier. Probably forty-odd years earlier. You see, we had thought we would never be able to have children. We'd been married fifteen years, and were in our mid-thirties. All our friends had families by then. Joan was very depressed about it, we both were, and we had pretty much given up hope. There wasn't as much medical help in those days, and we'd already tried everything available. We'd always been good churchgoers… most people went to Church in those days. We were Baptist, but there was a breakaway group from our Church called the New Age Christians. A friend of ours suggested we go to one of their Church meetings. She said some members of the Church had experienced small miracles in their lives, after the congregation had prayed for them. She knew we were desperate to have children, and we were very vulnerable. We were ready to try anything.'

Kevin paused for a bit here, then continued.

'The NACs, as we were known, met on Thursday and Saturday evenings, and for most of the day on Sundays. We were soon heavily involved in the church. We made several new friends. There were lots of shared meals and everyone was incredibly welcoming and supportive. We had fun. Our pastor was about our age, and we thought he spoke our language. The Church took us on as a prayer project. Instead of just the two of us praying for a child, the whole congregation offered up praise and prayers to the Lord on our behalf.'

Joan gave an audible sob. Kevin sighed.

'Three months later Joan was pregnant with Cindy! We were over the moon and forever grateful to the church. It may just have been luck, but we chose to believe, and we still do believe the Lord had graced us with a miracle. We felt in debt to the NAC for all they had done. We embraced the Church totally. Even more than before. We believed in, and followed, every law and tenet of the church. We lived strictly by their guidelines and we brought our darling little girl up, to love and worship the Lord and the Scriptures. We were so happy!'

'The NAC became our life. We spent every spare minute working for the Church, and all our friends were from the Church. Our old friends, even our extended families, had dropped away because we had no time for anything other than the Church. We were totally committed. And if anyone tried to criticise it or question our beliefs, we wouldn't hear a bad word against it. We trusted in the Church and the Word of the Lord, as written in the Bible. We never questioned a thing. And we adored Cindy. She was such an easy child, an absolute delight. And she shared all our devotion to the Lord. We prayed together every evening as a family… until she turned fourteen. Then she started to change.'

Despite her reluctance to hear anything about Cindy, Amber was fascinated. She had no idea what Cindy's childhood had been like. She'd never spoken about it, and Amber had been so resentful of Cindy, that it never occurred to her to ask. Cindy had always said her parents were dead, and that she was their only child. It seemed the only child bit was correct. Kevin spoke of a happy childhood. He acknowledged they had been strict parents, possible over-strict, but Cindy had always complied, and given them little reason to question their expectations.

All through primary school, they had been able to maintain control over who Cindy played and socialised with, encouraging her to spend time only with the girls her age, from the Church. Kevin and Joan had been very protective, not allowing her any interests outside of the NAC, or to play sport because of the bad influences she may have come across. That worked well until she started high school, and being able to control her friends became much more difficult.

Kevin spoke of how she changed, midway through year eight. Little things at first, like new hairstyles. She'd always worn her hair in two modest plaits. Suddenly she had a high ponytail, that she tossed as she spoke. She wore more daring clothes, hitching up her skirts and cutting off T-shirts to show her mid-riff. Then there were requests to go to parties. But these were parties of friends who were not members of the Church. Soon enough, there were boy's parties she wanted to go to. Of course, they refused, and there were many fights about what Cindy could and couldn't do. Most of the time they said no, but they discovered too late that Cindy was an expert at slipping out at night. By the time she was sixteen she had an entirely secret life that they knew nothing about.

'You see, we had no idea of what was regarded as normal behaviour for teenagers. The teenagers we knew were docile…or so we believed. We had no friends outside of the Church so we couldn't relate to this new phase of rebellion. We just wanted Cindy to get through school, and maybe get a job at the bank in Geraldton. We never even considered that she would go away to study, or work in Perth.'

Kevin breathed out deeply, as if he could expel the memory of that time from his body. Amber could tell the recollection of this was painful for him.

Patting his knee in a quiet gesture of empathy, Joan found her voice, taking up the story. She went on to describe how all of a sudden, Cindy withdrew from everything. Suddenly there were no more requests to go out at night, and they could tell there was something troubling her. When Joan got up early one morning, she heard Cindy vomiting in the bathroom. It all clicked into place. The sudden tiredness, disliking food she'd always loved. And the new baggy clothes. Cindy was pregnant.

'I confronted her. She was pale and sick, she looked awful, but I shook her until she admitted it. She thought she was about five months pregnant. I demanded to know who the father was. I couldn't believe she'd had sex! She was barely sixteen! I didn't handle it well. I yelled at her. Kevin woke up and came rushing in. I thought he was going to have a heart attack. He was so red-faced and angry. He was furious! We both were.'

Stopping suddenly, Joan placed her hands on her chest as if she could stem the anguish she felt.

While Joan took a moment, Kevin continued, remorse clear in his voice.

'All I could think about was what the Church would say. How Cindy had failed us, disgraced us! How ashamed I was! Not for one minute did I consider how Cindy was feeling. That she might have been unhappy or afraid. And I hit her! I slapped her twice. Once across the face, and then I followed up with a slap to the back of her head as she turned away.'

Shaking his head in shame, Kevin could barely speak, whispering his last words,

'I'd never hit her – ever. I've never hit anyone before, but I hit my own sixteen-year-old daughter when she was pregnant. What kind of man does that?'

Silence ensued for a few moments, as each of them absorbed Kevin's story. Lexie was shocked. She was horrified at Kevin's behaviour, but she could also see clearly the heartfelt remorse of this old man, and a part of her wanted to comfort him. Amber couldn't have said anything, even if it were possible for her to speak. But really, she had no words. This was difficult to process. She felt for the sixteen-year-old Cindy – anyone would – but it was hard to reconcile the unfamiliar image of a teenage, vulnerable Cindy, with the tough, cold Cindy she knew. As difficult as it was to connect this sad old man, with the angry, cruel father he described.

Joan gripped Kevin's hand. She continued, the sadness in her voice, reflected in the sorry story she told.

'The only thing Cindy would tell us was that the father was a German back-packer, who was long gone. He was twenty-one and she was desperately in love, but when she told him she thought she was pregnant he had disappeared without a word. Not even his friends knew where he was…or so they said. We didn't offer her any comfort or even ask how she was. We just screamed at her. We said some terrible things and we told her to get out. She begged forgiveness, but we turned our backs on her. She was desperate. She pleaded with us to let her stay. But we were so enraged. An unmarried mother! Sex out of wedlock! Sex at sixteen! We couldn't get past it, and we were so afraid of what our Church friends would say. We were embarrassed and hurt. She was a sinner in our midst!'

Kevin, weeping quietly, was unable to articulate anything at this stage, so Joan described how they had forced Cindy to pack a bag and go – that very day. Abortion was not an option. They didn't even consider counselling or medical help for Cindy. Kevin went to the bank and came back with two thousand dollars. He thought this was a generous offer, enough for her to get a room somewhere, and tide her over until she could get a job. Then he drove her to the bus-stop and told her to get a bus to Perth. He said they never wanted to see her again. He told her not to bother returning to Geraldton; she was dead to them.

Amber was stunned. She was reluctant to give Cindy any sympathy but this was a horrible tale. Maybe this was why she had always been so heartless. How could Kevin and Joan have cut her out of their lives like that? She could readily imagine the fear the young Cindy must have felt, while she was pregnant with her. Did heartless behaviour run in the family? Kevin's voice was hoarse with emotion, tears streaming down his cheeks as he told the rest of the story.

'We told everyone she was going to school in Perth and would be living with my sister. Eventually, even our friends stopped asking after her. We certainly never mentioned her to anyone ever again. At first our anger sustained us. We had given her everything and she had let us down. She had let down the

Lord, and turned away from his Grace. We lived in fear of anyone learning our secret, we were so ashamed.

'But as the months went by, turning into lonely years, we began to see things differently. We saw other families embrace the 'sinners' in their own families. It turned out that Cindy wasn't the only teenager in Geraldton to rebel. We gradually pulled back from the Church and began to see a whole new world out there, where people made mistakes, and their families and friends gathered around and helped them. We realised too late what fools we had been! How could we have turned on Cindy, our only child whom we still loved desperately, just because she had made a mistake? Why did we abandon her when she needed us most?'

Lexie finally asked the question that nagged at her.

'But how did you know she'd had a baby called Amber? When you read the name in the paper how did you figure it out?'

Joan looked embarrassed and ashamed, but she answered,

'Cindy sent us a few letters in the early years, and every time, she asked if she could come home. In her first letter she told us she had a baby girl called Amber. She asked us for money so she could buy a ticket home. There was an address for a house in Armidale. We never replied.'

She went on to describe how Cindy continued to reach out, the return address changing with almost with every letter, as did the circumstances of where she was living. They kept the letters, but never replied. Cindy used to sign them 'Love Cindy and Amber' and the sender's name on the envelope was always 'Cindy and Amber Evans'; so that was how they knew she had given the baby her surname. By the time Kevin and Joan realised their own callous stupidity and drove down to Perth to the last address Cindy had left them, they were way too late.

Cindy was long gone, and they had no idea where she was. And they didn't know where to start looking.

'We used to come down here on weekends and holidays, just to sit in Hay Street Mall, or go to train stations near Armidale, in the hope that Cindy might walk by. We didn't ever give up on finding her. Then, by a miracle, we read the article about the car accident in The West, and saw the name Amber Evans, and the age matched! We had to try and find out if it was Cindy's Amber. And we've literally knocked on almost every house in St James to find you.'

Lexie looked at her watch. These poor people looked exhausted. She stood up saying,

'I'll make tea. Let's move into the kitchen and we can keep talking, but if I don't have a cup of coffee or a tea, I'll collapse.'

Needing to do something to calm herself down after listening to such a shocking story, Lexie headed towards the kitchen, leaving the others to follow. Joan and Kevin stood up stiffly from the low couch, showing their age. Amber couldn't exactly say why she decided to trust their story, but she went to Joan, putting out her arms and hugged her. Kevin stood awkwardly by, until Amber reached out to include him in the hug. They stood together for several moments, none of them willing to break the tentative bond of a first hug. Finally, Amber pulled back. Smiling she again hugged each of them in turn, and kissed them on the cheek.

Amber was by nature a loving, kind person. Words may have been stolen from her, but from her actions she hoped they could see she was willing and open to them. Why wouldn't she embrace them? She had never even imagined that she had any family beyond, Cindy, and her brothers. Yet, here were grandparents, in the flesh, like guardian angels summoned out of the blue.

Joan returned Amber's hug and holding her face gently, said, 'You cannot imagine how much we regret our actions. We've spent twenty years regretting what we did, and wanting to make it up to you and Cindy. We want you in our lives – if you'll have us. Our lives have been meaningless. We've paid a huge price for our folly, and nothing can bring back all those lost years. But if you'll accept us as grandparents, we'd like to try and make it up to you and Cindy, and your gorgeous children.'

Despite their harrowing, but brutally honest confession, Amber had a good feeling about these two oldies, as she ushered them into the kitchen where Lexie was taking orders for coffee and tea, and putting out more biscuits and Jeanie's cake. Ruby and Arlo were already beside her, demanding juice and chocolate milk respectively. Amber paused to take in the scene. Only three months ago she had been desperate, clinging onto Ruby and Arlo by a thread, facing homelessness and the threat of losing her children to family services. Now she had a home and friends who cared for her. Marco was gone and she was safe. And today she had discovered a family. Grandparents! And she could see a future with them in it.

***

Kevin and Joan stayed on for lunch, and late into the afternoon. There was so much to discuss and to discover about each other's lives. For a start, they didn't know anything about their other grandchildren, Robbie and Sam. There were fresh tears of joy when Joan and Kevin heard they also had two grandsons, and they listened closely to Lexie's description of the boys as they were now: teenagers at high school, hockey players, and living with loving foster-parents in Mandurah. With Amber's nodded permission, Lexie told as much of Amber's story as she could, up until she had Ruby and Arlo, but leaving out the details. If Amber decided later down the track to share how she ended up with two teenage pregnancies, it was her tale to tell.

In contrast to the situation of twenty-three years ago, this time there was no judgement from Kevin or Joan. They delighted in everything Lexie could tell them. Arlo being Arlo, soon had their full attention, as he showed them his Lego constructions and demonstrated, without a ball, how to do spin bowling. Kevin had been a keen spin bowler in his day, so ball in hand, the two of them went out to the back yard to teach each other a few things. Ruby was content to sit up at the kitchen table, drawing and colouring in, while Joan and Lexie talked and Amber listened. When Ruby gave Joan a picture, she had drawn of her and Kevin, together with Amber, Arlo and herself, Joan said it was her most treasured possession... a compliment Ruby readily accepted, because she had tried to do her very best and was quite pleased with the result. Ruby didn't quite understand this great-grandparent stuff. She had friends at school who had Nannas or Nonna's, and Emily had an Oma, but she'd only ever had Amber. This new old lady did seem nice, though.

They left several hours later, by which time everyone was exhausted. Kevin and Joan actually had a home in Perth that was ridiculously close by at Victoria Park, and they promised to return the next day. Lexie promised to ring Sally and tell her about the grandparents the boys didn't know they had. She didn't ring until that evening. It had been such an emotional day; she needed to recover somewhat before she could make the call. Amber had just put a very sleepy Arlo and Ruby to bed, when Lexie signalled her to come and sit in the loungeroom while she put Sally on speaker. Sally was astonished. Her reactions ranged from 'How were they not able to track Cindy down? How could they be so cruel?' to 'Do we really want these people in the boys' lives?'

Amber itched to speak. She wanted to reassure Sally; she knew instinctively that these were good people. That her heart told her, that even though they'd made shocking mistakes, they deserved a second chance. After all, she and Robbie and Sam had only had each other at one stage, how could it hurt to allow into their lives, someone else who wanted nothing more than to love them?

She listened, frustrated that she couldn't express herself. She tried, but the words choked and caught in her throat. After a while, Lexie managed to talk Sally round. She didn't quite say what Amber wanted to, but she did get Sally to promise to tell the boys the story, and ask them if they wanted to meet their grandparents. Lexie offered her house as a safe place where they could all meet, and offered to host an afternoon tea the next day. It took another little while for Sally to absorb the details of the story correctly, calming down in the process. She promised to tell the boys straight away, and she would text back if they wanted to meet them.

In no time at all, the response pinged back.

Boys so excited to find out about GPs. (Rolled-eyes emoji.) *We'll be there around 2pm tomorrow. Boys have hockey in Perth at 12, so it works out. See you then xx Sally* (Fingers-crossed emoji.)

CHAPTER 27

Sunday afternoon rolled on, a glorious Perth day with a blue sky that went on forever. There were tears of joy, and tears of regret. Hugs and laughter. Questions. So many questions! But, most of all, there was joy.

Kevin and Joan were brave. Lexie had to admire them for that. At no time did they excuse their behaviour, taking full blame for the disaster that was Cindy's life. And there was no getting past it: had they been decent, supportive parents, Cindy may never have made the choices she made, and all their lives could have been easier, especially Amber's.

As unfamiliar as they were in the role of grandparents, Kevin and Joan were good listeners, hungry to find out as much as they could about Amber, Robbie and Sam, devouring every snippet of information. Arlo and Ruby were quickly bored with all the talk and wandered back and forth between the loungeroom, where Amber and the boys were with Joan and Kevin; and the kitchen, where Sally and Lexie had thoughtfully stationed themselves in order to give the newly blended family some space. Still mute, Amber paid careful attention to Robbie and Sam as they told the story of their years spent with Cindy.

Robbie was brutally honest, describing quite dispassionately how Cindy and John, had neglected them for most of their lives. He didn't sugar-coat anything where Cindy was concerned, but he loyally spoke about Amber as the one person they could rely on.

Amber could see the guilt and despair written on Kevin and Joan's faces. This turned to astonishment when Robbie said off-handedly,

'We know where Cindy is, actually. You could meet her if you want to.'

Kevin and Joan looked questioningly at Amber. She hadn't mentioned this. Amber looked stunned.

'Amber hasn't seen her yet,' Robbie continued chirpily, seemingly oblivious to the bombshell he had just dropped on Amber.

'We only saw her last week, so it's crazy that you guys have also turned up at the same time. She's out of prison now.'

'Prison?' wailed Joan, clutching Kevin's arm. Amber realised they had no idea what uncomfortable truths they had yet to discover, when they got to know Cindy again. She also had no idea the boys had seen Cindy. This must have happened while she was in hospital. She was instantly furious that no-one had told her. Probably lucky for everyone I can't speak, she thought wryly.

'Yeah. Cindy went to prison for dealing. That's how we ended up with Sally,' Sam said with complete candour. 'But when we saw her last week, she seemed better. She doesn't look like a druggie anymore. And she wants to see us again… but we don't have to live with her, or anything.'

Amber froze. This was still a taboo subject with her. She really didn't want to hear any of this. Outwardly, she remained calm, but inside, a tiger paced, growling. Standing up, she quietly left the room. As she walked away, she heard Sam say,

'She was really sorry she'd let us down…'

Let us down! fumed Amber. *That's making it sound like she missed a goal at hockey! Well! The boys could see her, and so could Kevin and Joan. They could probably do some apologising themselves, she thought. To Cindy!* Not that she was going to give Cindy any excuse for her shocking behaviour. Cindy had chosen her path; she had never put any of them first. Amber, Robbie and Sam had come at the end of a long list of priorities… John, drugs, parties.

In the kitchen, Sally was just telling Lexie how Cindy had recently, and completely out of the blue, made contact with the boys. She confessed she had deliberately kept the information from Amber, planning to tell her once she was stronger, her injuries healed. She hadn't wanted to worry her beforehand, especially while she was still in hospital. Then all this happened. Continuing, Sally said, 'I'm not sure how much this will affect Amber, but I think you should know,' when Amber appeared unexpectedly, and heard Sally's next words.

'Robbie and Sam met up with Cindy last Friday.'

Betrayal hit Amber like a brick wall. She gestured angrily at Sally. Fighting the urge to cry, Sally blurted out,

'I'm so sorry, Amber! I wanted to tell you! I was just waiting for the right time!'

Amber ignored her completely and tapped the table emphatically as if to say,

'Out with it!'

With a worried look at Lexie, Sally took a deep breath and began.

'Apparently, Cindy was released from prison a few weeks ago and she's been trying to make a new life for herself. Obviously, she would have been given my contact details as the boys' foster carer. When she first emailed me, I wanted to send it straight to junk mail, but it wasn't my place to decide. So, I showed the boys her email. In it, she promises she's not trying to get them back, but she wants to have some sort of connection with them. They agreed to see her, even though, I told them I thought it was a bad idea.'

Sally rubbed roughly at her forehead.

'I shouldn't let this get to me, but I love those boys and I don't want them hurt. And I know they are really happy with us. This just brings it all back again… just when they are getting on with their own lives, she comes back!'

Sally broke off crying, as her emotions got the better of her. Lexie patted her hand, but Amber sat stiff and silent. Stifling a sob, Sally tried to recover.

'Sorry. It's really not about me. I'm okay. It just gets me, every now and then.'

Taking a moment to gain control, she dabbed at her tears with a tissue before saying,

'So, to cut a long story short, they saw her last Friday at our house. She only stayed maybe half an hour. She had a support lady with her, and I made sure I was there for the boys as well. They are such good kids. Big hearts. Despite what she did to them, I think they will see her again. She also mentioned you, Amber. She wanted to know if we had any contact with you. The boys hadn't said anything, but she knew about the accident. Bloody newspapers!' Sally rolled her eyes and continued.

'The boys are still processing the visit. I think they are glad they saw her, but I'm not sure what they'll do next. Neil and I will be fine. We always knew this could happen. It's not the first time we've had to take a backward step. At least this time the boys are old enough to exercise their own rights, and they can take some control over what happens,' she finished feistily

Lexie quizzed Sally for more detail, while Amber listened. Her head was spinning with this new information. Occasionally, she could hear snippets of the boys' conversation with their grandparents and she was happy they'd moved on from the topic of Cindy. Eventually, Joan came out to check on Amber.

Giving her a hug, she asked if she was okay. She told her she understood if she didn't want to see Cindy, but said that she and Kevin needed to see her. Taking Amber's hands gently in her own, Joan pleaded with Amber:

'We have to know if she wants to be in our lives again. We deserted her when she needed us the most. You understand that we need to make amends, if possible. We need to beg her forgiveness. That doesn't mean you have to see her. That's your choice. Totally your choice. But we want to be part of your life, and little Ruby and Arlo's lives too, if we may. We are not going to make you have anything to do with Cindy, unless you want to. We love you and we want to help you and your beautiful little family. Will you let us do that?'

Amber nodded and reached up with her good arm to touch Joan's cheek. Of course, she wanted these people in her life. She could see genuine pain in their eyes and understood they had suffered long enough for their mistakes. They were all a band of lost souls, carrying too much baggage. Lexie had saved her, but she had always craved a family of her own. Kevin and Joan needed a family. They needed each other. To make that happen, she could ignore Cindy's existence.

CHAPTER 28

Lexie finished hanging out a load of washing, cleared the sink of dishes and wiped down the kitchen benches. Right. No more procrastinating, she needed to get started on her half-yearly reports. She had the house to herself, a rare scenario. The formal assessments were completed, she had plenty of anecdotal evidence and informal test results, and she was ready.

It was week six; reports were due with the Vice Principal for editing, by the start of week seven. Second term had whizzed by. It was almost three months since Amber's accident and several weeks since the long-lost grandparents, Kevin and Joan, had arrived on her doorstep. So much had happened since then, and Kevin and Joan, like the proverbial fairy godparents, had proven to be an absolute bonus to everyone. Amber's arm and shoulder had healed well, and although she was still seeing the physio, she was making good progress.

Amber's damaged larynx, however, was not such a success story. Even though her specialist confirmed that the larynx had healed, and there was no longer any physical reason for her to not to speak, she remained mute. Amber was vehement in her conviction that she had tried, but wasn't able to speak. There was no more medication available to her; the injury needed time and rest to recover. She continued to use the humidifier in her room at night, and several times during the day, in the hope that the moist air would help with the healing.

Amber, Ruby and Arlo had gone to spend the day with Kevin and Joan. They usually visited on the weekends, and Robbie and Sam were often there as well. Occasionally, the older boys slept over at their grandparents', so far without any incidents. Sally monitored it all very carefully, and kept Lexie in the loop because Cindy was now living with Kevin and Joan, so she was also there when the boys stayed. So far, all reports were positive and the family seemed to be making connections, slowly re-building their fractured foundations.

Today, Lexie had offered to go with Amber because this was the first time Amber and Cindy would actually cross paths, but Amber was adamant she would be fine. Usually, Amber would stipulate that Cindy should not be there at the same time that she was, but Robbie and Sam had persisted, and finally worn her down to agree at least to meet Cindy. They promised her she could walk out if at any time she wanted to.

This was all in the back of Lexie's mind as she worked away at the reports. She had half expected Amber to have chucked it in and be back by now. Lexie kept glancing up at the clock. She'd been gone three hours, long enough for a dispute that would force Amber to return home. Knowing how she felt about Cindy, a reconciliation of any sort seemed impossible. Lexie had just decided to stop for a break, and had hit 'save' on the last report, when she heard a knock at the door. She didn't really want an interruption, she had been making such great progress, but when she saw it was Josh, she was pleasantly surprised. He'd completed his work on the house opposite some weeks ago, and between school and helping Amber with Arlo and Ruby, she'd been too busy to think about her own renovations. She assumed this was the purpose of Josh's visit, and apologised sincerely for not getting back to him.

Josh put up his hands good-naturedly. 'Oh! Don't worry about that. I had to call around to the Watsons' across the road. They had some trouble with one of the drawers in the laundry cupboards, so I said I'd pop in. I'm only here to check up and see how things are going with everyone. How's Amber? Has her voice returned yet?'

Lexie shook her head ruefully, ushering Josh inside.

'Come in Josh. I've just put the kettle on if you've got time for a coffee, or tea?'

Leading the way to the kitchen, Lexie quickly tidied the table, pushing aside the student files next to the computer to make space for him. Josh caught sight of the files. 'Report time?' he asked. 'I bet that's stressful,' he added sympathetically.

'Oh, it's fine,' Amber smiled. 'I actually enjoy reports. I'm a bit weird like that,' she laughed.

'I don't think you're weird. Anyone who cares as much as you do about a student you taught ten years ago, seems like a bit of a hero to me. I wish there were more people in the world, as kind as you.'

Lexie found herself blushing. 'Thanks, Josh,' she murmured, embarrassed by the compliment. Changing the subject, she asked if he'd met Joan and Kevin yet.

'Yes, I met them a couple of weeks ago. Did you know I'm doing some work for them?'

'Is this for the unit they are building for Cindy, at the rear of their house?' asked Lexie. When Josh nodded, she couldn't help but ask, 'Have you met Cindy?'

'Yes, I have,' admitted Josh. 'She's had a little input into the design, but she appears to be so grateful to Kevin and Joan for this, that it seems she doesn't like to impose any ideas. But she did make a couple of useful suggestions, and I've included them in the design. As to what do I think of her?' he shrugged.

'She's attractive, taller than Amber, but not much. She seems very quiet, older than I expected, maybe even a bit jaded, as if life has worn her down. She looks fragile, I guess,' he said, before adding,

'All of them seem very gentle with each other. I think Kev, Joan and Cindy are still working out how to be together after all that has happened.'

Josh paused, his serious expression turning to a grin.

'I was there one day though, when Robbie and Sam turned up, and the change in Cindy was immediate. She looked happy, and they were all very relaxed together, Joan and Kevin included. Mind you, it's hard not to be happy around those kids.'

'I haven't met Cindy yet,' confessed Lexie. 'In fact, Amber is only meeting her today for the first time, so I'm feeling a bit nervous about the result of all that.'

Josh nodded and offered an opinion.

'I don't think I'm speaking out of turn here, but it does seem that Joan and Kevin are prepared to do anything to unite the family.'

Lexie agreed. 'Apparently, they wanted to leave Geraldton for a long time, mostly because of the sour memories it held. They purchased the house here several years ago, but only ever stayed for short periods then returned to Geraldton, in the vain hope that Cindy might turn up there one day, looking for them. They are only now in the process of selling the house in Geraldton.'

When Josh asked Lexie why they hadn't tried to find Cindy on social media, Lexie shook her head, saying,

'They did try. Often. Both Joan and Kevin are savvy with social media. They trawled it regularly for any sign of Cindy, with no luck. It seems that Cindy and John had deliberately kept off all social platforms. The trail was completely cold, and as far as Joan and Kevin were concerned, Cindy and her baby Amber could have left Western Australia years ago. They might have been anywhere, their names changed, their identities a mystery.'

Lexie shook her head, finishing her story.

'They were well aware of the dreadful way they had treated Cindy, and they only held a faint hope that she would even want to see them again. They had all but given up, so this reunion is beyond their wildest dreams. Now, they are ready to help Cindy and her family, the family they thought they had lost, in any way they can.'

Lexie paused, gathering her thoughts, and took the first sip of the coffee she had made before continuing.

'They were so nervous about meeting Cindy, but amazingly she held no grudges. Joan told me that Cindy was so happy to be reunited with them that she was the one who apologised. Not for getting pregnant, but for never returning home and giving them another chance. Cindy confessed everything about her drug addiction and her role as a dealer, and that the boys had been put into care, saying she had not been much of a mother to them anyway.

Her time in prison apparently had been tough. She'd had plenty of time to reflect on her life and she finally accepted full responsibility for everything that happened. Of course, Kevin and Joan still believe themselves to be the ones at fault. After all, they had abandoned her in when she most needed them and, worse, had ignored her all her letters after Amber was born!'

Lexie shook her head in disbelief. It still shocked her to think of it, even more so when she tried to imagine the kindly Joan and Kevin acting in such a way. Lexie repeated Joan's story about their first reunion with Cindy.

'They were expecting her, waiting nervously at the front door. She'd arrived on her own in a taxi. She knocked, and when they opened the door, they stood back politely and asked her in. They weren't sure if she would stay, but were hoping desperately that if she did, perhaps they could all sit around the table and talk. But they were totally unprepared for Cindy, who threw her arms around them, sobbing, not letting go. Of course, they hugged her back, all sobbing and hugging, clinging on to each other before they eventually made it inside.'

Lexie sighed, 'So, in a nutshell they are all guilt-ridden, with so many regrets you could furnish a house with them.'

For a few moments they sat in silence.

'Heavy stuff,' mused Josh.

'On a happier note, though, I can tell you another story. Something that happened on the day Amber had her plaster taken off,' said Lexie, smiling at the memory.

'Kevin and Joan arrived in two cars. Joan drove their usual car and parked on the verge, while Kevin drove a lovely little white hatchback into the driveway. Amber came out to meet them, all excited that her arm was finally free of its itchy plaster, and demonstrating the range of movement she had. Out of the blue, Kevin says,

'Well, that's lucky because we brought you a little present!' and they presented Amber with the keys and the papers for the hatchback! 'It's not new, but it's in great condition and has less than 20,000 kilometres on the clock!'

Lexie laughed, a tear slipping out as she recounted Amber's response.

'She just stood there totally overcome, as if she didn't understand. She looked at the keys in her hand for a moment, then suddenly she started jumping up and down. She hugged Kevin and Joan so hard I thought she'd do their old bones some damage, or end up back in plaster herself, and then she burst into tears. Of course.'

Lexie continued, a big grin on her face,

'This has opened up her world in such an amazing way. It's mind-boggling freedom for her. For the first time in her life, she has some real independence. I know she desperately wants to get a job, so fingers crossed, eventually she'll be able to drive to work. It's made her so happy. She cleans it every week, and the inside is absolutely spotless; even Arlo and Ruby look after it,' chuckled Lexie.

'The other thing is, Joan and Kevin never arrive here empty handed. Ruby and Arlo had barely any toys of their own before, and now Joan and Kevin are intent on giving them everything they ever wanted. They love finding something they think the kids would enjoy. They must have missed out on so much over the years, and now they have grandchildren and great grandchildren to spoil, they've gone into hyper-grandparent mode. And even crazier…Joan and Kevin are talking about helping Amber out with getting her own home. I think the plan is that if Amber can get a job, they'll help her with repaying a mortgage. It's a pretty generous offer, but they seem only too happy to be able to help her,' confided Lexie.

'Well, why wouldn't they?' smiled Josh. 'They must have been so lonely before, and now Amber and her little ones have filled a gap. They must be such a welcome addition to their lives.'

'And Robbie and Sam!' reminded Lexie.

Lexie and Josh talked a while longer, until Josh looked at his watch.

'I'd better go. I've got a meeting with a client in thirty minutes. Thanks for the coffee and the chat. I hope I haven't held you up too much,' he said, gesturing at the pile of report files on the table.

'Not at all. I enjoyed having the chance to talk about this with someone who understands the situation. Most people wouldn't believe me, even if I tried to explain!'

Josh picked up his keys and phone and walked to the door, Lexie following. Opening the door, he turned and said, 'I've really enjoyed chatting as well. I know you're busy, but I wonder if you'd like to go out for dinner with me? Soonish, maybe?'

Lexie didn't overthink it, or hesitate, and her heart actually skipped a beat at the thought of an evening with this lovely, kind and very attractive man.

'I'd love to. I'm free most nights. Dinner would be nice.'

'Great. I'll be in touch,' said Josh, and bending forward he kissed her on the cheek, before jogging down the steps to his car.

Lexie waved him off before returning inside. *Well, that's something to look forward to.* she smiled to herself. Maybe she wouldn't be quite so lonely after all, if Amber and the kids got a place of their own. She went back to the reports, albeit with slightly reduced concentration than when she started them.

CHAPTER 29

Amber parked out the front of Kevin and Joan's house, which was, ridiculously, only a ten-minute drive from Lexie's house. She pondered on the six degrees of separation theory; only ten minutes away, yet without the car accident, they may never have met. She still thought of Kevin and Joan by their Christian names. Not having had grandparents all her young life, it was just too much of a stretch to call them anything else.

Ruby and Arlo undid their own seatbelts, and jumping out of the car, raced up the driveway calling out 'Granny! Grandad!' They'd had no problem adapting.

Amber followed at a slower pace. She knew that Robbie and Sam were already inside; they'd had one of their frequent sleepovers. This was one visit she was not looking forward to. She had finally given in to Robbie and Sam's constant nagging and agreed to meet Cindy; this was the first time they would be face to face since she had left Manjimup, four years ago. Pausing at the door, she told herself yet again, that Cindy could not hurt her anymore. Nevertheless, she defensively straightened up, chin forward and shoulders back, before walking through the open door.

She saw Cindy immediately. She had changed. The brown hair was an improvement on the bleached blond frizz she had favoured, for as long as Amber could remember. It fell naturally, shoulder length, and the colour suited her. She was kneeling in front of Ruby and Arlo, introducing herself to them. Her voice was husky, just as Amber remembered.

Cindy looked up and smiled at Amber, acknowledging her existence, but she didn't stand until she had finished explaining to Arlo and Ruby who she was. When she told them she was Amber's Mum, they looked around at Amber, visibly confused.

'So, you're another Granny?' asked Ruby confused, looking back at Amber for confirmation. Reluctantly, Amber nodded.

'Do we call you Granny, too?' asked Arlo, who appeared very unsure about this new person.

'We can work it out later,' said Cindy. 'I'm just so happy to see you both. You were only babies the last time I saw you. And now you're all grown up.'

'I'm six and Arlo's five,' Ruby offered.

Hovering close by, watching on fondly, but also anxiously, were Kevin and Joan. When Arlo caught sight of them, he broke away from this strange new granny and ran to give them both a hug. Ruby did the same. Cindy took her cue, smiling at Amber and moving towards her. Instinctively, Amber put her hand out, stopping Cindy in mid-stride. Amber wasn't sure what Cindy intended to do, but any physical contact between them was certainly not in her plan.

If anyone else noticed the awkward moment, they didn't make mention, and very soon the greetings continued as Robbie and Sam ambled into the lounge, creating immediate uproar, with Arlo and Ruby competing with each other for their uncles' attention. Amber chose to sit on a hard-backed chair at the table.

Silently, she watched the happy scene unfolding in front of her, her resentment escalating by the minute. Ruby and Arlo seemed to have accepted Cindy without question. Obviously, they were getting used to long-lost grandparents turning up out of nowhere. Sam and Robbie were clearly at ease with Cindy, their conversation a relaxed banter.

At one stage, Kevin put his arm around Cindy, joking about Joan's cooking. Not that they ignored Amber. They tried to bring her into the conversation, but her very soul felt it would crack like an eggshell if she did. It was all she could do to sit rigidly where she was. She noticed Cindy sneaking glances at her, just as she, herself, was furtively checking out Cindy. The new Cindy. The flashy tart of Amber's nightmares had been replaced by this pleasant, well-groomed woman. It was difficult to match the image she had of Cindy for so long in her mind with this new version.

Joan had prepared a delicious lunch for everyone, and the conversation was lively. Amber noticed that Cindy was subdued, a trace of sadness around her eyes, but as quickly as she noticed it, Amber dismissed it. Cindy was the last person she was going to feel any empathy for. Eventually, the ordeal of lunch was over, and before Amber could do anything about it, Joan and Kevin announced they were taking all the young ones to the shop for ice-creams. Within minutes, and ignoring the angry expression and gesticulations of a voiceless Amber, Joan had herded Arlo, Ruby, Robbie and Sam out the front door. Kevin slammed it emphatically behind them, and they were gone.

Not very subtle, but this was it; the crossroads moment for them both. Cindy moved from the kitchen where she had been loading the dishwasher, and sat opposite Amber. The table stretching like a safety barrier between them. Somewhere in the hall, a clock ticked. Otherwise, all was expectantly quiet. Cindy began to speak, haltingly.

'Amber, I know you hate me. I can see it in your eyes, in the stiff way you're sitting now, judging every word I say. And I deserve it. You have every right to hate me. I was a terrible mother to you. In fact, I wasn't a mother in any sense of the word. I treated you dreadfully and I am so, so sorry for it.'

Amber's first reaction had been to flee. She seriously considered just getting up and leaving. She had even pushed slightly forward in her seat, the pressure already on the soles of her feet to stand up. But there was a stronger urge inside her, that convinced her to stay; an old yearning that tied her to the chair. She needed to hear what Cindy had to say.

'I've had four years to think about this. A stint inside is good for that…and I wasn't sure if I'd ever get the chance to apologise.' Cindy looked into Amber's eyes. Eyes that were a mirror of her own. The likeness impossible for mother and daughter not to see. Amber stared back at her fearlessly.

'I'm not going to make any excuses for myself. I was completely selfish, and you deserved so much more from me. Right from the beginning, you were such a good baby, and I knew I was lucky to have you,' Cindy unconsciously clasped and unclasped her hands. She went on, her tone slightly pleading,

'Everything I did in those early days was such a struggle, and I had no money and no support. I'd worked until you were born, but I didn't have much saved up, and the single parent payment barely covered the rent. I had some bad relationships, made mistakes, and I couldn't seem to get anywhere… And then I met John. We clicked, but I know now we were not good for each other. We are both weak characters. John was the reason I got onto the gear in the first place.'

Cindy tried to catch Amber's eyes, but Amber steadfastly looked away. She wasn't going to make this easy. Cindy sighed.

'I know, I put John ahead of you. You were a cute little thing, and you'd sit quietly with your Mookie bear, playing with whatever toys you had, just waiting for me to feed you or put you to bed. John used to do things for you too, like take you for walks to the park. He wasn't so out of it in those days. And then when I had the boys, you were so good with Robbie and Sam… I was such a loser. God knows what would have happened to them, if it wasn't for you. Even when you were only little, you could change Robbie's nappy, or make him a bottle. And the more you did, the more I let you take over the role of mother. I was so selfish! And I don't think it ever occurred to me to think this was all wrong.'

Cindy's words rolled across the table to Amber, invoking memories of a childhood plagued by worries and constant vigilance for her brothers. She was surprised Cindy remembered so much. She'd thought she was so drugged out most of the time that she hadn't even noticed what Amber had been doing. It wasn't a choice for Amber. She loved her baby brothers, and a mothering instinct somehow kicked in, despite the fact that she'd never experienced much nurturing or love in her own short life. Amber had been down this road before, in her memories. She had already figured out that the unconditional love she received from her brothers was what made her capable of showing love in turn.

Cindy looked down at her hands, composing herself. Amber waited, her heart cold. Struggling with her emotions, Cindy raised her eyes and looked straight at Amber. This time Amber held her gaze.

'I could apologise for a year, eight hours a day and still not even come close to listing all the wrongs I've done to you. I don't deserve to be called your mother. Please. I beg your forgiveness. I'm begging you to give me the chance to make this up to you. I'm prepared to spend the rest of my life trying to make it up to you. We've got an unexpected second chance here.'

Gesturing with her hands at the house around them, she went on passionately, 'I never thought I'd see my parents ever again. I knew how dominated by the Church they were, and I didn't think they would be capable of change. I thought there was no way they would want to see me. After all, if being unmarried and pregnant was cause for kicking me out of their lives, I certainly never considered they would accept me back into the family, especially now I'm also a convicted drug dealer. Yet, here I am. I'm living in this house with them as if I'd never left. And we are happy together!'

Cindy's voice rose as she spoke, rushing and tripping over her words, anxious to say it all. A last-ditch appeal to Amber.

'Now I've found you, and the boys, and your darling little Ruby and Arlo, we could actually be a family! A real family! With birthdays and Christmas and all that stuff we've never had! Instead of all these separate sad lives, we could get to know each other. And maybe love each other!'

Looking Amber straight in the eye, Cindy gave it her final desperate shot.

'And Amber, I do love you. I always did and I always will. I remember when you were first born, I would look at you and marvel at the love I felt for you. Sometimes I was so happy, that I didn't even care that my parents had disowned me because I had you. Please believe me that I loved you, and when you were a baby, I tried to be a good mother to you. And I gave you lots of love and care… But when I started using, I lost sight of everything. I was a pathetic loser, a junkie… I was weak. I used up your love and threw it away. In my twisted logic, I thought I deserved to be special, that I was the one hard done by. Believe me, now I'm clean, I see it all clearly. Every day, I curse myself for all the ways I let you down…and for all the years I never showed you that I did love you. And how proud I was of you.' Cindy was crying freely now, the tears coursing down her cheeks.

'When I knew that creep Snowy was after you, I should have been strong. I should have taken you and the boys, and run, but I was too afraid to leave…'

Cindy was begging, her words punctuated by sobs.

'I understand if it's too much for you to forgive me, but I need the chance to love you now. To show you, now and forever, that I love you. The chance to be a proper mother to you. One day maybe, if you allow it, I could be part of your life again.'

Amber just stared back at her, her face implacable, an iron shield, her heart a locked vault. She asked herself if she cared at all about this woman who, in her own words, had neglected her almost from the day she was born. Did she owe her anything? And now she wanted forgiveness! It was too much. Time ticked away between them. Past injustices reared up like snakes, their bites as painful as they had been in her childhood and teens. Amber's eyes locked onto Cindy, the hatred in them visceral, accusing. Acknowledging defeat, Cindy closed her eyes, shamefaced and shattered.

Voices filtered in from outside. One by one the charged emotions connecting mother and daughter across the table, fractured and fell away. Robbie burst through the front door first, oblivious to the intense feelings that had circled his sister and his mother, only minutes before. He threw himself on the couch, and began telling a story about something apparently hilarious that had just happened. The others followed, also still laughing, while Joan rushed to the kitchen carrying the remains of Ruby's ice-cream that was now melting fast, like the hopes that Cindy had briefly dared entertain. Completely deflated, her dreams crushed, Cindy turned away from Amber's implacable fury. She could feel the anger radiating from Amber. She had given it her best try, and she'd failed.

Jolted out of her all-consuming rage by the family's return, Amber was slowly brought back to reality. She watched the interactions of the family members: great grandchildren, grandchildren and grandparents filling the room, their voices in harmony as they laughed, teased each other and showed their love. Love that was newly born, and growing with every fresh encounter; creating relationships and memories, where before there had been a lonely void. Already Arlo had run over to Cindy, smearing chocolate on her jeans, as he showed her the five cents he'd found on the footpath. A family. How much did she risk losing if she refused to be a part of this? Would they have separate birthdays and Christmases like those acrimonious families she'd heard about? Could she risk this fragile family unit imploding before it even got started? Gradually her rage began to dissolve. Her thoughts became calmer, more measured.

Would she be the one forever on the edge of it all, or would it be Cindy? Both of them had faced rejection by the people who were supposed to have loved them and fought for them. They'd both made bad decisions as they searched to compensate for the love they'd lost. She saw Robbie and Sam's acceptance of Cindy. She thought about what Sally had said to her about Robbie and Sam's attitude: that they thought Cindy deserved another chance. They didn't overthink it, or weigh up their grievances. They reckoned enough time had been wasted already. Boys! Amber looked at them, and rolled her eyes. How could they forgive so easily? She knew she didn't want to forgive Cindy. Her hatred had sustained her though many a tough time… but she loved Robbie and Sam dearly, and she knew they wanted this reconciliation to work. Could she deny them this one last request of her?

Watching Robbie and Sam, Arlo and Ruby, having fun together, filled her heart with happiness. Joan and Kevin had also enriched their lives with their love and affection, adding the precious gift of an older generation's devotion to their little gang. She was the only stumbling block… Amber glanced at Cindy and their eyes met. Cindy looked away; her eyes dull with defeat. Amber recognised that look. She'd seen it before, in her own eyes. Her heart thudding, Amber made up her mind.

Reaching across the table, she stretched out her hand towards Cindy, surprising her with her touch. Tentatively, Cindy responded, placing her hand in Amber's. No-one else noticed. Amber swallowed hard and cleared her throat. It was only a whisper, but it pierced the room like a siren, stopping everyone in their tracks. As one, all heads turned towards her. Did Amber just say something? She repeated it. This time it was louder, and although she had to swallow in between the words, everyone heard them.

'… for… give… you…?' Amber gasped, and shrugged. She shook her head as if she wasn't sure. Then, using each breath to push out the words, 'but… we… can… be… a… family.' She gestured to include everyone in the room Amber swallowed again, as Joan rushed to her side with a glass of water. She sipped, and pointing to Cindy and back to herself, said, '… maybe… we…. can… find… a way.'

Cindy grasped Amber's hands in both of hers, her smile slowly reaching her eyes; a faint light rekindled. It took a second or two until Amber's words sunk in, and everyone rushed over to hug them. There was talking and laughter; there were tears of joy. As love swirled around, reaching its way into hearts, easing painful memories, soothing and healing damaged souls, Amber felt the anger and resentment, she had held onto for so long, begin to lessen and fade away. Only a slight shift, but a definite easing of the pain in her heart.

Amber looked across at Cindy, the tears streaming down her cheeks as she was being embraced by Joan and Kevin. Their eyes met, and they shared a hint of a smile. She had hated Cindy for such a long time, but maybe it was time to stop, to heal. Didn't the love they shared for all these people finally override everything else? Maybe, it was time to stop jumping over waves and seek out calmer water instead.

'You talked, Mummy!' Arlo cried out when the hugging and crying paused a little.

'Yes. I did,' Amber whispered, hoarsely, her voice a little stronger as she began to trust in it.

'I think… I might… be better now.'

Amber looked around the jubilant faces of her family and she realised, better days had already begun.

Acknowledgements

This book has been inspired by the many brilliant and dedicated teachers I have worked with during my career. As all good teachers know, teaching is not a job that stops when the dismissal bell rings. It lingers with you on the drive home, as you prepare a meal for the family, and in those moments before you drop off to sleep. And it is the students who traverse these corridors in your mind, as you reflect on their behaviours, successes and failures; constantly questioning how to get them to be the best version of themselves they can be.

Primary school teachers in particular will get to know these individual personalities very well over the course of the year. It's not unusual to hold onto concerns for certain students, and to wonder when they catch a glimpse of them in high school uniform, or even many years later, how they are managing. No matter how much you may try in the classroom, you can't always fix everything… some things are out of your control.

It is an unavoidable fact, that children in any school, will come from very different backgrounds, and not all of them will have the same opportunities. *Jumping Over Waves*, is a tribute to those children, who endure, despite the obstacles they face every day.

Writing can be a very solitary process, and I thank my son Jacob who read an early draft, for his helpful comments and ideas. Also sincere thanks to my friend Gordon Muir, for his insightful and valuable feedback, and his encouragement for me to continue.

Thanks also to my editor Jo Smith for her suggestions and excellent work. It was an enjoyable process. Thank you also to my very knowledgeable publisher, Ian Hooper from Book Reality, for his understanding and flexibility. As always, it was a pleasure to work with you.

I am also indebted to my daughter Luci, who in between looking after her new-born baby and moving house, designed the stunning cover for *Jumping Over Waves*. Thanks, Luci, for the cover and my beautiful new grandson.

And last, but not least, thanks again to my husband Greg, whose optimism and good humour, I appreciate every day.

About the Author

Tricia Trevaskis lives in the South West of Western Australia. Born and raised in Geelong, Victoria, she studied teaching, before completing her Bachelor of Arts at Deakin University, majoring in Creative Writing. Apart from a short stint as a journalist, Tricia taught for over forty years, in various Primary Schools, in Victoria, New South Wales and W.A. As a teacher, she was always interested and enthusiastic about teaching children to love reading, and write well.

Tricia and her family have relocated several times, across Australia, but consider the beaches, and beautiful natural environment of the South West, home. She enjoys pottering in her garden, travelling, walking and playing golf. She is married to Greg, who she met at seventeen, and has four children and six grandchildren.

The Wildcards (Book Reality 2022) was her debut novel and she is currently working on a children's picture story book.